Peter Carey grew up in Bacchus Marsh, Victoria, and was educated at Geelong Grammar School and Monash University, where he read science. He now lives in Sydney and works, part-time, in advertising He is the author of the much-acclaimed collection of short stories *Exotic Pleasures* (also available in Picador); *Bliss* is his first novel.

Also by Peter Carey
in Picador
Exotic Pleasures

BLISS

Peter Carey

PICADOR
published by Pan Books

Acknowledgement is made to John Mavrogordato, the translator,
and Hogarth Press, the publishers, for permission to quote from
Waiting for the Barbarians from *Poems* by C. P. Cavafy.

First published 1981 by Faber and Faber Ltd
This Picador edition published 1982 by Pan Books Ltd,
Cavaye Place, London SW10 9PG
9 8 7 6 5 4
© Peter Carey 1981
ISBN 0 330 26785 X
Filmset by Northumberland Press Ltd, Gateshead, Tyne and Wear
Printed and bound in Australia by
The Dominion Press-Hedges & Bell, Maryborough 3465

Part One

Knocking at the Hellgate

Harry Joy was to die three times, but it was his first death which was to have the greatest effect on him, and it is this first death which we shall now witness.

There is Harry Joy lying in the middle of that green suburban lawn, beneath that tattered banana tree, partly obscured by the frangipani, which even now drops a single sweet flower beside his slightly grey face.

As usual Harry is wearing a grubby white suit, and as he lies there, quite dead, his blue braces are visible to all the world and anyone can see that he has sewn on one of those buttons himself rather than ask his wife. He has a thin face and at the moment it looks peaceful enough. It is only the acute angles struck by his long gangling limbs which announce the suddenness of his departure. His cheeks are slightly sunken, and his large moustache (a moustache far too big for such a thin face) covers his mouth and leaves its expression as enigmatic as ever. His straight grey hair, the colour of an empty ashtray, hangs over one eye. And, although no one seems to have noticed it, a cigarette still burns between two yellowed fingers, like some practical joke known to raise the dead.

Yet when the two fingers are burnt, he does not move. His little pot belly remains quite still. He does not twitch even his little finger. And the people huddled around his wife on the verandah twenty yards away have no justification for the optimistic opinions they shower on her so eagerly.

Harry Joy saw all of this in a calm, curious, very detached way. From a certain height above the lawn he saw the cigarette burning in his hand, but at the same time he had not immediately recognized the hand as his. He only really knew himself by the button on his trousers. The lawn was very, very green, composed of broad-leaved tropical grasses, each blade thrillingly clear, and he wondered why everyone else had forsaken it for the shade of the verandah. Weeping came to him, but distantly, like short-wave signals without special significance.

He felt perfectly calm, and as he rose higher and higher he caught a fleeting glimpse of the doctor entering the front gate, but it was not a scene that could hold his interest in competition with the sight of the blue jewelled bay eating into what had once been a coastal swamp, the long meandering brown river, the quiet streets and long boulevards planted with mangoes, palms, flame trees, jacarandas, and bordered by antiquated villas in their own grounds, nobly proportioned mansions erected by ship-owners, sea captains and vice-governors, and the decaying stuccoed houses of shopkeepers. Around the base of the granite monolith which dominated the town, the houses became meaner, the vegetation sparser, and the dust rose from gravel roads and whirled in small eddies in the Sunday evening air.

Ecstasy touched him. He found he could slide between the spaces in the air itself. He was stroked by something akin to trees, cool, green, leafy. His nostrils were assailed with the smell of things growing and dying, a sweet fecund smell like the valleys of rain forests. It occurred to him that he had died and should therefore be frightened.

It was only later that he felt any wish to return to his body, when he discovered that there were many different worlds, layer upon layer, as thin as filo pastry, and that if he might taste bliss he would not be immune to terror. He touched walls like membranes, which shivered with pain, and a sound, as insistent as a pneumatic drill, promised meaningless tortures as terrible as the Christian stories of his youth.

He recognized the worlds of pleasure and worlds of pain, bliss and punishment, Heaven and Hell.

He did not wish to die. For a moment panic assailed him and he crashed around like a bird surrounded by panes of glass. Yet he had more reserves than he might have suspected and in a calm, clear space he found his way back, willed his way to a path beside a house where men carried a stretcher towards an ambulance. He watched with detachment whilst the doctor thumped the man on the chest. The man was thin with a grubby white suit. He watched as they removed the suit coat and connected wires to the thin white chest.

"My God," he thought, "that can't be me."

The electric shock lifted his body nine to ten inches off the table and at that moment his heart started and he lost all consciousness

He had been dead for nine minutes.

Harry Joy was thirty-nine years old and believed what he read in the newspapers. In the provincial town where he lived he was someone of note but not of importance, occupying a social position below the Managing Director of the town's largest store and even the General Manager of the canning factory; he was not known to the descendants of the early pioneer families or members of the judiciary, but when he entered the best restaurants in his grubby suit and dropped his cigarette ash everywhere he was humoured and attended to, and pity help the new waiter who did not know that this was Harry Joy.

"Mr Joy, how good to see you. This way please."

The lank figure with his pot belly passed between the tables and left smiles and whispers in the air behind him.

"Are you happy, Mr Joy?"

"Yes, Aldo, perfectly."

And indeed he thought himself happy, and why shouldn't he? He had a wife who loved him, children who gave no trouble, an advertising agency which provided a good enough living for a man with an almost aristocratic disdain for mercantile success, and, most important of all, the right to the best table in Milanos.

Here on the outposts of the American Empire, he conducted his business more or less in the American style, although with not quite the degree of seriousness the Americans liked. Telexes which began their journeys in Chicago, Detroit or New York found their way to him up river, where he interpreted these requests in a manner which, he would explain (ash dropping down his sleeve), suited local conditions.

"Someone is joining you, Mr Joy?"

"No, Aldo."

"A half bottle of claret?"

"A full bottle, Aldo. You choose something."

His great talent in life was to be a Good Bloke. He could walk into a room and sit down and everybody would be happy to have him, even if all he ever did was smile, for they imagined behind that moustache, behind the smile it hid, something sterner, more critical and yet, also, tolerant, so that when he smiled they felt themselves approved of and they vied with each other to like him best.

It all came down to the feeling that he was intelligent enough to be critical of you, but was not. He laughed too, a rich deep brown laugh which made the laughs surrounding it or following it sound slightly too thin. He was something of a story-teller and no one ever thought to say that the way he told a story, his deep drawling confidence, his refusal to be interrupted, might have been a sign of selfishness or self-centredness, for to criticize Harry only had the effect of making the critic himself appear somehow mean-minded.

For his part, Harry was never heard to criticize anyone (or for that matter, anything). He exhibited a blindness towards the faults of people and the injustices of the world which should have been irritating but which seemed to have almost the opposite effect: his very blindness reassured those around him and made them feel that their fears and nightmares were nothing but the products of their own overwrought imaginations.

They chose to love his grubby white suits, the way he lounged, dropping his ash everywhere, let himself be seduced by women (which he did, with rather appealing vanity) and accepted their praises without embarrassment. Even when he began to grow a belly it did not stop the women, who could never understand how he had married Bettina, who always seemed to speak badly of everyone and everything.

Bettina, for her part, had infidelities of her own, although she did it so less cleanly, so less gracefully. For if Harry, drunk, adopted an almost feline grace, a looseness *so* loose that you felt that if he collapsed it would be like a big cloth toy designed to do it, Bettina was louder, coarser, with rips in her stockings and lipstick smeared on her face, and her aggressions, normally so well hidden beneath a pancake make-up of niceness, cracked and broke on the third martini. Her choice of lovers was never very good, limited as she was to men who were prepared to be unfaithful with the wife of a Good Bloke. Even this (particularly this) made her angry, this conspiracy of men, this almighty *brotherhood of frauds*, as she secretly called them.

Harry Joy was not particularly intelligent, not particularly successful, not particularly handsome and not particularly rich. Yet there was about him this feeling that he belonged to an elite and for no good reason (none that Bettina could see) he was curiously proud of himself.

When the patrons of Milanos saw his empty table on Monday

lunchtime they already knew the news. They felt a gap, an emptiness, as if something very important was missing from the place.

When the table in the corner was taken by Joel Davis, his junior partner, and Harry's wife, there was (although they could not express it) something not quite decent about it.

Aldo would not have given them the table, not that particular table, but the woman tricked him into it, and then, of course, it was impossible to take it away from her. She arrived first, by herself, and how was he to know she was lunching with that person.

"Ah, Mrs Joy." He beamed. He held her hand. He had not been told. Other people had been told.

"For two, Aldo."

"For two. Mr Joy will be joining you?" (He groaned, remembering.)

"Mr Joy will not be here."

She did not tell him. Of course she was upset (possibly she was upset). No one told him. He, Aldo, was the only one who didn't know. It was a Monday, a difficult day to know things.

His mistake (when he discovered it) offended him throughout lunch, made him scowl to himself, and while he made sure that the service was scrupulous, he sulked behind the bar, preoccupied and uncertain.

When Joel came up the stairs, the penny dropped. But it was too late to shift them to another table.

And still he did not know about Harry! It would be another minute before he would know, and then from a winewaiter. Now he merely looked at Joel with a sour sort of contempt. He smiled, a baring of teeth.

Joel bared his teeth in return and checked his cufflinks, a salesman's habit he would have done well to be rid of. He did other American things (for he was an American), like insisting on iced water at table and then drinking spirits throughout the meal, which was noticed by everybody and not always approved of. The town had an ambivalent attitude towards Americans, envying their power and wishing to reject it and embrace it all at once. In business you could never be sure whether it was an asset or a liability to be an American.

Joel was only twenty-six but there was about him the sense of something over-ripe and gone to seed. He was not tall, and not exactly fat. But one noticed, immediately, those large red lips, which hovered on that balancing point where sensuality becomes greed. His fleshy face was a trifle too smooth and the skin glistened like a suspect apple which had been waxed to give it extra sales appeal.

He saw Bettina waiting, noted Aldo scowling, and instinctively, with no calculation, chose a route through the pink tablecloths which would take him past a prospective client, who would, he assumed, be eager for news of Harry.

Bettina watched him with qualified pride. She saw that the client liked him but that other people at the table were offended by his over familiar manner. He had no real idea of the impression he made. He would never understand why he offended people, why they thought him too pushy, too loud, or why they would also think him refreshing and clever.

"Hello, Mrs Joy," he said.

"Mr Davis." She did not smile. She felt the disapproval of the restaurant, like a slightly off odour, collectively generated. There was discomfort. A glass of wine was spilt at one table, a fork dropped at another.

Joel was busy searching for a waiter.

"It's O.K.," Bettina kicked his shin gently. "I ordered you a daquiri."

He pulled a face. "You know I don't like daquiris."

"How are they at the office?"

The office, like the restaurant, had displayed a certain mute hostility towards Joel as if the whole business had been his fault. They had detected signs of a new pomposity in him. He had "borrowed" the little Birko jug Harry had kept in his office to make coffee and this, although he didn't know it, had created a minor scandal.

"It's O.K. in the office. Alex is looking for another job already. He doesn't trust me and if Harry . . ."

He didn't say "dies" and she lowered her eyes as if he had imprudently complimented her on the smoothness of her skin.

"And a couple of the girls were crying."

"Which ones?"

He looked at her and laughed maliciously.

The daquiri arrived. He sent it back and asked for a martini. He explained to the waiter how he would like the martini made.

"You bastard," she said.

"What?"

"I ordered the daquiri for you."

"I don't like daquiris."

"I would have drunk it," she said.

Only after the food arrived did he ask her about Harry, and, just as in any business lunch the entrée is reserved for small talk and the main course signals the commencement of serious business, it was at this point they began.

"Well . . .?" he said.

"He thinks he's going to die."

"And . . ."

"The doctor says he'll be fine. It's a dangerous operation, but he's confident it'll be fine."

"But he thinks he's going to die? Why?"

"You know Harry, it's like his hives. He decides he's going to get them and . . ."

"When he decides he's getting hives, he gets them."

"I didn't mean that. He looks good."

"Good."

"The doctor says there's nothing to worry about."

"Marvellous," he said, but kept looking her in the eye, his knife and fork lifted, as if looking for some secret sign. Joel, sometimes, lacked all subtlety.

Neither of them had the will or the strength to actually murder someone, although Bettina would certainly grow in leaps and bounds over the following year, and nor did they have the strength to say they would have liked Harry dead. In truth they wouldn't even look the idea in the face. Instead they flirted with it. They saw it pass sexily out of the corner of their eyes but did not, for a second, turn their heads to stare. They did not allow themselves to know what they wanted or why they wanted it. They were blind-worms pushing forward, entwining in the dark. One could, unfairly perhaps, imagine them as the instruments of someone else's pleasure.

"Here comes the little monkey."

He knew she was talking about Aldo and didn't look around. Joel had long ago given up trying to make Aldo like him.

"Mrs Joy," Aldo looked at her reproachfully, his small dark head on one side, "you didn't tell me . . ."

Aldo did not much care for Bettina Joy but he admitted to himself that she had something, a strength, a sexiness that was very rare for a slightly dumpy woman with fat legs. Her face was round and smooth and olive-skinned, her hair straight and dark, her eyes impenetrable.

"I'm sorry, Aldo."

"I understand, I understand."

"He's in the General. They'll be operating this week."

"Such a young man. He'll be better though, soon. My brother had a heart attack twenty years ago. He's been healthier since he had it." He laughed. "It's probably the best thing."

"Coronary by-pass surgery", Bettina said firmly, "is very dangerous, but we all hope it will be fine."

"Now perhaps he will give up those cigarettes."

"Perhaps, yes."

There was a pause and Joel thought: not a damn fool here knows I am fucking her.

("Your meal was enjoyable?")

When, of course, they all knew.

("Yes, thank you.")

They had watched it for months. They had seen her dull eyes glisten. They had heard her throaty laughter become a fraction shriller. They had not talked about the curious *ménage à trois* at the corner table, merely absorbed its possible implications so that later, when everything became obvious, they would realize they had known all the time.

Aldo, strangely irritated, passed around the tables, making his way towards an inept food-writer who had also been sent to haunt him.

Bettina said: "He's a cretin." She was being unfair, but she was sick of being patronized by idiots who couldn't tie up their own shoe-laces. She wanted power and success, not vicariously, not through a lover or a husband, but directly, for herself alone. Joel, at least, accepted this in her, and in this respect at least she felt equal with him. There was some perverse honesty she shared with him. She no longer had to pretend to be generous and kind and loving. She didn't want to be good, she wanted to be successful. She explored the border territories of pain and pleasure with him. Smeared with shit and semen she felt herself to be standing at new doorways with new possibilities.

All around her were clean pink tablecloths.

Harry Joy was suckled on stories in those long lost days in the little weatherboard house on the edge of town. The world he was born in had been fresh and green. Dew drops full of visions hung from morning grass and old Clydesdales stood silently in the paddock above the creek. Crickets sang songs and everything had meanings. The sky was full of Gods and Indians and people smiled at him, touched him, stroked him, and brought him extraordinary gifts from the world outside where there were, he knew, exotic bazaars filled with people in gowns, strange fruits piled high, the air redolent with spices, and Jesus Christ, and the Good Samaritan, always dressed in his dusty grey robe with its one red patch on the left sleeve, and the soldier offering the dripping wet sponge of wine to Jesus, and there were small boiled sweets and white sheets and the smell of bread, and floor polish and, far away, New York, its glass towers trembling in an ecstasy of magic which was to become, his father said, one day, after the next flood, a splendid book read by all mankind with wonder.

His father came and went three times, the first to sire him, the second to drain the swamp, the third to see his son with vaguely disappointed eyes.

His father had lain in bed while the Shire Engineer had knocked on the door. He remembered his mother giggling and how happy it made him feel, those sounds like drops of water suspended in sunlight, and how his father, pulling on his tall boots had come to the door laughing, to admit the tight-faced engineer.

"You'll be dead a long time, Brophy," his father told the engineer.

His father was tall and had a big moustache. He had been born in New York State and had travelled the world. When Harry and his mother went to church, his father stayed in bed.

"I can talk to God from here," he told the child, who never doubted that his father had a special relationship with the Almighty. He would have rather stayed in the warm bed beside his father than venture out to the little wooden church with its gothic texts written on the arch above the nave, a cold austere place where people left to drink communion wine and returned with solemn faces and a slightly frightening smell. The church was always nearly empty and only his mother's soft contralto rose like a bird and warmed its empty spaces with its trembling wings.

Here he heard about Heaven and Hell and the tortures of Jesus. He sat aghast at such terrible cruelty and more than once wept in sympathy for the tortured God or fear for what the God might do to him.

He preferred the stories of his father.

"How I met your mother," his father said, "is a story you should know, but first you must give me blue bread or a sapphire."

"I haven't got any," the boy wailed. "Tell me the story."

"Don't tease him, Vance," his mother said.

"Don't tease me," the boy said petulantly.

"You must always give something for a story," his father said. "Either blue bread made from cedar ash, or a sapphire. That is something I learned from the Hopi. All stories come from the Holy People and you must give something for them."

"What is a sapphire?"

"A stone."

The boy ran outside and found a stone, a small brown stone with a white vein in it. He gave it to his father, who accepted it solemnly.

"Thank you, now we will sit on the floor."

"No, Vance, not the floor."

But they sat on the floor, the father and son, the boy folding his legs the way his father showed him. Occasionally his father would stop the story to feed the wood stove.

"This", said his father, "is the story of the Vision Splendid. It had been dry for eight weeks and the whole of the air was full of dust, bright red dust that settled on everything. Nobody thought it would ever rain again. And then one afternoon we saw the storm clouds coming from the south and we prayed for it to rain. Your mother, who I didn't know, went to the church and she prayed. And I prayed too, but not in the church."

"Did it rain?"

"Did it rain? When your mother asks God for rain . . ."

"Vance," his mother said, but she giggled.

"Did it rain? The rain poured down. It rained so heavily you couldn't see your hand in front of your face. It rained like all the air was a river and the drains in the main street filled up and then the water, red water, the same colour as the dust, crept out across the main street until there was just a white line going down the centre and red water all around it, and then there wasn't even the white line and the main street was a river three feet deep."

"Captain's Creek flooded and I went down there with some other fellows to help the shopkeepers. We had old Malachy's clinker boat, half-gone with dry-rot, and when we got to the Co-op it sank on its mooring (we tied it to the verandah post). We were shifting the flour and grain up on top of the counter, away from the water, and I just looked out the door, just glancing up, and that was when I saw the Vision Splendid."

"What was it?" asked the boy. "What was the Vision Splendid?"

"It was your mother, lad, her long black hair blacker than coal, standing in the front of a boat which was piled high with all the things from the church vestry. She was standing in front of the boat holding the cross and her eyes, her eyes, my boy. Ah ..." he stopped. "All that red water and such luminous eyes."

It was only a small house and when the February winds blew it rocked on its wooden stumps and it is a measure of their sense of their own specialness that they did not envy their neighbours' larger houses but found theirs in every way superior. To walk into that little cottage was to feel something that was available nowhere else in town: old oiled timbers, mellow lights, curious old rugs, and chipped plates with pretty patterns, which visitors would fondly imagine were the remnants of a misplaced fortune. Where everybody else bought glossy white paint and threw out their kitchen dressers, the Joys were seen removing the last vestiges of paint and fossicking out at the tip for their neighbours' rejected furniture.

They should have been hated, or at least ridiculed, but they weren't. Seen fossicking at the tip they were granted the right to eccentricity normally given only to aristocrats, and there were rumours that they were, in some not very clear way, almost aristocratic. Perhaps Vance Joy's English middle-class accent gave them this idea, or at least provided a core on which other layers of fantasy could be coated, creamy layer on creamy layer. Yet at the heart of it all was this: Vance Joy was a big expansive man with a generous spirit whom it was impossible to dislike; he would never say no to anyone who asked for help; he could, if need be, drink like a fish and, most important of all, knock any man down. Patricia Joy was at once very beautiful and very modest; she was well educated but never displayed it; she taught piano on Thursdays and Saturdays and once did a water-colour copy of "The Last Supper" for the Sunday School, a work of art so highly valued that a departing clergyman had forever muddied his reputation by taking it with him when he left the town.

As everyone would say, as if expecting the contrary: "They're hard-up, but not stuck-up."

The Joys, charming, beautiful, educated, eccentric, played a part in this little game and in ways too subtle for anyone (themselves least of all) to notice, they encouraged it. They did feel themselves to be aristocrats of a sort: free-spirits, moralists, artists, bon vivants; and one must acknowledge, at least, the strength of character required to live their very slightly bohemian life in such a small and often intolerant community and, what is more, to get away with it.

When Harry thought of that house afterwards it would always be night and the wood stove crackled and made dull thumps and hisses and it shifted its burning innards to make itself more comfortable. A soft yellow kerosene light threw benevolent shadows across the room and his father (who lived in the house for a total of four years and two months) would always be there, telling a story in a languid way, stuffing a pipe with tobacco, feeding a stove, or cooking some unappetizing peasant porridge that he had taken a liking to in India or South America or Oregon.

And stories, always stories: Wood Spirits, lightning, the death of Kings, and New York, New York, New York.

"In New York there are towers of glass. It is the most beautiful and terrible city on earth. All good, all evil exist there." He could say the word "evil" so you felt it, a cold sinuous thing that could come in under a locked door and push up into your bowels. "If you know where to look, you can find the devil. That is where he lives. If you keep your eyes peeled you can see him drive down 42nd Street in a Cadillac with darkened windows. He lives in Park Avenue, surrounded by his servants. But New York is full of saints, they . . ."

"Vance!"

"My darling Patricia, you know it's true."

"He believes everything you tell him, stop it." She was sitting at the table, darning socks. She brushed her dark hair from her eyes and smiled.

"When God makes the next flood," his father said, "he will leave New York as a lesson to those who survive. Every other thing on earth will be destroyed except the buildings in New York. It will be a bible of buildings, a much better bible, a holy place which only the very learned will know how to read."

"One day," Harry said sleepily, "I will go to New York."

"You will too," his father said, and read his palm to prove it to him.

He grew into a tall thin boy who had been at first what children (or at least the children in that town) called "Gooby", by which they meant someone who is a little slow and introverted and is likely to stand at odd places with his mouth open staring at things that no one would look at twice. But later, fed by the deep wells of his own self-regard, he became much liked. His height was a positive advantage in the type of football they played, and that too all worked in his favour. He was a deadly accurate kick and scored many goals; which was nothing less than what he had expected of himself, for he had been raised to expect excellence, and he did not, even for an instant, think it ridiculous, when confronted with some problem, to ask himself: what would Jesus have done? In fact he did it all the time. He sometimes had quiet dreams of martyrdom for some greater good.

They had wanted him to be Van Gogh, Jesus Christ and Zapata all rolled into one.

But somewhere there was something lacking, and as he grew older he came to show too great a regard for his father's maxims about not working yourself to death. His mother took him to a city specialist to see if he had a problem with his thyroid gland, so lethargic did he begin to appear. He was like a wonderful racing car with a severely underpowered engine, and whether it was his father's final departure, or simply the onset of puberty, his idealistic concern for goodness seemed to have fallen away. He did not ask himself what Jesus would have done. In fact he hadn't asked himself what Jesus would have done since he had been faced with the prospect of Jeanette Grandell's wonderful fourteen-year-old breasts.

But although it would be a long long time before he concerned himself with goodness again, it did fall into the sediment of his character, and at times over the years he found himself wondering what God would like him to do.

But now he was a man of thirty-nine lying in a hospital bed and contemplating death. He could not allow himself to know that he was sickened with his life. He was like someone who has lain in bed too long eating rich food: within his soul there was suddenly a yearning for tougher, stronger things, for ecstasies, for the thrill of goodness perfectly achieved, to see butterflies in doorways in Belize, to be part of the lightning dance, to quiver in terror before the cyclone.

But it was too late for all those things, far too late. He stared out at the sunlit garden and listened to a banana leaf flap against the rain-water spout on the verandah. In the garden, an old woman with swollen arms picked roses. Beside his bed a man with a striped suit and eyes like weak tea dropped, for the third time, the card that contained the details of Harry's medical condition. The man picked up the card with thick sausage fingers and yet it was not the surgeon's clumsiness that convinced Harry Joy he was about to die, nor was it the admission that the operation entailed something like a 5 per cent risk. In fact he was less worried about dying than where he would go after he died.

He watched the surgeon's unnaturally red lips move and could not bring himself to talk about the lingering taste of heaven and hell, explain that hell was like chrome-yellow flowers, that there were worlds in the afterlife like layer after layer of filo pastry, that he, Harry Joy, lay now at the cross-roads, that he had been warned.

What happened to him now, what he thought, what he decided, would determine whether he entered Heaven or Hell.

Vance Joy's stories had drifted like groundsel seeds and taken root in the most unlikely places. They had rarely grown in the way he would have imagined, in that perfect green landscape of his imagination, intersected with streams and redolent of orange blossom.

In certain climates they became like weeds, uncontrollable, not always beautiful, a blaze of rage or desire from horizon to horizon.

All these Harry had carried innocently, passing them on to his wife, his son, his daughter. Not having understood them, he transmitted them imperfectly and they came to mean quite different things. Vance Joy's stories of New York contained apocalyptic visions and conflicts between Good and Evil, but to Harry they were merely stories to be told, and to Bettina they were something else again.

New York was her antidote for the town she hated. She hated its wide colonial verandahs, its slow muddy river, its sleepy streets, its small-town pretensions. She loathed the perpetual Sunday afternoons, the ugly people, the inelegant bars and frumpy little frocks. Here, marooned on the edge of the Empire, she had spent ten years waiting for Harry's promise that they would go to New York.

"How could you?" she had asked (how many years ago?).

"Easy," he said.

"How?"

"Sell up the business and go there."

"When?"

"One day."

He hadn't not-meant it, but he hadn't really meant it either. His business was a grand, slightly decrepit, old boat drifting with the current down a slow muddy river and every now and then he would get out and, with a long pole, push it away from the bank. Sitting back in the wheelhouse he could afford to dream about New York, but the thought of really competing in that turbulent water filled him with fatigue.

Bettina did not give up her dreams so easily. She spoke of New York to no one. She secretly married it to another dream, rolled the two together, harboured them within her and let them grow. She cultivated Americans and read their magazines. She saved money and put it in a special account. She did exercises to preserve her body for that time of arrival. And there had been times – how could she deny it to herself – when she had imagined, dreamed, the easiest solution to her problem would be if Harry would quietly die in his sleep. And sometimes, sitting in the kitchen at Palm Avenue, waiting for him to arrive from some late conference, she had watched the clock-hand edge its way sideways around the dial and she'd thought – of course she was drunk – he's dead. And there was such lightness in the thought, such relief.

Ah, she was not a nice person. It was obvious. Nice people were usually boring, always boring.

She was drunk, and hated the town. She hated Harry's Fiat: it was ten years old and full of cigarette butts and old newspapers and, for some reason she could never understand, he was proud of it. He bought a Jaguar and gave it to her, but he kept that Fiat for himself as if it were somehow vulgar to display any wealth.

"But why? Why? For Christsakes, why?"

"I like it." And you could see that he didn't even *know* why he liked it, but that he clung to it like an old teddy bear, some piece of damn rubbish Crazy Vance or Silly Patricia had scrounged from the tip.

But the Jaguar was (again) in the garage having its cooling system fixed (the cretins) and she had to drive this little joke car.

She grated the gears going into the hospital. She saw no charm in the old building, smothered in bougainvillaea and surrounded by big old flame trees, frangipanis and mangoes. It was only Americans who found it charming and when they did she suspected them of being patronizing, just as now, parking beside a particularly large and rather gross Ford, she thought she detected a certain superiority, a certain condescension directed towards her by its owner.

Fuck you. If I'd arrived in the Jaguar you'd have known who I was.

The woman left the Ford and minced towards the hospital. (Look at the mutant in her black Crimplene pant suit!)

Bettina stood beside the Fiat and picked cigarette butts off her white linen jacket. She was late. As she hurried across behind the Crimplene pant suit, she remembered that she had a pussy full of semen. It was only held in by a Kleenex and a pair of panty-hose. He would smell it. He would know. She wondered whether she should go home but hurried forward, catching her five-inch heel in a metal grating and falling heavily.

"Fuck it." She had grazed her leg.

The Crimplene pant suit, summoned by the urgency of her obscenity, had hurried back.

"Are you alright?"

Bettina, her leg bleeding, her linen jacket ripped, sat up and gave her most charming middle-class smile. "Yes," she said, "thank you so much."

In the hospital she had to fight off the nurses who wanted to fix up her knee. If they had known she didn't have knickers on they'd have been scandalized. If they got a sniff of her pussy, God knows what would happen.

She backed away from them, her knee smarting, her lips smiling politely.

"Thank you ever so much," she said, emphasizing the "ever" in an English sort of way. "But I'm in a hurry. I'll fix it when I get home." She would have liked to have picked the nurses up by their necks and shaken them for their dreary ambitions and their dreary lives. Their sunburnt noses irritated her. They carried their bedpans and buggered up their insides lifting heavy weights. They went back to the suburbs and had families. They ran around answering buzzers and falling in love.

There, Bettina thought, but for the Grace of God, and so on.

"Sit closer."

"No, no," she smiled. "I'm fine."

"Why are you sitting so far away?"

"I think I'm getting a cold," she lied. The fishy smell rose from between her legs and in her guilty imagination it assumed the splendid obviousness of a smoke flare spewing upwards from her discreetly tailored lap

"Had any visitors?"

"Oh," he laughed, that famous deep brown laugh, and for a moment he looked so *happy* with himself, sitting up in bed in his silk pyjamas. "It's been a circus in here. Tom Flynn and Ernie from the cleaners, Jack and Belinda, Mike, Dee, the Clarkes. We played poker dice. I won ten dollars."

The table in the corner was piled high with fruit. There were pineapples and bananas and passionfruit and grapes, so many grapes, and custard apples and avocados. He was proud of these offerings, she saw, but when Bettina looked at his table, she thought only that it represented the monstrous lack of originality of his friends.

"Eat some," he said. "I can't eat it all. Please come and sit here."

He stretched out his hand. He would never believe, in his wildest dreams, that she no longer loved him. She had said it once, but he would dismiss these sorts of things as "temperament" or "wine" as if a bottle contained an infusion of foreign thoughts with which she had innocently poisoned herself.

"Come and give your old man a kiss."

She kissed his hand, making a joke of it.

"On the lips."

She leant across the bed and kissed him quickly. Of course she loved him, a little at least.

"Phew," he said, wrinkling up his nose.

Betrayed, she burnt red.

"What have you been up to?"

"Nothing."

"You've been drinking whisky," he said.

"Oh, yes," she said, and added bravely, "with Joel. I got a bit drunk. I fell over in the car park." And she withdrew a little to show him her bleeding knee. "I ripped my jacket." She could feel herself still blushing and he was looking at her with those big dark eyes, as if he knew. But that was a trick of his, not an intentional trick but a misleading sign. He saw nothing. It looked as if he could see everything and people always gave him credit for it.

She dragged the horrible plastic orange chair another inch closer and leaned forward to hold his hand.

"You can bring it closer than that."

"I'm alright." She stank. "What's the matter?"

"Nothing. I'm fine."

"You've got something on your mind."

He never knew what was on his mind until he was questioned about it. He would not let himself see his own worries and even his own mind, she thought, was a strange territory to him and it always needed someone else to come along and sift through it and point out interesting or painful things to him. Often she would find him frowning, and, after due questioning, he would say: "ah, I think I must have a headache."

But she would not question him today. That slight contraction of the brow could be caused by, probably was caused by, the fishy smell he would not acknowledge.

"I'm going to die," he said.

"Why do you go on with that?" She didn't mean to snap, but she felt accused. There was no logical, medical reason for him to think he should die.

"Don't be angry."

"I'm not angry." Yet she was. Unreasonably angry.

"You're frowning like a bulldog."

"You're only talking yourself into it. It's like your hives . . ."

"I don't talk myself into hives."

"You always know when you're going to get them."

"I can feel them coming on. I can feel them before you can see them, that's all."

"You're not going to die."

"You don't understand," he said, "listen to me: I don't mind dying."

Why did he always give you the feeling that he knew things, that he knew she had dreamed his death a hundred times and now, meekly, he held out his throat to be cut. He would make himself die to show her how wrong she was. She looked at that long sinewy arm, the hairy wrist that emerged from the pyjama coat, and thought about its life and saw, before her eyes, how it would be dead, decaying. She saw maggots, crawling things, and looked up at his face.

"I don't want you to die!" she said as if her secret wish were the core of the problem and once she had said this the problem was solved.

He looked at her with astonishment.

"Why don't you believe me?" she said.

When he didn't answer her (he couldn't think of what to say) she lapsed into angry silence.

"Do you believe in God, Bettina?"

She winced. If she had been religious she would have believed in

Satan and would have found him, in her terms, "generally less boring". But religion represented all the goody-goody two-shoes and she found it embarrassing even to talk about.

"You won't die," she said. She had torn the crotch of her panty-hose somehow.

"Something very strange happened to me when I had the attack," he said. "I haven't told anyone."

"You should tell the doctor," she said warily. If her panty-hose had torn . . .

Bettina shifted in her chair.

"I had a vision."

"It was lack of oxygen," she said confidently.

He had a distant look in his eyes like he did when he watched *Casablanca* on the television. "I left my body and went up in the air."

She looked at him with alarm. "Maybe you should see a psychologist."

But he did not appear to hear her. He began speaking very quickly, with none of the grace notes, none of the velvety drawl that he would bring to a story; he rushed through the events of his death and described to her, exactly, who had stood where on the lawn, who had carried his body, what the doctor had worn, the details of everything that had happened while he was dead.

"It was a warning," he said finally. "I saw Heaven and Hell. There is a Heaven. There is a Hell."

"It was lack of oxygen," she insisted, but he shook his head with uncharacteristic stubbornness.

"I'll get him fired," she said firmly.

"Who?"

"The doctor. He's a clumsy fool. No wonder you're frightened."

"It's nothing to do with the doctor."

"He's got sausage fingers."

"I know."

"He drops things."

"I know."

She moved her chair closer to the bed and patted his hand.

"You won't go to Hell, Harry. You're too nice to go to Hell. If anyone's going to Hell it'll be me."

And Harry, not for the first time, failed to recognize the resentment in her voice.

★

When he was about to die in a foreign country, years later, Harry's son would tell his captors that he had been born in an electrical storm. Like so many of the things he had said throughout his short life, the story was not quite true.

David Joy remembered the night his father took him to see lightning. It was his first memory.

He could still remember the stale musty smell of the raincoat wrapped around his tiny body. It was hard and nasty and would always make him associate mildew with terror. His father held him and laughed. His great moustache had tickled his face.

How the earth had shaken! What monstrous shapes the lightning showed.

"Lightning."

Could he speak? Did he answer? There was only the memory of mildew, tobacco, and rain needles on his uncovered head.

His father always maintained that he had not cried, that he had pointed with pleasure and gurgled with delight, but that was not quite true either, not at all true, but reflected what Harry would have wanted of his son.

No, he had not gurgled, he had stared with big dark eyes full of terror.

His mother said he screamed, yet he did not scream until, in the middle of a rolling thunder clap, a monster came rushing through the night and seized him from the precarious safety of his father's arms. And then he screamed. Held tightly in the foreign arms he was transported through the storm.

It was only when they entered the house that he saw the monster was his mother, her face white, her eyes wide with fear and anger. With what urgency she kissed him, with what fierceness she hugged him. He knew something terrible had happened. He smelt sheets drying by the fire, warm and sweet, and his father, standing, smiling, saying: "I was only showing him the lightning."

And his mother, wrapping him in a milk-soft towel: "Oh you fool, you fool."

When he was older he would go and stand in the lightning by himself. They told him he was like his father. He was pleased. He did not confess that the lightning had always filled him with fear. He stood in raincoats of different colours, with different smells, and forced himself to confront the most violent storms of the monsoon. Seven seconds between thunder clap and lightning meant the lightning was one mile distant. He stood and counted, his wet lips moving. He stood rigid and confronted Mount Sugar Loaf while the lightning hit its peak and danced like a devil around its dark dead shape. He stood while it marched closer, surrounded by mildew, alone in the storm.

But later, in the warm house, he would be told he was like his father and he would look with masculine superiority at his mother who drew the curtains to cut out the storm.

David grew tall and thin and they said he was like his father. They did not notice the dark eyes that trembled with dreams, the smooth olive skin of his mother. It was better to be like his father, that was what they all wanted. He went to his father's office and sometimes, if there was an empty desk, sat in a big chair and wrote advertisements like his father did. Did they never notice that he was in no way like his father, that he did not make friends easily and was full of secrets?

At school he told lies. They found him out. He told them that he had been to New York. He stood up in the classroom and described it as his mother had described it to him. He mentioned bars where people drank a wonderful green drink (his own invention) from tall thin glasses he had quietly stolen from Bettina's *Vogue*. Yet when Lucy came home and told his mother, while he stood and listened, rigid with panic, bright with shame, no one had reproached him seriously.

"Ah," Bettina said, cutting shortbreads, "he is like his father, always telling stories."

Yet the dreams that shone most brightly in his imagination were often gathered from his mother who, without really meaning to, taught him about the meanness, the insignificance of the town he lived in, the smallness of his life and thus, in her own perverse way, showed him the beauty of the world or, at least, the beauty of Other Places.

He read adventure books and bought an atlas with money stolen from his father's bedside table.

When Harry told him Vance Joy's story of the Beggar-King he heard the story with his mother's ears.

"There was a king," Harry said, "a long time ago in a country full of tall mountains. The winter was full of ice and the summers were so hot that children and old people died. There were many beggars in the country," Harry said, repeating, thirty years later, the exact words of the story, "and the king felt sorry for them. At night he could not sleep. He lay awake thinking of the beggars. Like all kings," Harry said, forever ignoring the political implications of what he said, "it did not occur to him to give away his wealth, but rather he wished to punish himself for being rich." (Don't you remember, Harry, the lovely ice-thin malice in your father's voice, or were you too young to hear it?)

"One day he decided to dress as a beggar and go out amongst the people."

At this stage of the story it was necessary to pull a coat or a woollen sweater around the head, to cover the face, to wander dolefully around the room. (But don't you remember how your father did it, how he managed to get that unbeggarly strut into his walk so that beneath that old brown sweater you *knew* there was a king pretending to be a beggar?)

"He had a dark cloak made and wandered the streets. He didn't fool anyone. They all knew he was the king, even the little children knew it was the king. When he came down the street in his dark robe calling piteously for alms they rushed from their houses and gave him gold.

"Each day the king returned to his palace laden with wealth. When he counted his gold and saw how much one beggar could make in a day, he became very angry. He felt that the beggars had tricked him and so he made a law forbidding them: anyone found begging would be put to death, by the sword.

"All that winter," Harry said in his father's doleful voice, "the beggars slowly starved to death and when the spring came there were no more beggars to be seen."

And that was the story, in Harry's hands a poor directionless thing, left to bump around by itself and mean what you wanted it to, although it was not without effect and young David Joy sat silently before its sword-sharp edges.

"But why?"

Harry felt uncomfortable before such questions. "It's just a story."

"I will be rich," his son said, "and have jewels."

Can we blame this story for David's avarice? Hardly. He was already stealing silver coins from his father's bedside table when he was six (Too young, you say? Not a bit of it.) and one should not think him lacking in sympathy for the beggars, quite the opposite: he brimmed full of emotion and saw that sharp-edged sword come down on the pitiful skin of their blue, cold necks.

As he became older, people came to think of him as cold, yet he was so full of emotions he could not speak. He dared not reveal his destiny. He read books and hoarded their contents. He chose South America as his special domain. He knew Paraguay and Patagonia, Chile and Brazil. He dreamed of wealth and adventure, and yet he was frightened of almost everything. On the football field he cowered and cringed. Confronted with fist fights he ran away and hid. In dark corners he rehearsed his triumphal return from South America when he would make presents to his family (his enemies too) and tell them stories of his adventures.

He hoarded money and counted his bank balance. He sold newspapers in the evenings (a long-legged boy fearfully dodging peak-hour traffic) and saved everything he made. When he was fifteen he began selling marihuana to his class-mates. It brought him money and prestige, yet he dealt with damp hands, fearful of discovery and punishment. He told his father he wished to study medicine because his father indicated it would please him. His business broadened to tabs of acid, speed, and lignocaine which he sold as cocaine. He never took drugs. He was frightened of going mad. And yet the cocaine entranced him because it (if it had been real cocaine and not lignocaine) had come from South America.

This then is Harry's son, who in his father's words is "a good boy, going to be a doctor". He contemplated arrest and murder by knife; he stood before these visions with his hands clenched, his body rigid, while the lightning danced around the nearby hills.

"The story of the butterfly.

"I was in Bogotá and waiting for a lady friend. I was in love, a long time ago. I waited three days. I was hungry but could not go out for food, lest she come and I not be there to greet her. Then, on the third day, I heard a knock.

"I hurried along the old passage and there, in the sunlight, there was nothing.

"Just", Vance Joy said, "a butterfly, flying away."

David Joy had decorated his bedroom in the style of an office. The walls were covered in brown felt, the floor with a dark brown carpet. A black desk occupied a central position in the room, which was illuminated solely by a small chrome desk-lamp. Beside the desk was a chrome and leather swivel-chair and in front of the desk there was another chrome and leather chair, but in this case it had no swivel.

His bed, tucked away in a dark corner, was covered with a large brown rug. With the curtains drawn and the desk-lamp on, one could forget the bed was even there.

His parents could not see that it was not a bedroom but an office.

He was seventeen years old. Now, sitting at a desk, wearing a fawn cashmere sweater, his dark hair conservatively cut, he might have been a student from any good middle-class home, except that the top of the desk was covered with money, some of it in large denominations. It was, in this quiet and private moment, arranged from the highest to the lowest denominations, from left to right, from far to near, one note occupying one space.

The notes glowed magically. He sat perfectly still, had already sat perfectly still for fifteen minutes with only those dark eyes sweeping ceaselessly back and forth along the eight rows in front of him: additions, subtractions, dreams that swept the Americas from New York to Tierra del Fuego.

He heard his sister approach and although she may just as easily have been going to her own room he gave himself five seconds to clear the desk. He did it in eight polished, rehearsed movements, as graceful as a card sharp, with no hint of panic or fear, only this wonderfully svelte movement. He was not, however, perfect: as Lucy entered the room a single note was still floating from desk to floor and David would have found it undignified to grab for it.

Lucy saw it but she knew better than to touch it. Things had changed in their relationship since the time when she had teased him about his tears and his lies. She walked around the note and sat facing her brother across the desk. She was fifteen years old and still in her school uniform. She resembled her mother except that the slightly desperate quality that Bettina carried was totally missing and, in its place, a rather dream-like detachment which would make the lips in her plump olive face more sensuous than her mother's, the eyes somehow wider, the dark hair fuller and richer.

"Aren't you going to pick it up?" she said.

"Why should I?"

"So you can take it and put it with the other money in the back of the Fiat."

Something in David's body tightened, and Lucy, who knew him well, stiffened. Her eyes did not, for an instant, leave his.

If she had thought him incapable of hurting her, his behaviour would have been melodramatic. For he now revelled in the threats he posed her, the darkness and danger he might represent, and he applied himself to this with the same single-mindedness that he would, outside the door of this room, bring to the role of a sensible intelligent boy who wished to be a doctor.

"Who told you?"

"I found it," she said. "I was looking for a pencil I dropped."

"When?"

"Two months ago."

"If you tell anyone, I'll kill you."

"I know." She shivered. She was not exactly sure that he would kill her.

The tension went away for a moment and David bent down and picked up the money.

"What are you going to do with your money?" she said.

"Why do you ask questions when you know the answer?"

"You're still going to New York?"

"See ... you know." She didn't know. She didn't know about South America and he would never tell her because she would laugh.

"To go into business?"

"Haven't you got anything else to do?" he said coldly; yet he didn't want her to go. His sister's presence charged him with a strange erotic energy. He was not thinking about what he said. He spoke, merely, to keep her there. She had boyfriends. People liked her. He wanted to touch her hair.

Lucy shrugged. You couldn't talk to David. He wouldn't talk. Except once, a long time ago, he had told her his dream, his secret, his vision of New York. She had wanted to hear about it again, this glistening dream he had made in the darkness of his discontents.

"When you are rich in New York, will you send for me?"

"No," he said, "what do you want?"

Lucy smiled.

She had not come to see him because she liked him. She was being nice because she wanted something. That was the way the world was. Yet in his dreams he returned with presents for her: a sapphire necklace worked with Inca gold.

"The answer", he said, "is no."

"Oh ... please, David ... just a deal."

"I'm not doing grass any more."

"Oh, David ... please."

"All I've got is some flowers and beads and I'm keeping them."

"What else have you got?"

"Coke, MDA, speed."

"Go on, please, give me some grass. I'm feeling low."

"Take a Valium."

"I don't want a Valium. I want some grass. Oh, please . . . be nice to your sister."

"My sister won't be nice to me." His voice was hoarse. He hardly knew what he was saying.

She stopped smiling for a moment because she recognized the voice. A harshness came into her face.

"Is that what you want then?" she said.

"I just want my sister to be nice to me." For a second his hard-locked eyes shifted uncertainly and his mouth wobbled before it fixed itself again.

"I've got forty dollars," she said. "why don't you just take the money?"

She saw him hesitate. She thought he was weighing it up, the pros and cons, putting a dollar value on pleasure, assessing the pleasure in profit.

"If you blow me," he said softly, "I'll give you some." Her lips tightened. "How much?"

"A bag, a deal."

"A full deal? Show me."

"No. You want it: yes or no?"

She shrugged. She didn't like blowing him, but there were worse things. He came quick and then she'd have the grass and the money.

"O.K.," she said, "get it out."

"Don't talk like that."

"Like what?" She had him now. Now she was the one with power.

"Don't talk tough, talk soft. O.K.?"

"O.K.," she said.

She sucked him then, with neither passion nor revulsion, thinking what a stupid thing it was to say: don't talk tough, talk soft: how could she talk? It did not occur to her for a moment that he wanted her affection and love.

"Sister," he said, "little sister."

He was miming affection, she thought, simulating love. It was necessary for him and she felt sorry for him. She could imagine him, in a brown shirt, being a Fascist, his hair slicked flat, the dark irises of his eyes stopped down to exclude ordinary people, to include nothing but the fiery bright light of some impossible hero, some unvisited place. This hate was all he had managed to pick up from his mother, who, at this very moment, was entering the front door.

Lucy stopped. "Betty's home," she said.

He forced her head down and she knew, as she heard the footsteps and her mother's voice, that he would not let her go. The footsteps were coming up the stairs when he finally shot his 10 ccs.

When Bettina opened the door she found David sitting at his desk with a book and Lucy brushing past her. David was smiling. Before she could ask him what the joke was she heard Lucy retching in the toilet.

"Hello, Mummy," he said, "how's Daddy?"

"What's the matter with Lucy?"

He shrugged. "I guess she's a bit sick. How's Daddy?"

Bettina looked at him sharply. "You little bugger," she said. "What have you done to her?"

It was not a question that would have occurred to Harry, who had never seen his family as you, dear reader, have now been privileged to.

The fluorescent light cast green over everything. The apples and bananas and grapes and biscuits and Black Forest torte and smoked trout were all placed on a small table and arranged like flowers. Why did everybody bring him food? Why, now, did they all look so sinister, the dead green things he had been given?

He sucked on his sheet and lay quite still.

The apple had once been connected to a tree. Now it was disconnected. Did it die? What was death to an apple? It had never occurred to him before that there was a vast distance between the apple on the tree and the apple on the table. Nor had he thought of the trout as connected to a river, a silver and pink being in cold blue water, eating, breathing and fucking, now laid out in a morgue under green light, a place as unimaginable to the trout as his vision of Hell had been to him.

But these things were gifts, given to him by people who loved him! They wanted him, needed him, wished him alive. As John Spearitt said, "You always make me feel happier, Harry. Even now, when you're sick." These were no polite little lies. And how about old George Meaney who ran the newspaper kiosk below Milanos, who had travelled by bus and tram to reach him, had hobbled painfully up the steps and stood awkwardly in this room to give him (how had he known?) smoked trout.

Yet what power would these people (coughing John, hobbling George) have to save him? Why, even the green light could suck the life from their gifts as if reality itself (hadn't he seen it? Wasn't it proven?) was only something as thin as a tissue paper and you put your foot through (like glass, quicksand, ice) and you were, suddenly, like the trout.

For the hundredth time he clenched his eyes shut against the terrors of infinite space. He was going to die! He felt himself sucked down long green corridors of despair where he could not define his "I" except by a dull pain which would not stop. The room began to be not a room at all, but a construction caught in the wafers of undefined space. The apples ceased to be apples, the trout was merely the external form of pain.

"Hello, Daddy."

He looked with staring eyes at his son who held a wrapped parcel in his hands.

"David," he sat up. He was still half-caught in his waking dream. He tried to smile. He took the parcel. "Well, well, this is nice."

He busied himself over the parcel, hiding his confusion. "Chocolates?"

"No, not chocolates."

He ripped at the paper. "Ah, a book." He felt confused. People did not give him books. He did not read books.

"I know you don't read," David was saying, "but it's a very unusual book. It's about drugs."

"Ah."

Looking at Harry's puzzled face, David began to wonder at the wisdom of giving him the book. It was a thrilling, adventurous book about cocaine smuggling and the drug business. Yet when he saw the book in his father's hands he knew he would never understand it. To Harry it would be a book about criminals.

"Medical drugs?" Harry smiled at his son and turned the book over and over, wondering about its title: *Snow Blind*.

"No. It's about drug smuggling."

"Ah," said Harry and turned it over once more. "Ah, I see."

In spite of himself, David felt irritated. The father he imagined was never the same as the father he spoke to. He had crept out of the house, so he could come here without Lucy, so he could be alone with his father. He had imagined a different conversation, which he

34

now tried to induce: "It's really very exciting," he said. "There's a lot about South America."

"Ah."

"It seems to be quite an unusual business." He felt an almost overwhelming desire to tell his father what he was really like, that he gave not a damn about medicine or being a doctor, that he would be a son to be proud of, journeying to foreign places, confronting dangers, laughing at lightning, falling in love in Colombia. He would be a businessman adventurer and return with money and strange stories.

Harry looked at his son and was very proud of him. He was proud of how he looked, of his dark intelligent face and his rather shy gentle smile. He was proud that he had given him a book about an unusual business. He was proud of his academic record.

"How's school?"

"It's O.K. They treat us like kids."

"Well, you are a kid." Harry took his hand for a moment and neither of them quite knew what to do. They wanted to hug each other but it was not what the family did. They were not touchers. Sometimes they tickled. Harry, for instance, was known to have particularly ticklish feet and David was remarkable for being almost immune.

He did not want to burden his son with his father's death, and yet it seemed to him to be wrong not to tell him. They might only meet three, four, five more times and how would David feel to be cheated of this time, to squander it while his father tore up wrapping paper into little nervous strips.

And yet when he did say it, it was so unreal, so lacking in feeling or conviction that he wondered, for an instant, if he wasn't just making it up.

"David," his son was still smiling, "I've got to talk to you about what plans I've made," the smile had gone, a frown begun, "because there is some chance I'm going to die." The dark eyes wide with shock, the mouth open, the head shaking.

"No."

Harry took his hand. "Don't be frightened. I'm not frightened."

"No." Tears streamed down his face. "You can't."

And suddenly they were in each other's arms and Harry held the hard young body as it was ripped with sobs.

"Daddy, Daddy, I love you."

The trout lay on the table. The fluorescent light washed green.

Everything Harry Joy thought about became more and more complicated, less and less clear.

He no longer knew if he was going to die, if he was play-acting at dying, if he felt frightened or brave, because at this moment he felt an enormous strength, a curious triumph, as he held the body of his weeping son in his arms. He held him firmly, full of joy, the pair of them in a room full of gifts.

There was toughness in Harry Joy you may not have yet suspected, and although he appears, lying between the sheets of his hospital bed, surrounded by food and friends, to be mushy, soft, like a rotten branch you think you can crack with a soft tap of your axe, you will find, beneath that soft white rotted sapwood, something unexpected: a long pipe of hard red wood which will, after all, take a good saw and some sweat if you are going to burn it.

Harry Joy, for all his vanity (watch him look sideways now, trying to catch an impossible evasive profile in the mirror), his blindness, his laziness, all his other foolishnesses, brought a surprisingly critical cast of mind to the question of salvation and damnation.

For if you had thought he would go running back into the skirts of his childhood church (what would Jesus have done?) weeping, asking for forgiveness, last rites and so on, you were in error. Which is not to suggest that the thought did not enter his mind — and cross it, most attractively, its sweet-smelling wool skirts swishing softly — for it did, on many occasions, and on more than one of them he put his hand to the buzzer and, once, pressed it, to ask them to bring him a priest.

"Yes, Mr Joy."

"Nothing, Jeanette. I pushed it by mistake."

He could not (for all his fear, for all his proof of Hell) bring himself to fully believe. He had never rejected the Christian God. But now, to believe just because he was frightened of hell seemed to him to be unreasonably opportunistic, and he could not do it.

(He hoped, just the same, that God saw him and at least gave him some marks for his honesty.)

Scratching around in that overgrown mess which constitutes his mental landscape, we might find a few undiscovered reasons for this. This is not to take credit away from him, for he hasn't seen them, and is acting by his own lights, bravely.

But, look: the place he went to when he died bears absolutely no resemblance to the little wooden church of his youth, and the smells are not the smells of his Christianity, which were dry and clean like Palestinian roads through rocky landscapes, scented with cheap altar wine, floor polish, and the thin, almost ascetic, odour of his mother's perfume. It did not fit. It did not fit anything at all, except perhaps some stories he has since forgotten, but since retains, so one day he will remember them, even though they never appeared to him to have any religious intent.

Here, then, a fragment, dredged up from some dark corner of his memory: Vance Joy pretending to be a Hopi Indian.

"You may need a tree for something – firewood, or a house. You offer four sacred stones. You pray, saying: 'You have grown large and powerful. I have to cut you. I know you have knowledge in you from what happens around you. I am sorry, but I need your strength and power. I will give you these stones, but I must cut you down. These stones and my thoughts will be sure that another tree will take your place.'

"The trees and the brush will talk back to you, when you talk to them. They can tell you what's coming or what came by, if you can read them."

Thus, Vance Joy, many years before. And perhaps it is the force of fragments like these, his father's unconfessed pantheism, that kept his finger away from the buzzer for another day.

But, as the Reverend Desmond Pearce would say tomorrow, and as Bettina implied two days ago, there was no reason to think that, even if there was a Hell, Harry Joy should be sent there.

What monstrous crimes had he committed? A little adultery perhaps, an amount of covetousness when it came to other men's wives, but that was about all. So why should he lie in bed and gnash his teeth when, in all likelihood, he would be a Good Bloke for all eternity? And that, too, would have been the argument of his friends if he had ever been able to push through the dark curtain of embarrassment which surrounded the subject and actually lay down his frightful secret — there, disgusting thing! — before them.

But he could not, and did not, and instead the pressure of daily life in hospital crowded in upon him and he found time, all the time, being stolen from him in thin, wafer-thin, slices and great fat slabs during which he was placed on metal tables, had catheters inserted along the length of arteries and into his very heart, while wires connected him to dials and screens, and life itself contained enough terror to push his heart, one afternoon, into a dangerous arrhythmia.

He had seen his mother's sin on her death bed and he carried it with him for ten years knowing that when his time would come it would be the same for him, that her sin would be his sin, but worse, for although she feared damnation he knew she would be spared it.

He remembered now (in this antiseptic cold room full of dials), that dull grey hospital room of his mother's which smelt of cheap soap and the yellowed pages of old women's magazines. When he had arrived (puffed because he had run from the car park) she could no longer recognize him and thought that he was his father. He did not disillusion her, and had he tried she would have, in any case, maintained the illusion, for she was a stubborn woman when she had set her mind on something.

"Vance," she wept, "I have committed a terrible sin."

He remembered how guilty he had felt, listening to her, as if he was prying into confessionals, opening letters not addressed to him. She clutched his hand, her skin was almost transparent, a dry crust of spittle marked the corners of her mouth.

"No," he said, and then: "What sin?"

"A terrible sin."

"Don't tire yourself." How stupid a remark. A few hours of life left, a few things to say, and what does tiredness matter? Don't talk, he had meant, be quiet!

"Vance . . ."

"Yes."

"I have wasted my life waiting for you."

"No!" But it was true.

"Waste, waste, waste," she said. "Oh, Vance, it is the only sin that cannot be forgiven." And he saw, in the wrecked remains of her splendid dark eyes, his mother confront the shining steel orbs of hell.

It was not the buzzer which brought the Reverend Desmond Pearce but the good man's own blunt brogues, clumping down the hospital verandah as if testing for rot in its ancient planks. His swinging hands were rough, coarse with nicks and scabs, a hint that the saving of souls required something a bit more muscular than his 4Ps, which — to get them out of the way here — were Prying, Preaching, Praying, and Pissing-off-when-you're-not-wanted.

Harry looked up from his cane chair, saw Desmond Pearce's face, and liked it immediately. It was a rugged, pock-marked face with a slightly squashed nose and a crooked grin. His hair was a curling mess and he showed the proper disregard for sartorial elegance which Harry had always seen as a sign of reliability in a person. Neat men always struck him as desperate and ambitious.

"G'day."

"Hello," Harry smiled, and noted the little gold cross, tucked away where a rotary badge might normally go, on the lapel of the crumpled grey sportscoat.

"Join you?"

"Go for your life." There was something about Desmond Pearce that attracted such slanginess.

He dragged up a cane chair and sat down, pulling up his grey trousers to reveal footballer's legs and odd socks.

"What are you in for?"

"Heart," Harry grinned. "How about you?"

"Armed robbery."

They laughed a little.

"Harry," Harry said and held out his hand.

"Des."

"The Reverend Des?"

"You bet."

Harry tapped his fingers on his chair.

"It's a beautiful day," said Desmond Pearce surveying the sun-filled garden. There was still dew on the coarse-bladed grass and honey-eaters hung from the fragile branches of a blue-flowered bush. "And a good place to be sitting too." He shifted his bulk around in his creaking chair, crossed his legs one way, then the other. "Odd socks," he said, leaning forward to take off his coat without uncrossing his legs. "I've got odd socks."

But Harry wasn't looking at the socks. He was staring intently at Desmond Pearce and making him feel uncomfortable.

"Well," Desmond Pearce said, and slapped his big knees. He had only just (four weeks now) arrived from the country, where he had been very successful. He could talk to men in sales yards and paddocks, in pubs or at the football.

Harry was still staring.

"I have a lot of trouble with odd socks," Des said. "Sometimes I go to the laundromat with matched pairs and come back with all odd socks. Sometimes I go with all odd socks and come back with pairs."

"Have been making a list," Harry said, "of religions."

"Oh."

When you talk to a man in the middle of a paddock, you look off into the distance, or at the ground, you do not stare at him like this.

"And seeing you are here," Harry continued, "I might . . . ah . . . ask your help."

"Ah, yes," said Pearce with a feeling of inadequacy, not to say dread, in the face of this velvety urbanity.

"The problem begins", said Harry, closing his eyes and talking as if the whole thing had nothing to do with him personally, but rather about some character in a much-told story, "with the high probability that I shall shortly die, mmm?"

And he smiled a slightly apologetic, but none the less charming, smile.

Des Pearce was not good with dying.

"Shall shortly die. Now, I think there is also a likelihood that I will go to Hell and that . . . ah, I wish to avoid. But," he pulled a battered notebook from his dressing-gown pocket and waved it at the clergyman who was beginning to wonder if he wasn't some ratbag atheist out to have some fun, "but there are a lot of religions." A pause. That dreadful stare. "You see my problem."

"Well, you've got a bugger of a problem," he said carefully.

"I've had fifteen milligrams of Valium, I'm ashamed to say."

"And you're not a Christian?"

"I was, but I think you'd call me lapsed."

Was he an atheist?

Harry Joy folded his arms and Desmond Pearce was shocked to realize that his eyes were wet and that his face, half-hidden by his fringe, spectacles and moustache, showed real fear, that the dry rather indifferent tone had been adopted to get through a difficult subject.

"Lapsed as buggery," said Harry Joy and they both watched a cabbage moth alight on Desmond Pearce's leg.

"Are you scared?"

Harry nodded.

"Of Hell?"

"Mmmm."

"What have you done to make you think you'll go to Hell?"

Harry shrugged.

"Have you murdered someone, something like that?"

"Good heavens no."

Des Pearce was feeling better now, better in the way you felt when you knew there was something you could actually do. "Look, old mate," he said, "do you really think God is such a bastard he wants to punish you for all eternity?"

"Why shouldn't he?"

Des Pearce grinned. "It doesn't make sense. It's like you wanting to torture flies, or ants."

"Yes."

"Do you?" he said, joking.

"That's my point. People do. Look, I read the Bible in there," he gestured into the hospital. "It doesn't muck about. It says you either believe or you go to Hell. And look," he took from his notebook a grey, much folded pamphlet he had found as a bookmark in the library Bible. It was titled: *Memory in Hell*. "Listen to this: 'As the joys of Heaven are enjoyed by men, so the pains of Hell be suffered. As they will be men still, so will they feel and act as men.'"

"Harry, this was written in 1649."

"I know. I saw that."

"Well...it's a bit out of date isn't it? This is the twentieth century, not the Middle Ages."

"We're talking about eternity," Harry said incredulously, "and you're talking about three hundred years. That's a drop in the bucket. You can't just modify Hell. You can't change it."

"I haven't. The churches have."

Harry was beginning to get hives. He could feel them now. There was this tightening in his throat and this curious swelling which always preceded them. His fingers moved, as if he wanted to clutch something. "How can you change your mind about Hell?" he smiled. "If it was true once it must always be true. What about the people you sent there in the Middle Ages? Have they all been allowed to go home?"

"It's the twentieth century," Des Pearce grinned, but he felt irritated.

"Are you saying there is definitely no Hell?"

"I..."

"There is a Hell." He said it with that lunatic brightness Desmond Pearce had seen in the eyes of Mrs Origlass who had seen a flying saucer land beside the railway line at Anthony's Cutting.

"I can't imagine God wants to punish us, Harry."

"Ah, but maybe not your God, you see. Maybe," Harry looked around furtively (just like Mrs Origlass, he thought, that darting movement of the head), "maybe another god. Maybe it's a god like none you've ever thought of. Maybe it's a 'they' and not a he. Maybe it's a great empty part of space charged with electricity. Maybe it's a whole lot of things in a space ship and flying saucers are really angels."

(Landing beside the railway line at Anthony's Cutting.)

"Look," Harry turned over the pages in his notebook. "I made a list of religions, and do you know what I think?"

"What, Harry?"

"They're all wrong."

"All of them?" he smiled.

"Every damned one of them," Harry said, "maybe." And felt the hives swelling up beside his balls, like twenty nasty flea bites on top of each other.

"You must have done a lot of study," Des Pearce said, looking at the list and noting the absence of Animism and Zoroastrians before he handed it back.

"Study," Harry waved his arms, dismissing the hospital, its garden, certainly its library. "What good is study?"

He made the gestures of an angry man and yet, Des Pearce saw, he still smiled charmingly.

"A God for people who read books?" Harry was saying. "No. Definitely not. I will tell you two things I know: the first is that there is an undiscovered religion, and the second is that there definitely is a Hell."

"Then", Des Pearce held out his arms sadly, "I can't help you..."

"But maybe I'm wrong. Don't you damn well see, I might be wrong. Tell me what to do..."

"I can't."

"Tell me to believe."

"I can't."

"Well you better go," and he stood up and shook his hand warmly, still smiling as if the meeting had been a pleasure for him

Desmond Pearce stood up. "Is there a Heaven?" he asked.

"Yes, yes, there's a Heaven. There's everything." And then he slumped back in his chair, his hand on his forehead.

Des Pearce had an almost uncontrollable desire to pick him up in his arms and comfort him, to carry him back to his bed, to give him absolution, to have him confess the sin that was eating at him. He would gladly have taken all Harry's pain in the palm of his strong plain hands and held it tight until it died there. But he also realized, looking at this peculiarly frail figure in the cane chair, that Harry Joy could not give up his pain to anyone, that he would carry it with him to the operating theatre and to wherever place he went to afterwards.

"Maybe I should have talked about cricket," he said softly.

Harry tried to smile. The peculiar tortured twisting of his face was to stay with Desmond Pearce for a long time for it was now marked by those unsightly weals which Harry called hives; they would haunt Desmond Pearce and make him wonder if he had witnessed a warning from God, a proof, a mark signifying the existence of Hell.

Dull grey bats swooped, darting, catching insects above his bent head. His stomach gurgled. In the yellow lighted wards off the verandah, nurses cast shadows and served unappetizing meals. He whispered. He leant towards her, talking quickly. The dew was already on the grass. Outside the garden walls the river ran sleepily carrying heavy metals past ships with humming generators. The air contained lead and sulphur but Harry noticed this no more than the heavy honeysuckle which, for Bettina, filled the evening air.

"You'll miss dinner," she said.

His stomach gurgled again but he merely shook his head. He was not to have dinner tonight. Tomorrow was the day of his operation, a piece of information he could not bring himself to share.

"I'm not hungry," he said. He patted his moustache and hugged his knee. He rocked back and forth and rubbed his aquiline nose. His eyes were slightly feverish and he had the beginnings of a headache. There were so many things he had to tell her and now, at the last moment, she had to listen. And no, not about death or about Hell, he had stopped all that four days ago.

"Are you listening, Betty?"

"Yes."

He had talked about Joel for half an hour. He was talking about Joel still. He would not stop. Joel was not the man to run the agency. Joel was a bad leader. Joel was selfish. Joel was a good salesman, no doubt about it. Joel was lazy. Joel was not a good strategic thinker. Joel was too pragmatic. Joel wouldn't look after the staff. Joel had been very good with the Spotless people. On the other hand he had lost the margarine business. Joel was too flashy. He should try driving a cheaper car, something like a Fiat. On the other hand you could trust Joel. Joel would not lie or deceive anyone. If you had to sell the agency, Joel would not deceive you.

Bettina wanted to tell him he was wrong. Was it only pride that prevented her? Was it simply that she couldn't bear her husband to know she was having an affair with someone he thought was a fool? Anyway, he was wrong. He was so wrong about so many things. Joel would deceive anyone if it suited him (she liked him for it, her un-goody-goody lover). But then, why did she keep on believing Harry about the rest of it? When he said Joel was a bad strategic thinker, maybe he was right. She believed he was right and she felt angry with Harry for having tricked her with his good opinion of Joel and then, just when it was important, withdrawing the sanction totally. Joel had always been the hot-shot. she assumed he was the hot-shot. Now he was saying the business couldn't survive with Joel alone and she would have to sell out the business to the Americans (fuck that!) if he died. If he died. He'd gone as pious and maudlin as his looney old mother.

He took her hand and looked into her eyes (was he really going to die?) just as he had done when he courted her. He would not permit her eyes to leave his. They had talked about America and he had known the names of famous bars and that was a long time ago and she was Bettina McPhee and she was going to be a hot-shot.

"You talk to me like I'm a fool," she said.

"You should know these things."

"You should have let me come into the business", she said, "when I wanted to."

"No."

It was their old argument, a bitter one for Bettina, now doubly bitter. (But he wouldn't die. Nothing would change on its own.)

"We wouldn't have this trouble," she said.

Harry regretted not having found someone better than Joel to run the place, but he was not sorry that Bettina had never joined the business. He had offered her enough money to start a little boutique instead, but she did not want that.

"I offered you money," he said now, years later, on a verandah, the night before an operation.

"You should have let me come in."

"No."

"I was more clever than Alex."

"You still are."

"I'm as clever as Joel."

"More clever."

"Then you were wrong."

"No," he said, "you didn't have the experience." But the truth was not that, it was painfully simple: he did not want his wife around the office undermining his dignity. He never thought about it like this, but when he imagined her there he became irritated.

"I think", Harry said, "the thing to do would be to find an American buyer this year. Don't let them talk you out of it."

And then he went on, droning on about the provisions he'd made, his will, the formula to sell on, who was best, and on and on about Joel. She stopped listening. She started to wish he damn well would die.

"Do you understand that?"

"Yes," she lied. She was bored. She wanted to see Joel. If he dies, she thought, I will run the business and I will run it well and the only shame will be that he's not alive to see it. And then, shocked at her thought, fearful of its magical power, she embraced him.

Leaning across the uncomfortable cane arm of the chair, a lump of loose cane sticking into her breast, she felt his fear. It was gnarled and sour and as she held his handsome head in her hands she found herself handling it as one handles over-ripe fruit, being careful not to squeeze too hard.

He wasn't ready. He would never be ready. His mind was full of unfolded shapes and twisted sheets and it was too late to put them into order.

He wrote his farewell note on a piece of cardboard torn from the box his slippers had come in. The address was printed on one side: to Bettina and Lucy and David Joy, 25 Palm Avenue, Mt Pleasant. His whole world was contained in those ten words written on grey cardboard. It seemed nothing, a life so pitiful and thin that it was an insult to whoever made him. It was not so much that he had achieved nothing, but that he had seen nothing, remembered nothing. A series of politenesses, lunches, hangovers, dirty plates and glasses, food trodden into carpets, spilt wines, the sour realization that he had made a fool of himself and done things he hadn't meant to.

Yes he had been happy. Of course he'd been happy. But he had always been happy in the expectation that something else would happen, some wonderful unnamed thing which he was destined for, some quivering butterfly dream soaked in sunlight in a doorway.

And now: only this sour dull fear, this lethal hangover.

But he remembered. He remembered the day they went to the bank to sign the mortgage, a rusting gutter he had tried to fix, the lawn, all those weeds he had laboured over, the trees she planted (trees most painful of all), layers of wood, one layer for each year, the cambium, the sap, the roots and those other ones (What were their names? The ones near the bottom fence?) she had planted the first year they were married, the year she lost the twins and he went to see them in their humidicribs, each tiny feature perfect, and went home to change the sheets and blankets on the bed, wet with the broken water from her womb, and those flowers, like bottle brushes, were out then and he took them to her.

They had beautiful clever children but there was no satisfaction in that, no pleasure to remember that he had bathed them and read them stories.

"Now," the Kodak advertisement said, "before it all changes." He had always admired the line but never taken the photographs. Just as well, just as well. Why would details make it any better?

He could hardly write. He had to force himself to spell each word fully. He dug these words in soft cardboard: No farewell. Sorry. Operation today but could not bear to say farewell. Love you all. Fingers crossed. Bless . . . Harry.

He pressed the buzzer above the bed.

"Envelope," he asked, and waved the cardboard.

Denise came from the country. Her father and mother kept poultry. She was used to milking cows and finding eggs under bushes. She looked at Harry Joy with his ash-grey hair, his huge moustache and his piece of cardboard and couldn't imagine how he had been made.

"Wouldn't you like some paper, Mr Joy?"

"No."

His smile was so painful it made her want to be able to do something, anything. The smile was worse than a scream. In the matron's office she found a huge Manila envelope, nearly sixteen inches long. She brought it to him gently and watched him drop the tattered cardboard inside and write in large careful letters the names of his family.

"Stamp," he gave her money.

"I'll fix it in the morning, don't worry."

"Now, please."

"O.K., stamp now." And she went plodding off in her soft white slippers and stole stamps for Harry Joy. She covered the envelope with stamps, giving him the only thing she could give. She brought him a pill too and he didn't even ask what it was, but ate it almost greedily, his hand shaking and spilling water down his front.

The pill soon reduced his world to a hazy blur, within which, in the sharpest detail, the seeds of Hell, long ago planted and recently nurtured, began to sprout and unfold their chrome-yellow petals.

Under Pentothal, he tried to name things. He tried to name the garden but could not do it properly. As he went deeper the names were lost and there were only shapes, tied with yellow string, revolving on a Ferris wheel.

He existed with white shadowy forms and sharp astringent odours. He had died again and he waited, fearfully, wondering. Lost, he felt nauseous, a floating feeling, his body without substance.

He closed his eyes, conscious of being handled with mechanisms, an object in space, without time.

Instruments were applied to him cruelly, without love.

He was split by pains, small and sharp, long and monotonous.

He was pervaded by a full consciousness of punishment and the curious certainty of death enveloped him like a shroud.

Sometimes he cried with self-pity. Frightened as a child, he begged for mercy.

He was on a shuddering railway of merciless steel, voices echoed coldly. There were noises of silver wheels or distant thunder.

He existed nowhere in solitary terror.

Visions of days before his death moved towards him and receded: his mother in that dusty street giving him the cheque. "Now go," she said, "now go. I've won the lottery." And in that white empty room, the Sunday School, the single sentence he had carried with him like a limpet since his youth: It is harder for a rich man to enter the Kingdom of Heaven than for a camel to go through the eye of a needle.

When he saw the shapes around him it was through grey veils. He was tormented with shifting images of his wife, his children, of Desmond Pearce. Joel circled him. With what intention?

Someone said: "He will be confused for a while."

Yes, he thought bitterly, I will be confused; it will not be as they described it. He knew himself to be ripped with huge wounds, a vast punishment down his chest. Thin wires and tubes. A poor weak Gulliver.

He looked bitterly at those around him, forms which became more and more distinct, but he was ready for them before he saw them. He was in a room beside a verandah. Is this what they did to you? He demanded they state his sins although he could already guess them. They never answered directly, never once. "As they will be men still," he thought, "so they will feel and act as men."

Slowly, during his convalescence from his successful operation, Harry Joy became totally convinced that he was actually in Hell. He watched them, as cunning as a cat, silently indignant that fate should play such a trick on him.

Part Two

Various Tests and Their Results

He moved around the house in sandshoes and tracksuit and exhibited a curious stealth and — if you had not shared the general trauma at Palm Avenue, had not felt those creeping, inexplicable irritations — you may have found his antics funny.

Look at him: sneaking up the stairs you might have thought he was impersonating a cat in a pantomime, or even without a costume, a lizard. But this is all deadly serious, and what he is doing is throwing the whole emotional balance of the household out of kilter, tipping the axis of his world and producing peculiar weather.

Is he mad?

A question he has asked himself. And if you follow him now, as he turns, for no apparent reason, and begins to go downstairs, hesitating before he crosses the shining expanse of living room, out on to the creaking verandah, down the steps, you will see him slip, like a shadow, into the garage.

There are a number of dusty old ammunition boxes lying higgledy-piggledy in the corner, so dusty that they might have been there for years; and have. Yet those shining new brass padlocks give his secret away, and in a day or two this will occur to him too and he will come down here at five o'clock one morning and paint with khaki paint, clogging up the keyholes and giving himself new difficulties. But now the key slips into the padlock smoothly and the shining hook flicks open, and the lock is removed, and softly pocketed. Inside there are notebooks, fifteen spiral-bound, but at this date only six have been filled and a seventh started.

They contain all manner of peculiar observations. These are tests for madness. He is making them himself.

Harry Joy is running checks. He is comparing his life (termed "life" in the books) with his other life, that is the days and years before he entered the operating room, the days before this cruel scar on his chest. If he had found someone he half-trusted he might have confessed, initially, that the chances of this being Hell were about sixty/forty. But as the weeks have rolled on, the evidence has mounted and he is not, according to his own checks, mad.

This is not the childish Hell of the Christian Bible with its flames. Here, obviously they planned more subtle things, and it has already occured to him — a flush of panic as he stared into the 3 a.m. dark — that this, these boxes, locks, etc., are to be his punishment. He contemplated the possibility of Hell in a universe made like an infinite onion until he became as sick and frightened as he had once, as a child, lying on summer's black night grass, trying to grasp infinity of space.

But to return to these books, and their entries. Here, on page 16 of the first book: FIAT IS WRONG.

While he was in hospital Lucy and David decided to clean the Fiat. It was a present. And they waited, like children, for his delight or at least his thanks and if not his thanks, his acknowledgement. They encouraged him to walk beside the garage, to enter the garage, to drive the car, but nothing they did could induce him to mention the Fiat, and Lucy, whose idea it had been and who had contributed most of the hard work it took, became angry and thought he had taken it for granted.

FIAT IS WRONG he wrote and, on page 20: THEY MADE MISTAKE WITH CARPET. Possibly they had, all things considered.

In the notebook he also recorded observations concerning "Lucy", "David" and "Betty".

Some selected entries concerning "David".

23. I notice taking money.
25. Talks money.
26. More money talk.
36. Mean streak exhibited again.
39. Caught him lying.
43. Rattish face, quite different.

This last description could be made (uncharitably) to describe not only David but Harry's own handsome face, which the Indonesian Consul had once favourably compared to the god Krishna in the Javanese Wayang Kulit. Krishna, the Consul said, had an almost identical aquiline nose and the same finely chiselled chin.

There he is now, locking himself in the toilet to make more observations, and it looks comic, the way he crouches so earnestly over the book, crabs his fingers around that little stub of pencil, holds his head to one side, sticks out his tongue, and gives a number to his latest piece of evidence. He is in torment. If he shits it will be watery-thin and black.

His family, in moments of clarity, saw and sensed his pain. They did the most absurd things to please him. David, who was fastidious enough to be repulsed by the black hairs that grew on Harry's big toe, cut his father's toe nails while Lucy, simultaneously, began to read him an amusing story about Don Camillo which, from an ideological point of view, she strongly disapproved of.

But he withheld his love — his vast, blind, uncritical love — from them, and they were like children withdrawn from the breast. When their love was not reciprocated they punished him with a fury that puzzled them and left them guilty and shaken, offering apologies that could not be accepted, the rejection of which, in turn, produced greater hurts, ripped scar tissue before it was healed, and ended in scenes of such emotion and frenzy that the neighbours turned off their lights and came out into their gardens, where they stood silently beside fragrant trees.

They were like heavy cigarette smokers suddenly denied their drug. They raged at the slightest rejection. They saw no light in Harry's eyes, and got from him no talk, no story, no smile. Depression spread like an insidious fungus through the whole family. The depression interacted and created a synergistic effect, each amplifying the other, and one can see, here and there, traces of quite mad behaviour in those members of the family whom one might expect to be sane.

Lucy was fifteen years old, a dialectical materialist, rational, sensible and, of all of them, the least given to hysteria. Yet it was she who decided that Harry had been given the wrong operation.

"Don't be absurd," Bettina said when Lucy confided in her.

"It's true. I know." They were whispering in the kitchen. In the next room Harry was recording "mutterings" in his notebook.

"Lucy, stop it. You can see the scar on his chest."

But Lucy exhibited the tenaciousness of the truly desperate. "When I was rubbing his head, I saw a mark."

"Nonsense."

"It's true. They did something to him. You don't know what happens in hospitals."

"Rubbish."

That evening, as they sat around in the living room, Bettina got up and rubbed Harry's head. She stood behind his wing-backed chair and went through it as thoroughly as native women look for nits. As she worked you could see, if you were looking for it, the temper building up in her smooth round face, which became, as rage approached, smoother and smoother.

"You silly bitch," she screamed at Lucy who was sitting on a big cushion in front of the television. "Why do you make up stories?"

Harry sat very still in his chair while inexplicable things happened around him. Lucy wept and hugged his legs. Bettina threw her favourite Royal Doulton jug across the room. It slammed into the plaster wall, left a hole, and dropped to the floor without breaking, DID NOT BREAK. Lucy left his legs and picked up the jug.

"You harlot," she screamed at her mother.

Bettina danced up and down. Pranced. Stamped her small feet. "You little slug," she screamed at her daughter. "Slug, slug, slug."

Harry sat very still and made mental notes while "Lucy" and "Bettina" acted out their roles in Hell.

David leaned indolently across the front-verandah rail and watched Joel waddle as he walked up the drive. He did not acknowledge the chubby wave (delivered at the flower beds) but silently criticized the display of bad taste as it crossed the front lawn: the poisonous green cravat, the ostentatious ring, and, worst of all, Gucci slip-ons accompanied by white socks. David winced. Joel was someone, he thought, who should never be allowed to escape the safety of a conservative dark suit, and whose ties and socks should always be purchased for him once a year, in advance, by someone with enough love and concern to stop him committing outrageous errors.

"Where's your father, Davey?"

He pointed downwards, towards the garage.

"In here?"

David nodded, that cold, distant, masculine nod with which older boys had once so intimidated him. He retired from the edge of the verandah and sat on a wicker settee while, beneath him, Joel banged on a door which would be opened to no one, him least of all.

Later Joel ran the gauntlet of David's disdain before scurrying into the house, where Lucy would make him coffee while Bettina had her shower. Joel was trying to talk to Harry about business. Harry did not wish to discuss business.

David, hearing a creaking door, leant across the edge of the verandah, and saw Harry emerge from the garage and slip silently down the side of the house.

*

It wasn't until just before lunch that Joel caught up with him just as he was making a run for the toilet. Harry, in tracksuit and sneakers, sped softly along the back verandah whilst Joel struggled along beside him like a reporter trying to grab an important "no comment".

"I've brought the balance sheets, Harry."

"Uh-huh."

"What do you want me to do?"

"Just continue."

"Come on, Harry, I can take advice."

"Continue," Harry said, "that is my advice", and the last half of the sentence was uttered from behind the snibbed safety of the toilet door.

It had become very obvious that Harry did not wish to go back to work. Just as it also became quite obvious that the business needed him. In this climate of upset and emergency, with everything threatening to crack and collapse around him, David decided it might be safe to sacrifice his famous medical career before it began. The pressures had built up on him, year after year since he was ten, and now he saw his chance to slip sideways, and away to freedom.

He approached Harry on the subject, waiting until he was securely ensconced in the hammock, which stretched from the red flaming poinciana to the side fence.

"Daddy."

Harry, making a rare entry in his notebook, started, and shoved it stupidly up his shirt, in full view of his son.

"Don't creep up on me."

"Sorry."

The air was so fragrant that day, one could have imagined that the grass was perfumed. It was about twenty-eight degrees and their backyard was thick and glossy with the luxurious semi-tropical vegetation people fly half-way round the world for, but neither of them noticed it.

"Daddy," he swung the hammock for his father, "I want to go into business."

His father's dark eyes frightened him when they came to bear on him like that. They recalled, too sharply, those recent scenes of hurt and confusion, "And I thought I might go and help in the agency. It'd be interesting work," he said, "I guess."

"You guess?"

"Yes."

"And what about this doctor business?"

"I'm prepared to give that up."

"For what reason?"

"For family reasons. For the family business. I could help. You know..." and did not say (did not think he needed to) anything about the current business problems.

"For the money?" Harry said in a neutral tone, as if that were quite a reasonable thing. He swung a little in the hammock.

"O.K., for the money, that too."

"Ha."

"What?" David frowned.

"Ha."

"All I said was money, money too."

"Yes, precisely. I noted it."

And then, as he was wont to do on these occasions, Harry arched an eyebrow and cocked his head on one side just to let them know that he understood what was going on, that he knew where he was. But he was quite likely, in the middle of this protective cynicism, to be struck with confusion, and the least display of pain or tears could make him wonder if his real family had not, after all, been sent to Hell to accompany him, just as the families of the Pharaohs accompanied the Pharaoh into heaven, and this confusing tendency to switch from one view to the other was to stay with him for a great deal of his time in Hell.

"You noted it?"

"Your interest in money. I have noted it", Harry said, "many times."

"And I think the ad business could be better than medicine," David said, pleased to be discussing finances, rather than the sloppy old-fashioned view his father had once brought to the idea of medicine.

"The prime attraction of medicine is really the money?"

"Most of it," David admitted, relieved.

"Its main attraction."

"Yes."

This was not his son. This was someone pretending. In the pay of someone.

"Who do you work for?" he asked his son, oh so casually, but the timing of it was wonderful: just slipped it in there, like so.

David looked at him, his eyes wide. How many times had he

wanted to discuss his business activities, his interest in drugs, the trips to South America? He wanted to talk business with his father, not business business, but adventure business. "You mean," he said, "who do I work for?"

"Yes." Harry waited tensely. It was only a hunch. But look at him, look at him swallow, and his throat is dry when he talks: "Who do I work for now?"

"Yes." A single red poinciana flower dropped on Harry's white shirt and lay there like a pretty wound.

"You know?"

"What do you think? Who do you work for?"

"Abe da Silva," David Joy said melodramatically.

Harry Joy did not know the heroes or the hierarchies of organized crime, so he did not understand either the size of the boast or the field of endeavour, neither could he judge that his son's claim was only true in the loosest most indirect way, just as a service station attendant might have once claimed to work for Aristotle Onassis.

But what he did get was a name, his first name in Hell. He was an explorer, a cartographer, and on that great white unmarked map of Hell he could put this name, although quite where he did not know. Although, when David finally left him (his question unanswered, his private business undiscussed), his father would go back to his mental map, and beneath it, where one might expect the scale to go, he produced this key, this code, by which he now expected, like a zoologist, to classify the creatures he found there. Generalizing from his experience, he made a note of these:

1. Captives. (Me)
2. Actors. "David" et al.
3. Those in Charge. da Silva. Others?

Finally, of course, the expected happened: his family kept out of his way. He prowled the lawn, haunted the garage, stared at the TV, and found himself isolated by his madness. David slunk home to get drugs and departed silently. Forever in the house you could find someone slinking up a stair, departing by a back door, running across a lawn with imaginary eyes burning into their back while Harry, the mad master, masturbated dully in his hammock or sharpened his pencil in the anticipation of some rare tit-bit of evidence.

Bettina, once so fastidious about the house (for she had a strong streak of very-small-town politeness and a serious concern for what the neighbours thought, although she would have violently denied it), left pictures to hang crooked, floors unswept and meals, also, uncooked. She spent as much time as possible in Joel's flat viewing its idiosyncrasies with eyes similar to her son's, but having other, fleshier, compensations.

Lucy was up early to sell the *Tribune* and up late at meetings, some official, some secret, in which she plotted to reform a Communist Party branch. But, like David and Bettina, she could not pass through the dead dusty heart of the house without feeling a certain sadness, a cold shivering melancholy similar to that which might be produced by an old orange tree growing next to a wrecked chimney.

When she came home one night she found her room had been searched She suspected the Special Branch, wrongly as it turned out.

"Are you a Communist?" her father said.

"Yes." It was about time!

"Good," he said truculently, and turned briskly on his heel.

He continued to do his exercises as instructed and, with a lot of walking and no regular meals, lost his belly. On his walks, he saw ugliness and despair where once he would have found an acceptable world: goitrous necks, phlegmy coughs, scabrous skin, lost legs, wall eyes, dropping hair, crooked spines, lost hope, and all of this he noted, but when nothing actually happened, he became bored.

And then, one morning, he woke feeling optimistic. There was no reason for it, unless it was that he was tired of the game, the staleness of the house, being lonely and cranky and isolated. Perhaps he was like someone unmechanical who turns on a defunct TV every now and then to see if it has healed itself, but, for whatever reason, he did not wear his tracksuit (stinking thing) or his sandshoes (worse) but showered and scrubbed himself and washed his hair and shaved fastidiously. He ironed a shirt and took his baggy white suit from the wardrobe where it had hung since the day he died in it.

The Fiat, the wrong Fiat of course, started immediately, and he was too happy to be suspicious.

He backed down the driveway, nearly ran down the postman, and accelerated down Palm Avenue, only pausing to clash his gears in a style that had once been familiar to those who lived near the bend in the road.

*

Bettina had given up on Harry.

She sat amongst the heavy Edwardian furniture of The Welling-ton Boot and listened to Joel argue with the waiter about the bill. In a moment she was going to order another drink, but she waited, swilling the last little drop of Gewürtztraminer around the bottom of her lipstick-smudged glass. Joel was trying to write new figures on the bill and the waiter was taking offence.

"Here," the waiter was saying, "I will bring you a new piece of paper, sir. I will get it. You can write on that."

Bettina looked out the window wondering if she might, this once, see someone particularly elegant or glamorous walk past, someone with some damn style, but she was rewarded with the same stream of heavy, dowdy, frumpy-looking people who she had always despised. Prague 1935, she thought, and found little except the motor cars to contradict this idea, although she had never been to Prague and certainly not in 1935.

She heard the tooting. And then five sets of brakes locked in squealing harmony, and through the middle of the intersection sailed a small red Fiat Bambino with Harry at the wheel. It looked so carefree and eccentric that she forgot her animosity towards him and smiled. Dear Harry. She laughed out loud.

"What's so funny?" said Joel, who was now standing beside the waiter. They both looked down at Bettina with hurt expressions. "I argued with the man because he charged us for a salad he didn't bring us. He admits his mistake." His voice rose an octave, pro-testing at the injustice of her laughter.

"It was Harry," she said. "He must be feeling better. He's going to Milanos."

Joel sat down very heavily and left the waiter standing. His head was wobbling. "We are not going to talk about Harry any more," he said.

Bettina held up the empty wine bottle to the waiter and smiled. "One more," she said, and didn't bother to notice his expression.

"We talk about Harry in bed. We talk about Harry while we fuck. We talk about Harry in the shower. We can't even come to our own goddamn restaurant . . ."

"Don't shout, honey," she said in perfect American, "and don't wobble your head."

"I'm not shouting." He adjusted his tie. "I just don't want to talk about Harry any more."

"Well don't talk about Harry. Talk about us. Talk about how

we're going to set up our own agency. That interests me more than Harry."

"Don't be a bitch."

"Bitch, why bitch?"

He compressed his fleshy lips. "You know the problems."

"You want a business . . ."

"We need money . . ."

". . . I want a business."

"We need money."

"Didn't you say we could get the money if we could get a client or two. Isn't that what you always say. Because if we . . ."

The waiter had arrived with the wine and was busy pouring it into glasses.

"Did you order this?" Joel asked her.

"Yes, darling."

"Why didn't you order it before?"

"I wasn't thirsty before."

Joel turned to the waiter. "May I have the bill, please."

The waiter raised his eyebrow a fraction of a centimetre. Joel looked at him for a moment and decided it wasn't anything definite enough to pick a fight on.

But when the waiter returned he smirked.

"Excuse me," said Joel, "but didn't I notice you lift your eyebrow in a disagreeable way?"

"I beg your pardon, sir?"

While Joel continued his conversation with the waiter, Bettina looked out the window. She saw a woman in a white linen suit and red shoes. She gave her seven out of ten.

He had always parked his car behind the public toilet in the park opposite Milanos. He had done it for fifteen years, and for fifteen years different parking inspectors had received a yearly present and turned a blind eye.

But today there was a circus in the middle of the park and he had to enter the park from the wrong side, and drive across the grass. He parked, as he had always parked, next to the MENS sign.

Then he walked across the road and up the stairs.

He had always like Milanos. The walls were the colours of smoked salmon, the tablecloths the same. He was reminded of the inside of vaginas, of peace, and for no good reason, of a large blue lake. He liked the roses and the carnations in their old fashioned silver vases which sat on each table. He liked the mirrors, and the tasteless little shaded lights on the walls, which somehow looked so elegant here. All this, his favourite place in the world, was unchanged and he breathed an almost audible sigh of relief to see Aldo sitting behind the bar as usual, to feel (more than see) the rush of waiters, the rolling chrome marvel of the dessert trolley, the soft exciting noise of a long French cork being drawn, the muted clink of long-stemmed wine glasses.

When he found five people sitting at his corner table, he took his notebook from the pocket of his baggy white suit and began writing straight away.

Aldo, his dark face like a clenched fist, decorated with two intense intelligent eyes, watched him. He was irritated by Harry's apprehensive face, the tentative way he came in, poking his nose around the coffee machine like a rat. Aldo, who was famous for his prickliness, had always been polite to Harry. He had been pleased to see him; he had even liked him. And Harry had liked Aldo without reservation. He had made Aldo feel good. But now Aldo's antennae twitched and he wanted to smash Harry across the mouth. He wanted to smash him across the mouth for even being alive. He sent the new waiter to give Harry a table. It was a provocative act. He watched its effect.

Harry was led to a window table, where he seated himself without protest. The meekness with which he accepted the table irritated Aldo even more. So when Harry looked over and smiled uncertainly Aldo pretended not to see him. He let him wait five minutes and then, as he circulated the room talking to customers, appeared to find him by accident. Harry was waiting for the drink waiter without complaint.

"I cannot keep a table empty for three months as a monument," he said, watching Harry writing in his book. "If you tell me you will be here you can have the whole big table and what in the hell do I care that the other five seats stay empty? Did I ever complain? Now you have this table, a good view. Many people ask for the window. Today, in particular, you can watch the elephants. There, see."

"Hello, Aldo."

"You are tanned. You are thin. Your operation is over. You should be happy, but look at your face. What do you want to drink? The Meursault again?"

"Thank you."

"There is no Meursault. How about a Mercury Blanc?"

"And pearl perch with sorrel sauce."

Aldo shrugged. All his creased dark face showed pain and discontent. "Let me advise you not to open the window. It stinks of animals' shit." He pocketed his order book. "We eat, we shit, we die. I myself have cancer."

"No, Aldo, that's terrible."

"Terrible? How is it terrible? It just is, that's all. Aldo will die. They tell me you died once already, but you came back. Maybe I'll come back too," he laughed coldly.

"Ah," Harry said sadly, "you think so?"

"I think so?" Aldo said. "I know you did. I know so."

Aldo retired with the order and sent the Mercury Blanc to Harry's table. When the perch and sorrel sauce passed him on its way to Harry's table he did not, as he should have, send it back to the kitchen, but shrugged to himself and let it go. Harry who had been a mountain had become a pit. Aldo watched him play with his pearl perch and when he had nearly finished he wandered over.

"How was the meal?"

Harry made a see-saw motion with his hand.

"Pah. What was the matter with it?"

"Oh," Harry said, "nothing. Don't worry, Aldo." He suddenly felt very sad, sad either because Aldo had been replaced with an Actor, or alternatively had not been replaced by an Actor and had cancer. In either case it was depressing. He had made notes of both options and put the notebook in his pocket.

Aldo took the plate away. Harry hadn't finished, but Aldo was embarrassed to see it on the table. He retired to his bar and watched Harry drink wine. He was ashamed of himself. He liked Harry. He wanted Harry to smile. He wanted energy from Harry, but Harry sat at his table like a man with his forebrain cut out. So later, when the Mercury Blanc was nearly finished, Aldo came over to the table with a couple of cognacs. He sat down opposite Harry. He tried not to be prickly. He tried to talk to Harry as he remembered him.

"My Joy," he said, sliding the glass across the tablecloth, "they are giving me chemo-therapy and it makes me ill. So, to prevent the illness which is caused by treating the illness, they give me this." And he pulled, from his pocket, a little plastic bag full of green herb-like substance.

Harry picked it up and fingered it. It crunched inside its bag.

"Marihuana," said Aldo. "Illegal, except for fortunate people like me who are dying of cancer. It is for counteracting the chemo-therapy. Have you ever smoked it?"

Harry shook his head. He had always believed what the city's tabloids told him about marihuana. He clutched the notebook in his pocket. DRUG ADDICT.

"It's not bad stuff," Aldo admitted, sipping his cognac. "In comparison with wine, of course, it is definitely below par. I mean: no nose, no colour, no complex taste. But as a euphoric: very good, probably better than wine. I tell you this, Mr Joy, because I see you are not on top of the world for the first time in fifteen years, it probably would not hurt, at your age, to try a little."

"No thanks, Aldo." PUSHED DRUG. INSISTENT.

"Come on. What do you think will happen? You will turn into a heroin addict? You will rape little schoolgirls? Have some. Makes you feel nice. Trust me, I wouldn't lie to you. Just mix a little with your cigarette. You roll the cigarette like this, see, so the tobacco falls out the end, then you can put a little pinch inside. It's easy."

"Why are you talking so much, Aldo. You never talked so much." V. PERSUASIVE.

"Well," Aldo paused thoughtfully, "I am stoned as a matter of fact."

"Ah," said Harry and regarded Aldo closely.

"Do I look like I rape schoolgirls?"

"No." SMALL PUPILS.

"Well take it."

Harry pursed his lips and then bit his moustache.

"Take it, take it."

"Thank you, Aldo," said Harry. He slipped the little plastic packet into the big pocket of his voluminous white trousers.

"You will enjoy it and think of me."

Harry wondered.

"But," Aldo went on, "let me tell you about this cancer business, Mr Joy, there is a great deal of it around and it makes me wonder." He narrowed his eyes. "A lot more around than before. My theory is that it is being sent to punish us for how we live, all this shit we breathe, all this rubbish we eat. My theory, if you are interested, is that cancer is going to save us from ourselves. It is going to stop us eating and breathing shit."

"What shit?" Harry wondered about the pearl perch.

"What shit? You name it. But listen, you know George Bizneris from Shell, he has it. You know Betty Glover, she has it. You know," and he started counting off names on his fingers, "David McNamara, his wife too, the man who runs the news kiosk downstairs, my own father, and that man there, sitting in the corner with the woman with red hair, he says three children at his daughter's school have it. Three children, eh?"

Harry shook his head mournfully, wondering what it all meant.

"Ah," Aldo stood up. "I can't stay here with you, Mr Joy, you're too depressing. Come and see me when you have a smoke."

Harry had a weakness for Bisquit cognac and no matter who told him it was not a great cognac, nothing could diminish the pleasure it gave him. When, sitting by the window, he dropped his nose into the brandy balloon it was like the proboscis of some creature whose evolutionary success had been based on its ability to live on the fumes of volatile fluids. It did not matter what they had done to Aldo (there he goes, the dark little man, flitting across the restaurant with his hidden drugs) because Harry was warmed and soothed and Milanos still had its magic, even now, at three o'clock in the afternoon as they set up the tables for evening and one could imagine oneself the first guest rather than the last.

He felt at once brave and (was it possible?) contented. The second-rate table by the window had its advantages: he could watch the Captives limp and struggle along the crowded street below, observe the laughing face of the occasional Actor, and even (once only) the impassive masks of Those in Charge hiding behind the glossy windows of a Mercedes Benz.

On his white map of Hell he was pencilling in marks, crude, inexact, tentative at the moment, but surely even Livingstone must have become lost occasionally and needed some high ground to see the lay of the land.

And also, perhaps, a sanctuary like this where one could momentarily forget the tribulations and terrors of the unknown continent.

He heard coarse laughter. It came from the bar. It was not Milanos-type laughter. It was the laughter of street spruikers and early morning markets, not the laughter of crystal glasses and pink tablecloths.

He cocked his head on one side, watching carefully; Aldo pointed towards him. Then he led this other person (this wrong-laughter) towards him. It was a big red-faced sandy-haired man. He had huge bushy sandy eyebrows and large sandy-haired arms sticking out of a dirty yellow sleeveless sweater.

"Found you at last," the stranger shouted to Harry when he was still only half-way across the restaurant. "It's extraordinary."

"This is wonderful," Aldo said. They came and sat at his table without being asked and Harry had to put his notebook away again.

"This is Mr...?" Aldo began.

"Mr... Billy, Billy de Vere," said the sandy man holding out a hand which felt like it had been stored in a bag of unwashed potatoes.

"From the circus," Aldo explained. "Mr Joy."

"Harry."

"Pleased to meet you, Harry." Billy de Vere placed a fistful of notes on the table. "If you'll allow me," he said, "what will be your pleasure?"

"No, no," Aldo said, "this is on me," and he waved a waiter over and whispered in his ear.

Harry sat motionless. His flicking eyes didn't miss a thing, not the nod to the watier, the wink of Mr de Vere, the removal of the notes from the table, or the faint aroma, like wet dog, which came from the direction of the yellow sleeveless sweater.

"Alright, alright, Mr Joy, don't worry, cheer up," Aldo said. "Cheer up, cheer up, it's just an accident. A funny story..."

"What happened?" Harry asked thickly.

A bottle of Grande Armagnac was placed on the table and they all watched the waiter take his knife and break the green-wax seal on the cork and then pour the dark brown liquid into three brandy balloons. The bottle was left on the table.

"Drink first," Mr de Vere said, clapping his hands together like a hungry man. "Or you'll think I'm lying."

Harry and Aldo shared a momentary comradeship, a shared astonishment as Mr de Vere downed his Armagnac in one fast dis-respectful swallow.

"Good brandy," he said, "very smooth."

Aldo giggled (out of character) and poured him some more.

"A drink for a man," said Mr de Vere.

"This must be some story," Harry said nervously.

"It is almost the same as the original story," Mr de Vere said, placing his empty glass on the table with an appreciative sigh, in spite of which gentle compliment it was destined to remain unfilled for longer than he had hoped. "It's like lightning hitting the same place twice." He picked up his glass and looked at it. "Which", he said, his huge eyebrows rising, "I've heard can actually happen, in spite of what they say." He looked at Harry inquisitively as if he might prefer to discuss lightning for a while. "This is almost the same as the original story," he said.

"No," Aldo said, "certainly not. In the original story it was a red Volkswagen."

"What story?" Harry said.

"No," Billy de Vere said, "it was a Fiat. I remember distinctly. A Bambino. A Fiat 500, the same as Mr Joy's."

"I think you're mistaken, Mr de Vere. But, in any case..." Aldo relented and gave him a little more Grande Armagnac, "in any case ...close enough."

"Life", Billy de Vere raised his glass, "imitating art. Or should I say," he lowered his voice and winked, "life imitating bullshit."

"Do you know the story about the Elephant, Mr Joy?" Aldo said. "Because very soon you are going to have to tell it to your insurance company."

Aldo and Billy de Vere roared laughing.

"Go on..." Harry said, all the pleasure gone, only watchfulness and suspicion left.

"It was trained to sit on red boxes."

"Big red boxes."

"Big for a box, small for a car. It's what you might call an apocryphal story."

"It never really happened," Billy de Vere said. "This elephant was trained to sit on red boxes, see, and one day someone came and parked near her."

"In a red Volkswagen," Aldo said. "Surely you've heard it?"

"Or Fiat."

"And she sat on it."

"An elephant sat on my car?" Harry said glumly. "You're laughing because an elephant sat on my car." He had never heard the story before. He was not interested in precedents. All he could see was that he had suffered an outlandish misfortune and that these people were sitting there laughing at him because of it. In Milanos!

"You've opened a bottle of Armagnac because my car has been ruined. What sort of place is this?" he said to Aldo.

"Look on the bright side," Aldo told him darkly. "You're not dying. You're drinking good Armagnac, and you are the first person whose car has really been sat on by an elephant. What a story. You like stories. Come on," he gave Harry a little more Armagnac, "drink up. Have fun."

"Your insurance will pay," Billy de Vere said. "We have witnesses."

"You are a ninny," Aldo said, talking to Harry as he might talk to any customer who irritated him.

"A what?" said Harry, who had never been spoken to like this.

"Ninny," Aldo said, his eyes dark and dangerous.

Later Aldo was to regret this, to realize that he had gone too far, even for him, and that marihuana and Armagnac can be a tricky combination.

"A moony ninny," he said, wilfully tormenting his best and oldest customer. "A dill, a drongo, a silly-billy."

It was to prey on Aldo's mind, and later, when he was dying, he tried to get a message to Harry Joy, but by then Harry Joy was nowhere to be found.

"A dingo," he called after the departing figure in the white suit. "A po-face," he told Billy de Vere, "a dim-wit, a poo-pant," but by then he was laughing too much and further speech became impossible. Through a curtain of tears he watched Billy de Vere pour himself another Armagnac.

"Look at this fucking cretin, will you," Senior Constable Box said.

He brought the patrol car into the lane beside the crushed Fiat 500 which was making a painful-sounding 50 kilometres an hour. Sitting behind its wheel, his head and shoulders emerging from its crumpled sunshine roof like the tank commander in some private war, his white suit splashed with the black grime from passing buses, his hair slicked and flattened by the heavy rain, was a man with the profile of the god Krishna.

"Give him a wave," said Box who was probably not technically drunk.

Hastings closed his eyes and sighed. Box was giving him the shits. "Watch . . ."

Box tooted the horn and waved and the lunatic waved back, smiling and nodding.

"O.K.," Hastings said, "that'll do. Stop fucking about with him. Pull him over."

And he made Box get out in the rain and talk to him while he watched the conversation in the rear-view mirror.

Presently Box came back, opened the door, and burped.

"What is it?"

"He said an elephant sat on it," said Box, grinning.

"Is he a smart arse or a looney?"

"Don't know."

"Take him back to the station."

"I'm not going in that," Box said.

"No-body is going in that," Hastings said slowly. "It is an un-roadworthy vehicle. Now will you ask the gentleman if he would like to accompany us to the station in a nice new car?"

The police station was not what he had expected. It was like a house. A small neat path ran between borders of flowers. A sprinkler threw little jewels of water through the rain. The sun came out as they walked up the path. Harry, Senior Constable Box and the second policeman who had not introduced himself.

Inside the station innocent people filled out applications for drivers' licences. They took Harry through a side door and down a passage. They took him to a room at the end of the passage and left him alone. There was a table in the middle, scuffed vinyl tiles on the floor, a kitchen sink in one corner, and a number of kitchen chairs which had the appearance of newly delivered furniture. The wall had two different types of cream paint: shiny at the bottom and flat above the shoulder line. Sellotaped to the wall was a small printed sign which explained, in ten sarcastic points, how to produce a juvenile delinquent. A light with a frilly shade hung above the table, on which were an ashtray full of butts and a coffee cup with lipstick on it.

There was a curtain rod but no curtain. Harry sat on one of the chairs and looked out the window. He was wet and miserable. Water dripped on to the floor. Outside the window there was a clothesline and a young woman was hanging clothes on it. Harry watched her peg a pair of very large pyjamas on to the wire, a brown sock with a diamond pattern, and three small pairs of white panties.

A small fair-haired boy dragged a yellow plastic red-wheeled tricycle across the grass beneath the clothesline. It was all wrong. Water dripped from Harry Joy as he waited for his punishment.

After ten minutes the second policeman entered the room. He was Sergeant David Hastings but he still did not introduce himself. David Hastings had also been born in a small country town. Looking at him you could still see the fair-haired boy with sandshoes on his feet and scabs on his short, skinny legs. His face was freckled, his hair stood up at the back, and although he no longer blushed as readily as he had, his face would still go red when he felt he was being mucked around. A gentle glow suffused his face.

"Now, Harold," he said, "here's a cup of coffee."

"Thank you."

David Hastings pulled up a chair and sat with his back to the window. "We're very busy," he said slowly, playing with his own cup of coffee, turning the cup a full 360 degrees on its saucer. "We don't have time to muck around."

Harry patted his pocket, hoping that the marihuana had some-how vanished, but when Hastings looked pointedly at his hand he pulled it away as if he'd scorched himself.

"Now, Harold, would you just tell us the truth about your accident and everything will be O.K. You'll get a little fine and we'll phone your wife to come and get you."

"I told him."

"Tell me," encouraged the policeman, his face becoming a little redder.

"An elephant sat on it."

The policeman closed his eyes and sighed. "Oh Harold," he said, "don't be silly. If you're going to tell stories to the police, tell us something original. Don't come and tell us old elephant stories, and if you do, get the car changed. The car in the story was a Volkswagen."

"An elephant sat on it," Harry insisted, but he no longer believed the story himself. "The guy from the circus came and told me."

"Name being...?" Hastings opened his notebook with a tired flick of the hand.

But all Harry could see was de Vere drinking Armagnac and his name would not appear.

"I forget."

Outside the small boy rode his tricycle into a wet sheet. He stayed immobile with the sheet wrapped around him, blowing little white linen bubbles. The sun shone brightly, illuminating the white-wrapped boy and the three wheels of the tricycle.

"Weren't you going to claim insurance? Didn't you write down his name?"

Harry didn't say anything. He knew he was in for it. He had been planted with drugs and he could only wait for his punishment. He started to think about the two different kinds of cream paint they used on the walls, the flat above, the gloss below. It was the same scheme they had used at school. He didn't like the flat paint. It reminded him of finger nails being dragged across the blackboard.

He pulled a face, remembering it.

"What's that in aid of?" David Hastings stood up, took Harry's coffee, and walked over to the sink where he emptied it.

"What?"

"Pulling that silly face. What's that in aid of?"

"I just remembered something."

"You better do a lot of remembering very fast, Harold, before I charge you with driving an unroadworthy vehicle, resisting arrest, obscene language, and obstructing a police officer in the course of his duty."

"Phone the circus," Harry said, "they'll tell you."

Hastings put down his pad and walked across the room to Harry. He put his hand on Harry's chest and twisted his shirt and skin together. When he had twisted it tight enough for his satisfaction he picked him up and forced him against the wall.

"Now," he said, "don't tell me what to do. Second, don't muck me about."

Harry burped.

"You filthy bastard."

Harry, pinned against the wall, raised a questioning eyebrow.

"You've been eating garlic. You fucking stink." And he slammed Harry against the wall.

"I'm sorry," Harry said. He was frightened. He waited. He would not be punished for stinking. He would be punished for the real offence.

Hastings walked to the other side of the room. Harry undid a shirt button and looked at the scar on his chest. It was bleeding. He felt he was getting hives. He felt them massing inside him. He stood still, trying not to attract attention to himself.

Senior Constable Box entered the room. He was no longer wearing his raincoat. His belly bulged out over his belt. He had combed his black curling hair and washed his face roughly. There were still two little drops of water clinging to his small moustache.

"Still telling funny stories?" he asked.

"Not very funny stories," Hastings said. "Very old stories."

Box pulled in his belly and hooked his thumbs over his belt. "Maybe it could think of something original."

Hastings shifted a chair around. "Don't know if it's capable of it." He looked up at Harry and his freckles were almost invisible in his red face. He gripped the chair and placed it an inch further to the right. "Maybe all it can do is tell old stories. Maybe I better pass him over to you."

Box nodded in the manner of someone receiving a specific instruction. Harry watched. It was like a dance. Box retreated, Hastings approached. Hastings pulled Harry out from the wall and then stood behind him.

"Now," Hastings said, "I'll pass him over to you, Constable."

He pushed hard. The sharp edge of the table jabbed Harry between the legs.

He backed away from the table as Box moved behind him. "No," said Box, "I might just pass him over to you."

Harry hit the table again and Hastings pulled him back then shoved him forward, shoving him hard into the table with his boot. The corner of the table hit him in the balls. He tried to vomit. A boy stood on the tricycle, looking in.

"No, I think I'll pass him over to you."

"No, I don't deal with drowned rats."

Harry started to howl. He could not stand. They picked him up and sat him on a chair. His hives raged within him. He put his head back and howled to the heavens. He howled like someone locked in a dream. This, at last, was where he was sent to. Actors would punish him for all eternity while a child gazed through glass.

They were sitting down. They waited for him. He could not stand waiting for it to get worse. He had vertigo. He had to jump. He pulled the packet of marihuana out of his pocket and threw it on the table.

"There," he yelled, "there. That's the truth. That's the truth."

There was a long silence while Hastings picked up the bag and Box leaned over his shoulder. Hastings had lost all his red colour. He tried not to smile. He sniffed the marihuana (a pitiful little packet, he thought, maybe half an ounce) and handed it to Box who looked like he was going to get the giggles.

"Alright," Hastings said, only keeping a straight face with some difficulty. "See if you can tell us something original this time."

"Don't give us that old shit about elephants, Harold."

"Something new."

"A story."

"Something interesting."

"Something we haven't heard before."

"We heard such a lot of stories, Harold," Box said, sitting back-to-front on a chair, putting his arms on the table.

The man in the filthy white suit brushed his hair out of his eyes. "About marihuana?" he said. "About this marihuana?"

"About anything, Harold," Box said, "anything at all."

"Alright," the prisoner said, and shifted in his chair.

"But it must be totally original," Box said.

"Come on . . ." Hastings said to Box. "Let's just get his statement and . . ."

"No," Box winked. "You tell a story, Harold."

The prisoner's face was showing huge red weals and Hastings looked at the tortured face with embarrassment. He stood up.

"I'll be back in a moment," he told Box. He was going to walk out because he knew something nasty was going to happen, one of Box's degrading little tricks. Box didn't have a temper. (A temper, at least, was something clean and hot and fast.) Box liked tricks, slow, drawn-out entertainments.

"Alright," the poor bunny was saying, "I will tell you a completely original story." Hastings had his hand on the door-knob as the man started his story; but that brown voice held him, like a cello on a grey afternoon, and he found himself releasing the door-knob and leaning against the wall.

He did not realize, for an instant, could not have guessed, that Harry was extemporizing the only original story he would ever tell. In fear of punishment, in hope of release, glimpsing the true nature of his sin, he told a story he had never heard about people he had never met in a place he had never visited.

There he is, a tightrope walker in the dark.

"He was very short," Harry Joy began, "and also short-sighted, although no one knew that then, not in the beginning, and that was why he always got into trouble for being late to school because he couldn't see the hands of the town hall clock.

"The town hall," he decided, "was across the road from the school.

"He did badly at school. He was not good at anything. Not sums, not writing, and not games.

"His mother was short too. She was a Cockney from Bow in London and she was only four foot seven tall; almost, but not quite, a midget. This story is set long ago, and one year there was a competition on the beach — the beaches were different then, with bathing boxes and competitions — the people were more easily amused — a competition," he said, "for the shortest woman.

"Now Daniel, or Little Titch as he was usually called, persuaded his mother to go into the competition. The women were all lined up, ready to be judged, eyeing each other up, bending their knees, digging their feet down into the sand and so on, and everything was calm enough. But when they saw Little Titch's mother walk towards them a great cry of despair went up.

"Oh, no.

"And half the line of women just walked away. And Little Titch's mother took her place at one end of the line, very modestly, with that serious look she always wore on her face, and, naturally, she won.

"When they went home on the tram that night Little Titch carried the silver cup his mother had won. Although it tarnished quickly you could still read the inscription years later. It read: *The Shortest Woman, Queenscliff, 1909.*

"Little Titch was both proud and puzzled by the cup. He was proud that the people had smiled at his mother and given her the cup. He was proud that the cup was silver and there, where it was engraved (and he traced the words with his grubby finger), it was gold. But he could not understand, as much as he might think about it, either then or in the months that followed, that his mother should be rewarded for the very thing he, her son, was punished for. People did not kick his mother because she was small, or pull her ears (let them try!) or her nose. They did not pinch her when she was asleep and then laugh at her when she cried. But these things, these punishments, were the daily lot of Little Titch. His brothers were bigger and older, more like his father, and they took it in turns to box his ears and tell him how stupid he was. So when he walked back into the house that day it was not with happiness but with his habitual sense of fear, which was laced with cunning and not a little slyness, and he crept off into the corner under the big grey laundry trough where he would hide, with his dirty little arms around his scabby knees, for hours on end. When this hiding place was discovered, and they were always discovered — under the tank stand, beneath the house, in the smelly space behind the outside toilet — he would find another one.

"He was not lazy. He always tried hard. And later, when his father took up aviation and bought a second-hand Bleriot monoplane, Little Titch would repeatedly break his arm, getting it caught by the great wooden propellors which had to be swung by hand.

"But at the time of this story his father did not have aeroplanes, or even taxis, but a stables with horses. So the work of the family was all to do with horses, backing them into the shafts, tightening their girths, doing their shoes, mucking out the stables, feeding them, and so on.

"Little Titch tried to do whatever work they gave him but they said he was timid and stupid and only fit for shovelling out the stale straw and shit which he had to do each night after school and often he went to bed unwashed with only the cold smell of horse dung for company.

"The most difficult and troublesome horse in the stables", Harry said, "was a gelding named Billy-boy who was not only prone to kick, but also to bite with a ferocity unusual even in a horse. It was nothing for him, one morning when his girth was being tightened, to turn and bite the arm of whichever elder brother was doing it, not just the nasty bruising bite of an ordinary horse, but a ripping horrible bite that drew blood. And there was also the chance, in the confusion, of a kick or two for whoever came to the rescue.

"You could not touch Billy-boy's face, or go behind him, or beside him, and it seemed that most parts of his muscular anatomy had received beatings at one time or another and he was not eager that they be repeated.

"Little Titch's father said that Billy-boy had once killed a man, which was why he had been so cheap, no other person daring to deal with such a brute.

" 'It's good training for the boys,' the father said. But after two bitings and a nasty kick the mother forbade the bigger boys to go near Billy-boy and the father had to do it himself.

"So, life went on. Billy-boy bit the father, the father hit the boys, and the two big boys hit Little Titch and pulled his nose and boxed his ears and Little Titch looked for places to hide.

"But on this night, this particular night, the brothers could not find him, and in the end the whole family turned out, looking high and low, waking the neighbours calling out: 'Little Titch, Little Titch.'

"It was the father who found him," Harry said.

"The horse killed him," Box said.

"Billy-boy was standing there," Harry insisted, "and behind him, right next to his hind leg was Little Titch, his arms around Billy-boy's huge rear leg, his face pressed into the deep black warmth of his flank.

" 'Come here, Little Titch,' they said, 'come here at once.'

"But Little Titch," Harry said, "didn't have to do anything at all because the bastards couldn't touch him," he said, "and that's the end of the story."

There was a silence in the room and the two policemen looked the way people look when the lights come on in the cinema. Hastings looked out the window and saw it was raining again. Box yawned and stretched.

"I think you better piss off now," Hastings said quietly to the story-teller who was looking as perplexed (who was Little Titch?) and as embarrassed as any of them.

As he was escorting Harry out the door Hastings noticed Box, almost absent-mindedly, slip the packet of marihuana into his pocket.

Hastings thought: You silly cunt, but he escorted Harry silently to freedom.

As the taxi drove him across the bridge, the river below appeared as black as the Styx. Barges carried their carcinogens up river and neon lights advertised their final formulations against a blackening sky.

Harry Joy, his face ghastly with hives, his suit filthy, his chest bleeding, his back sore, lounged sideways in the back seat, drugged with sweet success. The buildings of Hell, glossy, black-windowed, gleaming with reflected lights, did not seem to him unconquerable. It seemed that a person of imagination and resources might well begin to succeed here, to remain dry, warm, and free from punishment. The old optimism flowed through him, warming him like brandy, and allowed him to feel some sympathy for the poor Captives who crowded the darkening streets, holding newspapers over their bowed heads in pitiful defence against the hail which noisily peppered the roof of the cab.

The rewards of originality have not been wasted on him and if he is, at this stage, unduly cocky, he might as well be allowed to enjoy it. So we will not interfere with the taxi driver, who is prolonging his euphoria by driving him the long way home.

*

Harry sat on the kitchen chair with the towel around him, red Mercurochrome marking the edges of his bleeding scar. There was a strange quiet when Bettina asked the question again.

"Now," she said, "tell me what happened."

He wanted to tell her, but he dare not repeat the elephant story. He looked upwards. He shut his eyes. He sat in total mental blackness and waited for originality to visit him. A lost blow-fly circled the kitchen table until it settled above the door frame where Joel leaned.

The silence was terrible to him.

No new story would arrive. He sat on his hands and looked down at his feet and, after waiting a minute or two, Bettina and Joel went away.

He heard them talking in the next room, their words hidden in a hiss of television.

Harry was meant to start work at the bank on Monday. Then, on the Wednesday before, his mother won money in the lottery. And now, it seemed, his whole life was to change: he was going to art school instead.

He would rather have stayed in the town and worked in the bank. But he was going to art school tomorrow and he pretended to be pleased. Everyone knew. They shook his hand and were proud of him.

When he came home he found his mother dressed in a long gown, deep blue with splendid embroidery on the back and on the edges of its long wide sleeves. She had put her hair up, that jet black hair which was never to be quite so black again. Her eyes shone with excitement and she pulled up her sleeves, trying to keep them out of the cooking.

"Into the dining room, go on."

She banished him. He sat alone in the dining room which was the living room, the parlour, the study, the drawing room. He sat in a corner in an old armchair and lit the fire.

He did not want to leave. He wanted to stay here. He loved this little room with its black polished floor boards, the old floral carpet which lifted in ghostly waves in a high wind, the tiny fireplace with its metal grate which had to be blacked every Sunday, the ancient wireless with its vast round dial lit by a soft amber light. He walked around the table which was now covered with a spectacular white starched cloth, resplendent with shining silver knives and forks. Two candles sat in the middle of the table and he lit them.

That night his mother showed him things he had never known, as if she were giving him a dress rehearsal for another life. She cooked food of a type he had never eaten, a mousseline, light and delicate, duckling with whole green peppers. And there was wine, a golden wine in an elegant long-necked bottle.

"Ah," she said, "wine." He was overcome with pride at his mother, yet he never asked her how she knew about such things, just as he never asked her who owned the house, when she was married, where the money came to live on, why his father had gone and when he might come back. And yet, that night before he left, she began to talk and he caught glimpses of other worlds, her wants, her loves, her disappointments. He was thrilled but also embarrassed. She drank the wine with pleasure and her eyes glowed with it. She danced like a butterfly through fields of conversation, fluttering for a second over one memory, barely touching it before she was on her way to the next.

"Ah, Harry," she said, "your whole life is in front of you. How I envy you. Do you mind your mother envying you? Of course not."

She insisted on dancing with him. He was giddy from the wine. They whirled around the room and fell over each other. "Oh Harry," she collapsed on to the tattered couch, "I'm so happy for you, so happy for you."

But had he ever thanked her for sending him to the art school? Years later he tried to remember. Had he ever thought about what she had given up to send him there? She had pushed him on to the train, almost desperately, as if given a second thought she would have taken the money and travelled the world, visited his father at what ever place he was in then, seen the great galleries of Europe, the Uffizi, the Villa Borghese. Did it ever occur to him that she was the one who wanted to go to art school, that she had given him her dream and he had taken it without realizing what it was?

He had asked her if she'd be lonely.

"Lonely?" she laughed. "How can I be lonely? All my friends are here."

Yet it wasn't true. She had no close friends. She had people she helped, others she did favours for. There were those she felt sorry for and those she liked a chat with. As time passed pity would be her dominant emotion as she tried to help those she felt sorry for. She took to religion with a new enthusiasm that he soon found almost embarrassing.

Yet that night there was no talk of God, just giddy dancing and golden wine.

"Throw your glass into the fire."

He didn't understand.

She showed him.

The glasses crashed in ecstasy. The wine sparkled in the lantern light. Outside the wind moaned in sheer pleasure and the great fir trees swayed under the night sky and great white clouds skudded across the heavens and Orion's belt lost its handle.

She found more glasses, long-stemmed and delicate, hidden in the back of a cupboard. She splashed a little wine into one and threw it.

"There," she said, "the end. Finito."

It felt dangerous and thrilling. He followed her example. "Finito," he said.

"Now," she said, and they toasted with two more glasses. "Now, for both of us, a new stage."

He did not understand. He looked at his mother's glowing eyes, her laughing lips and felt nervous, alone in territory he did not recognize.

"Now," she sipped the wine and wiped her mouth with the back of her hand. "Now, you go to be an artist and I," she emptied the glass and hurled it into the fire, "I go to polish floors."

"Oh, no." He stood up and hugged her. "Oh, no."

But she did not look unhappy. She was bright, almost feverish. "Oh yes," she said, "Oh Harry I want to. I am happy, happy, happy."

"You don't want to polish floors."

"Polish, polish," she waved her hand. "Not just polish. I am trying to explain, Harry, this is a new stage. I have planned it. Harry, I am going to be good."

She was crying now but still smiling. Tears sprang to his eyes in sympathy.

"No, no," she said, "don't cry. I'm happy. I'm crying because I'm happy. This is my new life. I'm going to be good."

He did not understand.

"I promised God," she smiled, "if I won the lottery." The wine was drunk. His childhood over. Few things ever happened afterwards to match this moment of tingling promise where Harry and his mother had trembled on the edge of life.

Alex Duval spent his Saturday morning as usual. He was the only person on the floor occupied by Joy, Kerlewis & Day and so allowed himself some laziness in dress. His grey gardening pullover was unravelling at the neck and a bright red shirt shone through the holes in the elbows. As he walked along the corridor to his office he carried two Italian doughnuts (the kind with a big blob of apricot jam hidden in the middle) and triple espresso coffee. Soon he would go down for another coffee and he'd probably (certainly) buy another doughnut or two.

The last of the corridor's neon lights finished its nervous flickering as he entered his office. He pulled a face at the stale aroma of pipe tobacco and placed his coffee and doughnuts on his large clean desk. He took from the top drawer a little L-shaped metal key which he now used to unlock the double-glazed windows. It was raining. He sniffed the air, yawned, and stretched.

Today, as usual, Alex Duval would write his second set of conference reports. A conference report is written in an advertising agency any time the agency and its client decide to take action on anything. It can record a budget allocation, the acceptance of an advertisement, approvals and rejections of media schedules, marketing strategies; all the business of a client and the agency's role in it is documented and then kept for up to seven years. In disputes between clients and their agencies, the conference report is regarded as a binding document.

And every Saturday morning for the last ten years Alex Duval, Account Director, had sat at his desk and written and typed a set of conference reports in which his role, seen by the revolutionary investigators he imagined would one day sit in judgement on him, would be blameless.

He was physically a large man, but there was a softness about him, the look of someone who has just stepped out of a hot bath. He was unnaturally pink, and his face with its pale intelligent eyes still carried, in some marks as subtle as the smell of white camellias, the signs of defeat. Alex Duval was a man of principle who had decided, a long time ago, that men of principle can never win. Yet he hoped and feared he was wrong. He voted for the Communist Party and rewrote his conference reports every Saturday morning. He ate cakes. Now and again he had an affair with a secretary.

He no longer expected anything good to happen to him and sincerely hoped that the world would not be destroyed until after his death.

In spite of such pessimism, he derived real pleasure from the doughnut, which was perfectly oily, and the black coffee, which was very strong. He did not rush this second breakfast, but savoured each mouthful of it, and if he was impatient at all it was only to contrast the slightly bitter taste of the coffee with the sweet oiliness of the doughnut.

Before he began work on his conference reports he washed his big soft hands and carried a heavy black IBM electric typewriter from his secretary's desk to his own. Although she didn't know it he could type faster than she could: one hundred and thirty words per minute.

And so he began, his belly sagging over his trouser belt, the natural stoop of his shoulders inclining him towards the black machine, the high intelligent forehead marked with creases of concentration. The hands flew. An observer would never have remarked that this was a man involved with a tedious chore, but rather one in the throes of a sometimes difficult but often exciting creation. For as he wrote these conference reports Alex Duval emitted a strange series of little cries: an ejaculation of triumph, a snort of disgust, an attenuated giggle. He typed quickly, perfectly, in complete command of his material, using the fixed language of the conference report with consummate ease: Client requested that Agency should prepare such and such. Agency expressed the opinion that such and such. Agency warned client that this practice was unprincipled, that this promise should not be made, that this chemical was carcinogenic, that this product could cause liver damage.

He was not so mad as to not know he was mad. He knew, almost exactly, how mad he was. But he also allowed himself the 1 per cent chance that he was taking a useful precaution, and so his Saturday morning sessions had continued. Later, going down in the lift, he would feel the damp sour shame of a perversion finally practised, a lust satisfied. And in the street, walking amongst other men, he would feel at once self-hatred and a strange sense of superiority.

So when Harry Joy came to find out who were Actors and who were Captives on that Saturday morning, he came down the corridor walking softly on his sandshoes. He had adopted a white shirt and white trousers, and he walked loosely, not at all like someone come to spy. He heard the typing and imagined one of the copywriters. He followed the metallic clatter through the stale weekend air to Alex's office, where, standing at the doorway, he watched the process of creation.

Alex was chuckling. He kept typing with one hand while he reached for the coffee. Harry thought of Winifred Atwell playing "Black and White Rag".

Harry had left Lucy sobbing in her bedroom because he had remembered to treat her like an Actor. He could no longer act consistently — treating everyone as his mortal enemy one minute and then, totally forgetting where he was, as an old friend the next.

He hadn't seen Alex for three months and he smiled now, forgetting he had come to spy. He leant against the doorway and watched him work, giggling at his manic energy.

"Christ . . . Harry." Alex rocked back and held his heart, dropped his head. "Oh shit."

He tried to cover the paper, to stand up, to shake Harry's hand. He was flustered and couldn't pay attention to what he was doing or saying.

"Harry, Harry." He came and hugged him. Harry smelt the wet armpits around his ears, for Alex was a very tall man. "Harry, Harry, we've missed you, Harry." He started to lead Harry out of the office, away from the paper, out into the dull light of the corridor. "Out here, where I can see you. Harry, you've lost weight. You look wonderful."

Harry couldn't stop smiling. "Thank you, Alex, it's good to see you."

"Harry, Harry." He put his big hands in his pockets and rocked to and fro on his creased old black shoes. "The place hasn't been the same. It needs you Harry, you old bastard. Are you back?"

"Almost."

"Harry, Harry, everyone will be so happy. You wait till you see them smiling. Nothing against Joel, but it's not the same. It isn't fun without you. What we miss, Harry, is your bleeding blind optimism."

"Come and sit down, Alex." Harry slipped into Alex's office before he could be stopped. He picked up the conference reports. Alex, flustering in behind him, tried to act as if they were nothing important, told himself to make no move towards them, to draw no attention to them. He was pleased to talk to Harry but he felt like a radio tuned to two stations at once.

"You look so well. You've lost your belly, you old bastard."

"I've been walking."

"And swimming. That tan makes you look ten years younger."

"Sometimes I go to the beach with Lucy," Harry flicked idly through the conference reports.

"So how is Lucy?"

"Mmm."

"And Bettina?"

"Fucking hell, Alex, what's all this?"

"Nothing, Harry, just a joke."

"*You* told them that saccharin causes cancer? *You* told them that, Alex?"

"It's a joke, Harry, that's all. I was just having fun."

Harry sniffed. He could smell Alex's fear. He saw the big slumped sad man with his red shirt showing through his gardening sweater and saw him light one more Low Tar Cigarette. "This isn't a joke, Alex. You're not doing this for a joke." His eyes narrowed, wondering what category of torment was contained here. "Tell me the truth, old mate," he said, using his genuine affection as bait in the trap.

Alex sat down behind the desk and looked up at him.

"Oh Harry, you know me . . ." Alex felt as if someone had filleted his soul and thrown it on the desk. It was pale and slippery, a pitiful thing.

Harry was still reading the conference reports with astonishment.

"Harry, it's not real. I didn't do it."

"What happens when you send this out? We lose the business? Is that it?"

"No, no, Harry you don't understand. Here, take this key. Take it. It's the only one. You open that filing cabinet behind you. That's the key to it. Go on." He waited while Harry did it. "There are seven years of conference reports with stuff like that. They don't get sent out."

"But why?"

"I guess I'm crazy." He tried to smile, the smile of a fat schmuck who thinks he's a fat schmuck.

All Harry could see was his pain. It was almost a visible aura, a pale trembling force that burned around him. "No," he said, "you're not crazy. You're frightened."

"Harry, Harry, I'd rather you found me sucking cocks."

"Alex, tell me . . ."

"How can I tell you, it's so crazy."

"You've got to tell."

"I can't damn tell you," Alex thumped the desk and a tear ran down his shining face. "I can't damn fucking tell you. It's ridiculous. It's my punishment, Harry, that's all."

Harry sat down carefully on the edge of the desk. "Punishment for what?" he said.

Alex was really crying now and Harry handed him a handkerchief impatiently.

"Punishment," Alex said, "for what we do here."

"Ah."

"You'd never understand. You're right. You're the normal one, Harry. I know you're right and I'm wrong, but I'm just crazy. It upsets me. I write . . . I write these conference reports for when they come to get me . . . to punish me."

Harry felt cautious. He didn't move quickly. He accepted his wet handkerchief back and didn't say a thing. He was like a man watching a splendid bird perform rare rituals in deepest forest.

Even when he spoke it was softly, and very carefully, as if the jab of a consonant or the scratch of a vowel might break the spell.

"Come on," he whispered, "let's go and get a drink."

He walked softly on his white sandshoes and Alex squeaked behind him carrying a box of Kleenex tissues. They went first to Harry's office, where they found ancient layouts stacked all over the desk. The refrigerator was missing and two dirty glasses and a quarter of a bottle of campari were gathering dust in the once-generous bar.

"Joel's got the fridge."

Harry nodded. "Tell Tina to tidy this up and stock the bar."

"Joel fired Tina."

They went to Joel's office and found the refrigerator locked inside a newly built cupboard. It wasn't much of a lock. They broke it with a screwdriver and went back to Alex's office with a bottle of Scotch and a big bucket of ice.

Alex sat down in the chair behind the desk, and Harry lounged in the low guest's armchair. He crossed his legs and put the tumbler of Scotch on the arm of the chair. He looked like a man on holiday. He looked handsome.

"Tell me who is punishing you?" he said.

"Don't, Harry . . . please."

Harry saw the humiliation in his eyes.

Alex stood up and shut the door, but when he sat down again he obviously didn't know how to start talking. "I guess," he said, and then stopped. "I guess I'm just punishing myself."

"I don't think you're crazy," Harry said softly. "I don't think you're punishing yourself."

"Then you're crazy too," Alex said sourly.

"No," Harry said and narrowed his eyes.

"O.K., O.K., don't get mad."

"Do you believe in Good and Bad?" Harry asked.

A slight hint of irritation showed itself on Alex Duval's face, and for a moment it was possible to see he was also an arrogant man. "You know I do," he said. He took out a cigarette, worried about it, and put it back in the packet.

"And you're being punished for being Bad."

The simplicity of this made everything sound so childish that Alex Duval was almost angry. "Yes," he said. "If you want to put it like that."

"So," Harry stood up. He was smiling. "So we'll be good."

"Oh Harry, that's very nice, but not very sensible."

"Sensible?" Harry's eyebrows rose alarmingly. "Sensible? How isn't it sensible? We'll be good."

"We."

"Both of us."

Alex blinked. "You'll be good?"

"Alex," Harry sat down again, but he hunched over his legs and looked down at the floor, "Alex I'm a bit crazy too. I think I'm in Hell."

There was a silence.

"You're the first person I've told. I don't know who to trust. I've been trying to work out what to do."

"You mean you know you're in Hell."

"Yes," Harry said.

"Oh Christ, Harry."

"You think I'm crazy." Harry stood up. He looked bereft. His face was suddenly very white.

"No," Alex Duval said quietly. It did not for a second occur to him that Harry meant everything he said literally. He was distressed merely because Harry was the last person he had ever expected to reveal deep unhappiness.

"Since when?" he asked.

"Since," Harry smiled encouragingly but his voice was choked off with emotion. "Since I was in hospital."

"Ah yes." Alex remembered that it was at about this time that Joel and Bettina's affair became public knowledge.

"It's good to talk to you, Alex."

"It's good to talk to you, Harry."

The two men lapsed into an embarrassed silence. Alex Duval finally lit his cigarette and Harry ate the ice in the bottom of his glass.

"I have a theory," Harry announced when he had finished the ice.

"Tell me." Alex lit a cigarette.

"There are three sorts of people in Hell. Captives, like us. Actors. And Those in Charge. What do you think?"

"Who are the Actors?"

"Most of them. They work for Those in Charge."

"To persecute the Captives?"

"Yes."

"They're Actors; acting; not what they seem."

"Mmmm. What do you think?"

"Brilliant," said Alex Duval pouring himself another Scotch. "Exactly right." As he sipped the Scotch he wondered if he and Harry might finally end up being friends, real friends, after all these years. He liked Harry's theory. There was no room for optimism in it.

"Joel is an Actor?" he asked.

"Definitely."

"And Bettina?"

"Yes."

"We are Captives?"

"Yes."

"Have some more Scotch, Harry."

"Thank you, Alex. The question is," Harry dropped a fist full of ice into his glass, "the question is who are the Captives and how can they be freed?"

"Harry," Alex said, "it is good to see you. It is nice to talk to you. We haven't talked like this since the Old Days. Remember how we used to sit around till all hours and talk?" Alex stuffed tobacco into his little bent pipe and lit it. When he had it glowing he leant back in his chair. "You old bastard," he said. "It's so nice to talk to you."

"Let me ask you a question," Harry said. "An opinion . . ."

"Yes," Alex settled down comfortably.

"The relative merits of Goodness and Originality ... what do you reckon?"

"Harry," he shook his head, "you're amazing. I don't believe it."

The two men smiled at each other proudly.

"Originality, without Goodness," Alex said at last, "is nothing, of no worth."

"That's what I was thinking," Harry said. "Originality, by itself, is nothing?"

"Not a pinch of shit."

"But with Goodness?"

"Dynamite."

"I think we should fire Krappe Chemicals," Harry said. "I think that's the place to start."

"Yes ..." Alex said cautiously.

"How much are they billing?"

"Just under two million."

Alex began to feel that there was something in the conversation he had not heard, as if he had dozed off and missed some vital piece of information. He sat for a while puffing on his pipe and looking at the hockey match in the park across the way. Harry fished a piece of ice out of the bucket and crunched it up.

"Why?" Alex said at last.

"Why what?"

"Why fire Krappe Chemicals?"

Harry looked at him in astonishment. "So you don't have to write your extra conference reports. I'm damned if I'm going to be punished for ever. Do you want to be punished for ever?"

Alex took the pipe out of his mouth. "No," he said, and held the pipe about three inches from his mouth, where smoke issued forth from both ends. "Still," he said, "it's a lot of money ..." And, when Harry didn't comment: "It might seem a little inconsistent ..."

"How inconsistent?" said Harry through another mouthful of crunching ice.

"To suddenly, after all these years, fire them."

"Ah, but they weren't doing it before."

"Doing what?"

"Making you unhappy."

Alex blinked. "Harry, I've been doing these for ten years."

"Mmmm," said Harry Joy vaguely and poured himself a Scotch. "Here's to us," he said, "we're going to be good."

At night, lying in bed, Alex read Rousseau and Pascal, Bertrand Russell and Hegel, Marx and Plato, but now looking at Harry Joy, whom he had worked with for fifteen years, he was frightened that he had understood him.

"You mean Good, don't you? Capital G?"

"Capital G," grinned Harry and wet his moustache in the Scotch.

"You mean GOOD."

"Bet your arse."

As a dream, as a possibility, this would have made Alex smile. Reading at night while his wife snored beside him he would have luxuriated in the ridiculous possibility of Harry Joy deciding to be Good. But now, facing the possibility of it in this stuffy Saturday office, he was filled with fear.

"You're really serious?"

"Sure. Why not."

"You'll go broke."

"Who cares." Harry felt as if he had opened the windows in a locked-up house. He could smell fresh-mown grass.

Alex smiled a hurt ironical smile. "Well I might. I need a job."

Harry stood up and put both his hands on Alex's soft shoulders. "You'll have a job. I'll make sure you have a job. We don't need a lot of money."

Alex had always been given strength by Harry's enthusiasms but they had always promised him safety, not danger. And besides, there was something in him that was irritated by Harry's new discovery of morality and punishment, as if he were moving in on a territory that didn't belong to him, a territory where he, Alex, was much more familiar with the nuances of right and wrong, the details of the crimes of their clients, the exact nature of their own criminal compliance. It was Alex's field and he resented Harry's crude enthusiasm and his childish determination to be Good. A year ago, three months ago, Harry had had no interest in anything but a successful business and now he was acting as if he had sole proprietorship of the moral dilemmas of life. He had ignored Alex when he nervously, tentatively, suggested there was something wrong with various Krappe Chemicals products.

Now he, Harry Joy, was taking control.

"Still," said Alex, "it's good to see you, you old bastard." But his smile was uncertain.

"Don't worry about the money, Alex. I'll make sure you don't go out on the street."

"Sure," said Alex and Harry decided not to hear the sarcasm in his voice. Instead they sat and talked about who were Captives and who were Actors and as afternoon came on and the bottle of Scotch gave up its last drinks, they composed a list, based on Alex's information.

Outside the streets were flooding and cars were stalling and being abandoned. But when the list was complete Harry Joy rolled up his trousers and went out to find a taxi.

Alex stayed in his office trying to open his filing cabinet with a screw-driver, cursing Harry Joy who now had the key.

It was one of those hot still mornings that come in the beginning of the wet season: the sky a brilliant cobalt blue, and beneath it legions of green all freshly washed or newly born and only the rustling dry leaves hanging like giant dried fish from the banana trees might suggest death, and then only to someone hunting eagerly for its signs. The air that blew through the open windows of the old wooden house was sweet and warm, and honeysuckle and frangipani lent their aromatic veils, which billowed like invisible curtains in the high-ceilinged rooms.

Harry Joy whistled and spread the old newspapers across the kitchen table and set up the boot polish (dark tan, light tan, black and neutral) and the matching brushes and the polishing cloths. He brought to his goodness the slightly obsessive concern with method which is the hallmark of the amateur. He picked up the first pair of shoes and was pleased to see them muddy. He took an old knife and scraped them carefully; then a slightly damp cloth to wipe them; then the brush and polish; now the cloth. Then considering he had rushed the job and perhaps done it badly, he removed the laces and began again.

In the hour before eight o'clock he had cleaned the whole family's shoes, and none of them had so much as stirred. He allowed himself the luxury of a cup of tea and while the kettle boiled he watched a family of honey-eaters attack the last of the previous season's pawpaws on the tree outside the kitchen window. He tried to memorize the form and colours of the birds but he knew he had no talent for it. In three minutes' time the honey-eaters would be a crude blurr in his memory and all he would know was that they had a yellow marking near the eye.

When he had finished his tea he began to clean the windows, beginning in the kitchen where a fine layer of grease lay across the surface of the glass. He was engaged in rubbing this dry with old newspaper when David, already dressed with his wet hair combed neatly, came into the kitchen.

"Morning," said Harry.

David took in the shoes which were now lined up on the back door step, the clean window, and Harry Joy resplendent in bare scarred chest and Balinese sarong, his taut body glistening with sweat, his yellowed teeth biting his lower lip in concentration. He didn't know what to be indignant about first.

He picked up his shoes. "Did you do this?"

"Yes."

"Dad, please, you mustn't."

"It's O.K., it gave me pleasure."

It was true. He couldn't remember ever having had so nice a time as this morning, alone with his family's shoes. He had enjoyed everything about it.

"You must not," his son said.

"They were dirty." He rubbed the window until the smeary marks had all gone. "It gave me pleasure," he said. "I liked cleaning them for you."

David's dark eyes shone. "No. I should clean your shoes."

"If you want to . . ."

"But it's wrong for you to clean mine."

"David, I enjoyed it."

He was not displeased with his son's irritation. It seemed to indicate the efficacy of the ritual.

"But you mustn't, Dad, you mustn't. Don't you understand? Why don't you understand?" He started shaking his head and smoothing down his wet hair.

"What is there to understand?"

"You're so insensitive, I can't believe it! It's like the Fiat. You never understood why that was wrong."

"It embarrassed you."

David was pouring milk over breakfast cereal. "Oh great," he said sarcastically. "After ten years you understand. Great."

"Well you don't have to tell your friends I cleaned your shoes."

"Dad," David pushed his bowl away as if he'd be sick if he ate any more, "you are the head of this household. Doesn't that mean anything to you?"

"It seems a funny sort of household these days," Harry said, "to me, at least. How does it seem to you?"

"And whose fault do you think that is?" David said, his eyes wide and challenging, his head cocked on one side. "Do you think it's mine? Do you think it's Lucy's? Do you think it's Bettina's? It's yours."

"Mine," Harry said happily. "It's my fault." The windows were so clean he could see the honey-eaters much more clearly. They had a grey underbelly and little red wattles hanging like earrings from the sides of their heads. He stared at them with fascination, looking at the hollow they had made inside the pawpaw.

"You are the head of the household. You should lead us. You should punish us."

"Jesus."

"Yes. When we do wrong, we should be punished."

"Christ."

"There is no discipline. That's what's wrong. That's why Mum is unhappy. That's why Lucy takes drugs."

"What drugs?"

"You mustn't clean our shoes or shine our windows. You've got to make us do all that."

"What drugs?"

"When we have our lunch today you let everyone else do the work. You walk in the garden. You'll make us all happy."

"No."

"You and I can play Monopoly."

"I thought you were going to work."

David retrieved his bowl of breakfast cereal. "Really," he said, "there's not an awful lot I can do."

Harry returned to his window and tried to forget about this painful impersonation of his son. He allowed his mind to focus on the merest speck of fly-shit, to think about nothing else but the problem of its removal. He vaguely heard David depart and he didn't hear Bettina arrive at all.

"You are about as subtle as a ton of bricks!"

She didn't look well. Her mascara ran over one eye. It gave her a crooked, slightly demonic appearance. She sat at the kitchen table and angrily smoked two cigarettes.

When she had finished the second cigarette she put it out very brutally. "You are trying to make me look like a tart," she said.

She was trying to make him angry but he wouldn't get angry. He was Good.

He put on the kettle and started to make the tea.

"Don't you damn well make me tea." Bettina was stumbling to her feet. "Don't you dare."

He clung to the tea canister determinedly. "It gives me pleasure," he said. "Please. Let me."

Bettina turned off the gas and threw the water down the sink. "Don't try and be a martyr with me."

"I'm just making you tea."

"I know what you're doing."

With a terrible chill it occurred to Harry she might know exactly what he was doing.

"Oh," he said. He pursed his lips and then sucked in his cheeks.

"Oh yes," she said, her wide eyes mocking him.

"Does it cause you pain?" He tried to appear disinterested.

"In the arse, yes."

"Ah," and he regarded her with interest, his head on one side, scratching his right leg with his left bare foot.

"Come and sit here, old mate." She patted the chair beside her. It was a term of affection from another time, and Harry, standing on one leg like a shy tropical bird, allowed himself to be induced to sit at the table.

She held his hand and kissed him on his splendid nose. They hadn't made love for two months.

"Harry . . ."

"Yes."

"Do you think you're going a bit loopy?"

Harry shrugged. "All I'm doing . . ." but he stopped, not wishing to show his hand.

"What are you doing, old mate?"

"All I'm doing is cleaning windows."

"So you can make me look like a tart."

"No."

"So everyone can see I don't do anything?"

"I'd have thought you'd be glad for me to do it."

"You're a sarcastic bastard aren't you," she said good-humouredly, "Alright, get out."

"Get out where?"

"Get out of the fucking kitchen and let me get on with it."

"No, let me clean some more."

Bettina pointed a single finger and started jabbing him around the edges of his scar. "Look, you, get out, out."

He retreated upstairs. He managed to clean half the bathroom before she came and found him.

She was going to be a hot-shot but she met Harry Joy and fell in love with him. They told her he was from the French Consulate and she watched him for a while, not in the least impatient, merely fascinated by him. He wore a beautifully tailored rather loose white suit. He had a huge moustache. He looked Splendid. She watched how he moved, gracefully, as if his feet hardly touched the floor, the walk of a dancer.

It was a party for a departing Trade Commissioner, full of businessmen with rotary badges. She had come with her boss who ran the local Ogilvy & Mather office.

"Come on, Tina," he had said, "grab your hat. We're going to a party."

She sat in a chair and began to watch Harry Joy. She was shy and had no plan for meeting him. She was happy enough to look and admire.

Even then she was offended by the drabness of the town, its dullness, its lack of style. Her only escape was in her stinking room above her father's service station. Downstairs Billy McPhee burped and farted, wise-cracked, giggled, ran between cash register and pump, pump and cash register; upstairs, his daughter turned the shining pages of the New York Art Directors' Annual.

Men sat beside her and engaged her in conversation but her eyes never left the exotic man in the beautiful white suit. It was not even possible, she thought, that he spoke English.

And then he was standing in front of her.

"You've been staring at me," he said and he was not French at all, but he spoke with such a low, slow drawl that she was not in the least disappointed.

"Yes," she said. She couldn't think of anything else. Yet the brevity of her reply probably struck him as bold.

He sat beside her and surveyed the motel room full of grey suits and striped carpet. "Mmmm," he said.

She thought he was the most Original person she'd ever met.

"It's a beautiful suit," she said. She was so tense her fingernails ached.

When he smiled, his eyes crinkled. "Why are you wearing gloves?"

She was nineteen. She said: "My hands sweat."

A smile stirred beneath that vast moustache. "Are you eccentric?" he asked.

"Yes."

He called a waiter and ordered vodka. Then he undressed her hands and wiped them with a handkerchief dipped in vodka. He borrowed a towel from the waiter and dried them.

"There," he said, "all you need is a splash of vermouth and you could have a very dry vodkatini." He was twenty-two. He had read about vodkatinis in the *New Yorker*.

She did not ask him what he did. She detested people who did it to her.

"Ask me in three years," she'd say.

"Why?"

"Because in three years I'll have something interesting to tell you."

Even the two men who ran Ogilvy & Mather did not know their secretary, receptionist and switchboard operator held ambitions to be an advertising hot-shot. She probably knew more about the history of American advertising than they did. She owned a total of fifteen annuals from the New York Art Directors' Club and she knew who had written every one of the Volkswagen ads since the first ones Bill Bernbach had done himself. She devoured the American trade papers and knew all the gossip. If there had been anyone to tell she would have told them funny stories about Mary Wells and Jack Tinker but there was only her father, bug-eyed on pills, scattering his own verbal garbage behind him: "ten out of ten, number one son, go for it Gloria." She lived in a wreckers yard of words.

"I'm in advertising," Harry Joy offered. "Harry Joy."

It was enough information for her to be able to place him exactly. He was only twenty-two and he was the Joy in Day, Kerlewis & Joy. He had been made a partner after only eight months when Mr Kerlewis died suddenly. She knew how much he was reputed to earn, what commercials he had written, and the names of three women he had been seen with regularly.

She did not want to tell him she was a receptionist at Ogilvy & Mather. She did not wish to be ordinary. Later, later, she would be exceptional, but now when it was important she was a little Miss Nobody with nothing interesting to say. She looked at him in despair as if he might, at any instant, be snatched from her and she acted quickly, with the outrageous courage of the very shy.

She stood up and put her gloves back on.

"Where are you going?" He looked hurt.

"I'm going to dinner," she said. "Want to come?"

"O.K.," he said as though he was asked out by women every night of the week. Her hands were bathed in nervous sweat and later that night when she kicked off her shoes they stank of all the hopes and anxieties that had never once showed on that smooth olive-skinned face which had so beguiled dear Harry Joy.

On the way to dinner he decided, without consulting her, that he needed petrol.

"No," she said, "not here."

But it was too late. They were already parked on the forecourt and Billy McPhee, a stinking rag in his back pocket, was bounding out of the office, his worn red head low, his arms swinging, whistling some piece of nonsense he'd misheard on the radio, and Harry was saying to her: "Why did you say that?"

"Nothing," she said. "It doesn't matter."

She tried to be invisible.

"Fill 'er up," Harry said.

"Oil, water, Captain's Daughter?" Billy said, peering into the car but Bettina turned the other way. "Fix your windscreen?"

She never forgot it. Eighteen years later it could still make her moan out loud. How could she have betrayed him? How could she, heartless cruel nineteen-year-old, have refused to acknowledge that the man looking at her through the windscreen was her father?

More than her father. Her mother too, because her real mother had left Billy and Billy had not missed a beat — he just brought her up, right there on the forecourt. He changed her nappies beside the cash register. He parked her pram between the pumps. While the gallons clicked over he talked to her continually. "You were born into this business," he told her. "It's in your blood. You are one hundred and twenty octane." He had been young once, keen, self-starting, go-ahead, with plans. But somewhere all his energy and his dreams got out of control as he gabbled around the forecourt making plans to buy a block of flats, then two blocks of flats, and then three. But he didn't even own their own flat. He stank of sweat and speed and perished rubber and his pale blue eyes bugged out his unnaturally white skin.

Bettina saw her father through the window. She looked right through him. Something, a spasm, a tic, wrenched Billy's mouth and then his eyes just clouded over and he finished wiping the window and filled up the tank.

"Could you check the tyres?" Harry said.

"Get fucked," Billy McPhee told his future son-in-law. "Give me the money and piss off before I punch your ugly head in."

Later when they knew each other neither of them ever got over the obstacle created by that night.

Bettina McPhee hadn't expected to fall in love with anyone. She hadn't been able to imagine it and it had played no part in her plan. Later, perhaps, in America or somewhere else, but not here and now.

But next thing she knew, she'd done it. Like that. Without even pausing to think. And then everything went out the window and she pursued her love with a reckless sort of enthusiasm and she suddenly didn't give a hoot about being a hot-shot or going to America because she was happy and her happiness seemed so perfect it needed nothing. She applied herself to marriage with wild enthusiasm, as if it might yield up treasures in exact proportion to the energy she plunged into it. She decided to find the town interesting. They bought an old stilted house in Palm Avenue and she became pregnant with David, she was still smashing out a central wall with a jemmy and a sledgehammer and ending her days with bloodied hands and plaster-covered hair.

Billy McPhee's daughter, without a doubt.

She did not abandon her interest in advertising; it was, after all, her husband's business. She read the American trade papers. She bought the new Art Directors' Annuals. She criticized Harry's work with a keen intelligence.

She was shocked when she realized how complacent he was.

"It worked," he said, defending a television commercial he'd written.

"So it worked," she said, "so what. Was it *great*?"

"Oh, come on, Bettina . . ."

"Was it great?"

"Alright," he said, "it wasn't great. But it makes us money."

"To hell with the money," she said. "I don't care about the money. All I care about is that you do witty, beautiful wonderful advertisements."

"You're right," he said, and she tried to accept that he would never do great ads.

She hadn't been quite so keen to become pregnant the second

time. She was going to be a hot-shot. Each year she told herself that she was still young. And while she waited she became more American than the Americans. She supported their wars, saw their movies, bought their products, despised their enemies. Even their most trivial habits were adopted as articles of faith and there was always iced water on the table at Palm Avenue. She believed in the benevolence of their companies, the triumph of the astronauts, the law of the market-place and the twin threats of Communism and the second-rate, although not necessarily in that order.

By the time Lucy was ten they were having arguments about whether Bettina could come into the business. In Harry's mind they had never been bitter arguments, and, in a superficial sense, he was right. But Bettina had been deeply offended by his refusal to consider it. It was a rejection more painful than any she had ever experienced and she could not forgive him for it.

In Bettina's view, it was that rejection which had produced their present unhappiness. Yet, even now, in the midst of Harry's madness, in the total ruin of their marriage, there were days when they would find themselves, almost forgetfully, on the verge of having fun (although something would always go wrong, some irritation would creep in and everything would suddenly go sour and hatreds and resentments would come spilling out of her and lie in a nasty slippery mess along with the water from the sprouts and the spilt pieces of cabbage on the kitchen floor).

"Who cleaned the shoes?"

"Your idiot father."

Her daughter was the wild, untended variety of the same plant, loose like a dog, her dark hair curling in masses, her movements still graceful but lackadaisical. She had her mother's almond eyes but her olive skin was nearly black from the sun. She sat on the kitchen table and watched Bettina rubbing at the glass.

"Have you been swimming again?" Bettina said, puffing a little.

"Yes."

She worried about the size of her daughter's shoulders. She turned and gave a crooked mascara look.

"Don't worry, Mum, I'll marry a gorilla."

"You might have to," she said drily. "Have a shower."

"I can't. Daddy's cleaning out the bathroom."

"Oh fuck him," screamed Bettina and ran up the stairs. She gave Harry credit for greater deviousness than he was capable of. She had heard him tell his methods for dealing with difficult clients and she now felt some subtle net was being drawn around her. Why was he polishing the bath in his sarong? Why were there clean shoes sitting in a line on the back door step? He made her feel like a tart, an adultress, a drunk, a failure. He was humiliating himself in order to humiliate her.

She found him in the bathroom and after she had hit him with the mop she asked him to forgive her. She held him then, and in spite of all her resolutions, all her determination, her ambitions, she felt the old stirrings of a familiar love.

"You won't let me love you," she said to the man she had decided to leave, who drove her crazy and sent her into wild displays of rage.

She felt him tremble. She liked his body since he had been sick: it was thinner and harder. She even liked the big silky scar on his chest.

"You won't let me get close." She was damn well seducing him, in the bathroom, with her hand up his sarong. She bit his ear. "Harry, Harry." She felt him resist, and then, without a word, he just unknotted, and it was like the old days, the old times when they had stayed in bed on Saturday morning, days before the invention of Joel, and with one hand he was locking the door and with the other he was tearing off her dressing gown.

"Betty, Betty," he said, "is it you?"

In the mythology of the family the McPhees were dark, discontented, poetic, and the Joys were placid and rather ordinary. In this classification it was necessary to forget Harry's eccentric mother and his wandering father. It was equally important to forget Bettina's sad bug-eyed father who had died of an overdose of amphetamines and anger, howling at a customer who wanted a dollar's worth of petrol.

"Dollar's worth," screamed Billy McPhee, literally jumping up and down beside the pump, "you expect me to give you a fucking *dollar's worth*." And Bettina, paying her guilty last respects, imagined she could detect, amidst the sweet-petalled aromas of funeral flowers, the more familiar perfumes of her youth: oil, petrol, and perished rubber. This pale dead man was not a McPhee.

David Joy was a McPhee, and was teased by his sister because of it: "How's the master race?"

"You," Bettina told Lucy, flying in the face of all physical evidence, "are a Joy." And, as if to compensate for this misfortune, it was always said: "Lucy is going to be happy." She made it sound as if there was something dreadfully wrong with being happy in this particular way.

Her mother's elitist attitudes irritated Lucy. "What's the matter with being ordinary?" she said. "Why do you want to be special?"

"I couldn't bear to be second-rate."

"I wouldn't mind being sixth-rate, or tenth-rate."

"Can't you do something about your appearance?"

"My appearance is fine." She bit an apple. She accepted herself so completely that she could not help but be beautiful, and even if her bum was already too big and her ankles too thick, there was something about her that made people calmer and better just to be with her. Men would always be attracted to her as boys were now. She liked fucking them too. Given her appetites it is a wonder – when you consider the provincial nature of the town – that she was not derided for them.

"You are complacent," her mother said (had said, would say, repeatedly). "You are going to be a social worker and you'll just get your degree and end up with a line of children and a house in the suburbs."

"I don't want to be a social worker."

"Don't you ever say that to your father."

"Yeah, yeah. I know."

"What *do* you want to do?"

But you couldn't tell Bettina McPhee that you were going to overthrow the Americans.

Harry set the table in the dining room. It was Georgian, made from English Ash and imported by a sea captain from a certain Percy Lewis Esq., who surely could not have imagined his table in this room with this monstrously exaggerated view of a mountain like a sugar loaf and a tree that flowered flame. Now, as Harry placed the silver on the table, the clouds slid in over the flat mangrove swamps to the south and, as if aware of the almost unbearable richness of the view, wrapped themselves around Sugar Loaf and covered the gleaming bay beneath.

It was drippingly humid. Lucy and David and Bettina sat out on the wide verandah and fought against or relaxed into the heat, according perhaps to the amounts of McPhee or Joy apportioned them. Bettina, certainly, did not enjoy the heat and collapsed back into her stockman's chair with her eyes shut. David affected the quality he thought proper for a Sunday Luncheon and although he wore a cashmere sweater, looked not in the least hot. Lucy sat on the verandah rail in a white cheesecloth dress and looked at the bangalow palms, which, in the absence of any wind, mysteriously rustled their fish-bone fronds, as if talking to each other.

Today was to be a real family lunch, a re-enactment of some tradition they imagined they had always shared. It had been Lucy's idea; she had guessed, not incorrectly, at the healing power of the ritual.

Harry drifted out on to the verandah with some more Veuve Cliquot and arranged himself in a large cane chair.

"Ah," he said, and sipped his champagne.

Like a dog who keeps sneaking on to a sofa it is forbidden, it was the nature of Harry Joy that he would always seek out comfort. So here we have him two weeks after his vow to be Good, to fire his largest client, to save his colleague from the tortures of Hell. The client is not fired. The tortures of his colleague, if anything, have increased: now he loses sleep, tosses and turns in unemployed nightmares, and wanders around a house in which neither his wife nor his Pascal can provide him with any comfort. And as for Goodness, it seems to have degenerated into something as silly as setting the table for a Sunday Lunch.

And Harry, meanwhile, can lie back on the verandah of his charming house at Palm Avenue and sip his Veuve Cliquot and wait for the rain to come and try to persuade himself that he may, after all, have been crazy.

Lucy went to sit beside her mother who held her hand contentedly. The lunch might just work, if Betty didn't get too drunk, if Harry didn't start taking notes again.

"What's the first course?" Harry said.

"Escrivée Amoureuse."

"Ah," he said.

The rain began to fall, very gently at first, making loud slapping noises on the banana leaves, where it collected in tiny dams which dipped and broke and then reformed. The poinciana, like so many feathery hands held palm upwards, let the rain brush carelessly through its fingers.

The Veuve Cliquot was old enough to have assumed a golden colour, and Harry was not unappreciative of its beauty, nor was he ignorant of its cost, nor the contribution Krappe Chemicals made towards its purchase.

He had reread his notebooks and found them a little extreme, a little frenzied, not to say unbalanced. And all their evidence, he thought, was insufficient to justify this terrible, risky strategy of Goodness which he viewed, just now, sitting before this gentle curtain of rain, in a little the same way as he might have thought of a slightly embarrassing sexual indiscretion.

But he is not quite ready to deny his notebooks. Even now, as he yawns, stretches, and points his sandalled feet, he has promised him himself One Last Test.

The bar wasn't quite right, but it would do. It was the best bar she knew but in no way equalled the bars she would have liked to sit in. The bars she would have liked to sit in had a chrome rail parallel to the smooth leather bar top. They had elegant art deco mirrors reflecting beautiful people carelessly dressed, and those little lamps with figurines by Lalique, each one valued at something like three thousand dollars.

But here, at least, they did put pistachios on the bar instead of peanuts and they made the Tequila Sunrises from real orange juice and it was the best bar in this town and as long as nobody told her it was a chic and elegant bar (thus forcing her to disagree violently with their provincial judgement) Bettina was very happy there. She didn't mind that Joel was late. She wasn't even mildly irritated. She looked at the bottles on the shelf, felt the shiny dark envelop her, and wondered (raising her eyes to the mirror) whether she mightn't just pick up someone. She looked, she thought, interesting. She was satisfied with her sleek dark hair which now, thanks to Edouard, came in two sleek sweeping pincers beneath the high cheek bones of her rounded face. Her large mouth (Revlon Crimson Flush No. 7) was very red. She did not look nice, or easy, but she did look interesting. She could have been anywhere (Budapest 1923, Blakes Hotel London 1975).

When she had finally gone through the agonies of leaving Harry, when she had her own business, she would go to Blakes Hotel in London and sit in the bar there.

She sat at one end of the bar and watched the door with a wonderful sense of expectation as if, at any moment, the most beautiful man might walk through the door, three days' growth on his handsome face, a loose linen jacket thown over his shoulders, a dark face, sensuous and violent, but an intelligent forehead.

So when Joel came scurrying through at the moment she was,

without knowing why, irritated and depressed. She was always disappointed when she saw him: physically he was not quite what she had remembered.

Joel always rushed. He had no cool. Harry had more style than Joel, who almost waddled, and there, there still, were those damn cufflinks he wouldn't take off.

"Hello, honey." The bar stool farted when he sat on it. She tried to tell herself it would have happened to anyone. "I've been getting your husband on to an aeroplane."

"Do you really have to wear those cufflinks?"

But Joel was ordering a drink. "He nearly missed the damn plane."

"If you really want to wear cufflinks why don't you come with me and I'll buy you some."

"I don't know why in the hell he wants to go down there, we could have done it on the phone. Hey . . . get your hands off my cufflinks. What are you doing?"

"I'm taking your damn cufflinks off."

Joel sat at the bar with his cuffs flapping at the bottom of his coat sleeves. "What in the hell do I do now?"

"Pull your sleeves up," she said and started giggling. "Did you have a nice day at the office?"

"Hell, honey, that isn't funny."

Bettina ordered another Sunrise and Joel removed his suit coat, put it fussily over the next bar stool, rolled his shirt sleeves up, and put his coat back on. He sulked for a while and Bettina looked around. In the end he started talking to stop her looking around.

"He's not in a very healthy state of mind."

"Who, honey?"

"Your husband."

"Ah," Bettina waved a ringed hand, "he's just growing up." She liked Harry when she was away from him. He towered over everyone else she knew.

Joel started laughing incredulously, "Oh that's good, honey, that's really good. Just growing up. He tells me in the car that he is going to be Good. Is that *sane*? Because, honey, if that's sane, then I want to be crazy."

"It's not your style, darling."

"What isn't?"

"Being crazy isn't your style."

"What in the goddamn hell do you mean by that?"

His chin was starting to wobble so she changed the subject. "Who did you take to lunch?"

"I'm taking George Lewis out to lunch next week. I've got a table booked at La Belle Epoque."

"He said he'd go last week."

"Well he had to cancel."

"Why can't we steal someone else's clients? Why do we have to steal Harry's clients?"

"We haven't stolen anyone's clients yet."

"Damn right we haven't," said Bettina bitterly, wondering if she had got herself stuck with a schmuck who couldn't even get one account. She had listened to Harry when she shouldn't have, and ignored him when she should have listened.

"*You* do it then."

"Alright, fuck you, I just might." The bastard. He knew she couldn't. He knew it gave her the shits to be unable to do this thing that she wanted to do more than anything else. But how could Harry Joy's wife phone up a prospective client and take him out to lunch.

"Well do," he said smugly. "Do it yourself."

"I just might."

But he wasn't even threatened by it. In fact it restored his good humour and a little colour crept into his face.

"What I was thinking," he said, and began to run his chubby finger around the wet rim of his Scotch glass.

Bettina listened. When Joel spoke like this she thought of an ice-skater. Suddenly the little bugger was so damn elegant it was almost unbearable.

"What I was thinking was it might be *better* and *simpler* and less *disruptive* for everyone if we just had him committed."

He took her breath away. Bettina, literally, could not speak. And when she looked at Joel she saw that he meant it: he had that strange little prim smile on his face and his eyes were wet but how or why they were wet she didn't know. Some emotion moved him. But she smelt no weakness, only a sly satisfaction, a boneless strength.

"Christ," she said, "you little creep." But her eyes were bright with admiration and the smile seemed to stay on Joel's face even while he sipped his Scotch.

That night, in the branches of the fig tree beside his house, Harry would conduct his Final Test.

It had not been easy to get there. Joel had been attentive and kind.

He had driven him to the airport and waited for him to board the plane.

"You go, Joel. No point in waiting here."

"No, no, I'm fine."

When the plane had finally begun to board Harry had still waited.

"You go," he said. "I'll go on in a second. I'll just wait for most of them to get on."

But still Joel wouldn't go, and Harry found himself both irritated and moved by his kindness. Joel waited to watch him walk down the boarding finger and waved him all the way on to the plane.

He took his seat and stood up again.

"I'm on the wrong plane," he told the hostess, and smiled wanly. "Sorry." She took the ticket from his hand.

"No," she said, "you're on the right plane, sir. Please be seated."

"I want to get off."

"But this is your plane."

"I don't care. I don't want to fly on it. I was only *pretending* to get on it."

"And you just got carried away?" the hostess said sourly, stepping back into the galley to let him past.

And now he was up the fig tree just as he had planned to be, ready to observe what Actors did when they had no audience. The final test was hardly worth all the effort.

It was not so uncomfortable. He had been in worse situations. From this particular branch he had a good view of his neighbour who was taking advantage of the late summer light to dig a hole. This was quite consistent with his behaviour in all the years before Harry had died and he found it, in a peculiar way, soothing to watch him scurrying and puffing around his garden like a little mole. The neighbour always enjoyed holes and mounds of dirt. The earth in his garden could never lie in peace, always on the move from one corner to another. Just when it was settled in, he would decide to shift it. It had all the senseless motion of a sadistic punishment and yet the man (known affectionately as "the Miner" by the entire Joy family) looked happy enough as he surveyed his mound of dirt and his hole in the ground.

Harry settled in against the trunk and lit a cigarette just as the Miner was walking across the back door. He stopped and stared up at the tree. He stood very still.

"Hey you," he called at last, "you, in the tree."

"It's only me," Harry hissed.

"Who's you?"

"Mr Joy."

The Miner replied in a similar style, in a piercing whisper "What's up?"

"I've lost my key."

The Miner's wife came and stood on the back step: "Who is it?"

"Mr Joy, from next door."

"What's he doing?"

"He's lost his key."

"The boy is home."

"Your son is home," hissed the Miner.

Harry knew that his son was home: he could see yellow light shining through the chink in the heavy curtains three feet above his head.

"I know," he hissed back.

Down on the back step of their house the Miner and his wife had an anxious little conference.

"He knows," the Miner said.

"I'm not deaf."

The Miner took a tentative step towards the fence. "Do you want me to ring the bell for you?"

"Stupid, stupid," the wife exploded and went inside and slammed the door.

"I want to surprise them," Harry whispered.

"He wants to surprise them," the Miner told the darkened screen door. Obviously she had not given up all interest. The door creaked outwards, inquiringly. Another whispered conference concluded with a sharp little bang as the screen door shut like a trap and the Miner, as in the manner of one reluctantly following orders, left his territory and came down the side path on the Joys' side of the fence.

It would appear that he wished a more confidential talk.

It was not an easy tree to climb and the Miner did not acquit himself well. The problem was the first branch.

"Stand on the chair," Harry whispered, deciding it better that the climb be executed quietly if it was going to be done at all.

"What chair?"

"There."

It was almost dark now but it was still possible to see bulges and creases in the Miner's bulbous form as it approached, heralded by wheezing.

"Hi."

"Hi."

Such American-style casualness in the middle of a tree. Was he going to remark on the weather?

"He's not here," the Miner said at last.

There were so many people who were not there. Harry couldn't think what he meant.

"The blue BMW."

Joel drove a blue BMW, but why would anyone climb a tree to tell him that Joel, as was perfectly obvious, was not visiting his house.

"The person you are trying to surprise," said the Miner, trying to take possession of Harry's branch, "is not here."

"Thank you, Mr Harrison."

"You're welcome any time."

"Can you find your own way down?"

"Yes, I think so." But he had only retreated by one branch when he stopped. "Mr Joy?"

"Yes."

"I must discuss the fence with you sometime. We are going to have to replace it."

"I'll drop in, Mr Harrison."

"No hurry."

He crashed his way through the lower branches and just when Harry judged him safely down, there was a sharp crack followed by a soft thud and a yelp of pain.

"Are you alright?" he called.

There was no answer, but he thought he saw the shadow of the Miner limping along the darker shadow of the fence and then saw it slide inside the still-dark screen door.

Harry, already, was doubting the wisdom of his final test and the Miner had reminded him, had let him see himself as he must be seen: Harry Joy was crazy. He fervently hoped he had been. His theory, so cleverly arrived at (if they are Actors they will reveal themselves when they think their audience is absent) seemed puerile to him, more affected by champagne than common sense.

So there he was, considering leaving his tree, climbing down, finding a bottle of wine, removing himself from that uncomfortable, undignified position, when Joel's blue BMW pulled up outside, and it was only the fear of being thought mad that stopped him climbing down and saying: here I am.

He waited, and, with no real interest, watched.

He heard Joel turn off his blaring radio. He saw Bettina lurch from the car. The clink of bottles. Bettina saying: "You open the door for me again and I'll break your bloody arm." Laughter. Joel locking the door and having trouble with his keys.

His partner kissing his wife. His partner's leg jammed hard between his wife's legs, in the glow of the street light, against the hedge, beside the footpath.

No.

Harry retreated up the tree in pain.

Joel, far below, said: "We should have gone to my place."

He did not want to hear anything. He came to escape pain, not find it.

But Bettina's voice insisted on reaching him: "I can't stand your bloody brass any more. If I have to look at your brass any more, I'll puke."

Eastern brass artifacts in Joel's bedroom. He had bought a crate-load of them in a market in Kabul and a woman was paid to polish them every week. In the living room there were books he had bought by the metre.

Harry kept climbing, away from voices.

He wanted normality and peace so badly that he could still deny he had seen this torture. He could have erased it from his memory. He wanted normality and warmth. Instinctively, seeking comfort, he put his eye to the chink in his son's bedroom curtain. Show me my son.

There: David Joy, his trousers around his knees and Lucy, her skirt beside her on the floor, sucking his son's pale-skinned penis.

Harry Joy at the windows of Hell.

He moaned and staggered on his branch like a man pole-axed. He began to descend, forgetting that trees should not be left in a hurry, but slowly, carefully, one leg at a time, even by those practised in the art.

But Harry, hurrying, left his branch too quickly and barely held the next branch for a second before he was on his way further down the tree. He crashed ten feet, was wrenched, and held.

The sharp end of the branch the Miner had broken in his fall now held Harry securely like a butcher's hook in the trousers of his suit.

He stayed there, suspended, and swung a little in front of one more vista. For in front of his eyes, the curtains properly parted, was a window where he was presented with one last glimpse of his partner's pudgy little hand disappearing up his wife's dress.

Bettina Joy looked up and saw her husband's head staring in the window, upside down.

Harry saw her mouth open wide and her eyes bulge a little. He thought of fish eyes in shop windows and Billy McPhee screaming about a dollar's worth of petrol.

Bettina Joy hit Joel Davis who misunderstood and would not stop.

Harry saw Joel Davis turn and saw his mouth wide open. Joel Davis wiped his hand on his handkerchief before he made a move towards the window.

"I put you on the plane," he said. And, indeed, he looked up into the sky as if Harry might have dropped out.

"Just cut my trousers."

They were there in a second: all the cast of tormentors: the partner, the faithful wife, the good neighbour, the loving children.

They fooled around with him on the broken branch, claiming to lack strength and height. He felt them circle beneath his blood-filled head like a congregation of Satanic dwarves come to perform magic rituals.

They discussed ladders. They made it a protracted affair.

He begged them to cut his trousers.

But, no: "I'll get the aluminium ladder."

"No, the wooden one will be better."

"Alright, you get the wooden one." Which was further away, next door.

Then, with the ladder, they fooled around some more and claimed they should not lift him off. He lifted his head upwards, trying not to black out.

Joel Davis knelt so he could look into his senior partner's bloodshot eye: "We're going to have to cut you down." He held up a rusty old razor blade. "O.K.?"

Harry closed his eyes. He felt them cut and then, suddenly, there was a loud rip and he fell into an untidy nest of elbows and arms with fingers poking out the top of it. Bettina poked a finger in his eye. David put an elbow in his throat.

When he had vomited, he spat sedately on the lawn and looked at them. They had all gathered in a little group beside the house, like people posed for a photograph, each one looking a little self-consciously into the lens, no one quite sure what expression to adopt.

The Final Test.

"I curse you," he said, and the anachronistic sound of the word impressed him with its power. "I curse you all, for all time, without exception."

They stood before him silently, giving him the respect awarded the holy and the insane.

Part Three

The Rolls Royce of Honeys

It was like a holiday. Everything seemed bigger than life: nice wine, dramas, whispered conversations, madness, maybe even love. The Joys' house at Palm Avenue felt like the headquarters of some ecstatic campaign in which madness played a vital role, but whether as an ally or assailant was not always clear.

Harry had retreated to a suite on the twenty-first floor of the Hilton, from which privileged position he managed to charm the doctors who were sent to commit him. They savoured the champagne, letting its acidity take away the feeling that they had almost been associated with something unclean.

They had disliked Joel and had found his cufflinks offensive.

The beluga caviar Harry Joy offered them helped erase the last of this vulgarity and they chatted about the Hiltons they remembered from other countries and other times. They remembered lost luggage at airports, cancelled flights, and bored each other a little until the champagne was drunk and they departed smiling, a little unsteady on their feet.

Even while Joel was complaining about the expenses Harry was running up, Bettina was ordering take-away food from Milanos and having it delivered by taxi. They all felt themselves to be trembling on the edge of something new and wonderful. Lucy saw all this and understood it instinctively. She couldn't understand why their happiness surprised them or needed to be denied.

"You were stuck," she told Bettina.

"How stuck?"

"Stuck. Now you're unstuck."

"You're too young to understand."

"You've got a new lover," she hugged her mother. "You're having a wonderful time."

"You've got no feelings. What about your father? Your father is crazy. He's insane." And she burst into tears ...

They ate chocolates and had curacao in their coffee. They made pancakes and mulled wine. They all put on weight and their faces became rounder, their skin tauter, and it made none of them less attractive but somehow tumescent.

They tidied the house as if they were expecting important visitors. They had conferences about Harry in which they pretended everything was being done for his good, as if even the chocolates would somehow help to bring about the cure they said they wanted. They sat around the shining Georgian table and, as they acted out their concern, they came to believe it. Joel's eyes shone with emotion and no one could doubt that he wanted his partner well.

To Lucy the conferences began to stink of hypocrisy and she could no longer enter into the spirit of things. She sat glumly at the table and listened to the unsaid things, the dark brown words with soft centres. There was something "off" about the meetings. She thought of stale water inside a defrosted refrigerator.

Lucy spoiled it for the others. They were happier and easier when she went off to bed, and as she left the room she could hear their chairs shifting and their bodies unfolding and, sometimes, a light clunk, as Bettina's shoes were dropped gently to the floor.

Lucy did not go to meetings (official or secret) of the Communist Party. She had resigned from the branch and her Comrades were disgusted with her. Comrade Dilettante, they had called her.

She lay on her bed and looked at the ceiling. She rolled a joint and turned on the radio to block out the conspiratorial murmur which reached her from the room downstairs.

You could not call it jostling, for they were all seated on chairs and the chairs did not move, except occasionally to scrape impatiently, or to see-saw back and forth on their precarious back legs; but yet what had happened with Joel and David was exactly like the jostling that takes place on the football field as two players position themselves for a ball that is still half-way down the field, an irritating elbowing sort of movement which can often flare up into a fist fight and then you have one player lying on the ground and the crowd wondering what has happened.

They vied for Bettina's attention, consideration, and rarely spoke to one another directly.

The subject, of course, was having Harry committed.

Initially David had taken little part in these conversations but as the nights went on he became more and more astonished at what he saw as Joel's ineptness. He listened with astonishment to the decisions that were made. If the world was full of people like Joel it was going to be a very easy life, a lot easier than he had ever imagined. If this was a businessman (an *American* businessman) then business was a pushover. Were they all so sloppy-minded and stupid as this little frog with the beads of perspiration on his lip?

But tonight he would not jostle. Tonight, he would hit.

Like an out-of-favour general, David waited to be asked to take command. He was in no real hurry and the irritation he felt was not unpleasant. He secretly rolled his eyes and curled his lip as he listened to the latest reports of failure to have his father committed. They were children. They couldn't bribe their way out of a traffic offence.

And now they were worried about money. It was pathetic to listen to Joel talk about money. He did it like a petty cash clerk who is two cents out. He was so frightened of spending money he could never, ever, hope to make any. He fretted. He brought bills to the table and threw them around.

"But he's taken a suite," Joel was saying, "That's what I keep trying to tell you, honey. It isn't a room. It's a suite."

"I know the difference," Bettina snapped. "I've probably stayed in more suites than you have. What do you think he is? You expect him to stay in a *room*?"

"How damn long will he stay there? You know the sort of wine he drinks."

"The Hilton's got a lousy wine list."

"Betty, that's not the point."

David stood up and walked around the room, looking carefully at the insect screens. There it was: an improperly closed insect screen on the front door. He clicked it shut with a small over-precise movement of his stiff left hand.

"Joel," he said.

Joel had taken advantage of his absence to hunch over into a conspiratorial whisper, but when David spoke Bettina looked up and Joel was forced to acknowledge him.

"Yes, Davey."

David rolled his eyes towards the ceiling. He could not stand being called Davey. It reminded him of a dog or a simpering little boy in a sailor's suit. He walked silently to the table where his mother held out her hand. He took the hand absent-mindedly but didn't sit down. "Joel, when you come in you must shut the door properly."

"Sorry, old mate."

"The mosquitoes get in."

"O.K., sorry."

David placed his mother's hand carefully on the table and walked out to the kitchen.

"He hates mosquitoes," Bettina said.

Joel pulled a face of ambiguous meaning.

"He's just upset."

"Oh, sure!" Joel thought otherwise, but if he was going to say anything else he was stopped by David who re-entered the room firing insecticide into the air from two aerosol cans, one held in each hand high above his head. He circuited the room and started up the stairs, the cans still firing.

"Put your hand over your drink," Bettina said.

Upstairs they could hear heavy footsteps.

"Lucy doesn't like insecticide," Bettina explained.

When David returned to the room he was pleased to see that Joel had his hand over his drink, although he couldn't have explained why.

David sat down. There was a silence. Joel lifted his hand off his drink and wiped the rim with his finger before drinking. The silence continued. David stretched his long legs beneath the table. He threw back his arms and yawned. He was loose and relaxed. The silence continued further. It was quite delicious.

"I know how to do it," he said.

Joel clicked his tongue in irritation but Bettina was looking at him.

"How?" she asked.

"Oh come *on*," Joel said to her, "now you ask a boy: what does he know? Who do you want to listen to?"

David shrugged. "O.K.," he said, "I was only offering."

"Tell me," Bettina said and Joel moved his chair angrily.

"Well, you won't get anyone to commit him the straight way, that's the first thing." His mother was looking at him in a way she had never looked at him before.

"Go on," she said.

"Davey, I don't want to be rude," Joel said. "But you are seventeen years old. You are hardly an expert."

"Well you're not an expert either. That's why Harry is still in the

Hilton." He turned to Bettina. "I know how to have him committed but it'll cost money."

"Ah well, there you are," Joel said, "... money."

The petty cash clerk!

"Five thousand dollars," David said, enunciating the words very carefully and looking straight at Bettina.

"Look," Joel said to Bettina, "do I have to listen to this." He sifted angrily through the American Express and Diners Club bills that littered the table. "Look at these."

A mental dwarf! Look at him stacking his little bills into a neat pile. David curled his lip and revealed a neat row of small white teeth.

"I'll pay the five grand," David said. He hadn't planned this, but it didn't matter. It was worth every cent of it.

Look at Joel, his frog mouth wide in disbelief, and Bettina too, staring at him. But she, his mother, had a smile waiting to accompany her astonishment.

"Where would you get five thousand dollars from?" Joel said.

It was wonderful.

"I want something," he told his mother. "When Harry is committed, let me drop all this university thing. I'm not going to go. I want to go into business."

"You're astonishing," his mother said. "I don't believe it. For God's sake," she turned to Joel, "don't you ever tell Harry about this, or I'll kill you."

"You must really hate your father," Joel said to David.

"No ..."

"Five thousand dollars," Joel shook his head. "That's a lot of money."

"I don't hate him," David said, "he's sick."

But Joel was sitting there, smiling smugly, shaking his head. "Oh boy," he said.

"You're a hypocrite," David said hotly.

But Joel was smiling that big revolting red-lipped smile, as if *he* had won.

"I didn't want to do it," David told his perplexed mother, "I didn't want to have to do it ..." And startled everyone by bursting into tears.

He waited to be acted on, as he always had, having the peculiar good luck to be at once passive and attractive, so that he had rarely been left to moulder by the roadside, but had been picked up, cared for, involved in schemes, affairs, businesses, the conception of children. Even love had come to him like this, delivered to him where he stood in his wonderful white suit. Appearing to need nothing, he attracted everything, women in particular, who found in him something feline, graceful, as slow and sensuous as a snake.

He waited and doctors came to him. He said nothing to them of his pains. He knew their game and played it and they went away. In those first few days he felt, like the plotting members of his family, that he was on the brink of something new, although in his case he did not anticipate improvement, but the reverse.

Yet the days passed and nothing happened. He watched the ugly goods yard beneath his window and looked out over the whole expanse of Hell which lay under a poisonous yellow cloud. The doctors ceased coming. The phone did not ring. Actors came and went. They carried food, emptied ashtrays, vacuum-cleaned the floor and made the beds. Their performances were lack-lustre, their eyes dull. They were thinking about other things they would rather have done. They did their jobs and would not talk to him.

This had never happened to Harry Joy before, and it was only happening now because the whole hotel knew about the madman in room 2121. There had been conversations between doctors and management, management and family, and so on. You cannot keep secrets in a big hotel. The staff treated him politely, but with great caution and great reticence.

He bought himself little treats, like his family: magazines, flowers, candies, Premier Cru Bordeaux wine. He had more white suits made and ordered an exercise bicycle which was delivered by two youths who giggled before and after entering the madman's suite.

The pain was continual. A tightness across the chest produced by some invisible steel bands so he could hardly breathe. He drank heavily to eliminate the visions of his family. But somehow, it seemed, he could not get drunk, or not drunk enough, for they remained before his eyes and would not go away.

It was in this painful mood that he at last telephoned Krappe Chemicals, but not, one would guess, having any great faith in Goodness, but simply to find a diversion, a person, some action that would take his mind away from the razor-blade tortures of Hell.

When Adrian Clunes, Marketing Director of Krappe Chemicals (Consumer Products), was summoned to meet Harry Joy at the

Hilton, he did not ask why. He assumed he was at the Hilton because he had left his wife. (Everyone had been waiting for it.) Adrian was surprised and pleased that Harry had turned to him.

All he said was: "When?"

"Whenever you like. How about today?"

"I'll be there at one."

And at exactly one o'clock Adrian Clunes slouched through the door in his donnish uniform of grey slacks and leather-patched tweed sports coat, a style only made possible by his air-conditioned car. He dumped his unfashionably large briefcase on the middle of a table, pushed his round tortoise-shell spectacles back on to his slightly melted nose, and clapped his hands together in the manner of one about to get down to hard work.

"Well," he said, squinting across at Harry who was reclining in a white towelling dressing gown. "This is a jolly nice place to be doing business. What are we going to do? Drink champagne?"

Adrian Clunes, as is obvious enough, was English. He had not, originally, made a thing of being English but finding himself admired for it, he had ceased trying to hide it. His Englishness gushed from him untempered and brought him a reputation for an intelligence he did not possess.

"Nice dressing gown," he said quizzically.

"I'm having a new suit made. I tore my trousers."

There was a flatness about Harry Joy he had never seen before. The man looked dull. Even his voice seemed to have become tighter as if there was a constriction in his throat. He was taking it hard.

"Beer then," he said, "if there's no champagne."

"I got a special fridge," Harry said mournfully. "They have these damn silly little self-service things full of rubbish. Would you like San Miguel?"

"Thank you."

Harry walked to the bar slowly and then poured the beer slowly; then he seemed to forget why he had done it. He sipped the beer himself and put it down on the bar.

"I didn't want to talk on the phone," he said, "or in the office."

"Are you drinking alone?"

Harry looked at the beer and then poured another one which he handed to his guest.

"They can all go to hell," Adrian Clunes said, collapsing into one of the Hilton's low chairs.

"I'm not going back there today. Let them stew," he said. "Let's have a nice lunch."

Harry leaned against the bar and played with his San Miguel. He did not bother about who Adrian Clunes was, although he remembered with some sadness they had once, somewhere, enjoyed each other's company.

"Jolly nice beer," Adrian said with froth on his big lips. "Why don't we go somewhere and have dozens of oysters." He giggled and freckles jumped around on his face. He was shocked with Harry Joy. He would not have thought it possible. "God it's nice to get into the city, Harry, it's so horrible out there. It is ghastly. They live on curried egg sandwiches! What a disgusting thing to do to an innocent egg. They don't even taste of curry."

Harry Joy's face expressed nothing.

"Come on," Adrian said, "let's go to Milanos and terrorize Aldo."

"Adrian, I can't have you as a client any more. I have to fire you."

"Well, *I'll* pay for the lunch."

Harry came to sit opposite him. Their knees (Harry's bare, Adrian's flannelled) nearly touched. "No," he said with a feeling of unreality, "I'm serious." But all he could think about was the nights he had gone on drunks with Adrian Clunes and ended up at the Spanish Club, drinking vodka at three in the morning. "I'm serious," he said again. "It's not you. It's the products."

"Is this what you got me here for?" Adrian put his beer down slowly and it made a sharp clink when it touched the low glass-topped table. He started to wipe the beer froth from his top lip and then, half-way through the motion, stopped. He whistled and a little froth sailed through the air.

"Holy Jesus," he said quietly. "You're serious, aren't you?"

"Yes." No he wasn't, no he wasn't. His chest hurt.

"You got me to drive twenty miles so you could fire me. I came here to jolly you up because I thought you'd left your wife."

"Why would I leave my wife?" Harry said narrowly.

"No reason, that's all I thought."

"Seems a funny thing to think. We've been married eighteen years."

"Yes, now you mention it. It's just what I assumed."

Their chairs were low, designed so that matrons would not have to reach far for their handbags. The two men, knee to knee, looked slightly ridiculous.

"You are here to be fired," Harry said coldly.

"Holy Jesus. You're mad."

"No."

Adrian lifted a bushy ginger eyebrow. "*Are* you?"

"No," said Harry Joy but looked too cunning when he said it.

"You've landed a competitive account. You got General Foods!"

"No."

"Well why are you firing us?"

"I have evidence", Harry Joy said slowly, "that three of your products cause cancer."

"Oh, shit . . ."

"You deny it."

"Of course I don't deny it. For Christsake Harry, it's been going on for years. It's been in the papers. The tests in America. You remember."

"Ah, those tests. Those tests didn't mean anything. They used too much saccharin."

"Oh, Harry, Harry, Harry."

"What do you mean: Harry, Harry, Harry? That's what you told me. Or somebody", he said levelly, "who resembled you."

"Harry, you know and I know that's the company line. No one believed it. We all had to pretend we believed it."

"You don't deny it?"

"Deny what?"

"You make products that cause cancer."

"Oh shit . . ."

"Come on."

"Of course not."

"Then," Harry Joy said standing up, "you're fired."

"You're impossible," Adrian Clunes said at last. "People like you don't exist. You cannot exist, Harry. You handle our business for ten years and then you . . . Look, think about it. Consider it. You make 17½ per cent of two million dollars. Every year. What do you gain by resigning it?" He put his head in his hands. "The rest of us went through all this seven years ago."

"I just found out."

"Oh, rot and rubbish."

"I *just* found out. I won't do it."

Adrain Clunes sighed and stood up. He walked to the bar and brought back more beers. He filled Harry's glass and then his own. When he sat down again he was laughing.

"It's impossible," he said. He lifted his beer. "To Harry Joy, the newest, most impossible idealist in the world. Laugh, damn you," he said, "it's a joke. Oh, God help me, don't be miserable as well. Look," he walked to the phone and picked it up. "If you can throw away money I can help you throw away some more." He ordered Bollinger and oysters.

"Now," he said to Harry Joy, putting his arm around his shoulders, "do you feel better?"

"A little, yes."

They drank beer and waited for the oysters and champagne.

"Ah," Adrian said, as he squeezed lemon juice over the flinching oysters, "bloody marvellous oysters in this country. You know, Harry, where are you going to draw the line? If you fire us, you'll have to fire all your clients."

Harry was feeling better. He didn't believe a word Adrian Clunes said. "Oh yes," he said sarcastically.

"Harry, you're astonishing. You're a child. I can't understand how you've survived so long. Listen, they release something like eighty thousand totally new organic compounds every *year*. They're not properly tested. God knows how many cause cancer. Cancer takes years to show up. The whole of the Western world is built on things that cause cancer. They can't afford to stop making them. For Christsake, look at your client list. Mobil have benzine in petrol which is carcinogenic. Firestone use it making tyres too. We use saccharin, and even if we switch across to cyclamates instead, that's carcinogenic. ICI make dieldrin which is carcinogenic and that mob, your dry-cleaning client, use carbon tetrachloride which is the same. And every time an announcement is made that something causes cancer, it makes people *less* worried because they can't believe that half the things they breathe and eat are carcinogenic. And there are you," Adrian rested, breathless, "resigning our business because we use saccharin."

Harry sipped his champagne. He smiled. It was the smile of a man who is smart enough to know when he's being bull-shitted to.

"You don't bloody believe me," Adrian Clunes said in astonishment. "Look at this man. He does not believe me."

He leapt up from the table. "I will damn well prove it to you." His voice was high-pitched. "I will prove to you how bad it is, and how piddling you are being. What you are doing", he went to his briefcase, "is nothing."

He pulled a map from his case and spread it on the floor.

There: before him: the actual map of Hell. Harry did not need to be told. He looked hard at the colours, the hot red centre, the vermilion, the crimson, the hard industrial orange, the poisonous yellows radiating out from its hot centre.

They knelt on the floor beside it.

"This", Adrian Clunes said, "is a cancer map. It shows the incidence of cancers according to place of residence and place of work. There is a damn cancer epidemic going on, Harry Joy. They will not even sell these maps any more, let me tell you, they are shitting themselves."

Harry watched it in horror. He could not disbelieve the map. He did not bother to study the relative proportions of tumours or understand all the accompanying statistics. He noted only that they were, at this moment, in the epicentre of Hell.

"It is an epidemic," Adrian Clunes said angrily. "And wait. You wait for another five years. This", he tapped the paper, "is what we get for how we live. And believe me, it is just hotting up."

When he went back to his half-finished oysters he had become chalkish and pale.

"My wife has cancer, Harry," he said quietly. "She weighs four stone and six pounds and everyone comes, like ghouls, to look at her. Our friends are nice enough to stay away," he held up his hand. "It's alright. Don't say anything. But don't preach to me about cancer. I know about cancer, dear Friend, from both sides." He pushed his oysters away. "I've lost my appetite."

"I have to fire you," Harry Joy said softly.

"I admire you," Adrian Clunes said quietly. "You are eccentric, and most surprising, but I admire you. I wish you well."

And as things turned out that day it became Harry Joy's task to think of a way to cheer up Adrian Clunes. He started by filling up his glass.

Lucy, it must be remembered, was only fifteen and a half years old, so although she was capable of some maturity, not to say wisdom, she was also capable of acting just like a fifteen-and-a-half-year-old.

Lucy is standing by the Mobil Station, hitching a lift to see Harry in the Hilton.

And there, right on the bend of the road, rolling hard and squealing its tyres, is a rusty Cadillac Eldorado with an unemployed motor mechanic named Kenneth McLaren at the wheel. He is twenty-two years old and his false teeth have been made to reproduce the crooked, oddly spaced teeth he had before. His cheeks are hollowed. He has a wizened, slightly old face, a mess of curling tangled hair and, in the centre of this wreckage, two doe-like brown eyes.

In the backseat of the Eldorado, together with fan belts, old radiator pipes, and reconditioned fuel pumps, is a great pile of papers.

There are two coincidences involved here. The first, the biggest, is that Kenneth McLaren has just, five minutes before, resigned from the Communist Party; the second, hardly a coincidence at all when you consider that Lucy, in her cheesecloth dress looks at once romantic and attractive and that she has her thumb out, is that he stops for her. And right now, it may as well be revealed: Lucy Joy will *never* get to the Hilton.

Comrade Dilettante, meet Comrade Doomsday.

Adrian Clunes's high-pitched laughter filtered through the shut door.

Harry Joy sat on a low chair in his dressing gown and watched his girl. She was tall and straight and everything about her was vertical, even her profile, which was almost flat, interrupted only by the bump of her nose and lift of her lips. She was, from instant to instant, severely plain then astonishingly beautiful, and her most beautiful and obvious feature was her very large, almost impossibly large, brown eyes, which glistened with what Harry, entranced, chose to believe was suspicion. He was not wrong. She was like a cat that has come in a window. He knew her. He knew how she felt when she walked across the room touching things with her curious, long-fingered hands, stroking lamps, feeling fabrics, smiling absently. She was someone with a notebook in her hand. He felt that if he had jumped up from his chair she would have bolted, left in one silky movement: the leap of the cat from chair to window ledge.

"This your wallet?" It was sitting on top of the bar amongst some melting ice.

"Yes."

"Your credit card in here?" She had a funny shy, sly smile.

"Is it the Diners Club?"

"American Express," he said contrarily. He let her touch the wallet, open it, remove the card. He trusted her suspicion.

"Don't worry about me if I talk too much," she said. "I've just got all this city shit in my system. It makes me speedy."

"Are you from the country?"

"No," she said sharply. She brought a bulky credit card machine from her handbag. "I'm not from anywhere."

He smiled.

She smiled back, but uncertainly. "I'm not into any funny stuff. No Golden Showers."

"I don't want any funny stuff."

"Change your mind, it's O.K. I'll just call the office, they'll send someone else."

"It's O.K.," he said. "I don't want anything funny."

"Better to get all that up front."

"Cards on the table," he teased her.

"All hanging out."

"Et cetera," he said.

She laughed, and ruined her third Diners Club form.

"Fuck it," she said.

But she got the fourth one right and brought it to Harry to sign.

"Well," she said, "that's that."

She went back to the bar and turned her back to him. She dropped a spoon and picked it up hurriedly.

"You wonder what I'm doing, don't you?"

Harry shrugged. She had a Band-aid on her leg, under her stocking.

"It's not what you think."

"I didn't think anything."

"It's not cocaine."

"What is it?"

"Honey." She held up a little jar about as big as an expensive shoe cream. She raised an eyebrow and he saw in the twist of her pale pink lips a drollness — this was a face that could be anything. She took a teaspoon full of honey and held it up before she ate it.

"This is very powerful honey. You shouldn't have more than a teaspoonful." She screwed the lid back on and dropped it back into her bag.

"What does it do?"

"You people," she said. Which people did she mean? "You people are amazing. Look at my eyes. No, come here. Come over to the mirror."

She held out her hand and he stood up. She led him to the vanity table where, sitting side by side, they put their faces up to the mirror.

"Put your face closer to mine," she ordered. "So you can see your eyes and my eyes."

Harry looked into his dull grey eyes and looked at her glistening dark ones, the iris of such a dark blue it was almost black, the whites perfectly white.

"Your eyes are beautiful," he said sincerely, looking at the reflection of her solemn face.

"Honey," she said. She leant back from the mirror and looked at him critically.

"What do you eat?"

Harry tried to tell her.

"Christ," she said in amazement. "Let me look at your eyes. Hold still."

She held his head and peered closely into his eyes while Harry was overwhelmed by the aromatics of her powerful honey. "You eat a lot of salt," she said.

"It's all there, in your eyes, years of salt. But you have very nice eyelashes," she said. "And you look a little like . . . turn that way . . . Krishna."

"So I've been told."

"You know who Krishna is?"

"Certainly."

"You do?"

"Yes."

She raise her eyebrows in surprise. "Well," she said, "would you like some of my honey?"

She brought the spoon and fed it to him. "This is leatherwood honey," she said. "The Rolls Royce of Honeys, from the leatherwood tree. Are you in a hurry to fuck me, or what, because if you want to, I'm you know, free any time." She held out her hands, indicating the presence of a body. "I guess this talk isn't very erotic for you."

"More than you think," he said rolling the honey around the inside of his mouth.

"Do you have lots of whores?" she asked him.

"A few."

"Well you're lucky today," she grinned, "because you have struck a gifted amateur."

What Honey Barbara said was not really true: she was not, strictly speaking, an amateur. Whoring was her one commercial talent and once a year, for two months, she came down to the city and signed up with the Executive Escort Agency. She felt as ambivalent about it as she felt about the city itself, sometimes looking back on it with nostalgia and forgetting that daily life was normally spent in fear and homesickness.

Sometimes she liked her clients, but usually she didn't and when things got really bleak she would spend her time, against all her principles, doped to the eyeballs so she didn't feel a thing.

But this was her first commercial fuck of the year and he wasn't fat and flabby and when he got undressed she wouldn't get that unpleasant feeling that comes, like a sour gas, from bulging white flesh and nylon socks. Besides, he looked like Krishna.

She saw his passiveness and knew he was easy to handle, that she could walk away from him and it would be O.K. or she could take him, right now, and spread him out, like that, and have him lie, like so, on the floor, and devour him, first of all with her mouth and that there, at least, he would not smell too bad for a city man, and he would not fuck like someone running for a bus.

He was just a businessman, but she felt at home enough with him to put her heart into her work for an hour or two while she tangled her long legs with him, and when he brought his big moustache against her face, she did not mind kissing him.

She would never know, if she lived to be a hundred, how a big glob of come could be worth three hundred dollars. Three hundred dollars was enough to live on for six weeks. It was a roof. A water tank. A stove. It was thirty avocado trees. Half a horse.

"Was it worth three hundred dollars?" She snuggled into him. He looked pleased with himself. He had a crinkle in the corner of his eye.

"Every cent," he said.

"Would you see me again?"

"Well," he said, "what do you think?" He was a thin man with a roly-poly voice. He was so foreign she couldn't imagine what his thoughts might be. Even his clothes felt foreign. She could not understand someone with a silk shirt.

"Oh," she rubbed her head. "I don't feel a thing."

"Nothing?"

"Not a thing."

"You must feel *something*," he insisted, touching the nipple on her small breast. They both watched it grow erect.

"Something." She pulled the sheet over the offending nipple. "It's my Karma. You don't know what Karma is, do you?" she grinned. "You know you look like Krishna. But you don't know what Karma is?"

He bowed his head humbly.

"Karma means that what you do in one life affects what happens to you in the next. Maybe I was a whore in the last life, so this life I don't like fucking much. It means if you're Good in this life you'll have a better time in the next one. Hey," she hit his arm, "are you taking the piss out of me?"

He was doing an imitation of a staring man. "If you're Good?" he said.

"Stop it. Stop taking the piss." She pulled the sheet up over her nose.

"No, tell me. If you're Good in one life you have a better time the next one?"

"Yes," she said cautiously. "Right."

"That's what I'm doing."

She started to laugh, but when she saw he was serious, she stopped. "But you're a businessman."

"Advertising."

"That's *really* bad Karma."

"No," he said, "no, I'm being Good."

"You can't," she said stubbornly. (How conceited. How stupid.) "How can you? How could you?" She pulled the sheet down and let him see the straight thin line of her mouth.

"I just fired a two-million-dollar client because his product causes cancer," he said. "That's him in the next room."

Two million dollars!

"Really three hundred and fifty thousand dollars, I get 10 per cent commission from media and $7\frac{1}{2}$ per cent service fee, which is three hundred and fifty thousand on two million."

"Christ."

"That's Good," he said. "It has to be."

"I don't know," Honey Barbara said, "I suppose it must be." It was more than you got for a good dope crop.

"And I'll tell you something else." He jumped out of bed and ran across the room on tip-toe. "I'll tell you something else." He picked up a brightly coloured map and brought it back to bed. "A cancer map."

"Shit."

Cancer Maps were part of Honey Barbara's folk literature, just like the Dream Police (a legendary squad of psychiatrists) and the whole cast of Cosmic Conspirators, the CIA, flying saucers, multi-nationals with seed-patents.

She had never seen a cancer map in her life. She looked at Harry Joy with new respect. "Where did you get it?"

"I stole it," he decided, "from him." He nodded his head next door.

"You're one hell of a businessman," she said.

He bounced his bum around the bed.

"I trusted you when you walked in," he said. He paused. He smiled. "It is my opinion," he said, "that I am living in Hell, that this, all this," he waved his hand around the room, "is Hell."

And sat there, with his eyebrows arched.

Where Honey Barbara came from, people believed many different things about the nature of reality. Christopher Rocks believed in Wood Spirits, and Edith Valdora understood how flying saucers propelled themselves; she was going to build a flying saucer herself and no one thought (no one said) she was crazy. John Lane had been a fish in another life, and people believed in Jesus Christ, the Buddha, reincarnation, levitation, and feared the three 6's on the Bankcard as a sign of the Beast of the Apocalypse. Bart Pavlovich had been Astral travelling for years and would think nothing of opening a conversation by saying, "I was on the Moon last night." Which, as everybody said, was his reality.

When Harry Joy told her he thought they were in Hell she did not, for an instant, think that he meant it metaphorically. She understood him perfectly.

"Far out," she said.

"But," he said, "what do you *think?*"

The connecting door was opening. She pulled a blanket up to hide the cancer map as the naked figure of Adrian Clunes stumbled across the room and lurched into the toilet. They waited while he vomited.

"Sorry," he said when he emerged, "she's using the other one." He picked up his briefcase and walked back into the other room.

Honey Barbara threw the blanket back.

"Do you think I'm crazy?" he said.

"You're not crazy."

"They're trying to lock me up."

"I bet they are." She had never met anyone who had refused 350,000 dollars. She was more than a little impressed.

And then Honey Barbara, who knew a lot about such things, gave him his first lesson for survival in Hell, which dealt, for the most part, with psychiatrists and the police, and went under the loose heading of keeping yourself clean, by which she meant: no drugs, no funny books, no funny friends, just clean. Don't be a smart-arse with the cops, don't argue with them, don't let them search your room without a witness. Be nice to them, make them tea, don't let your voice shake when you talk to them, try to think of them as human beings. Always have money, never write down the names of lawyers but memorize their phone numbers and make sure they're up to date. If they send the Dream Police then don't fight with them because they're unhealthy and unfit and will use drug-guns on you and not their fists and you will arrive unconscious and not be able to admit yourself voluntarily (always admit yourself, always sign yourself in, and then, with luck you can sign yourself out later). Most of all, never admit that anyone is trying to threaten you, get you, attack you, hurt you, poison you, radiate you, punch you, pinch you, fuck you, or, in any way at all, do you the slightest bit of harm for these are the symptoms of paranoia and they are, Honey Barbara said, illegal and you can get locked up for showing them even though you really are being radiated by the air and poisoned by the water.

Harry was overcome with this gift. He looked at her, smiling, shaking his head and holding her hand.

He was in love.

He wanted to give her a present, something glistening and wonderful. He brought it out and displayed it, revealing it shyly, the way one draws back the tissue paper from around an opal to display it lying in its fragile nest.

He told her what it was like to die.

When he had finished the room was totally dark and all he could see were Honey Barbara's two huge eyes.

"I'm going to leave you some honey," she whispered at last.

It was only later that he appreciated it, what it meant; leaving the honey behind, and then he only appreciated a little of it and it would be another full year before he knew the whole truth about Honey

Barbara, who may have been only an amateur whore but was more than a little knowledgeable about other things.

She became Harry's trusted guide to Hell, and he became her client, so that every morning at around ten o'clock she would enter his room and run off a Diners Club card.

Honey Barbara lived not far from the Hilton in a small crumbling house with fifteen green plastic garbage bags of marihuana stashed above its bulging plaster ceiling. She shared the house with Damian who had come down with her and whose job it was to sell the crop, something he seemed to have stuffed up. He was immersing himself in a whole lot of city shit that Honey Barbara didn't understand. He was eating Kentucky Frieds and Big Macs and she noted with disapproval that he was starting to put on fat around his hips.

She woke him to tell him.

Maybe, she thought later, that hadn't been very nice, but he was always asleep when she got home and in the mornings, of course, they always had to get up at four a.m. and get out of the house, just in case.

He shouldn't even have been there. He should have sold the crop and been on the road home.

"You're getting really fat, man."

"What?"

"The whole house stinks of dead chicken."

"You woke me up to tell me that?" Damian sat up in his bed and she could *see* that layer of fat just sort of *hanging*, nothing really noticeable yet, but soon he would be covered with poisonous fat from cancered chickens and Big Macs. "You're fucking unreal."

"Come on, Damian. I'm doing my job. I'm working. I've got a right to know. What are you doing about the dope? Why are you eating all this shit? You should be home by now. They need the money, you know that."

"Did you wake me up to have a fight? Are you so full of city shit you have to fight someone?"

"I am *not* full of city shit. Who's been eating Big Macs?"

"Well go to sleep."

"I want to talk now. It's the only time we can talk."

"Spend some time here tomorrow."

"I've got a client."

"Who's full of city shit then?" He smiled his big white smile and raised a guru-type eyebrow, or at least that was the intention of the eyebrow. "Maybe that's just your projection, Honey Barbara, because you're into this bad trip fucking fat businessmen."

"It wasn't my decision."

"It doesn't matter whose decision it was because in the end it's your decision. It's your Dharma."

"My client isn't fat. You'd *like* him, Day. He's astonishing."

He rolled over and left her to look at his hairy back. "You're really into a bad scene, Barb. I don't want to hear about the fucking..."

"Come on, Day," she sat facing him. "You know I don't feel anything..."

He laughed into the pillow.

"I was hypnotized," she yelled, "you know I was hypnotized. It cost fifty dollars so don't you laugh."

He stopped laughing but he lay still.

"What's happening with the dope?" she asked quietly. She waited for a while. "Day?" He didn't move. "You're lying here all day getting radiated with television and smoking cigarettes and eating sick chickens full of antibiotics and God knows what shit you're breathing. You're meant to be *home*. They need the *money*."

Damian rolled on his back and stared at her. "We got ripped off," he said. "They had a gun. They took it all. I can't go home." And there, in the middle of the dead chicken carcases and the Big Mac boxes, he started crying.

"Good old Honey Barbara," she though bitterly as she held his weeping body in her arms.

She always forgot the fear when she remembered the city afterwards. She did not forget its existence, but she forgot the intensity of it, its total gut-wrenching, dull-eyed, damp-handed presence. It was not the run down in the truck with the bags of dope in the back. That wasn't so bad. They dressed like farmers and drove the back roads.

It was the time of waiting to sell it that she always forgot: the fear of the police, the fear of narcs, spies, the fear of being ripped off, so that everyone they spoke to was potentially an enemy and there was no such thing as "just a police car" or "just a visitor". Everyone looked like a narc. Every parked car seemed occupied by big men reading newspapers. Every public phone box contained strange clicks and faint voices. When the front door bell rang your guts went tight.

But each year when the wet ended she found herself looking forward to it again, and if she remembered the fear about the dope at all, there was no chance of her recalling that other, duller, perhaps more dreadful fear she felt in the city.

She remembered the bars and restaurants and movies and even the junk food seemed tasty in her memory and the businessmen didn't seem so bad and she remembered the good times and ones who danced. And when it was almost time to go people said, "Look at Honey Barbara," for she was high as a kite just at the thought of it and when they hit the wide yellow plains going south and there were no hills, just this wonderful yellow sea and huge sky her heart damn near burst with happiness, and she had forgotten.

She had forgotten how damn miserable they all looked and how dirty the air was and most of all she had forgotten the anger. They seemed knotted in anger, and the whole of the city seemed like it was about to uncoil itself in a paroxysm of fury.

She went to the movies but no longer understood the lives on the screen and she felt a lack of sympathy which would have enraged the rest of the audience who laughed or cried on cue, as expected.

"They're so fucked up," she said. "How can I identify with that? It's all so depressing and ugly. I can't stand all this negativity."

To Honey Barbara the city was a force, half machine, half human, exuding poisons.

And this year it was worse. This year they had been ripped off. This year there had been a gun. This year there was no money, and a whole season's work, all those bags of manure they had carried on their backs along bush tracks, all those little plants they had nurtured, protected from wallabies, hidden from the air, all this was wasted.

This year the only money would come from Honey Barbara, lying on her back, staring at the ceiling, too doped-up to feel a thing.

She sat in the Hilton in Harry's room and not even the long blue stripes on the carpet, the turqoise Thai silk covers on the chairs, none of the carefully chosen blues or greens did anything to give her peace because they were cold and synthetic and looked poisonous to touch.

Harry was talking on the phone and lying to Adrian Clunes about the cancer map. It was probably bad Karma. They had discussed it seriously.

The map lay on the table, and somewhere, somewhere she wouldn't tell Harry, was the place where Honey Barbara lived. She looked longingly at the cool (safe) yellow of the north and the fine blue line of the unnamed creek she knew, and imagined, for it wasn't shown on the map, the rutted track that ran up to Mount Warning and the Silky Oak plantation where Bog Onion Road had once been and the smell of the mill when it worked in the winter and the good clear hard noise of the blade as it cut into a tallow wood, beside whose stump, in the bush, another tree had been planted. And most of all she thought about the blossoms which grew through the swaying green umbrellas which made up the roof of the forest, and on which the bees feasted: the stringy-bark with its characteristic sharpness, the sarsaparilla which was sweet and heavy and a little dull, and the showy red flowering gums bending in the south-easterly which swept the hill above the valley.

She did not, thinking about all this, forget bad things and a number of deaths salted the memory, one in particular: the bloated body of an unknown man hanging from a casurina above the falls. Nor did she ignore the presence of neighbouring people who thought differently: Ananda Marga, the Orange People, the Hari Krishnas and others, not all of whom could be trusted to be peaceful and some of whom had armies of their own, weapons, deadly secrets, secret rituals, ritual killings. Witchcraft was practised in the bush and the head of a sheep, or a pig, writhing with maggots, lay often in the path of Honey Barbara's horse, and the night was a less innocent place than it had once been.

Yet Honey Barbara, in the Hilton, wanted only to tell Harry how it was to wake up in the morning and hear those giant tallow woods talking to each other.

He put down the phone and smiled at her.

"I'm pleased I met you," she said, looking up at him from the synthetic floor.

"I'm pleased I met you."

"I don't think I could hack it otherwise."

"Likewise."

"How about," she said, "we go out today, to the park, and I tell you the names of trees."

"They're taking their time coming for me," said Harry who could not have appreciated the difficulties a seventeen-year-old boy has in being taken seriously, especially when he is carrying five thousand dollars in cash in his back pocket and runs the risk of simply having it removed from his person.

"They'll come," Honey Barbara said. "Just when you think they've forgotten, they'll turn up. That's why you've got to get up early."

"I've never been able to get up early," he yawned. It was certainly true that he had shown a remarkable facility for ignoring alarm clocks, telephone calls and the sound of the human voice.

"The alarm goes off at 4 a.m. and I get up and sit in the park till seven."

"They might come at seven thirty, just when you get home."

"No, they never do."

"Or seven fifteen, or lunchtime."

"No, they only come early in the morning. Even in the country, when they have to drive hundreds of miles, they never come after seven. Your alarm clock", she said, "is your key to freedom."

It was one of her expressions. The other was: "One in every three is a spy," a statistic she quoted with great confidence.

"I feel safer in the Hilton," he said.

"You are safer in the park with me."

So every morning they sat and shivered in the pre-dawn grey of the park, arriving too late for the warmest places which were inhabited by winos. They wrapped themselves in Honey Barbara's blankets. Their teeth chattered. Sometimes they made love. They were not unhappy.

Harry was more alive than he knew, and his life was filled with more delights than he could ever remember, and all of this took place in a climate of fear and watchfulness, where every waiter was a spy, every wino an informer. His eyes improved. He learned to recognize the glittering poisons the city placed in his path. Gleaming fruit had DDT lying just beneath the surface of its tempting skin.

He gave up meat, coffee, salt and anything they cooked in the Hilton kitchen. They ate fruit with spots and bread with lumps in it. He gave up everything his guide suggested except wine and it was he who introduced her to it: at the end of weeks of tuition she could truly appreciate the crushed violet nose of a 1973 Cheval Blanc.

Honey Barbara submitted to the evils of alcohol with a guilty flush. Dropping her perky little nose into a glass of Mouton Rothschild, she murmured: "It's probably organic" before she took the precious fluid into her mouth and closed her glistening eyes with pleasure.

*

It was three thirty in the morning when the phone rang.

"Hello."

"Harry, it's Alex."

"Hello, Alex."

"Got to talk to you, Harry."

"Where are you?"

"Reception. Downstairs."

"O.K., it's 2121. The twenty-first floor."

He hung up and dressed quickly.

He turned on the light in the sitting room and opened its door a little. Then he retired to the bedroom, locked the interconnecting door, turned off its light and opened the door just a fraction so he could see out of the lift. He had his shoes on, his wallet in his pocket.

But when the lift door opened it revealed the large soft stumbling figure of Alex Duval.

"In here, Alex." He turned on the light in the bedroom and held open the door.

"Sorry, Harry."

"Don't be sorry."

Alex had a big, pale, sick face. "Harry I've got to talk to you. I'm drunk. I'm *sorry* I'm drunk," he said belligerently as he stumbled into the room and sat heavily on the bed. Harry went into the sitting room and brought back a bottle of Scotch, a glass, and a jug of water. Alex drank greedily from the big tumbler. Harry leant against the window, waiting silently.

"You don't talk much any more, Harry."

"Not so much."

"You were a good talker, Harry. That's what made you, you know that? Not what you said, no." He paused and considered this. "It was the damn way you said it."

"I'm learning to listen," Harry smiled, but he was cautious.

"I'm leaving the agency."

"Ah."

"That's all you can say? Ah?" he mimicked nastily. "Ah." He poured another Scotch, half Scotch, half water, the tumbler filled to the brim. While he occupied himself with this, neither of them said anything.

Alex sipped and looked up, his white face sweating alcohol.

"You're a smart-arse, Harry," He had Chinese food spilled down his shirt. "You're a cold fish."

Harry appeared to lean against the window without a tight muscle in his body. He was ready to run.

"You were never cold, Harry, you were warm. You were such a warm person. You were a fool," he lifted his finger, careful that his argument should proceed honestly, "you were a fool, but you were warm. Now you're cold. All you care about is yourself and you've left us in the lurch. What's in there?"

"That's the sitting room."

"Fuck it, we go there. I didn't come here to sleep with you."

Harry followed the big man into the sitting room and watched him lower his sizeable arse on to the little Thai silk chair.

"Didn't come to sleep," he said, arranging his bottle and his jug on the floor, "How much does all this cost?"

"Two hundred a day."

"Fuck you, Harry. You've left us in the lurch. You fire Krappe Chemicals. Poor Joel, poor little schmuck, poor dumb ambitious little schmuck. It's not his fault. You don't even tell him, you just talk to the client and fire him. Two million dollars. Poof. Like that. What's in there?"

"That's the passage."

"Ah."

"Alex," Harry said cautiously, "don't you remember we had a talk one Saturday morning, I promised I'd fire them for you."

"I didn't ask you to." Alex sprang from his chair and then forgot why he'd done it. The Scotch in his hand swayed dangerously. "*You* decided to do it. You stole my fucking key," he said incredulously. "You stole my key. You interfered in my life. So I'm crazy. So what? So I write funny conference reports and never send them to anyone. Was it doing any harm? Did it hurt you?" He started to sit down but stopped. "You are so naive, do you know that? All your life you walk around and never see anything bad. Anybody who says anything is bad looks like a sour grape. That's what you do to people. I say, 'Oh, so-and-so's an old cunt' and you look at me, Harry, like *I'm* a cunt. You don't want to hear bad about anything. The papers are full of this cancer stuff and what do you say, 'Oh, it's nothing, just a scare', because you think they're cunts for calling Krappe cunts. Now you bloody wake up. God knows why. Why?" he asked.

"Doesn't matter why," he answered. "You don't know why. I don't know why. But when you suddenly realize what the world is like, then you go around destroying all the people who've known all along. Why do you want to destroy me?"

It was five minutes to four, five minutes before Harry had to leave the room. Now Alex's hand was twisting his shirt just the way Hastings had done. Alex was a big man. He stood over Harry and twisted his shirt with more strength than anyone would have guessed him capable of.

"Why do you want to destroy me?"

A look of indescribable contempt passed over his soft fleshy face, turned in on itself, and collapsed into nothing. His hand unclenched and he left Harry with only pain.

Alex lowered himself into the chair, letting himself drop the last six inches. "I drove round all night because I was frightened to tell you. Why should I be frightened of you? You're pathetic. You're not worth being frightennd of. I'm going to work at Ogilvy's. They like me. They damn well like *me*. Adrian Clunes phoned me and asked me if I would handle his account. You see, it's amazing isn't it? It's bloody amazing. All these years I've handled the account and you've taken the profit. Well now they're making me a director. That's what I'm worth to them."

"I fired them for you," Harry said, and came and sat opposite him in just the way he had, a week before, sat opposite Adrian Clunes. "I fired them to save you, damn it. Don't you remember? I fired them because you were a Captive and . . ."

"Ah," Alex waved a hand and spilt whisky down his shirt. "Captives . . ."

"Were you trying to trick me? Did you trick me into firing them?"

"Harry . . ." He opened his big pink palms and held them out.

"Because if you did . . ."

"Harry."

". . . I don't mind."

"You're looking at your watch and I'm trying to tell you I'm sorry."

"I've got to go soon."

"Everything's shut. I'm fucking saying I'm sorry. Doesn't that mean anything? I've got to live, that's all. I've got to make money. You would have fired me in the end. You would have had to. Don't blame me."

"I'm putting you to bed."

"I'm not an Actor, Harry. I'm just Alex, fuck it," he sniffed. "Fuck it."

He did not resist when Harry led him into the bedroom and he began, without any hesitation, to get undressed. "I betray you, you betray me," he said. "Oh, fuck." He fell over one leg in his trousers and Harry helped him out of his big grey socks and his surprisingly fine silk underpants. He registered, in a moment of shock, the enormous size of his flaccid penis and, as he tucked him into bed, he thought how unused it looked, fed on doughnuts and cream cake.

It was three minutes past four.

Doctors Hennessy and Cornelius travelled up in the lift bound for the twenty-first floor. They did not like each other. Cornelius's squashed little face was hidden behind a trimmed black beard and his shirt was open to reveal a hairy chest. He looked up at Hennessy and winked for no reason.

"How is it, Ace?"

Hennessy regarded him from pale, pale blue eyes. "Well enough," he said coldly, "well enough."

On the twenty-first floor they knocked, and when they were not admitted, entered with the key which had been provided. They found their mark sitting up with the sheet held the way women do when they want to hide their breasts.

"Good morning," Hennessy said formally, "I am Dr Hennessy and this is Dr Cornelius."

"You've come for Harry, haven't you?"

"Yes," Cornelius said, and opened his bag on his unmade bed, looking at the mark and guessing his weight at 200 lbs or 400 mgs of Pentothal.

"He's really gone crazy."

"So they say," said Cornelius, drawing up the required 400 mgs into the hypodermic.

"Well . . . are you going to wait . . . or what?"

"Or what, I should think," Hennessy said drily, taking his papers from his bag, watching while Cornelius fitted the charged hypodermic into the dart gun he had personally invented.

"Now, Mr Joy," Cornelius said, "we would like you to come with us very quietly and we will take you somewhere where they will make you better."

"No," Alex said, "you don't understand."

The bedclothes trailed out into the corridor like guts from the disembowelled room.

Neither Harry Joy nor Honey Barbara said a word. They stood for a moment and listened. Only the muffled noise of the lift dropping down the shaft broke the stillness.

Harry entered the room first. When he saw the broken chair in the doorway, the blood on the floor, the gaping guts of the television set, and the hunk of hair on the bathroom basin which looked pubic but had actually come from Dr Cornelius's bleeding face, he merely nodded, and although he was shocked he was not surprised.

Honey Barbara put down the box of food on the ruined bed. "Poor man," she said. "He fought them."

Harry nodded. He felt ill. He stood the bedside lamp upright and put the phone back on its hook.

"Come on," she said, "other room."

They pulled the blankets back into the bedroom and shut the door on it.

"Want food?" she asked, carrying the box.

He shook his head.

"He fought them," she said. "Good on him."

They both looked ill. They didn't know whether to sit or stand. Honey Barbara finally put the box down at the table and sat there in a chair. Harry leant against the window.

"They'll let him go," he said, "when they find out."

She shook her head. "Don't count on it. The hospital gets a subsidy. They'll try and keep him."

He picked up the phone.

"What you doing?"

"I'm going to ring my family and tell them."

"What?" She was already standing and walking towards him.

"They got the wrong person."

She snatched the phone from his hand and put it gently back on the receiver. "No."

"I can't have this on my conscience. I've got to."

"Darling, they'll come and get you."

"They can't get me. I get up too early." He picked up the phone and began to dial. He had more confidence in Honey Barbara's theories than Honey Barbara did.

"Hello," Joel said sleepily.

"It's Harry Joy here," Harry told his junior partner. "I am phoning to tell you that whoever you sent to lock me up has just taken Alex Duval instead."

He could hear Joel laughing. "Really? Really? Oh Harry . . ."

"Did you hear me?"

"Harry you don't know how funny it is."

"I said you got Alex Duval . . ."

". . . instead of you."

He hung up. "What happened?" she said.

"He laughed."

It was like a room in which someone has died.

They made love but it was somehow funereal and they looked into each other's eyes with sadness and nuzzled each other for comfort. Everything had suddenly become full of insurances and precautions. He ran off sixteen Diners Club bills for her while she watched tearfully.

"I should take you back home with me."

He smiled painfully.

"But you wouldn't like it: mud and leeches," she said, "no electricity, no silk shirts."

After a pause, she said: "Anyway, they wouldn't understand you. They'd think you were a spy."

She wrote down the address of the house where she was living and made him promise to memorize it. There was an air of emergency in everything and when Honey Barbara went to have a shower she was sure it was her last shower in a Hilton Hotel.

Doctors Hennessy and Cornelius called on Harry two weeks later at four o'clock in the afternoon, injected him swiftly and carried him off without the slightest struggle.

When Honey Barbara let herself in the next morning she found the suite as he'd left it, including a little piece of paper on which she'd written her address.

She did not have another shower at the Hilton.

Part Four

Some Unpleasant Facts

Alice Dalton had not been expecting Sea Scouts. She told Jim and Jimmy that she had no appointment marked but the Sea Scouts, it appeared, were insistent. She had imagined a bus load but when she discovered there were only two of them and that one of them was very small, she had them shown into her office and let them sit and stare at her vases while she brought the admission forms up to date. She wanted them to see what it was really like.

Mrs Dalton was a woman with a mission, which was to demystify the treatment of mental illness. It was her experience that a lot of sentimental garbage was spoken on the subject and she herself had spent many unhappy years until she had finally realised that Mental Illness was a business, just like anything else.

Once this decision had been made, her life had become more satisfying. As for the treatment itself, her greatest axiom was derived from a psychiatrist who had explained it this way: the ones that are going to get better, get better; all the rest is psychiatrists being neurotic or self-important or anxious or guilty; effectively they cost a lot and achieve nothing.

"Now," she said, "what did they tell you about me?"

It was a question she would have liked to have asked many of her visitors — but one couldn't ask such questions of adults, more's the pity — because Alice Dalton was fascinated by her own notoriety. "All I do", she beamed at her questioners until her little round face was so tight it looked as if it might split, "is what is obvious." But she could never ask them what they really thought of her. What she thought of herself was simple: she was a pioneer in the Mental Health business, an opinion obviously shared by Mr da Silva who had recently purchased 30 per cent of the stock.

But the Sea Scouts were having some difficulty in remembering what, if anything, had been said to them on the subject of Alice Dalton. They looked at her pale blue eyes as they swam behind her bright pink spectacles and felt that they had probably done something wrong.

"They never told us," the smaller boy said.

"Have you seen me on the Television?"

They shook their heads almost imperceptibly.

She felt irritated but smiled and nodded. The bigger boy took out a notebook and held a pencil in readiness. Somehow this cheered her up and she was thoughtful enough to speak slowly.

"This is a Mental Hospital," she began with a bluntness that always gave her pleasure, "where we lock up mad people."

She folded her arms and leant forward: "First unpleasant truth," she said to the smaller boy because the first one was bent over his notebook. "Second unpleasant truth: this is a business and I am doing it to make money, just like everybody else. What is the purpose of a business?" she asked the smaller boy who had a strange stunned quality about him. "It's to make money," she answered herself. "At the end of the year," she tapped her pencil on the pile of admission papers, "we must declare a profit."

She decided against her third unpleasant truth which went like this: "It's a garbage disposal." Pause. "Do you find that shocking?" Terribly, almost always. "Because that is what it is. Do you want to look after the old men? They're soaked in urine. They are garbage. Someone threw them out. Do you want me to love them as well?"

"Do you find that shocking?" She asked the Sea Scouts who seemed unsure.

"It's not shocking to me. It's life."

The small Sea Scout put up his hand.

"Yes?"

"When do we get our ginger coffee?"

"I beg your pardon."

"He means ginger *toffee*," the bigger boy said, looking up from his notes. "He wants to know if we get our ginger toffee before the tour or afterwards."

"There is no ginger toffee here," said Mrs Dalton firmly, in the manner of an aunt impolitely asked for biscuits.

"Oh yes there is," the small boy said, "that's what we chose this project for. This is the one with the ginger toffee."

There was something in Mrs Dalton's expression that frightened the smaller Sea Scout terribly. He had been frightened since they came into this room with its vases and flowers and funny smell. He looked at Mrs Dalton and began to cry.

The buzzer sounded and a big man in a white coat came into the room.

"Take them across to the Ginger Factory," the woman said.

The small Sea Scout began to shriek hysterically and even his bigger friend let a tear roll down his ruddy cheeks.

"It's only the Ginger Factory," Mrs Dalton tried to smile. "He's taking you where you are meant to be."

She was not believed and finally it took both Jim and Jimmy to pick up the two screaming Sea Scouts and deliver them bodily to the Ginger Factory across the road.

In Hell his sense of smell was the first to be truly awakened.

He was too giddy to stand up, but he could smell, and even though he had never been in a mental hospital in his life he knew without having to be told that this was the distinctive odour of a mental hospital. Floor polish, methylated spirits and chlorine seemed to dominate, but were given character and colour by the smallest concentration of stale orange peel, urine, and something very closely related to dead roses. There was no sympathy in the smell and every one of its components recalled, in different ways, in different degrees, fear (even if the fear was as petty as that summoned up by the methylated spirits with its associations of cotton swabs, cold skin, doctors' surgeries, steel needles, and chrome surfaces).

Without him knowing it, Honey Barbara had taught him to smell, and when he thought of her now it would not be in terms of how she looked but rather in relationship to the whole wonderful array of smells he associated with her: strong and salty as goats' cheese, rich and flowery as leatherwood honey.

He fought against the Pentothal but could not better it. For perhaps an hour he lay on his back, during which time, in giddy reconnaissances, he managed to gather that the room contained four beds, one of which was much larger than the others, that the walls were a yellow perhaps intended to be "sunny", that the fly-wire screens over the two small windows were torn, that the vinyl-tiled floor had a long black rubber skid-mark which ran from beneath the windows to the door on the opposite wall, and also: that he was wearing pyjamas which were not his.

He was not so much frightened as impatient to know what would happen next, and it was irritation with his drug-induced weakness which finally drove him, wobbly-legged, across the room to the window.

He had expected walls.

What he saw reminded him of a number of country railway stations all moored in a park of dwarf trees, covered walk-ways leading from one to the other. The red-brick buildings were long and thin and seemed to be only one room wide, with fading green doors opening out on to verandahs. Sometimes, he saw, the doors had signs such as "Social Workers" instead of "Station Master" or "Waiting Room" but there was, amongst the people he saw, the same melancholy one finds amongst passengers who have just missed the train to the city and know they will be marooned here for the next four hours. They paced up and down, sat still on benches, talked to each other, or more commonly established a hostile isolation amongst the dwarf trees. The sun sank below the roof of the Ginger Factory (although Harry took this ugly rusting corrugated-iron building to be part of the hospital) and the very green, perfectly mown grass assumed a darker, blacker coloration.

It was then that he heard the Sea Scouts screaming. Absolute bowel-loosening terror cut through the air and hung there, vibrating. The patients, like grazing animals, suddenly froze. Harry crossed the room in two strides and opened his door. There was no grass here, only bitumen, across which black expanse two large men hurried, carrying the struggling bodies of two small male children. A notebook was dropped. A pencil, somehow pitiful, fell and rolled across the bitumen. A woman descended the steps of a box-like aluminium building and, with a slight hop, like a magpie scavenging beside a busy road, picked up the pencil. As she rose she caught sight of Harry Joy, who, instinctively, shut the door.

The screams now came through the open window as Jim and Jimmy carried the kicking Sea Scouts across the grass towards the Ginger Factory. Harry saw patients move out of the way and then close behind in curiosity. The Sea Scouts screamed as if they knew the secrets of those smoking chimneys.

Honey Barbara had rules for survival in this particular quarter of Hell. They were as follows: Do not aggravate them, be quiet, smile nicely, don't let them know how smart you are. Eat all your food and don't steal jam. Fuck whoever wants to be fucked and then forget about it. Never tell a doctor the truth but make everything you tell them interesting. Never say you're not sick. Keep your nose clean and do not write complaining letters.

Harry was determined to follow the rules exactly and it was his desire, made more intense by the frightful screaming, that led him, so early, to his first mistake. His heart was racing. He was panicked and still dizzy from Pentothal. Yet he saw it clearly, there plain as day, on the end of the big bed. It was not the bed he had been sleeping in, but there it was: his name: Mr HARRY JOY, in metallic tape.

Already he was courting disaster. He was in the wrong bed. ("Never tell them," Honey Barbara said, "that a thing is their fault, even if it is.") A mistake had been made, or a trick. Perhaps he had been delivered to the wrong bed or a prankster had shifted him while he slept.

Quickly, dizzily, he made the bed he had been asleep in and shifted himself into the correct bed.

And there he was: keeping his nose clean, obeying the rules, not complaining either verbally or in writing. He was in the right bed, only worried now that he might have been given the wrong pyjamas and, in fact, he was sitting up in bed, peering over his shoulder and trying to read the label on his pyjama coat when Alice Dalton entered the room, already a little on edge.

She had a pencil in her hand. It was the Sea Scouts' pencil. She held it without feeling and he watched her narrowly as she approached the bed, thus ignoring one of Honey Barbara's many rules: "Always give out a good vibe, never let them think you hate them."

She stood at the foot of his bed for some seconds, her head bowed, her temples held delicately between thumb and middle finger. When she looked up at last, her mouth was drawn very tight.

"Mr Joy, I am Mrs Dalton. This is my hospital and you are here because you are sick."

Harry waited. He had remembered Honey Barbara's rule about vibes but all he could think was that he didn't like this pencil woman. He disliked her self-importance, her mottled red face, her pink glasses, her tightly permed indifferent-coloured hair, her sparrow legs, her fussy voice, her black shoes, and he would have gone on, finding more things to dislike, except that she started to talk and he had to concentrate on her ridiculous words.

"Unpleasant fact number two," said Mrs Dalton, "is you are in the wrong bed. Please don't interrupt. Now when we assign you a bed we do it for a good reason, probably a whole number of reasons. We know things, Mr Joy, that you could never possibly know so if you start changing your bed . . . well, it's impossible."

"It has my name on it," Harry said. He wasn't meaning to argue. He was simply trying to clarify. He did not wish to argue.

Mrs Dalton sighed. She held her temples again, in the same delicate way, between thumb and middle finger. Harry kept a respectful silence.

"I will not argue, Mr Joy," she said at last. "You see, this is a perfect example. How could you possibly know that there are *two* Mr Joys in this room? You see how silly that makes you look? You thought you knew it all, and now you find you don't. You find there are *other factors*. Even", she said, "if you were healthy you could not know. So", she said with some attempt at friendliness, "be a love and get back into your own bed."

He did not want to argue. He knew it was not politic, but the fact remained:

"But I *am* Harry Joy."

"No, you're *Mr* Joy."

"Mr *Harry* Joy."

"You are not Mr Harry Joy. Kindly do not tell me my own business."

"I should know my own name."

She smiled and allowed herself two good seconds before she answered.

"If you knew your own name, Mr Joy, you probably would not be here. I am here because I *do* know my own name. Not only my own name, but also the names of all my patients. You see, Mr Joy, this is my *speciality*. It is my *business*."

"I am not Harry Joy?"

"No. You are *Mr* Joy. Now why don't you get out of Mr Harry Joy's bed before he comes back. You don't want to start off in his bad books too."

Harry climbed out of the bed which was bigger and more comfortable than the one the horrible Mrs Dalton wished him to sleep in. When he had done that she tucked in the other bed and smoothed it obsessively. Then she came and sat on his bed.

"I'm sorry to growl," she smiled.

For one horrifying moment he thought she was going to take his hand.

"That's O.K."

"It's confusing, I know: two Mr Joys in the one room."

"My name is Harry too."

"Well you'll have to give it up for a little while," she said. "Let him have it for a while. Do you have a second name?"

"Stanthorpe."

"Alright, Stanthorpe. It's a very aristocratic name."

Stanthorpe!

"You can be Stanthorpe."

"I don't want to be Stanthorpe."

"Then you'll damn well have to be plain Mr Joy," she said, standing up irritably. "I can't spend all day arguing. Good afternoon, Mr Joy."

He wished to be polite but he had forgotten her name already. "Goodnight," he said vaguely. The only name that came to mind was Pencil.

When he woke up he was hungry, and later, looking back on all the indignities and irritations in this part of Hell, he was to remember the hunger as the predominant thing, the melancholy gurglings of his empty stomach.

It was night and there was someone else in the room. He heard the sound of a page turning and a loud hearty chuckle.

"Oh dear," said a familiar voice, "oh dearie dearie-me."

He propped himself up on his elbow and saw the person who had been designated as Mr Harry Joy.

"Jesus. Alex."

Alex was lying on his bed and reading. He did not stop reading just because he had been spoken to. In fact he continued to read for a good thirty seconds before he dropped his book down on to his lap, and then his face showed none of the pleasure his jovial "dearie me's" might have suggested. His high white forehead was creased up like a piece of rejected writing paper and the beginnings of a moustache accentuated the down-turned line of his mouth.

"Christ, Alex. What a fuck-up. I'm sorry."

"I thought they told you."

"No, no. I just found out. I mean, I just found out you were here. Alex, I'm sorry."

"I thought they told you", Alex said slowly, "that my name is Harry Joy."

There was a long silence and Harry Joy stopped smiling.

"Oh come on, Alex, don't be silly."

"I am not being *silly*. If you think I'm being *silly*, talk to Mrs Dalton."

"I don't blame you for being mad, Alex. I shouldn't have left you in the Hilton. You're quite right for being angry with me."

Alex shut his eyes and rubbed his big hand across them. Harry was reminded of Mrs Dalton.

"This is a wonderful place if you are reasonable about it. So don't go around the place saying you're Harry Joy because you'll only get yourself into trouble."

Harry's stomach gurgled. "I'm Harry Joy," he said. His name was his name. His name was more than his name. In short, it was him. It could not be stolen from him.

"You're new here. You don't understand yet."

"Understand what?"

"You have a primitive attitude towards your name."

"I don't know what you're talking about. Talk in plain English."

Alex hesitated, hearing the voice of Alex's employer talking to him, a voice that could no longer be used against him.

"It's a therapy", he said at last, "to find the right name. But first you have to give up your old name. You see, when I came here I was really stuck on being Alex. I didn't want to give it up. No damn way was I going to give it up," he smiled, remembering. "I didn't want to be Harry Joy. No way was I going to be Harry Joy but, finally, I just stopped fighting. And it worked, you see, the damn thing worked. I'd always *hated* being Alex."

"That's not therapy. That's a fuck-up. They called you Harry Joy because they got you by mistake. You're not meant to be here. They meant to get me. They thought you were me."

Alex smiled and shook his big head. "Sorry," he said, "save your imagination for someone else."

"It's true."

"You can't be destructive with me any more. I'm free of you."

"You're insane."

"You can't run my life and pull the strings any more. They've put you in here as a final test, that's obvious. It doesn't fool me. Well, I'm ready for you. You see: you can't affect me."

"Did they actually *tell* you it was the final test."

"Well there'd be no point in *telling* me would there. No, of course they wouldn't tell me. I don't have to be *told*."

"Alex . . ."

"Please call me Harry."

"Alright then, Harry. Harry you don't have to be in hospital. It's not you they wanted. Go home."

"You want me to go, don't you," Alex smiled cunningly, "You

don't like having to share a room with Harry Joy," he laughed. "Oh, what irony, what irony."

"Everyone knows you're not Harry Joy," said Harry, who, in spite of his growing conviction that Alex had been put there to torture him, was rattled.

"Who?"

"Everyone at the office. Your wife. My wife. My children. Aldo . . ."

"Don't see any of them here."

"Of course not."

"All the people *here* know I'm Harry Joy." He picked up his book to signal the end of the conversation but after a moment or two he put it down again. "You know," he said, gazing at the ceiling, "I'm not at all surprised to see you end up here. I knew you were crazy. All that bullshit about firing clients and Captives and Actors. You've been crazy for years. You've made everybody else crazy."

"I've been trying to be Good."

"How naive," Alex said. "The most dangerous thing in the world: an untrained mind deciding to seek salvation. The most astonishing thing about you is that you kept your ignorance as long as you did. It's probably a record."

"All that business about Hell . . ."

"We're all in Hell, you silly ding-bat," said Alex, playing his idea of Harry Joy. "It's a question of making yourself comfortable. I mean, if you want to be tortured, you've come to the right place. But look . . . it's *nice* here. We can stay here for *ever* if we want to They need the money they get in subsidies from the government. They *need* us, Harry." He stopped petulantly. "Fuck it."

"What?"

"I called you Harry."

"I didn't hear you."

"I don't care what you heard. *I* heard. I called you Harry."

"Don't worry about it."

"Of course I worry about it. You don't want me to worry about it. But I've got to worry about it, because I'm happy now. I feel really happy with being Harry Joy. I'm a successful advertising man without the smallest scruple. I've made money, made a name and don't worry about a damn thing. I'm crazy and happy." He had started to cheer up as he listed the advantages of being Harry Joy. "I can relax," he beamed. "We could get up a darts team and beat the old men."

"Are they going to torture me?" Harry did not expect an honest answer.

"No, they like us. They want our subsidies."

One in every three is a spy.

"They'll give us electric shocks and put electrodes in our brains. They'll give us pills and make us zombies."

"Harry, you are part of the biggest growth industry of the decade. You can have peace here. No one will hurt you."

Harry Joy considered it. As he watched Alex it occurred to him that he had the healthy pink glow of a pregnant woman. He plumped up his pillow and made himself comfortable, considering the implication of this amazing transformation.

"Fuck it."

"What?"

"I called you Harry again."

The real Harry Joy's stomach gurgled mournfully, dreaming of wholemeal bread and Honey Barbara.

Alex Duval had this dream only once but it had been so vivid that it had pushed its way through into his conscious where it occupied an important corner of his waking mind, metamorphosed from a dream to a memory.

There is a plush green carpet and a svelte grey cat with silky fur. On the cat's back is a large crayfish, about the same size as the cat. The crayfish is digging its sharp claws into the cat's body. There is a crackling sound. It is the cat tearing off those of the crayfish legs it can reach with its mouth. Alex Duval is watching. He believes at first that the crayfish will die, but then it occurs to him that this is stupid — dream-logic — and that the crayfish is in agony and cannot scream. The noise of the legs in the cat's mouth is the same noise you hear when you bite a cooked crayfish leg.

It was a portrait of his marriage Who was the cat? Who was the crayfish? He didn't know.

He had wanted to leave his wife for ten years. Daily, nightly, he had been on the very brink of doing it and daily, nightly, he had failed, he had been defeated and fallen into bed drunk. Viewed in this light his guilty conference reports can be seen to be less of a punishment and more of an escape. He was like an unhappy man who retires to his dusty garage to play war games.

At first it is difficult to see why he didn't leave her or why, when he had left her the first time — and this is where the trouble really started, ten years before – he ever went back.

It was "friends" who had persuaded him to return the first time, and his own oversized conscience as he thought of her getting fatter and less desirable, alone in that vast house, and he, Alex Duval, responsible for the destruction of a life.

But although this is important in its way, it has nothing to do with why Alex Duval stayed there still, year after year; for the only really important factor in his continual imprisonment and punishment was the ingenuity of his wife, who everybody thought of as a slow, bovine sort of woman, not very intelligent, always unhappy, and all the words they used to describe her suggested something large and blunt and totally lacking in elegance.

Yet she played games with Alex Duval more cruelly elegant than anything her critics could have dreamed of, and had this "dull" woman applied herself to something more public in life she may well have been called a genius.

It is impossible to describe the games she played with Alex Duval: they could centre around something as everyday as a torn postage stamp, a crumpled piece of paper, a blue towel and proceed by a series of moves as imperceptible as the hands of a clock. ("Did I move?" says the clock. "Look at me." "Yes, you moved." "I am perfectly still," the clock insists, "you're crazy. You're imagining things.")

A game concerning odd socks took two days of moves and countermoves to reach its conclusion.

At which point Alex Duval would explode with rage and fury.

But this is not the end of the game. Now, for this brief time, this is the whole point. Here one needs skill. Now he is dangerous. He can walk out the door. He may kill her with a blow.

Martha Duval's great slow face closes down and in the slitted eyes one might glimpse passion, fear, and as her shoulders finally relax, triumph.

Time after time, game after game, he was trapped, cornered, and could only turn his anger on himself.

She watched him break a dainty piece of china he had collected or stab the nib of his beloved pen into the wall where the blue ink mark would be, could be, if needed, the introduction to another game.

She had devoted her life to paying him back for having left her once. The scales would not balance. No amount of pain she inflicted on him could balance the hurt and terror of those thirteen days, ten years before. He could not leave her. She would not let him. She played him as if he were a ten-pound trout on a three-pound line.

And into this life, by mistake, without meaning well, doctors Cornelius and Hennessy had come.

Alex Duval wasn't even a fraction mad. They wanted him to be Harry Joy, he would be. To the whisker. He made notes on Harry Joy: his manner of speech, the quality of his voice, his eyebrow habits, his floating walk, his folding limbs. He sloughed off his Pascal and his Rousseau and felt a great lightness.

He immersed himself in the part and nothing gave him more pleasure than finding some mannerism, a gesture of the hand, a flick of the head, that made him more perfectly Harry Joy. He laughed and told stories. He made stories up. Better stories. He sat in quiet corners inventing Harry Joy-type stories.

He had assiduously paid court to Mrs Dalton, had even made himself pretend he liked her. It was Mrs Dalton who decided on who got Electro-Convulsive Therapy (the only therapy available) and who did not. They discussed her Clarice Cliff collection together, taking out the little triangular-handled cups and cooing over them.

And then he had his illicit pleasures, those books Alex Duval loved which Harry Joy would never have thought to open: Tolstoy, Dostoevsky, Dickens, Flaubert, Chekhov. These had to be read in secret, but this only increased his pleasure. In public he flicked through *Reader's Digest* impatiently, only showing an interest in the ads. He sat in the television room and told anyone who would listen how TV commercials were made and how much they cost. He did it so realistically, so charmingly, that he was more popular than the programmes.

And now the real Harry Joy had come to interfere with his happiness. He would not succeed. This time Alex Duval would turn all the resources of his considerable mind to the problem of this parvenu Joy, a problem which was to become more pressing when the two Harry Joys were noticed by the Social Welfare's computer.

No matter what Honey Barbara had told him about mental hospitals, he had not been ready for the depression and boredom. There was nothing to do. There was no tennis court, no swimming pool, no dart boards. There wasn't even any basket weaving. There was a library which was controlled by some racket he didn't even try to understand. Alex, he noticed, always had books under his pillow.

There was only television and that was made difficult by the bad state of the sets, which would break down and then take weeks to be repaired. There was nothing to do but walk up and down in the midst of mad people. In the mornings the Electro-Convulsive Therapy patients were wheeled, some protesting, some passive, to the place where they were "done". This procession of trolleys along the concrete paths was watched with morbid curiosity and had something of the attraction of a public hanging, although the ceremony itself was private.

One old man with long grey hair and a big bulbous nose always seemed to be there, grimly riding the trolley to this much-feared therapy. His name was Nurse and Harry was to meet him later.

Not even the meals provided any relief. The food was wheeled out into the echoing dining room in big electrically-heated aluminium trolleys, inside which, in cylindrical containers like bulk ice-cream drums, would be mashed potato, mashed pumpkin, minced meat in watery gravy, and an endless variety of custards, all concocted in the belief that they were not only mad but also toothless. For breakfast they would have reheated fried eggs with hard centres. For an extra five cents you could purchase a sweet orange cordial to take away the taste.

And Alex was always at his elbow waiting for him to share some mindless enthusiasm.

"Isn't this a wonderful trifle?"

"Look at that tree. Must be a hundred years old."

"Look at that fellow play chess. They say he beat Granscy in Poland."

Harry saw no logical reason to deny Alex the happiness that came from being Harry Joy, and yet it ate at him. It upset him to see the changes that had come over Alex as he grew into the part. It upset him in puzzling, contradictory ways.

Alex had grown a creditable moustache which might, in time, develop the authentic droop. And even now one might have believed, if one had been charitable, that he was an uncle of the first Harry Joy, fatter, older, slightly slower, but also (and this was one of the things that hurt) more authoritative, less passive. He had managed to adopt certain mannerisms of the original character so that, like a good actor called upon to play a famous man he does not physically resemble, he managed to give an unnerving impression of being Harry Joy. The original Harry Joy found even this disconcerting, like being endlessly mocked and criticized by an ageing child. He watched the second Harry Joy laugh and joke with Jim and Jimmy and Mrs Dalton, watched as an outsider excluded from a favoured circle, watched the familiarity with which he patted Mrs Dalton's arm, the confidence with which he jabbed Jimmy's chest with his finger, the expansive, jolly way he laughed. There was a largeness, a warmth, a freedom in his movements which seemed to indicate that the second Harry Joy was genuinely happy and this brought nothing to Harry but irritation.

Was Alex totally blind? Couldn't he see that his bumbling stupid optimism was out of place? It showed no sensitivity, no regard for the feelings of people here. When he saw him strut in that white suit or laugh with Mrs Dalton he was reminded of a film he had seen about Nazi collaborators.

Alex did not talk to the patients. He talked at them. Harry could hear his loud booming voice across the courtyard, intoning some interminable story with a self-satisfied air. He began to hide from Alex, to seek out odd corners of the grounds where he would not be found. He became furtive, and developed a habit of walking close to walls.

He was escaping from Alex's "Harry Joy" voice one morning when he saw Nurse, a wiry, bony sixty-eight-year-old with enormous strength in his limbs, holding himself rigidly against the jamb of a doorway while Jim and Jimmy pummelled him to get him out. He said not a word. He did not even grunt. He stood there, like a Christ in a doorway, and when he collapsed and went limp it was because he chose to.

The next day Harry found him in the dining room. He sat next to him. They talked about E.C.T. It was not an uncommon topic of conversation.

"You don't get breakfast the morning they come," he said. "They don't give you nothing. That's how you know, see. Then they come and try to get you before you can struggle. They get you anyway, doesn't matter what you do. I don't fight them to win, because you can't win. I fight them because they're bastards, see." He ran his hand through his great mane of grey hair and flicked it jauntily out of his eye. He jutted his jaw. "Then they take you to the shock table and they put these two bits of tin, bits of metal, on your head. Here. And then the doctor turns on the juice." He had stopped eating, held his hands together, as if they might have contained dice, and beat them up and down. "It is a darkness you can't imagine. A blackness. Cold black ink. Like death."

Across the other side of the dining room, the other Harry Joy was laughing.

"They steal your memories from you," said Nurse, mixing his mashed potato with his gravy. "They take away all your faces, all your pictures."

He must have liked Harry Joy. He took him outside and showed him his book. He was writing down all the memories he had left. He wrapped them up in plastic bags and buried them in the garden when they were full. Later Harry was to find out that Nurse told everyone his secret and thus even his notebook memories would be stolen from him.

Harry developed pains across his chest and he began to stoop. His shoulders rounded and his chest hollowed, and it may have been because Alex was breaking him down or it could have been that the pain he felt was not his pain, but the pain of the people he moved amongst, and he adopted it with a sympathy quite new to him. In any case, his shoes had been stolen. They had given him slippers instead.

Alex came and sat on his bed one night just after cocoa time. He was flushed and exuberant. He had just beaten the so-called Intellectuals in French Scrabble. He talked about it happily for a quarter of an hour and became irritable when Harry would not share his triumph.

"It's irritating," he said, "both of us having the same name and the same moustache, and now," he smoothed his baggy white trousers, "we have the same suit."

"Yes," Harry agreed, "very irritating."

"So," the big man said, his legs dangling loosely from his bed, "you could be Alex."

Harry felt as if someone was sitting on his chest.

"Alex is a schmuck," he said truculently and felt his chest tighten another notch. There was a silence. He had hurt. He was pleased he'd hurt.

"He suits you," Alex said coldly. "He's worried about good and bad and doing the right thing. For Christ's sake," he said, "be reasonable."

"What's so great about being Harry Joy?" He was bitter and confused. He did not like the Harry Joy that Alex portrayed. He could not imagine anyone wanting it. But Harry Joy was his name. He was Harry Joy and no one else and he squeezed himself in some mental doorway, resisting having the name pulled from him.

Alex poured himself a glass of water and added a drop of his "privilege", a little blackcurrant cordial, superior to the orange type. "I'm a successful advertising man who's gone crazy. I've got power and money and I don't have to prove a thing."

"I know," Harry said. "I've bloody well seen you."

"But it wouldn't suit you any more," Alex said oilily. "Can't you see it should be repulsive to you? I think it is repulsive to you ... isn't it?"

What a crawling voice it was. "Alex," Harry said, "for Christsakes ..."

He didn't even put the glass down. "You call me Alex again," he said, taking a sip of blackcurrant, "and I'll hit you." He said it so quietly that Harry would never make the same mistake again. "It's not just for me. Mrs Dalton asked me to talk to you."

"Why can't she talk to me herself?'

This wasn't like Alex, this driving insistence. They were going to steal his name and leave him with the name of a flop and failure.

"There are two Harry Joys on the Social Welfare computer," Alex said, "and they want to reject one of us as fraudulent. So I suppose you could say, the hour has come."

"That's you. You're fraudulent." But you could hear the weakness in the voice. You could hear, already, the surrender.

"Mrs Dalton thinks you're being difficult." There was no nastier threat that could be made in the hospital. There was only one thing that happened to difficult patients. Alex, some of his old humanitarian principles still weakly showing, felt momentarily guilty. "Come on, Harry," he said, "please, for old times' sake."

Harry!

There was a silent lake around the island of the mistake. Had they been dogs they would have scratched themselves and looked at the ceiling.

"I'll think about it," Harry said, but he was already beginning to embrace the pale, shuffling unhappiness of an Alex.

There was considerable pressure on him to shave his moustache and adopt a different style of dress but he made excuses. He had made a silly decision and as time went on he resented it more and more. Only rich men seek salvation by giving away the trappings of power. If a poor man has a car, he clings on to it. If he has a penny he doesn't throw it from him. He dreams of making a fortune, having a good name. And here, he had given away the privilege of being Harry Joy, and the minute it was done, signed and sealed and tucked away in the computer, he was sorry. While he had still been the legitimate Harry Joy some power was attached to him and even if they had given him the Therapy he would still have been Harry Joy.

But once he was an Alex everyone knew he was a crumpled thing, a failure, defenceless. Three silk shirts were stolen from him and were worn, brazenly, in his presence.

He sat in the sunshine with Nurse and took over the pen for him when his fingers were cramped.

"A dog is a funny thing the way it trots along," Nurse would say, and Harry would write it in the book. "It could put its head up high and its tail, too. Then there are other dogs who walk with their noses down and they make me laugh too. I was in Cooktown and there was a fellow there with a black dog I used to feed scraps. I forget its name. Now, cats . . ." and he would move on to the next subject and Harry Joy, wearing his pyjama jacket, would bend over the notebook and write and neatly as he could.

In the afternoons, on the days when Nurse had not been "done", they would go the rounds of the traps, as Nurse called it, checking on what memories had been stolen. One day they found someone had written 3/10 in a book, and then reburied it.

The new Harry Joy conferred with Alice in her office and ordered the old men about. The new Alex heard him and was jealous. He envied his loud happy laugh, the way he threw back his big balding head and just laughed, laughed and laughed as if there was nothing in the world to worry about, no pain, no agony, no indecision, no one stealing Nurse's memory from his head and his holes in the ground.

They had authority over him. They made him sweep the concrete paths and he did it. They tried to feed him like an Alex. They did it for sport. For their amusement. They brought him big doughnuts and laughed at him when he pulled faces. He told Nurse the food was full of poisons. He told him everything he had learned from Honey Barbara and Nurse insisted it be written in the book even though it wasn't a memory but because it would be, should be a memory the next day, and therefore should be entered. He did not tell the new Harry Joy about the poisoned food in case they decided to give him Therapy. He wrote Honey Barbara's rules in Nurse's book, paying particular attention to her thoughts on paranoia.

Hunger, lethargy, and the anger he had not yet recognized came to be his constant companions. His shoulders were permanently rounded, his chest hollowed, and when he walked down the concrete paths beside the wings he shuffled in his slippers like a defeated man.

Seeing him shuffle around the place his enemies made the mistake of thinking him permanently defeated. Yet a small revolution was brewing inside the stooped man known as Alex, and depression and lethargy were probably as important for its proper conclusion as optimism might be at a later time.

The change which would, anyway, have come, was accelerated by the arrival of the formidable Mrs Martha Duval, who was not to be denied her husband by something as ineffectual as a bribed Social Welfare clerk. She arrived on a Wednesday morning and was, shortly after lunch, introduced to a person Mrs Dalton claimed was her husband. She declared this person to be none other than Harry Joy.

More officers of the Department of Social Welfare were called. Interviews were conducted. And finally, from the far corner of the garden, the real Alex Duval was somehow unearthed and presented to his wife in the bitumen courtyard in front of Alice Dalton's office.

Social Security men stood around holding their clipboards and Mrs Dalton attempted to usher various select people into her office, but they all stood their ground, watching in terrible fascination as the false Harry Joy began to moan. He pulled at his moustache and gnashed his teeth. He sat on top of one of the old men and pissed in his pants. He rolled across the bitumen and bit Jimmy on the ankle. He curled into a ball and wailed.

All he could see was a great grey cat with a crayfish clamped on his back. There was a loud crack as he broke a claw from the body. The crayfish felt like steel pins. He rolled up beneath the kitchen window and moaned, while the crayfish shrieked into his ear.

There was no getting away from the fact that he was an impostor. Jim and Jimmy lifted him up and carried him to the building known as "The Foyer" where he was declared sane and returned to the custody of the large motherly woman who was his wife.

Harry Joy returned to the room he had shared with the impostor. He lay in the small bed and ate an apple. His eyes were dark with hurts and cunning: envy, fear, jealousy, rage, all showed their colours.

Alice Dalton arranged the vases on the table. Normally she kept the vases separate from the cups, saucers, bowls, teapots, coffee-pots and so on, but tonight she put them all together as if she wished to concentrate their power, to intensify their colour. There was a gayness, a girlishness about the work of Clarice Cliff with its bright colours, its stylized little houses and trees and, also, an optimism about the mechanical future suggested by those strange triangular handles and spouts which had first been marketed under the "Bizarre" name as early as 1929. Now, perhaps the optimism did not appear to be well founded and was, therefore, all the more appreciated.

It was Mr Harry Joy who had pointed all this out to her, and he had been able to talk for hours about those triangular handles and their significance. They had sat here, in this very room, their knees almost touching, and there had been a sense of almost breathless discovery, and while they had not become lovers everything was laid out, like a feast, and they were merely arranging the table decorations and putting out the place names, the final little touches, so that when the feast began it would have been a splendid thing, not only satisfying to the baser appetites but to the higher senses.

But he was gone, snatched from her, and she was bereft. She knew it was, in one way, her fault and that she had been *unprofessional*. She had tried to cheat the computer. She was ashamed as well as angry. It was unthinkable that she should be so unprofessional. It would be spoken of. Mr da Silva might hear of it, and although he would not and could not *do* anything, or even *say* anything, his unsaid criticism, his disappointment, would cause her pain.

For Alice Dalton's great pride was in her business abilities, her talent for facing unpleasant facts. No one knew what it was like to run a place like this. Those who criticized could not have done it. In sheer administrative terms, it was as complex as a large hotel. They criticized her for her lack of feelings, but they did not see her feelings, not her real feelings, and so they could be surprised on those rare occasions when sentiment gushed forth from Alice Dalton in a great wave as she wept and held some unfortunate whose mind was filled with shards of madness.

Twenty years ago, as a young nurse, she had been very different. She had tried to believe that there was no insanity, merely a lack of love or understanding, and this could be remedied, her love given, her love returned. Perhaps paradoxically she also believed the world of the mad to be at once more intense and more beautiful and therefore, romantically, envied it.

She had had a lonely youth. She had read poetry and novels and when she learned to drive had avoided squashing the cane toads that gathered on the roads at night. She had released blow-flies trapped against the glass and was attracted to psychiatric nursing as soon as she knew such a thing existed.

And yet it was to prove too much for her: this dull, grey piss-soaked world of the mad where people did not get better or worse and where no amount of moist-eyed love seemed to do anything but invite rejection and derision.

At twenty-one she had a complete breakdown and was admitted to hospital. It was here, at last, that she was to develop her attitudes towards mental illness, her list of unpleasant facts. She grasped the nettle of commerce. She felt herself grow strong, and when she returned to nursing her superiors felt her to be mercifully free of the romanticism that had afflicted her before.

Alice Dalton had become objective.

She had never been a feminist. She was too much of an authoritarian to believe in any sort of equality. And while those around her came to regard her as strong, while they stepped out of her way, as she gathered power and influence, she craved to be recognized as a poor weak woman by a strong and sensitive man.

Yet such men rarely came her way. Mad people, she discovered, were not normally very bright, were more likely to be poor than rich, and were less likely to be sensitive (in her definition of the term) than sane people. Her marriage to the schizophrenic Henry Dalton lasted two weeks, and while she cried at his funeral, something inside her had acknowledged his suicide as beneficial to both of them.

The nights then were long and lonely and she felt it was not unreasonable for her to have Mr Harry Joy and she had expected more sympathy from the Department of Social Welfare. She arranged the Clarice Cliff and wiped the slightly dusty lid of the "Bizarre" sugar bowl. She wished she had been alive in 1929, working for Clarice Cliff and her girls at the pottery, painting gay scenes, travelling to London to promote their wares, wearing artists' smocks and smiling at the camera.

Did they meet men on their visits to the capital? Or were they too left alone as she was, at eleven o'clock at night, with this ... itch. She did not wish to ring for Jim or Jimmy. With her finger, she began, but in the end it was always the same no matter what the feminists said about masturbation and the clitoris, had always been the same, always would be. There was a hole. A damn hole. An aching emptiness that had not yet revealed itself, not yet, and for the moment, this moment, she could always delude herself into thinking that the final humiliating need to press the buzzer for Jim or Jimmy could be avoided. In her mind Alice Dalton had a mental picture of herself as something quivering, vulnerable, glisteningly pink: a garden snail without its shell.

Harry Joy watched Nurse walk towards him. He was a distinctive figure. He had no hips and no arse. He kept his trousers done up tightly with a rope belt but it still looked as if his backside had been stolen from him and when he arrived at the bench and turned to sit down there would be a big empty sack of material hanging from the back of his belt.

Nurse called Harry by the name of Mo because, as he said, "Anyone with a mo like yours is called Mo, always have been and always will be."

"Good news for Mo," he announced and placed a crinkled brown paper parcel on the bench between them. He made no invitation to open the parcel. Harry stared at it and looked away.

"Mo is getting out," Nurse said provocatively.

"How?"

When it came to answering questions, Nurse always liked to take the Scenic Route rather than the Freeway.

"To survive in this place," he said, "you've got to be mad as a spider on a thirty-dollar note. Are you mad?"

"No."

"No, you're not mad. You won't survive. See," he indicated the garden with outstretched hands, "this is my job here. It's my work. I've got my notebooks, all my memories. This garden is like my brain, full of memories. All my little rabbit burrows, full of memories. But look at you!"

Harry's trousers had food stains on them. His pyjama coat was filthy. The left-hand slipper had been stolen and replaced by an odd one. He looked cowed and rat-like.

"You've got your buttons in the wrong holes."

Harry redid his buttons

"There. That's better. You're a good-looking fellow."

Harry grinned coyly.

"Sit up straight. There you are. A good-looking fellow."

"You should have seen me when I had my suit."

"Forget your suit. Why are you always talking about your suit? You don't need a suit." Nurse was shaking his cupped hands up and down. "She's a lonely woman," he said, "and you're a good-looking fellah."

Harry didn't understand.

"You sweety-talk her and ..." he raised his eyebrows and grinned lasciviously. "You know what to do."

"She won't."

"Yes she will. Look," Nurse dropped his voice to a whisper although there was no one nearby, "they steal your slippers and your shirts. I can't look after you all the time. I'm too busy. You wait, they'll come and give you Therapy next time you lose your slippers. They'll take your faces and your pictures."

"Don't talk about the black."

"Alright then, but ..."

"She'd never look twice at me," Harry said, "she hates me."

But Nurse was grinning and shifting around inside his trousers. He thrust the brown paper parcel into Harry's lap. "There," he said, "open it."

The parcel contained one pair of shoes, one silk shirt, toothpaste, aftershave and hair oil.

"Californian Poppy," Nurse said holding the bottle of hair oil with a tenderness that Harry Joy had once displayed towards bottles of French wine.

Harry's trousers were smudged with his attempts to use soap on them, but his shirt was magnificent, silk without blemish. His shoes shone. His teeth sparkled. And yet she had chosen that the interview should be across the desk and not in the comfortable armchairs that surrounded the flower-burdened coffee table. She was still in mourning for the impostor. She rocked back and forth in her squeaking chair while fish swam in the aquarium behind her head and she played churches and steeples with her short-fingered hands.

He sat on the edge of his chair and smiled and nodded, raised his eyebrows, inclined his head politely and, when his nose ran, had a pressed handkerchief to wipe it with.

"You will never be the real Mr Joy," she said. "I'm sorry. I know that's unfair, but it's true."

There was a silence. Harry gave her a sly grin.

"There is something, don't you think, about successful men that is immensely attractive, a certain lack of desperation."

He pushed his shoulders back and let his arm hang loosely.

"I have been reading my back issues of *Financial Review*, and look, here he is." She pushed a torn piece of newspaper across the desk (there was no chance for fingers to touch) and withdrew to be closer to her fish. "Not a good likeness though. Some people take good photographs," she said. "My late husband never had a good photograph taken. I regret it now. I always meant to commission a portrait. If you're trying to butter me up with that silly grin you might as well forget it. I can't afford to let you out."

He rubbed his face, as if slapped.

"And don't try running away." She took off her pink spectacles and cleaned the lenses with a yellow cloth. "If you try, Jim and Jimmy will bring you back."

"The boys in white," he joked weakly.

"Sometimes they wear white, sometimes they wear grey," she said contrarily. "Sometimes they wear shorts and white socks and sometimes, should you try in the middle of the night, I must warn you, they wear nothing at all. Mr Duval," she sighed, and while Harry Joy was still flinching from this insult, repeated it: "Mr Duval, I try not to have favourites. I try not to have personal dislikes, but I'm afraid I do not take to you."

"I'm sorry." Surely many romances grew from such unpromising beginnings.

"It is not your fault. You have an unfortunate manner and you are, of course, sick, so it would not have occurred to you how inconsiderate your request is."

"I'm sorry." He would begin again, on the right foot this time.

"You don't have to apologize all the time. That's exactly the sort of thing I mean. If you apologized less you might listen more. Then you would ask me *why* your request was inconsiderate and then I would have told you."

"Please tell me."

"I'm not sure that I want to any more."

"Please, Mrs Dalton." He summoned up all his reserves of confidence. He had once been told he looked like the God Krishna.

"The nature of growth industries," she sighed, "is often cyclical. There is under-supply and then, next thing you know, everyone is on the band waggon and there is over-supply. So from a shortage of beds we go to a surplus of beds and people like myself, pioneers in the business, are the first to suffer."

"But in time," Harry said (here was his chance to establish himself as a man of intelligence), "it is bound to pick up."

"Ah, in time!" she said bitterly. "In time. But will I still be in business 'in time'? Those nasty little worms in Social Welfare expel my patients or put their clients into the cheapest place they can find. And believe me, there are some very cheap beds being offered, not the luxury we have here. Even the cancer patients don't make up the shortfall."

"Cancer patients? Here?" he asked. She was softening. He raised his eyebrows with great interest. Ah, he told himself, you greasy genius!

"They become quite upset poor dears. I advise you, by the way, to stay well away from L Block. They can become very violent while they've still got their strength, although as anyone knows, it's their own fault."

"Sorry. I don't follow you."

"Their fault," she said impatiently, her voice rising in pitch, "their own fault. Anyone who reads the papers knows what causes it."

"Ah, cigarettes."

"Cigarettes!" She swung in her chair and for a moment he thought she was about to leave the room. She put her thin arms along the arms of the chair and held them tight. "Cigarettes." Her eyes swam behind her glasses like gold fish. "Alice, you are being intolerant," she said. She bestowed upon him a smile which was obviously intended as a gift of some munificence. "I thought the press had covered it quite adequately," she said with buttered patience. "But it is generally recognized by more advanced members of the profession that cancer is caused by emotional repressions. Now if they would use us as a therapeutic, preventative force . . ."

Liar! Fart-face!

It was not the lie that did it. It was the weeks, the months of slights, insults as fine as razor cuts across his undefended ego. But it was at this moment, at this particular lie, that anger came to him.

He had known the quiet superiority of being a Good Bloke. But beside this there was a nagging doubt that something was missing from him, that he suffered an impotence. For instance, when he saw a chair raised above a head in a movie he felt both excitement and resentment that this passion was denied him. When Bettina became angry he felt a jealousy. When she threw a plate, he envied her.

When he should have become angry, he got hives instead.

And now, like a dream in which one can fly, he was angry.

A wall of wax had gone, a blockage removed, and the feeling of anger flooded through him and it was better than it had been described, was more like he knew it must be. It was pleasant. It was a gift, a drug as wonderful in its way as sexual pleasure. It made you feel bigger, stronger, taller, invincible.

But still he hid it, holding it like a hot chestnut in a cupped hand.

"Saccharine causes cancer," he said. He tugged at his moustache.

"Are you a Communist, Mr Duval?"

"No." He ran his hands through his California Poppy hair.

"That sounds very like a Communist to me. The Americans are a very fine race of people, Mr Duval, but they have filled their government agencies with Communists and liberals and they will not get rid of them."

The muscles around his neck were knotted into hard lumps and his eyes were red. Tendons stood out on his neck like lumps of straining rope.

"These people hate business," the liar was saying. "They are jealous of people with power, successful men who have made a name for themselves."

He stared at her, his eyes bulging.

"Perhaps I talk too much," she sighed, trying to consider her complicated character with some objectivity.

Harry Joy clasped and unclasped his hands.

He would have liked to strangle her with his bare hands. He would have liked to break her neck and jump on her head till her brains oozed out her earholes. He could have broken up her desk with an axe and eaten her vases for breakfast.

With a purr of pleasure, he opened his hands and let her escape.

He walked down the steps in a daze, surprised to find sunlight and myna birds scavenging behind the kitchen. He was so angry, he wanted to sing.

Jim and Jimmy were talking to a female patient. The female patient was about twenty-seven and dressed in baggy white pants and a yellow T shirt. She had a wide straw hat with a scarf around its brim, but not even that could hide the luminosity of her big dark eyes.

As he passed the group Harry heard her say: "I don't feel a thing, not a thing."

*

Honey Barbara remembered the first time she had seen a new car. It was in Bog Onion Road and she was still a child. It was a raining day right in the middle of the wet season, just at the time when everything is starting to get covered with mildew and a treasured book or favourite cushion will suddenly show itself to be half rotten with mould. Little Rufus came running through the bush to Paul Bees (Honey Barbara's father) to tell him there was an American with his car stuck on the second concrete ford and it was being swept away. If he'd known it was a new Peugot, Paul would have run even faster than he did. But he didn't know, so he slipped on a pair of shorts out of respect for the unknown visitor and jogged down the track. He had a small body, but it was wiry and strong, and the American, one would guess, would have been pleased to see him coming.

Paul Bees was also known as Peugot Paul and ever since Honey Barbara could remember there had been long boring community meetings in which someone would raise the question of his Peugots. He had a whole paddock full of them, or at least, a paddock devoted to five Peugots of varying ages, dating back to a time when it had seemed to him that only a Peugot would be strong enough and sensible enough to handle the rigours of Bog Onion Road. But by the time the American got stuck on the Ford they were slowly rusting, disappearing under the ever-encroaching lantana bush, and when they were discussed there were always those who thought them unsightly but there was not really anyone who didn't secretly agree with Paul's belief that they were potentially valuable. And indeed in those days it was not uncommon (yet hardly frequent) to find some lost man in an old Peugot looking for Paul Bees and he would be directed to the only sign in all Bog Onion Road. It read: Paul Bees, Honey, Bog Onion Road. That was in the days they still had visitors and her father and the stranger would spend an afternoon wresting some valuable part from an ancient Peugot 203 and often it would turn out that the visitor had no money and would stay for dinner, and once, in the case of Ring-tail Phil, stayed for a whole year and had to be told to leave and then, as Paul pointed out so bitterly, left behind the wiper motor he had come to find in the first place.

But on the day that Albert brought his new Peugot to Bog Onion Road he did not come looking for second-hand parts, but for land. Later he was to claim that he had smuggled a Range Rover from Mexico into America by driving it across the Rio Grande, but if this was true he must have forgotten the trick because he stalled his new

Peugot in two feet of fast water and then opened its bonnet to let the monsoon rain complete the job.

When Paul and Honey Barbara arrived at the creek it was raging high and Albert, his carrot red hair plastered flat on his head and his beard soaking, was standing on the downstream side of the stalled car, smiling a desperate gold-toothed smile at his rescuers, and trying to push the car back against the current.

Soon Robert arrived, and Dani, and Sally Coe turned up with five bedraggled cockerels in the back of her ancient Peugot. They pushed against Albert's Peugot and had a conference. The rain poured down harder and harder but they kept their clothes on from respect for the man with the new car.

The electrics were wet beyond saving and in the end it was agreed that Paul would get his winch, but the cable on it was broken and had to be repaired and while that was done Honey Barbara and the others leant against the car. The creek was stronger. It pushed the car towards the edge an inch at a time while they waited for Paul to fix the winch.

Her father was a small wiry man who understood physics. In a problem like lifting a forty-foot-long tree trunk for a house's ridge beam or removing a Peugot from a flooded creek, his opinion was always listened to. If there was an argument about how best to pump water or difficult problems to do with mechanics, Paul Bees was the person to see. If he didn't know, he had three physics text books he could refer to and if they didn't know he would have a pretty fair guess. One year he had bought a second-hand electronic calculator with Sines, Cosines and Tangents on it. But the batteries had gone flat and he had made, or started to make, an abacus, but he gave it away and the beads now, ten years later, were part of a curtain in Honey Barbara's own house.

Honey Barbara's mother was not called on that day. Her expertise was in the area of healing and incantations and although, in one brief, disgraceful period, she had fallen prey to the Pentecostal Christians (it was said, jokingly, that she only rejected them because they insisted she marry Paul and stop living in sin), she espoused for the most part that peculiar hotch-potch of religion and belief and superstition which made up spiritual life in Bog Onion Road. Crystal was always called to adjudicate on such delicate matters as whether, when forming a circle to chant OM, the hands should be crossed right over left or left over right and whether the energy ran around the linked people in a clockwise or anti-clockwise direction.

From her mother Honey Barbara learnt something about healing and a little ritual, but not very much. She could, at least, stand in the middle of the circle and pick up all the energy being generated by the people and then beam it to whoever in the circle needed help or energy or love, as in the case of a bereavement. She could also take the energy and beam it to people far away, but these were hardly special skills and there wasn't a kid standing there pushing against the side of the stalled Peugot who couldn't do them too. From her mother she learned Tai Chi, massage, and from her also she inherited a strong straight body and beautiful eyes.

But from her father she learned how levers work and how bees live and how to look after them. She learned to tell what honey had been collected by taste and when to move the hives and how to do it. She also learned how to graft fruit trees, how to kill a hen, nail a nail straight, make soap, play the guitar, dig a post hole, sharpen a saw and fight a bush-fire with wet sacks.

So there was nothing in her education to prepare her for the American on the bridge and although she did not remember even talking to him on that day (she remembered only the gold teeth which she had never seen before) she was to formally marry him in two years' time, almost to the day. The marriage, as it turned out, was bigamous. In fact, a great number of things turned out differently from how they appeared and from Albert Goodman she was to learn candle-making (he set up a factory in Bog Onion Road) and the hit-and-miss art of running from the police, who were looking for him constantly. At sixteen, standing on the bridge, she had never seen a city, never been to a restaurant or stayed in a hotel; she had never been a whore; she had never been in jail or in a mental home.

All she understood was why that car, now connected by a winch to a large blood wood, was slowly inching its way out of the stream. She helped her father dry off the electrics and rode in her first new car up to their house where they all got stoned and Paul made everybody laugh by climbing under the new Peugot with a torch, lying in the warm mud, admiring the ruggedness of its construction.

They did not know then, giggling in the twilight with that damp, mildewy, warm smell that everyone lived in then, that in two years' time that Peugot would lie wrecked at the bottom of a valley and that later still Honey Barbara would strut across the bitumen with ugly high heels strapped to her beautiful feet, an expert on fear, poison and the city-life.

*

Harry Joy slunk across the bitumen and sat beside the kitchen gully trap where the air was redolent of grease and cabbage. Steam issued forth from the metal grating in front of him but did nothing to obscure his greasy ratty Californian Poppy hair which fell across his collar in little tails and left dark brush-strokes of oil on his silk shirt.

His ears stuck out. His once-proud nose had three pimples hovering just beneath the surface. His shoulders were hunched. His eyes bulged.

This greasy-looking spiv is examining his anger like a beggar who has found a jewel. Look at his cunning face, the way it darts sly looks at Jim and Jimmy, and at Honey Barbara who is flirting with them.

Honey Barbara thought she'd lost him for ever, and then she saw him sitting amongst the cabbage steam and her emotions were confused. She was so flustered she didn't know where to look and her smile, she knew, took on an idiot quality as she looked at Big Jimmy without even thinking what it meant and saying goodbye and walking across to Harry. She'd thought she loved him. She was not pleased with him. She had intended to punish him for his stupidity, but when she saw his rat-face held down with guy-rope tendons, she was too upset to punish him.

"Fuck," she hissed, "what have you been eating?"

"Christ I missed you," he said fiercely. "I fucking missed you."

"What have you done to yourself? You look revolting."

He gave a street-rat's lift of the head, a pick-pocket's nod. "Trying to sweet-talk her."

She folded her arms across her chest and squeezed all the colour from her lips. "Harry, *no one's* going to fuck you looking like that. You left my address in your room." She squatted down and looked into his eyes. "That was very uncool."

"I should have had my suit," he said. "If I'd had my suit she would have been a walkover."

"Did you hear what I said? You left *my address* in your room."

"They came in the afternoon," he sniffed. "It's not my fault."

"They only come in the morning."

"But they came in the fucking afternoon."

"What's the *matter* with you?" She stared at the wreckage of his irises. "You've been eating shit. Buckets of it."

He bent his fingers back and clicked his knuckles. "I'm angry," he said with self-satisfaction.

"Your muscles are knotted."

"It's fucking fantastic," he said, "it's wonderful."

"And your hair stinks."

"I have erotic dreams about you," he said, "all the time. I miss you. I dream about honey and brown bread and fucking. Where have you been?"

"Here," she said. "Where else? Because you left my address I had to get rid of the money."

"Why?"

"Don't *you* start."

"You've been here all the bloody time?"

"I thought they'd come and bust me for the money. I burnt it. I started to burn it and fucking Damian called the fucking cops." Her voice rose involuntarily and Jim and Jimmy, squatting on the other side of the yard, looked up and grinned. "And they bloody did an involuntary admission on me, for burning money."

Harry felt his penis grow hard and fill with blood.

"I want to fuck you, Honey Barbara. Come and fuck with me." He wanted to kiss her nipples and eat her pussy and fuck like they had in those paradise days in the Hilton Hotel.

"I thought you wanted to fuck Dalton."

"Only so I could get out."

"Whose brilliant idea was that?" She was grinning.

"Nurse."

"Nurse is crazy."

Harry shrugged.

"If she liked you, she would have kept you, stupid. The only way to get out here is money. M-o-n-e-y."

"Come and fuck with me, Honey Barbara."

"If you pay for me to get out, I'll fuck you for three years," and she grinned a wide wonderful grin that even Harry, caught in the confusing cross-currents of anger and erotic need, could not help but echo.

"Miss Harrison," Jimmy called across the bitumen.

"The bastards," she hissed, "they don't waste any time."

"Time for your bath, Miss Harrison."

"I'm coming," she called and then in a whisper: "That'll be the day."

"Honey Barbara, I love you."

She looked at him, stunned. "I love you too," she said, her eyes brimming with tears, "and you've gone and made yourself look like a creep."

"I'm not a creep."

"Miss Harrison."

"I've got to go. I'll see you tomorrow night. I'll come and get you."

"O.K.," Harry said and when he saw her walk across the bitumen towards C Block and saw Jimmy saunter after her he felt jealousy, pure, undiluted, come to fuel his anger.

Later that afternoon a delegation of Christian Scientists passed Harry and Nurse in the gardens. They were not in time for the early part of the conversation in which the power of m-o-n-e-y was compared with that of sweety-talking. They arrived just in time for the end.

"I'm not a creep," the ratty-looking man with the moustache was saying to the one with the bulbous nose and long grey hair. "On that point, she is incorrect."

"But," the man with the bulbous nose said, "you are creep-like."

It was at that point, they thought, that the fight started.

Money.

Plus anger.

Equals success.

When you knew, it was easy, and Harry Joy did not waste a second of valuable time putting it into practice. He had bathed his cuts, washed his hair, and by the time the Christian Scientists had reached Ward L he was sitting opposite Mrs Dalton once again.

He shook her hand and looked her in the eye. No threats of Therapy. No tut-tuts about violence. It was settled. The amount was fixed. The source of the money arranged. Mrs Dalton even complimented him on his business acumen. She had no interest in the cut above his eye.

He had dirty trousers and a silk shirt spotted with hair oil but as he emerged from Mrs Dalton's office, a connoisseur might have noticed a certain jauntiness in his pick-pocket's walk, and if he'd had a coin in his pocket he would have flicked it in the air and caught it with a snap.

Gene Kelly would have danced it, all the way across the bitumen and out along the concrete path.

A creep?

No sir!

Creep-like?

Not nearly.

His hair was clean; it positively flopped up and down as he

walked. He was not a lot like the Harry Joy who had come here. He had a cut above his eye, pimples on his nose, sore ribs from Nurse's knuckles. He was older, wiser. He had it worked out. He knew the game. And now he was going to be released, he was going to have a fuck, he was in love.

Honey Barbara traded certain favours to get a deserted staff flat from Jim and Jimmy, and other favours to buy candles, oil, bread, fruit, cheese, incense. While she waited for him she cleaned herself, cleaned her mind of their grunting red faces, washed out their simpering smiles, her stoned pretences, their moans, their cruelties, their fantasies, disfunctions, bulging eyes, the poisons exuding from their skins.

She scrubbed her skin with a hard brush and then did breathing exercises.

When it was dark she lit the candles to make a circle. Later when he arrived, he would want to know how she knew it was a magic circle, how it worked, why it was there. She wouldn't answer. She knew. She had always known how to make a magic circle.

He came into the room and brought a chill with him. It was like a cloak of cold gas. He was not a devil. He was the victim of a devil. She had met a warlock once, in the city, with a coven of seven women who served him. The warlock was as calm and relaxed as possible. He had great power. Under his power another visitor, a young man, babbled sexual fantasies and was humiliated.

"There is a devil in you," she said.

He asked too many questions and meant none of them seriously. He wanted to touch her. She didn't know the answers and it didn't matter anyway. Was it a Christian devil? Devils were devils. They did not belong to anyone, not Christ, not the Buddha – they were devils, malevolent spirits. They existed everywhere. Devils, goblins, evil forces. People say there is no evil, but they are wrong. Honey Barbara had seen the maggots in the heads of decapitated pigs, sheep, a horse once, animals killed for the sole purpose of an evil ritual. On the spot you could feel the evil. It was not the sound (the buzzing flies), not the smell, but a damp, dark feeling in the middle of a sunny clearing and the horse she was riding (Sally Coe's George) felt it as much as she did. It was not just death. Death is everywhere. There was a ghost down in the rain forest where an old man had lived alone and it was a good ghost, nothing cold there at all.

He thought he was in Hell and he had gone looking for the devil.

He had sired the devil and given birth to him and now the devil was in his guts like a parasite.

First he had to be washed. He did not understand. He tried to kiss her. She kept him away by force of will. Tonight, she had the power of incantation and knew she could heal him. She scrubbed his back hard and talked to him. She soaped him. She removed the smells from him. She was not known to be a healer.

But tonight she had a golden ball of light at the very centre of her being. She could heal.

She wasn't stoned. She was Honey Barbara, pantheist, healer, whore.

When a devil has your body he knots it, makes ropes, pulls it together, ties it up, braids it, circles you, makes you strangle yourself with your own neck muscles, cut yourself with your own tissues, burst your own organs apart.

The muscles are the devil's ropes. The Christians don't know that, but it's true.

She made him lie on the mattress on the floor in the middle of the circle of candles.

Rain was falling on the roof, ever so gently. She warmed coconut oil. He lay on his stomach on his erection. When she returned with the oil he tried to kiss her but she pushed him away. Not yet. He was grasping and his eyes still showed a dulled, ash-covered sort of anger, like the snakes you find, still alive, in the forest after fire.

Honey Barbara scented the coconut oil with a few drops of lemon

She wished she had real words for a ritual, but she had only her hands. She sat beside him, both of them naked, and rubbed some warm oil into his back. Then she set to rattle-out the devil. She put the palm of her hand on his spine and hammered up and down. She knuckle rapped, bang, bang, bang, along his spine, and then she used the edges of her hands to hack up and down. A drum-roll. She broke up the words that came from his mouth and let them float away.

She pressed into the skin of his back with thumb and forefinger and gently squeezed the flesh together. Then released it. A hundred small pinches in a light pattern over his back and the back of his legs.

When she turned him over he looked a little better.

She fast-stroked his knees, drained his thighs, her lips pressed determinedly together and Harry Joy exuded, like one giving up evil spirits, a gentle sigh.

She stretched his neck, and lifted his head. A beatific smile came over his face.

She lifted his arms and felt them — loose muscles.

She circled his nipple with her tongue. She rolled him over and ran that pink wet tongue along his spine, down the skin and bit him, gently, on the back of his knee. She brushed his back with her small firm breasts.

And then, kissed him.

And then, in one smooth acrobatic motion that seemed to take ten slow, oiled, minutes to achieve, like two snakes entwining, she took his penis into her and smiled as he shut his eyes and gasped softly. She nestled her lips into his ear as he entered her (lips into a shell, lips into a rose), and as the slow long strokes began she talked her spell.

The rain was on the roof.

She told him it was another roof, not this roof, Harry, my roof at home, the rain is much louder, really loud, you're with me, and there is plenty of dry wood and you can hear the creek, Harry, and the goats are in their shed and they're very quiet and the big tallow woods up the hill are bending in the wind and if you have your arms around them you can feel their power, and even the old carpet snake has stopped hunting for hen eggs, Harry I love you, and you're really happy.

"I love you," she moaned, "I don't know why I love you but when I take you home they'll think I'm crazy. Will you come home with me?"

"Yes," he said, "Oh yes, yes, yes."

The words came in waves ("And be my lover, Harry") like rain ("Yes, yes, yes") and he was where she said he was, far away, in a tin-roofed hut with candles flickering in their safe magic circle and up the hill the tallow woods bent in the southerly wind and the water ran down to the creek which would show itself a clay yellow tomorrow and the hens and the goats and perhaps even the carpet snake lay still and in the morning the trees would glisten clean in the morning sun and the steam would rise off Bog Onion Road.

For the rest of his life he would remember the night when Honey Barbara drove out his devil. Then he thought it was gone for good and she was the rain on the roof, the trees he had never seen, the river he had never tasted.

Later, washed by candle light, she said, "Now we can drink wine."

They sat on the mattress. She put on the white silk gown she had bought in the Op Shop. It was embroidered with two large golden flowers and one small bee. She had bought it because of the bee, which was executed in the most faithful detail.

They sniffed their Cheval Blanc and entwined their legs together.

"Will you really come home with me when we get out?"

"Of course," he said.

"Why?"

"I love you. I've missed you. I've got nowhere else to go."

"When do you get the money?"

"Tomorrow."

"On your credit card?"

"She won't take credit cards. She wants cash."

"Have you got that much cash?"

"My wife's bringing it."

He felt her stiffen.

"Does that upset you?"

"No," she said, "that's fine."

But when he looked at her she was frowning.

"It's alright," he said, "really."

"What does she want?"

"Nothing."

"Did you tell her about me?"

"Yes."

"What did she say?"

"Nothing. She's bringing the money."

"And she knows about me?"

"Yes," he kissed her ear. "Yes, yes, yes."

He was shocked to see Bettina: her face was puffy, her cheeks collapsed, her eyes rimmed, her skin a bad colour. When they kissed, her lips were tight and hard. A peck, quite literally. She smelt of stale tobacco.

"Christ," she said, "you look terrible."

And it was true that he had a scab above his eyes and pimples on his nose and that there was, in his eyes, a quiet glow of anger that had not been properly extinguished by Honey Barbara's magic, and was lying there, waiting for the first little touch of wind to set it sparking again.

Yet he felt wonderful. All night long he had stayed awake, tossing and turning with the sheer excitement of his life, reliving his fight with Nurse, the rain on Honey Barbara's roof, the future on Bog Onion Road. He was a child on the day before school holidays begin.

They sat in the small sunless room in the building called "The Foyer", although it was a detached building and used for nothing but admissions.

"Well," she said.

"Well," he said.

She wore black: a jacket, skirt. She had always distrusted pretty colours although they suited her very well. In black she could look at once severe and beautiful, but today she merely looked severe and unattractive and if you'd seen her in the street you might have thought her newly widowed.

She sat on an ugly red chair and fidgeted with her hands. He sat opposite on a couch upholstered so tightly it had no inclination to receive his body.

"I don't apologize for what I did," she said, "so don't try and punish me."

He hadn't expected this tone. On the telephone she had been different.

"I wasn't trying to punish you."

She pointed a finger. "Not silently, not in words, not with distance, not any way. I won't be punished. Do you understand me?"

"Yes," he said nastily. "I understand you, Bettina. I won't punish you." He imagined, vividly, slapping her hard across the face.

"And not that either."

"Not what?"

"Not that nasty shit you got in your voice then. I don't know where you learnt it, but I won't pay money unless you stop it."

On the telephone she had been tearful and full of remorse. Now she sounded as if she'd consulted a lawyer. She was hostile, wary.

"Bettina, Bettina," the Good Bloke said and held out his hand. Her hand was damp. "Bettina, it's O.K."

Her chin wobbled uncertainly and then firmed. She took her hand back.

"I am going to do a deal."

"Sure," he said, but now it was his turn to be wary. She had said nothing about any deal on the phone.

"I want to do ads," she said. He held her chin up.

He rolled his eyes.

"I'm not joking."

"O.K.," he said, "do ads."

Advertising seemed to him completely alien. He had seen advertisements while he was in hospital and he had found it astonishing that he had once thought they were important. Now all he could think of was the rain on the roof, Bog Onion Road, Honey Barbara, wholemeal bread. He wanted to be safe. He did not care about his house, his business, his car.

"O.K.," he said again, "I agree. I accept. You do ads." He was impatient. Honey Barbara was waiting behind the kitchen with her bundle.

"And you sell them for me."

She was smiling. He stared at her with his mouth open.

"If you don't come back to the business I won't give you the money."

"You didn't say anything about this on the phone."

"I'm sorry."

"I can't. I've made a promise. It's not on."

"I'm sorry Harry. But that's the deal."

"Fuck you," he snarled. He clenched his fist and curled his lip. "Fuck you."

"You want me to leave?" She stood up.

"No, no, sit down. Bettina," the Good Bloke said, "what's got into you?"

"It was always *in* me," she said. "Always, from the beginning. I was never a sweet little wifey. I was a hard ambitious bitch."

"It's because of the girl. You're pissed off at that."

"No."

"Well what the fuck is it?" he shouted and she looked with amazement at his twisted face.

"You're good at sellings ads," she said, "and I'm good at making them."

"You've never done an ad in your life."

"You don't know what I've done," she said. "Now that's the deal. It's the only deal. And if you start going crazy again I'll get you locked up for a long time."

"Christ Almighty," he said to his wife.

"Come on, Harry." Now it was her turn to hold out a hand to him. There was a glitter of excitement in her poker player's eyes. "We'll kill them, Harry. We'll clean up."

She felt she was back at the place when their hands had first touched, ready to be washed with vodka. She was going to be a hot-shot.

She took the bundle from Honey Barbara. It was wrapped in yellow crushed velvet and tied up with a burgundy-coloured strap. She threw it on to the front passenger seat of the Jag and thus, in one casual move, eliminated any indecision about who was to sit where.

She was not unkind to the girl. She had smiled at her and shaken her hand. She had found out everything she needed to know on the phone.

"Do you love her?" she had asked.

"Yes," he had said. He did not even pause. Just: "Yes."

Something happened then, something she had been almost planning, and by now everything was O.K. and she had it all worked out, she did not think it unreasonable that Harry should have fallen in love. But there was a deal about that one, too. The deal was that it was not unreasonable for Harry to do what he had done as long as it was not unreasonable for her to have Harry (Good Bloke) committed. She was not unreasonable. She was not bad. She had thought a lot about whether she was bad or not and most of the time, sober, early in the morning, she knew she wasn't bad.

So the girl was all right. She had, at least, some style: a funny, not particularly acceptable sort of style, but it was style (California, 1968) at least and even if she *reeked* of drugs, she had *something*.

Bettina gave her eight out of ten.

Honey Barbara had never been in a Jaguar before and she was not ready for it. She didn't understand what was going on. She tried to ask Harry questions with her eyes. They sat together in the back seat and held hands. There was something strange going on. There was something she could only describe as "off".

"I've hijacked you," Bettina said to Harry and laughed into the rear-view mirror. "After all these years, I've shanghaied you."

A game was being played. Honey Barbara didn't understand it. She was simply shocked at how old and unhealthy Harry's wife was. She was laughing. Honey Barbara couldn't imagine why. She should go on a fast.

"Barbara," Bettina said, "I have finally shanghaied my husband so that I can work with him. I had to buy him back to work with me." She turned her head to smile and Barbara wondered if her thyroid might be slightly overdeveloped.

"Oh," she said. "What work?"

"To do ads."

Honey Barbara looked blankly at Harry who was chewing his moustache.

"Advertisements," he said.

Everything felt horrible. There was shit in the air.

"He never let me do ads," Bettina explained. "But while he's been in hospital I've been doing them, and now he's going to sell them for me."

"I'm sorry," Honey Barbara said, and leaned forward in her seat, "but you've lost me."

She smiled, to show she meant no harm.

"I did a deal with his highness. I do the ads. He sells them."

"That was the deal," Harry said and squeezed her hand. She could feel how guilty he was. "I'm sorry but it was the only way we could get the money."

"What was what deal?" Honey Barbara's voice was rising. She looked from one to the other. "I don't know what you're talking about. I can't even understand your language. I don't even know what your words mean."

"I'm going to work again, selling Bettina's ads to clients," Harry said mournfully.

"You said you were coming home with me."

"I can't. Not yet."

"I've kidnapped him," Bettina said. "But you can come home too. I don't want him for anything but work."

Honey Barbara could smell evil in the air. She had been around witches before, people who practised magic, black and white. She had felt wills like this before, wills you could not resist. She had lived amongst them. She had gone riding in the mornings and found the heads of pigs writhing with maggots. The poisons from the free-way flooded into the car. She felt the lead take up its place, the carbon monoxide do its work.

"You mean", she said to Harry, "you're going to stay in the city."

He would not look at her.

"That's right, isn't it? You're not coming with me. You're staying here."

"You can ...."

"Well fuck you."

She dragged the bundle from the front seat and jammed it tight on her knees. For a moment Harry thought she only wanted the bundle to cuddle. She held it tight and rested her weeping eyes in it.

He knew she was crying. He could see the wet spots on the crushed velvet when she moved her head. She held out her hand to him without looking up. She squeezed his hand. She squeezed it hard.

When the car stopped at the next light she opened the door and got out. She walked back the way they had come, against the traffic.

When the lights changed, Bettina hesitated. The cars behind tooted, first one, then all of them. She was watching Harry, to see what he wanted. But he sat there stunned, not moving, and finally she applied her foot to the accelerator, very slowly, and when she moved off he did not protest. Thank Christ, she thought, one less complication.

But after a while he said: "She was right. I broke my promise."

There was nothing to say to that. All Bettina could ask was the question that had been in her mind since she met the girl. She knew it was the wrong question even when she was half-way through it.

"Was that smell," she asked, "was it marihuana?"

"It was Sandalwood Oil," he said at last.

"I always thought that smell was marihuana."

"Well it's fucking well *not* marihuana."

She was surprised by his tone. She looked into the rear-view mirror.

"You think I'm a creep, don't you?"

"No," he said tiredly, "I don't."

"You think I'm a conniving bitch?"

"No." He wasn't even interested in the conversation any more. He wasn't interested in Bettina's projections.

Projections!

Even the way he thought belonged to Honey Barbara. He had never known the word before he met her. He had broken his promise. She had walked out the door. He was full of shit. He should have just run away, run away with her.

"Harry, I'm not a bad person."

"Bettina, I don't give a fuck if you are."

"But I'm not."

"Alright, you're not."

"We *had* to lock you up."

"Thank you." He had decided how to find Honey Barbara. She would go to the house where Damian lived. He had memorized the address. Not the street number, but the name of the street.

"Harry, will you look at my ads?"

"Yes," he said. "Yes, I will look at your ads."

"Harry, we're going to kill them."

"Good."

He wondered how bad the ads would be.

"Do you want me to go back and find . . . Barbara?"

"Thank you," he said, sitting forward, "thank you."

As she turned the car Bettina knew that no one would understand her, turning around to look for the woman her husband liked fucking. But no one ever did understand that Bettina would sacrifice *everything* for this deal. They had never understood her ambition, not her bug-eyed father, not her languid husband, not even Joel had understood what it meant to her. No one later on would understand either. They would never know what weight she had put on it. They never saw an advertisement the way she did, nor did they have her glittering visions of capitalism which she merely called by the pet name of New York.

She would rather not have the complication of Harry's girl, but it was only a detail so she did not mind looking for her either. She had decided not to be jealous and when she had decided something like that she always had the strength to stick to it. She could isolate whole areas of the brain and mentally amputate whole organs if that was what was needed to achieve what she wanted.

She had decided she did not want to fuck Harry or Joel. She had decided that she had no need to fuck anybody. She did not fuck Harry because it was now impossible, and Joel because he was too mediocre to consider, and no one else because life would become too complicated and it would only get in the way. So she had disconnected herself, and it was detectable already in the way she kissed Harry and even in the way she walked: the signs of celibacy, subtle, delicate, would show themselves to people who shook her hand or passed her in the street.

She did not mind looking for the girl. Which is not to say that she was totally free of jealousy or that she wasn't hurt by Harry's anger and irritation. But as she prowled up and down the factory-lined streets, while Harry questioned rows of workmen having sandwiches on the footpath, she was as conscientious as she could be. In the end, however, she could not stop herself from suggesting they give up and go home. It wasn't that she was frightened of finding Honey Barbara, or even that she was bored.

She just wanted to show Harry her ads.

Part Five

Drunk in Palm Avenue

The house was in disarray. Harry had always liked it neat: the grass trim, the floors polished, the magazines in their rack, but today he was pleased to see it looking different. At least there was some external sign of change. There was a mattress on the floor in the living room (Joel – he won't go home) and another upstairs folded against the wall (friend of Lucy's). There were empty tins everywhere and, on the front lawn, an ancient Cadillac with a crumpled tail fin (some nonsense Lucy's going on with: tell her to shift it). The back garden was high with weeds (had to fire the gardener) and Bettina glowed.

She was a hot-shot.

"Let me show you ads," she said. "Let me show you ads."

"Where do I sleep?" he asked, looking around the blanket-strewn living room.

"You have our old room."

"What about you?"

"Don't worry, don't worry, it'll be alright. Come on, Harry, look at my ads."

He sat down at the table, his heart heavy with thoughts of Honey Barbara, while his wife stood up near the fireplace and presented him with some forty comped-up magazine advertisements.

A comped-up ad is not a final ad. It is, technically, a rough. It is the sort of rough that is done when a client has no imagination or, more often, when the person doing the ad is too much in love with it to show it in any way that is really rough and does everything to make it appear finished, taking "rough" photography and getting colour prints, ordering headline type and sticking down body copy in the exact type face (if not the correct words), carefully cut to give the appearance of the final paragraphs. And over all of this is placed a cell overlay, so that a comp ad, framed with white, mounted on heavy board, covered with its glistening cell overlay, looks more precious to its maker than it ever will again.

But as Bettina said, presenting her work to Harry, "It's only a rough."

For a moment Harry forgot his pain. "Who did these?"

"I did. I told you."

"I mean, who did the art direction?"

"I did it all. I wrote them. I laid them out. I ordered the type."

He was silent for a long time, rubbing his moustache.

Bettina stood at the end of the table, holding an ad upright.

"You did it all?"

"Yes," she said.

"Oh Bettina," he said, "I'm sorry. I'm so sorry."

She had dreamed of this moment for years and still she was shocked to hear the pain and remorse in her husband's voice. He was like a dead man's friend speaking to the dead man's widow.

She did not need to ask him why he was sorry. It was damned right that he be sorry. But it was shocking. And embarrassing. She could not look him in the eye. She became frightened he might display weakness and weep. But it was right, he *should* weep for all those wasted years when he wouldn't listen to her.

She did not regret the years. She valued them. She valued the strength they had given her. If she had spent the years working with him she would, probably, have had her skill blunted, her perfectionism tainted with pragmatism. There were no greater teachers than the Advertising Annuals she studied, no harsher critic than herself. If she had worked with him, she would have been good. But now she was not just good: she was great.

"Don't be sorry," she said. A cold, polished consolation she gave him, a hard-starched handkerchief for his tears. And anyway, she did not want to veil his eyes with tears or remorse and blubbering about the past. She wanted nothing to come between his eyes and the crystal clarity of the images in the advertisements. There was nothing in the past to discuss, only the future.

"I'm really sorry," he said slowly.

"Don't be sorry." She lined up three cardboard-mounted ads on the mantelpiece. "Are they great ads or are they great ads?"

She arranged them around him in a magic circle, along the couch, propped on chairs, along the skirting board. She did not intend a ritual. She was merely being practical. He stood in the middle of the circle and blew his nose.

What he saw in those advertisements, in their shimmering reflections, was the possibility of safety. With advertisements like that you could make a lot of money. You could be rich and even, in a limited way, famous. You would be undeniably Harry Joy and there would be no one to take it from you. No one was going to steal your shirts or suits or shoes. If anyone tried to give you Therapy you could give them money. The principle was so simple, it delighted him.

He did not, for an instant, forget Honey Barbara. He would find her. He would bring her here. She could be safe too. There were so many silk shirts here, so many suits.

"When do these appear?" he asked Bettina.

"They've been rejected. We can't sell them.'"

"We?"

"Joel, me," she still had the vulnerable air of the amateur. "We."

The cretins couldn't sell them. Other morons couldn't buy them. He (money plus anger equals success) would sell them. He, Harry Joy.

From nowhere, for no reason, an erection forced itself up sideways along his leg and he eased it upright, secretly smiling at Bettina. He wanted to fuck her, to celebrate their life, their power, their joys of freedom, fame, riches, safety, no Therapy, anything and everything.

"I'll sell them for you, Bettina. They're beautiful ads." He knew how to survive here. He stood up to hold her, to forgive her, to be forgiven, to congratulate her, to push his hard cock against her little stomach.

But she made it a stranger's embrace: all angles, bones and stiff hard lips.

"Thank you," she said.

Honey Barbara would have understood this ceremony: the powerful circle of advertisements surrounding him.

Had the neighbours been able to see the advertisements the way Bettina did they would have been in no way surprised. They knew that something decadent was going on in number 25 Palm Avenue and the only firm sign they had of it was this great derelict Cadillac parked in the middle of the once neat lawn. Around this Cadillac they had watched Lucy and her new boyfriend dance with wrenches and electric drills, but they did not see that as the problem, more as a symbol.

It was a straight-laced suburb where people brought home alcohol in special little cases. And only the clink of two bottles as they went through their front gates gave them away. The children, what few there were, all had clean nails and in many houses they still said grace.

Perhaps if they had stumbled into number 25 on this night at half-past six and found the stove unlit, the fireplace full of cold ashes and only two lights turned on in this big empty room where Harry and Bettina (madman and wife) stared at these cellophane covered mock-ups of advertisements, they might have *guessed* at their black magical powers, but they would not have seen. Few people in the world could see, perhaps fifty in England, eighty in America. Most of the people who made advertisements for a living could not see. Even Harry could not see what Bettina saw: the combination of all the complexities of a product, a market, competing forces, the proposition, the image, this writhing, fluxing, struggling collection of worms all finally stilled, distilled and expressed in its most perfect form, which, to Bettina's taste, was in one big picture and one single line of type running underneath it.

But the neighbours could not see this witchcraft, nor could they ever understand what these advertisements meant to Bettina who sought, as the apotheosis of her endeavours, something as unbearably perfect as the English Benson and Hedges advertisements, which had, against all possibility of government regulation, produced a totally new language with no words, only pictures.

As English society had broken slowly apart it had produced these wonderful flowers which grew amongst the rubble. But Bettina had never seen the rubble, merely these flowers, as exotic as anything stolen from a landscape by Rousseau.

Bettina had known how to see advertisements since she was Billy McPhee's daughter living in her vibrating little room above the air compressor, which switched itself on and off throughout the long hot afternoons. And she had known then that one day she would be a hot-shot and this afternoon, at half-past six, she could not get the smile off her face. Her eyes crinkled and her large mouth could not keep in its place. Even Joel's arrival could not take the shine off her happiness. He, poor man, could not see advertisements, and failure had done bad things to him. She felt sorry for him. It was her fault, her bad judgement, that had brought him unstuck. She had given him a chance too big for him. Bettina was amazed at what fragile props held up some personalities, tiny twigs, a frail hope, an almost possible conceit, not enough, you would think, to hold the whole structure together until you pulled it out and you not only snapped the twig, you brought everything down around your ears.

"Harry."

"Joel."

She watched them for animosity. She saw the glint in Harry's eye, a slight squint almost. She was not to know that when he squeezed Joel's hand he did it with a punishing viciousness, so she did not understand the red "O" of surprise Joel formed with his fleshy lips.

"You look well, Harry."

"You too."

"Hospital doesn't seem to have hurt you."

"Done me good."

"You're feeling better?"

"Yes, much."

"That's good."

But in the middle of this awkward exchange Harry noticed Joel's damaged suit. He had always admired the effort Joel put into his suits. Joel had an excellent tailor and he followed the most conservative lines and used only the best material. His suits were like his business card and people who did not really trust him still, somehow, could let themselves trust him because of his suits. For a man blessed with no natural taste, his suits were a triumph.

Harry had already stooped down. "What in Christ's name have you done to your suit?" The burnt fabric crumpled in his inquisitive fingers. It was pure wool and still it had burnt, right up one trouser leg, one arm, and half across one breast. It was a dark material, or he would have noticed immediately.

"It's nothing, nothing." Joel shook his head. "Come on, stand up. Tell me your news." And he walked away and drew up a chair at the table, shifting one of Bettina's ads to make room.

Bettina winced. She winced for shame, not at Joel, but at herself. She knew about this burn. She did not know its details, but she knew. It was as if she'd been left to look after someone's cat and let it be run over or savaged by rats. She had not acquitted herself well with Joel.

"What happened, snooky?" she asked softly.

Harry heard the word and saw how Joel liked Bettina. He looked out of his tiny eyes as if he adored her. His fleshy face lit up when he talked to her. "Ah," he said gruffly, "it was nothing." It was obviously "something" and Harry against his will, coaxed the story from him. He was worried that it would make Joel appear in too good a light.

Harry moved another ad and sat down opposite him and Bettina, equally reluctant, did the same.

"Well," Joel said, lighting a cigarette, moving an ashtray close to him, offering Harry a cigarette, closing the packet and standing it neatly beside the ashtray. "I was just crossing the road near the office, Harry. (Really it's nothing, don't worry) and this little kid, must have been about three, came running out of that big brown block of flats and an old man — you often see him there sweeping the footpath — well not so old, a bit older than you, came out and this woman . . ."

He stopped to draw on his cigarette and Harry noticed Bettina shift uncomfortably in her chair. She caught his eye. He didn't know why. He looked back at Joel.

". . . had one of those plastic buckets and she threw the bucket full of . . . I thought it was water but it wasn't . . . over the little kid. Ask me why?"

He was staring at Harry challengingly.

"Why?"

"I don't *know* why," Joel said. "That's the terrible thing, but she did, and the old man starts yelling out in Greek. He must have been saying, it's petrol, it's petrol. He dashed over to pick the kid up and you see, he'd forgotten. He had . . ."

Joel held up the cigarette.

Harry hit his hand down on the table. "No."

"Yes. Cigarette. In his mouth. They both went up."

"Shit."

"Burst into flames."

Harry shook his head and squeezed his eyes shut to eliminate the vision.

"But it's alright," Joel said, "because I threw myself on top of them and put out the flames."

There was a silence. Harry stared at his partner.

He heard Bettina's voice say: "Joel, that's bullshit."

He saw Joel look down at the table.

He looked at Bettina who was now staring at Joel.

"Joel?" she said.

"Alright," he said, "it's bullshit. You don't have to say it's bullshit. I know it's bullshit, but Harry didn't know it was bullshit."

Harry got up to have another look at the suit. It was really burnt. This beautiful English pure wool was burnt. Behind the burnt wool he could see Joel's red flesh.

"You've burnt yourself," he said.

"What the fuck. Who cares?" Joel said.

Heard steps, running and suddenly he was being hugged.

"Daddy." It was Lucy, clinging to him, apologizing for not having visited him. She smelt like her grandfather, the late Billy McPhee. "Daddy, welcome home."

Joel was taking off his burnt suit and dropping it on the floor. He looked tired and dejected, an artist scraping down a failed canvas.

"Get out," Bettina yelled at Lucy, "Get out. I can't stand that damn petrol smell."

"This is my father," Lucy said to a young man with broken teeth and a wizened face, wearing greasy overalls. "Kenneth McLaren, this is my father Harry."

"Mr Joy," said Ken.

"Out," said Bettina, gathering up her precious advertisements and removing them from this contamination. "Outside."

Joel sat on his mattress in his underpants and rubbed antiseptic cream on his burns. It was getting cold. He gave his suit to Lucy.

"Use it for rags," he said. "It's no good any more."

"Thanks, Joel," Lucy said.

"You bring that suit back here." Bettina dropped a pile of comped-up ads on the floor and ran across the room to grab the dark woollen bundle from her daughter's greasy hands. She stood in the middle of the room smoothing the suit out against her body. She lay the trousers carefully across the back of one chair and hung the coat on another.

She walked across to Joel and sat down beside him on his mattress. "Now," she said, "let's see what you've done with yourself."

Harry didn't know what to feel. It was like the aftermath of a war: everything shattered but people going about their lives with a certain optimism. He went up to his room and found his suits and shirts. He changed without showering and came down to find his wife sitting on the living room floor rubbing analgesic cream into the naked, shining, battery-fed body of his partner, well – not quite naked – his joke underpants were down around his pudgy hips and his burnt body gleamed in oil.

Harry stroked the collar of his silk shirt and marvelled at the richness and variety of life in Hell.

Bettina, as she explained to Harry later, no longer found Joel sexually desirable. (Harry didn't listen. He found it painful that she ever had.)

Joel was no longer admirable and it was admiration (she called it love) that made her want to fuck people. It was a cold brilliant sort of emotion, this admiration, and was backed up, invariably, with the unpalatable tastes of self-doubt and inferiority. She had worried all her life that she was cold. She had never felt for her children what a mother is meant to feel. She had despaired at this coldness and criticized herself for it while at the same time she hated (literally) mothers who displayed their maternal qualities in too obvious a way.

But now, although she would never have used the word, and would have denied it vigorously if anyone had dared to suggest it, she loved Joel. She had not begun to love him until he had begun to fail and then, she believed, he became automatically sexually uninteresting to her. But it was only after he crashed, after he began to do these stupid, dangerous bizarre things to gain her respect, that she actually began to love him.

He was her responsibility. She had pushed him too far and now she would have to look after him.

She rubbed the analgesic cream across his back. The burns were not too bad.

"Ah, Betty, you think I'm a schmuck."

"You try too hard, baby." Physically they were alike, stocky people from peasant stock.

"You didn't have to say it was bullshit."

"No, no, I know. I'm sorry."

"Fucking suit. My best suit too."

"Never mind, never mind."

Harry watched this and felt jealous. It was the sort of jealousy a man can feel towards a child at a woman's breast. Sitting at the table by himself he was able to see the emotion clearly and know exactly what it was.

When David Joy arrived home with his two Big Macs at eight o'clock, his father was sitting by the fire. The sight of Joel's blubbery body stretched out at Harry's feet was as disgusting and terrible a reproach as any he had encountered in his nightmares. It was David's fault that Palm Avenue was like this. It was because he had paid money to have his father committed.

Yet he was struck with contradictory desires about his crime, for although he was remorseful he was also proud. He wanted to confess, be forgiven, chastized, admired, understood, sympathized with, everything at once. He wanted his father to see how grown-up he was but also to forgive him as only a father could.

He was hurt, immediately, by Harry's lack of effusion in the greeting.

"Which one is mine?" his father asked, leading the way to the kitchen table.

"Both," he said, although he had bought one for himself. He was starving.

David imagined his father looked at him suspiciously. Certainly he was opening the Big Mac box distrustfully. But now he lifted the hamburger to his mouth, bit it, and, "Oh, Christ!" spat half-masticated food all over the table.

He was madder than when he went. There he was, his mouth half-full of old food, trying to smile at him.

"It's poisoned. I nearly ate it." Harry tried to explain. How could he tell his son that he had thought of Honey Barbara?

"I didn't."

"It's not your fault."

"I didn't poison it," David yelled, that dark hurt look all over his face.

"I didn't say you did," Harry yelled back and started laughing.

"But I wouldn't do it to you," David screamed. "Don't you understand? I'll never do anything to you again. I'm sorry. I'm sorry."

Joel shut the door.

It was after the war. It was a strange time. People's nerves were all shot to pieces. Harry stood and embraced his son who wept ecstatically on his chest.

"Oh God," he said. This was not an Actor. This was his son, in pain. He could feel the pain as keenly as any he had felt in Mrs Dalton's hospital. And he knew something like jagged glass was slicing at his son and hurting him, not some little boy's cut finger, but some great gaping wound. "I didn't think you were poisoning me," he said.

"I didn't. I didn't."

"No, no, I know."

Everywhere the world seemed full of wounded.

"I had you put away. I had you committed. It was me."

Harry heard him and believed him but it no longer mattered. It was the nature of Hell that Captives were made to hurt each other.

"It doesn't matter," he said, "I don't mind. I forgive you."

Somehow the forgiveness seemed too off-hand to David who had yearned for something stronger. His father underestimated him. He would not imagine, for a second, that his son had spent five thousand dollars of his own money, had taken risks, been more businesslike than Joel. His father did not know him.

"So tell me", Harry was saying, "about this job."

"You're disappointed?"

"No, not at all." And it was true. He was even pleased that his son would not be a doctor. Doctors in Hell did evil work. He was pleased that his son wore a well-cut suit and that he could choose a maroon tie like that and wear it with a soft blue shirt. He liked the way his son held a wine glass and when he poured wine, as he did now, that he turned the bottle in his hand as he finished pouring so that it would not drip. His son was emotional, too full of pain, but that was probably a good thing too and it seemed more honourable to be like Nurse than to be like Mrs Dalton.

David did not know how to tell him about the job. Looked at in one way the job did not sound very splendid at all. The idea of a Sales Representative for the Hughes Poker Machine Company did not exactly glitter in anybody's mind. It involved driving around the suburbs in a car and learning how to drink and not get drunk. But it was also a foot in the door of the da Silva organization. They had marked him, they hinted, for something big and it did not occur to him that what they had in mind was training for management in the organization's legitimate businesses. It still hadn't.

It was the bigness he wanted to talk about, the ill-defined promised land of his future where he would not be afraid any more and where there was South America, New York, wide rivers, a future as dazzling and complicated as a Persian rug. And in its magical pattern there was now a new element, a new glow, a cast of a golden colour which suffused everything, the source of which was a character in a book he had read half of and would never finish. He was not interested in what happened to Jay Gatsby. He was only interested that Jay Gatsby should exist. And in all his dreams about the future he had added this element of Gatsby with his big house, alone, looking across the bay at night to the island of East

Egg and the woman he loved. Yet in his dream, in its pinkest most sensitive corner, there was not a woman across the water at all: it was Harry Joy.

"So tell me," Harry said again, "tell me about this great job. Do they give you a car?"

To his eternal chagrin David told his father all about the car. He told him all the boring, predictable everyday details about the car. He even described the damned upholstery. And he talked about his salary, his boss, the machines he sold.

"Wonderful," Harry said, "wonderful."

It was difficult not to be cross with him for being so excited at all the most banal things. This was nothing to be proud of. This was a car. A fucking Ford. These were things to be disgusted with, reasons to throw him out of the house. These were not reasons to be sitting there smiling and nodding.

This was dross, dreck, brown paper camouflage.

Yet they talked about this damned job for two hours, through two bottles of wine and now, as the second bottle finished, David teetered on the brink of telling him.

"Well," Harry said. He yawned and leaned back.

It was not yet too late.

"I think I'll go to bed."

"O.K.," David said clenching his fist, "Goodnight."

And sat alone with all those old dreams of Vance Joy's which have become such tawdry baubles that you might expect him, shortly, to abandon them completely. Yet he isn't going to give them up (these eyeless teddy bears) and they will finally lead him on to the Espreso de Sol and up to Bogotá, to a job as a waiter, to a wife called Anna, to his wife's brother's red Dodge truck, to the unlikely occupation of truck driver, which he will accept disdainfully, acting out his disdain by driving the muddy mountain roads from Bogotá dressed in an immaculate white suit.

Unknown to himself he became the romantic figure he had always wished to be, someone to swagger through one of Vance's stories with a cane beneath his arm.

On the road of crippled trucks and miserable towns, his perfect cleanliness seemed almost magical.

"What will happen," they asked, "if he has a flat tyre?"

"He never has one."

There were no saints' medallions inside his truck. They looked to see. Perhaps he was a Communist. One day in the town of Armenia two nuns, coming upon him suddenly, crossed themselves.

Then one night in the wet time of the year the long chain of stories he had so innocently begun brought a visitor to his door. His wife, now six months pregnant, was in bed asleep and he received the visitor alone.

The man at his door was short and dark, a man with such a dark beard shadow that David felt immediately sorry for him and, had he been receiving him in a restaurant, would have put him in a back table with his back to the window. The man had a long droll-looking jaw, small wire-framed spectacles on an almost Semitic nose, and very short hair. He had broad shoulders but he shrugged them humbly.

He would not conduct his business in the doorway and forced, with a curious mixture of will and humility, David to invite him in. They sat in the kitchen. He refused a beer but accepted a coffee, holding his square hands around the tiny cup and speaking with a thin voice.

David Joy found himself being asked to smuggle arms into the mountains. It was not put so clearly. It was circled around, prodded at, kicked, and in the end there was no doubt that the bulky wrapped unnamed thing their conversation kept brushing against was that.

He began by adopting a superior air with the man but could not, for some reason, maintain it. Even the shrugging humility of his visitor seemed, at the same time, arrogant.

Was he a spy? A provocateur.

"Why do you come to me?"

"That is your truck downstairs? You wear a white suit?"

"Yes."

"We have no money," the man said it softly as if this might be a compliment, an inducement, an advantage. It was ludicrous.

"I'm a businessman. I only work for money."

The man smiled and shrugged. "We have no money."

"I work for money."

He dipped his head. "We have none." And smiled.

"You wish me to work for nothing?"

"We did not think you would let us down."

"But who am I? Why do you ask me?"

"You are *el Hombre en el Traje Blanco* — the man with the white suit."

"I am a businessman," he said hopelessly. "I am only interested in money."

"But we have no money, you see," the man said.

"But it is dangerous. It is illegal."

"Of course," he smiled as if he were making fun of himself, ducking his head and raising his eyebrows.

"You have no money?"

"We have no money."

"You could be a spy. A policeman."

"If I were a spy I would have offered you money. A spy would not expect a man to do it for nothing. They don't understand such things."

"And I do?"

"Yes. Of course."

"But I am a businessman," he said for the last time.

When he had accepted the offer the man left and he realized he did not even know his name.

That night he could not sleep. He tossed and turned and Anna became bad tempered and swore at him in a language he did not understand. He went and stood in the living room and looked at himself in the mirror. He was aware of the striking contrast between his appearance and the reality of his life. He looked dashing, interesting, even exotic, yet faced with local gangsters he had lacked the courage for anything more dangerous than being a waiter. There had been no rivers to cross and when the lightning played around the hills it brought only dampness and a nasty fungus which grew down the long back of his beautiful wife.

Now he was thrilled to think that someone, through a misunderstanding, might think him brave.

Standing in Bogotá, on the edge of his story, he composed one more letter to Harry Joy.

Dear Daddy, he began.

It was not the walk of city women, who, even when released from the hobble of high heels, still walk with invisible silk sashes tied between their ankles.

Honey Barbara strode.

She strode like women who can cross a creek by walking along a fallen log fifteen feet above the water, and do it without hesitation or any apparent thought. She walked as one accustomed to dirt tracks. The whistles of panel beaters did not affect her. She slung her saffron yellow bundle over her shoulder and strode down the street and they, seeing her, thought her haughty: her back straight, her head thrown back, her arms swinging. But she was not being haughty, she was merely walking.

Walking was the best thing when you hurt. It was better than dope and better than eating. It was better than fucking and better than sleeping. You just emptied your mind of everything so that the inside of your head was like an empty terracotta jar and no matter what happened you kept it empty. You guarded its emptiness with your eyes and your ears and you did not even stop to consider where you were going. In this way you always arrived at the right place.

She strode through streets filled with used-car yards, and others full of warehouses. She walked through department stores, a fish market, and along the wide rich streets at the bottom of Sugar Loaf. It was a fast walk, possibly six miles an hour. It brought her up those early gravel streets at the back of Sugar Loaf, where the rich houses end and where the crash of a famous developer left half-finished houses and unsewered blocks full of tall thistles and strangled with morning glory.

Her feet welcomed the gravel. The gravel was like rain on the roof and she felt it and tried not to think about it, but she knew she was going up Sugar Loaf. She had known from the beginning. But she had tried not to know. She pitted her muscles against the mountain and felt them ache. Her feet were soft. Not soft by comparison with the panel beaters, for instance, but soft in comparison with their normal condition. The great pads of callus on her feet had gone white and spongey during her stay in the city. They were big feet, but perfectly proportioned, with high arches and curved heels. They hurt a little already, but it was not real hurt, not the hurt she really felt.

She carried her bundle slung across her back. Her bundle contained a blanket, an alarm clock, a pair of baggies, two T shirts, an old sweater and a separate brown paper parcel full of her whoring clothes.

She did not need anything else. She did not need to think where she would go, where she would sleep. She rose up above the coastal plain perhaps six inches in every step, a little higher, above the mangroves, the big brown ill-used river, the sapphire bay, and walked the unnamed streets on Sugar Loaf where the unemployed, hippies, junkies, and even the respectable poor lived amongst the smell of unsewered drains, half-buried shit, uncollected garbage, jasmine, honeysuckle and frangipani. Bananas grew untended and made their own jungles. Green plastic garbage bags lay in the grass with their guts spilling out. Morning glory tangled itself over rusting cars.

Once there had been beds here to welcome her, but today the humpies were either gone or empty or filled with strangers who eyed her with suspicion. She had not been looking for them anyway. She had been looking for no one. She was merely walking, her head as empty of desire as a terracotta bowl.

She strode through a paddock of tall grass, crossed the face of a small cliff wet with seepage, found a new road and began to walk downhill. She was breathing regularly but her eyes were slits.

Down at the place where the bitumen began, she sat. She examined her feet: they were cut, but not badly. Her legs ached, but she welcomed that. The real pain was elsewhere and she didn't know what to do with it.

She walked three miles to the Zen Inn and ordered an alfalfa tea. And although she should have felt soothed and at home in the Zen Inn, she did not. She was edgy and irritable when she should have been relaxed. They were her people. They had clear skins and good eyes. If she wanted a fuck or just some warmth this was the place to be, yet it was nothing. She wanted to groan out loud. She could not even talk about her problem. How could anyone understand that she loved an advertising man named Harry Joy.

She bought some baked veggies and ate them slowly. She willed herself to taste them, to be thankful she was not eating shit anymore.

When she left the Zen Inn she would have denied that she had made up her mind, but not that her mind had made up itself. She simply denied all knowledge of what her mind was up to. She wished merely to let it sort itself out and she would follow.

In the city square she found a phone box. There was only one Joy in Palm Avenue and she memorized the street number.

She crossed the square as it struck eleven. She stood in front of the huge glass-fronted street directory and turned the nobs casually at first, as if merely looking at what streets the city had to offer. Finally she found Palm Avenue: another three miles.

She did not stride so rapidly because this was a different sort of walking now. There was a drag in her steps which was produced not by tiredness but by knowing her destination and being frightened of it.

Cars cruised beside her and tooted their horns as if wishing to escort her to Bettina's side.

She did not approve of grass. It was a poison like any other poison, but she could not have been a whore without grass and she could not get her legs to Palm Avenue without grass. She dragged in rough lungfuls of the stuff, judging it to be very strong indeed. In the middle of the park her joint spluttered and glowed like a beacon.

The streets she then walked along reminded her of a row of mausoleums she had once seen in a city cemetery, row after row of structures devoid of life. Even the trees seemed heavy and dull and she felt, as her bare feet fell softly on the concrete footpath, as if she was the only one alive.

She turned the corner of Palm Avenue with a heavy heart. She had no plan. Dark house after dark house was bathed in the negative radiation of fluorescent street lights. She did not need Wilhelm Reich to tell her about Deadly Orgone Radiation. He might be the master of the theory but she knew exactly what it really *felt* like. She nearly panicked and turned. She should not have been there. Her heart beat fast. She should have been heading back north, walking dirt tracks, have hard hands and clear eyes and be out at five every morning smelling the high flowers in the towering eucalypts.

She stood in front of 25 Palm Avenue. There was no sign of life. But the Jaguar was in the driveway and she knew it was the car she had driven in and that Harry Joy was inside sleeping.

She saw the Cadillac on the front lawn. It was, she reflected, more her style. She crawled into the back seat and there, surrounded by the dangerous perfumes of oil and petrol, she made a bed with her single blanket. She put her whore's clothes under her head and set her alarm clock for four a.m. Then she lay there, looking at the place where the night was blackest.

He was shocked to recognize the sour stale smell of the bed he had once shared with Bettina. He had lived with that smell and never thought about it. Its smell must have once been comforting to him and he must have wrapped himself in it happily. But tonight it was unpleasant.

He could not find a place to lie and his head filled with won't-stay-still thoughts: Joel's blubbery body, his burnt suit, Bettina's ads, his son's tears, Lucy's unknown boyfriend and — sharp, so painful he sucked in his breath — Honey Barbara getting out the door of the Jaguar.

His thoughts were a merry-go-round. He tried to be definite, to pin down his problems and ideas and dissect them coldly, to adopt a plan, have an aim against which he could measure himself.

But he had never, it seemed, believed in anything but his comfort and even these silk shirts hanging in the cupboard were enough to seduce him away from Honey Barbara.

He could not sleep. He could not escape himself. He saw himself as worthless, so loathsome, shallow, hollow, as to be worth nothing. The idea of suicide whirled past him but he did not even look at it. Those unseen gods would simply send him back in for another round.

He rolled over, swaddling himself in his sheet. In the room across the hall he could hear his son talking in his sleep. When he was younger the boy had been troubled by nightmares. They sometimes found him sleepwalking, talking as he went. "I didn't do it," he told them. "I didn't do it." They had never asked him what it was.

He knew how the deal had looked to Honey Barbara. And now it looked the same to him. He could not claim ignorance. He had seen the cancer map. It glowed malignantly in his mind's eye. He had chosen not to see the subjects of Bettina's ads, but how could he ignore them? He had made the agreement with Bettina, he told himself, to get Honey Barbara out of hospital. But then why hadn't he gone to consult her about the deal when it was made?

What would he do? Was a promise worth anything? Hadn't he promised Bettina? And didn't he, anyway, owe her something for having stopped her in another life when doing ads was an innocent thing?

He went to sleep and dreamed about green ants.

Whe he woke it was ten minutes to three. He knew he would have to find Honey Barbara and leave the city. He could not live here.

The rooster crowing in the dim dark four o'clock did not sound like a real rooster but something more sinister, some mutilated thing with the top half of its call sliced off, an electric warning device which wouldn't start.

If he stayed in Palm Avenue he could be safe. If he could not find Honey Barbara he could, at least, protect himself. He got up and went down to the kitchen where he began to do profit projections. The big round noughts began to soothe him, to give him pleasure, like the crinkling sound of tissue paper around an expensive present.

When (at four twenty) he went out on to the verandah he was thinking of the uses of wealth, no longer merely relating them to the colours of wine and the quality of crystal. He had never wanted to be rich before. He had never quite seen the need. But now he thought of high brick walls they built around themselves, the grates, grills, jagged glass, Alsatian dogs, alarms, patrols and so on. Those were things that might be necessary.

Lucy's car sat beneath him, its great rococo shape a reminder of a more ignorant and optimistic time. He was curious about the car and walked down the steps wishing to touch it. He had hardly talked to Lucy. He did not know what she wanted or why she wanted it. He did not know how she was being hurt, who she was hurting. All he had seen was that she was carrying a dream and the car was part of it.

They were all carrying a dream except him. He had no dream. He wanted only safety. Why was he so empty? Why should everyone else have these passions and he have none? He stroked the car absently.

Inside the Cadillac, Honey Barbara stirred in her watch-dog sleep. The dope had hung curtains in her mind and she was not quite sure what was happening. Someone, she knew, was walking around the car and mumbling. She could not see if it was a man or a woman. She could only see the shape, and occasionally it would move and blend with other shapes, blackness on blackness, the shapes of witches transmogrifying. She breathed in the petrol fumes and felt damp with terror.

"Curious," Harry Joy said out loud, "Very curious."

He was talking to her. He knew she was in there. He was saying – she understood him with dazzling clarity – it is curious that you are lying there and I am standing here.

He turned on his heel and she slipped out of the Cadillac and followed him into the house. She was a little more stoned than she knew.

There are times when the lips seem to sleep, to abandon their role as the signifiers of happiness, while the eyes become almost electric and not only the lips but every other organ must be subservient to them in this, their most splendid and spectacular moment.

Thus: Honey Barbara, standing in the doorway at four thirty-two a.m.

Her mouth was pale pink and sleep-soft when they kissed and all the world around them assumed an impressionistic softness and everything they looked at was coloured with dusty pastels which gave no sharp edges to forms, and even the white refrigerator they embraced beside seemed as mellow as pearl shell.

When she was an old woman with crinkled skin, Honey Barbara would still remember this moment and how the refrigerator looked and how perfectly happy she was, to hold her lover in her arms in the midst of enemy territory and how his eyes had been as soft as those of an animal, a foal, something slim and strong and gentle, looking at her with such emotion.

He could not stop stroking her. He stroked her face, her arms, her shoulders. She knew it was right to have come back because she too had made her promise.

(He was ready to tell her. He had made up his mind. He would have gone with her then at that moment, not saying goodbye to anyone. He would have walked out the door and left those advertisements where they lay, in a great pile beside Joel's bed. But it was Honey Barbara who spoke first.)

"I will stay three months," she said.

"I will cook," she said, thus protecting them further.

Harry considered it for hardly an instant. The silk shirts won.

Later Honey Barbara was to think about how innocent she had been. To imagine she could hold him against the forces around her. Surrounded by the smells of animal fat, Baygon, Silicone, Fluorozene, Rancid Butter, Stale Beer, Cigarette Smoke, Ash, and even Oil and Petrol, bombarded by fluorescent light, enveloped by aggressive red walls, she had not been daunted.

Then he took her briefly into the living room to show her the advertisements he had promised to sell. They sat in a long room where a man with battery-fed hips slept on a mattress on the floor.

"Her lover?"

"Used to."

They carried the advertisements back into the kitchen where he made her sit amongst the remains of Big Macs while he tried to explain them to her. She was shocked. She knew there was something magical about these things to him and she sensed their power. Yet she imagined herself equal to it. She was young and strong and confident. Later she would think she had also been naive.

They put the advertisements away and stayed at the table holding each other's hands, kissing, confessing their angers and their doubts or, in Harry's case, some of them.

In Honey Barbara's mind Bettina was a witch: powdered, smooth, white-skinned, dressed in black. So when she came out to the kitchen at six thirty in a pink dressing gown with puffy eyes, an olive skin, and a throaty sleep-stuck voice, Honey Barbara didn't even recognize her and only knew it was her because it had to be. She was shorter too, without her stiletto heels, and she shuffled into the kitchen and saw, immediately, that they had been looking at her advertisements. It seemed more important to her than any other fact.

"Did you like them?" she asked. Honey Barbara saw how vulnerable she would be to any criticism.

"They're very nice," she lied. Bettina was a witch, but she felt sorry for her. Her lover was fat and slept on the floor. Her husband was holding hands with another woman. It hurt her badly, it was obvious: she swallowed and looked away and went to fuss about things over the kitchen sink.

Honey Barbara followed her and embraced her. It was an awkward embrace, not just because Bettina was considerably shorter, but it was not rejected.

"I would like to do the cooking for you."

"No, no, it's not necessary." Bettina turned and started fossicking in the sink.

"I want to."

"It's not necessary. We'll cope."

Barbara looked desperately to Harry.

"It's different cooking," he said.

This disclosure, his intimate and familiar knowledge of Honey Barbara's cooking, was more hurtful to Bettina than anything else that had happened. She filled a glass with water, drank half of it and threw the other half out.

"It's healthy," he said.

"Fine," she said. "That'd be good."

"What time do you like to eat dinner?"

"Eight."

"Is there anything you don't like?"

"Nothing."

198

Bettina left and slammed the door behind her and it was Honey Barbara, abandoning all principle, who made her toast with white bread, strong instant coffee with white sugar, and took it up to her room where she sat shivering on a single bed.

When David Joy came down to breakfast he found Harry and Bettina already gone and a beautiful young woman in the kitchen. She had lined up all the plastic garbage cans and was emptying the cupboards as fast as she could. Bread, sugar, cans of beans, jars of coffee, cornflakes, white flour, were all dispatched without hesitation. Only a small unopened packet of Torula Yeast seemed to have escaped her wrath.

"I'm Barbara," the young woman said.

"David."

"I'm a friend of your father's."

He nodded darkly.

"Do you want breakfast?"

He nodded again and shyly regarded her firm arse which the morning sun revealed beneath her white cotton baggy pants.

She went to the dining room and came back with a big cloth bundle. From this she produced four little paper bags which contained unprocessed bran, wheat germ, lecithin, and raisins. She put a dessertspoonful of each in a plate, mixed them up, added milk and passed it to David Joy who was sitting on the edge of his chair.

"What's this?"

She did not take offence at his curled lip. She told him.

"Why?" he said. "I have cornflakes every morning."

"I'm cooking now," Honey Barbara said firmly. "Today I'll make you some good bread but for the moment this is all there is. So eat it. It'll make you shit properly. It'll give you roughage and vitamins to make your intestine muscles contract. It'll make your shit float, you watch." And she smiled.

David pushed his plate away in disgust. "I don't want to talk about shit," he said, "and particularly not with a *woman*."

Honey Barbara shrugged and went back to tidying up the cupboard.

"Did he meet you in hospital?"

"Sure did."

David left his bowl on the table and went upstairs, where he tried to persuade Ken and Lucy (who were meant to occupy separate beds while Bettina was in the house) to come down to the kitchen and make some kind of stand.

The woman was mad. He was scandalized by her madness, her obsession with shit, her wastefulness, her firm arse, her pubic hair. Everything about her was wild and untrammelled and he thought, passing her, that he could smell her sexual organ, and he felt weak. Madness horrified David. Yet often he felt it press upon him. He felt soft fingers touch the outside of the concrete brick walls of his bunker. He could feel mumblings, murmurings, the passage of lightning through an unseen sky.

Ordinariness pressed upon him: he invited it, needed it, embraced it. Look at this suit, so conventionally cut he might be a mere clerk. Was it a disguise, or was it the truth? Would he be too weak for the lightning? Would he be too brittle, have bones like sparrow wings? Would he simply snap?

He did not want the mad person downstairs but he could not convince them. He saw they had private jokes about him and he regretted ever having told Lucy his dreams. He was stiff and formal in his suit but had she ever told Ken that she had sucked her brother's cock and swallowed his come, or did she simply tell him that he was a clerk who wanted to be a bandit, one more pathetic Walter Mitty. Was that why they lay there like that and smiled?

Lucy and Ken were very interested in Harry's mad woman. They came downstairs the minute David left the house and they watched her throw foods into the rubbish bins as if they were poisonous substances that should not be touched, let alone eaten.

They introduced themselves and sat at the table to watch her.

"David thinks you're crazy," Lucy said. "He says you talk about shit like it was food and food like it was shit."

It was an aggressive beginning but Honey Barbara liked her. Further this occurred to her: Lucy Joy was *someone*, not someone famous or influential or even talented, but just someone. She looked like a wild plant, something bred for a purpose now going its own sweet way. Honey Barbara did not even notice that she was overweight or worry that the whites of the eyes in that dark face were a little on the yellow side.

"He thinks you can't tell the difference."

"Sorry," Honey Barbara tore her eyes away from the face, "difference between what?"

"Shit and food," Ken said. He wore a Kentucky Fried peak cap and his curling hair rushed out beneath it, swept behind two large pixie ears, one of which held a small gold earring.

They were both smiling (when Ken smiled he showed a lot of broken teeth) and Honey Barbara smiled too.

"Everyone here is crazy," Lucy said. "I'll make you herbal tea."

"You've got herbal tea? Here?"

"Been there," Lucy said, "done that."

It was a long time, six months, since Honey Barbara had been around anyone as young as Lucy and she remembered what a charge you could get from fifteen-year-olds: how fresh they seemed, and confident and strong, and also, what a pain in the arse they could be.

"Why is everyone here crazy?" Honey Barbara noted that it was Ken who made the tea (with a lumpily rolled cigarette burning beneath his equally lumpy nose). He squinted down into the packet while Lucy talked.

"Bettina's crazy because she wants to be an American; Joel is crazy because he'll do anything to get sympathy; David is crazy because he wants to be a dope dealer; and Harry must be crazy because he let the others lock him up."

Honey Barbara was charmed. She pulled up a chair. "And why are you crazy?"

Ken brought the cups to the table and put a big bag of dope beside them.

"We're crazy because we like everything." He said "everyfing". That made Honey Barbara like him more.

"We like you throwing all this stuff out," Lucy said, "and we like David being pissed off. We like everything. We like herbal tea and Coca-Cola and dope. There isn't anything we disapprove of."

Honey Barbara thought they were decadent but she liked them anyway. Not even her rather Victorian morality could censor them. What she did not know, and what they never told her, was they were on holidays. They were doing what every Party member must sometimes, in some secret corner of his or her heart, feel like doing — stopping analysing, appraising, and to hell with it all.

At this stage, however, they did not know they were on holidays. "Afterwards," Lucy said, "when the world is over, no one will know that all of this was really beautiful."

Honey Barbara closed her eyes.

"It's not heavy," Ken said.

"We are into the late twentieth century," Lucy said, "and definitely not fighting against it. Enjoy it. It's incredible. The sunsets wouldn't look so beautiful if there wasn't all this shit in the air. It refracts the light and makes better sunsets."

"That seems pretty negative to me," Honey Barbara said. "You should be trying to change it." An uncharitable observer may have noted a slight primness in Honey Barbara's mouth.

"It's too late," Lucy said.

"With herbal tea?" Ken said.

"We are the last," Lucy said. "It was always going to end. We are the first people to come to the end of time."

Ken rolled the joint. He was the one whose "Catalogue of good things about the end of the world", an ever-expanding loose-leafed opus, had set Lucy off on her Apocalyptic Holiday.

"Our Cadillac will do ten miles to the gallon," Lucy said. "Dig it."

"How do you sleep at nights?" Honey Barbara said, in no way cut by Ken's jibes about changing the world with herbal tea.

"We fuck," Lucy grinned, "until we can't do it any more."

And they all laughed and Honey Barbara, in spite of her resolution not to, shared their dope with them.

"Well," Ken said, "why are you crazy? Why do you treat food like shit?"

He was not being unkind but he tapped a serious flaw in Honey Barbara's character: she could not joke about food. She divided the world into people who ate shit and people who ate good food.

"This food is shit," she said, "and if I'm going to live here, Harry and I are going to eat good food."

"What do you think is Good?" Lucy said, leaning over her folded arms.

"If you don't know, how can I tell you?"

"No salt? No sugar? No meat? No white flour? That sort of thing?"

"Fucking right," Honey Barbara said, standing up and transferring her attention to the refrigerator.

"Sounds boring to me," Lucy said. (Ken started bundling up his dope.)

Honey Barbara emptied the fridge in five quick throws, saving only the chilled alarm clock from destruction.

"Come back at dinner time, you smart arse," she said to Lucy, "and we'll see how bored you are."

Lucy grabbed a can of Coke from the garbage can. "I'll be there," she said.

She made spinach soup with spinach and potatoes and onions

and spiced it with a little nutmeg. She baked potatoes in their jackets, pumpkin, onion, and stuffed mushrooms. She braised the cabbage with onion and apple and garlic and (eager not to lose her first engagement) threw in a little red wine she found in the cupboard. When challenged about the presence of wine later, she denied it all.

She steamed the sugar peas and planned to serve them in a big bowl.

I'll give you boring.

She made her famous apple and rhubarb crumble and sweetened it with the Rolls Royce of honeys. She said "boring" out loud, like an incantation. She cooked with love and venom in almost equal quantities, the sweetness of one managing to offset the bitterness of the other.

She walked twenty-four miles and came home and baked a loaf of heavy dark bread. She cooked it in a flower pot she stole from the garden, muttering to herself while an electric drill penetrated the steel shell of the Cadillac Eldorado in the front garden.

At half-past seven she showered and washed her hair and applied a dab of Sandalwood Oil.

Everyone had assembled in the dining room except for Joel who had gone out on some errand of his own. Ken and Lucy had washed their hands in tribute to her. They had rubbed them raw with industrial soap and taken out their Swiss Army knives and cleaned under their split nails with the smaller blade. Ken shaved his battered face and attempted to penetrate his tangled hair with a comb. He put on a white shirt and even stole one of Harry's ties, which he then had to be taught how to do up. Lucy wore a clean white boiler suit. David surprised everyone by wearing an exotic shirt and Gucci sandshoes. He poured the wine, but not before he had given his father the cork to formally approve.

Not since the family lunch (which had ended less enjoyably than it had begun — the duck caught fire and David put it out with a fire extinguisher) had they spread a cloth on the table and even Bettina, her shoes kicked off her sweating feet, a strong Scotch in her hand, seemed relaxed and happy.

David engaged his father in an earnest whispered conversation on the subject of Argentinian cowboys, something he was exceedingly well versed on, but the details of which, it appeared, he had no wish to share with anyone but Harry.

"Tell us all," Lucy said from the other side of the room.

But David ignored her and Harry, in any case, found it hard to listen. He was too concerned that everyone should like Honey Barbara, who throughout all this strode back and forth, her face serious, her back straight, her wet hair flat on her head, setting odd things to right on the table and in the kitchen refusing all offers of help, as if, Lucy whispered to Ken, they might contaminate the purity of what would be offered.

There were marigolds in little jars on the table, and a small glass bowl of water with frangipanis floating in it. The wholemeal bread sat on a big piece of tallow-wood off-cut she had stolen from a building site, and around the table, in egg cups, she had placed, as a peace offering, sea salt.

Bettina was not displeased to see Honey Barbara in the kitchen. She suggested, in a quiet moment when the girl was absent, that Harry turn bisexual and get a chauffeur as well. The joke did not go down well. She drank a solitary toast to the death of humour. She did not like the moony way Harry followed Honey Barbara with his eyes, but she sat herself where she would not have to look at him.

She liked the way the table had been set. It had, in a naive way, style.

The Scotch was Bettina's first drink of the day and she let it evaporate somewhere at the back of her throat. She felt good. She had felt good all day, a tight, hard, relentless sort of good feeling, like a well-tuned guitar string. The feeling started after she had delivered Harry to their new offices: cheap warehouse space down by the river which she and Joel had personally painted in long evenings on high ladders until her back had ached and poor Joel, sweating away beside her, had gone to work in the mornings with his hair speckled pink. She had bought the desks from army disposals for eight dollars each and they had sanded and oiled each one. They laid black Pirelli tiles on the floor and painted the walls pink and the window frames Indian Red. The lights were second-hand — creamy spheres which hung at regular intervals and even the couches were from a junk shop, re-covered with remnant fabric in an opulent cream.

It was her first business decision. She had sub-let the old premises with all their expensive old fittings and furniture for a considerable profit. The profit from the old lease would pay all the rent for this one.

And into this stylish, elegant space she introduced Harry and sat him at his swivel chair behind his army disposal desk. He complained when oil from the desk spotted his suit, but by three o'clock that afternoon he had sold his first campaign and he had something about him, a vitality, an edge, an aggressiveness she had never seen in him before.

Imagine this: a colour poster thirty inches long and eight inches deep. A photograph of a match, very large, occupies almost the entire length of the poster. Beneath it, in Franklin Gothic type, these words: *All the wood you need to burn this winter*, and beneath that, the logo: Mobil LP Gas.

All this for stores in country areas, to stick on walls for flies to shit on, for mutants to stare at. But look at it there, lying against the pink wall with its cell overlay: a thing of beauty destined to take its place in the One Show in New York with these credits:

Copywriter: Bettina Joy
Art Director: Bettina Joy
Typographer: Bettina Joy
Agency: Day, Kerlewis and Joy
Client: Mobil

All the client had asked for was something cheap and nasty to shut up the country dealers who were complaining about a lack of promotional support. He had not asked for this pristine piece of art lying against the pink wall. It would cost five times as much to print, and there was no reason to spend the extra money, except that the damn poster looked so good.

It was not an easy sale for Harry Joy. The client had already rejected the poster twice and here he was, being presented with it a third time, and he was already shifting in his seat and unfolding his arms and tapping his pencil when Harry's total reserves of charm, good fellowness and cunning began to work on him and he saw (when it was expressed like that — why didn't they say so before?) the reason for the poster being like it was.

Bettina, watching this performance, felt ambivalent. She gave him credit for the skill but felt it was a shallow nasty sort of skill and did not really admire him for it. It was a skill like being born beautiful is a skill, in other words not a skill at all. She had never seen him at work before and so could not assess the enormous impact Hell had made on his technique. Gone was that dozy lethargic Harry Joy, the old tell-us-what-you-want-and-I'll-do-it-for-you pragmatist. In his place was a man who felt he must not fail, a cunning, slightly angry personality who hid his aggression behind the natural blanket of his charm.

Bettina resented all the years he had squashed her and resented the fact that he was now to share her triumph. Yet resentment was nothing new to her and this resentment was of a low enough order for her to accept, just as she accepted fumes in the air. She was happy. She sat alone and warmed herself with her Scotch and her triumph.

"Will we wait for Joel?"

David was asking her, in that particularly petulant manner that he adopted for all matters relating to Joel.

"No," she said, "start."

It was Joel who had stood on ladders and carried boxes of tiles up three flights of stairs, who had worked on a high plank until 3 a.m. Who else would have done that for her? Who else, if it came to that, cared about her?

Honey Barbara sat next to Harry. Bettina watched them and knew their legs were touching under the table. She felt too tense to taste the soup. Anybody could see that they were touching under the table and his stupid moony face was pathetic. Obviously everybody else was embarrassed too. Why else would they talk about food? Why else would anybody *discuss* a soup? They took the soup to pieces as if it were a child's puzzle and held up each component and talked about it.

The woman was a looney.

She was explaining that she'd walked six miles to get spinach from someone who didn't spray it, for Christ's sake. Bettina was pleased to see that Lucy was taking the piss out of her with some subtlety.

"And demineralized water," Lucy said to Honey Barbara. "You mean distilled water, with nothing in it but water."

"Yes."

"You'll still get cancer," Lucy grinned, "just like the rest of us."

"Shut up," Bettina said. Once a year she had a complete check for cancer. Her appointment was automatic. She was advised by mail on the week before and the rest of the year she did not think about it.

There was a silence. Everybody thought about cancer.

"I like your food," Lucy said to Honey Barbara, "and it isn't boring."

"Thank you."

"It's very good," said Ken. "I used to live wiv a lady who used to make soup like this and this is better soup and hers was very good."

It was a long speech for Ken and possibly it would have been longer except that Joel arrived and a fuss was made to make sure he had his soup and his place opposite Bettina.

He sat down and smiled a calm shiny smile.

"Joel . . ." Bettina said.

Joel beamed. Sometimes, Harry thought, he looked like a flesh-coloured frog.

"Are you alright, Joel?"

Or a waxy image of a Buddha. A marzipan Buddha. Harry thought, nodding politely at his junior partner.

"Pretty good," Joel said to Bettina.

Lucy was looking at him sharply, her dark eyes narrowed, and Ken, as if waiting for something, held his soup spoon in the air. David rested his censorious eyes on Joel's face. Only Honey Barbara, engrossed in the problem of finding a clean soup bowl for him, paid no attention.

"What happened?" David said.

"Nothing Davey."

Joel began to eat his soup and everyone gave up and began to worry about other things. As was the rule in Palm Avenue it was always easy to get two people to agree on any subject, but never three, so that whatever was mentioned there was always plenty of room for discussion and sometimes enough for a brawl.

Nobody noticed whether Joel and Bettina actually spoke to one another, whether an interrogation took place and Joel divulged, reluctantly, his secret. They were too busy talking about demineralized water and the high incidence of kidney stones caused, Honey Barbara claimed, by the current craze for mineral water and the high levels of sodium caused primarily by excess salt, when they heard Bettina scream.

It is possible she had asked Joel nothing. It is even likely that when the others became engrossed in the problems of mineral water he had simply smiled a sad resigned doggy smile and opened his suit coat for Bettina to see. The smile would have had an apologetic edge to it, as if he was sorry for causing the trouble, but something, obviously, had to be done.

For there, protruding at ninety degrees from his blood-stained shirt, was a pearl-handled pocket knife.

"You fool," Bettina screamed. "You damned fool."

"They won't be back again," Joel said. "I saw to that."

Honey Barbara watched with her mouth open.

"Don't worry," Lucy told her, "he does it all the time." But she did not sound casual.

"It's your fault," Bettina screamed at Harry. "You're such a rock-'n'-roll star flouncing about the office, you never think how he feels..."

She would not have an ambulance for him. Ken and David lifted him up and carried him down to the Jaguar. Bettina insisted on taking him to the hospital alone.

Honey Barbara knew they were going to turn on Harry. She sat and waited for it. They took their time. They complimented her some more on the cooking and she waited.

Bettina was a powerful witch.

"Poor Joel," Lucy said.

"You've got to hand it to him, he works hard," Ken said.

"What did you do to him?" David asked Harry.

"I didn't do anything," Harry said.

Honey Barbara watched, but what was happening was worse than she thought. She did not know that Harry had been, all his life, a protected species. He had not been nipped like this before. He had not been held accountable for anything.

Yet this was the way it was going to be at Palm Avenue for as long as they all lived there, not just nipping like goldfish in an overcrowded tank, although that would be common enough, but arguing, shouting, laughing, vomiting, attacking, counter-attacking, all too loud, too late, too abrasively. There was an irritable peevish excitement as if they were only a lie or a conceit away from some big discovery and once it was lanced or cauterized everything would become clear, but what revealed itself was never any more than the hungover morning of another day.

Tonight Harry would be "it". He would not accept any responsibility for Joel and Lucy wasn't going to let him get away with it. She didn't want him to be totally responsible. She just wanted to admit he was partly responsible like they all were. She felt irritated with him, as if he might be a hypocrite, and although it was a strength of her character to allow others to be weak and flawed without judging them, she now found it difficult to extend this to her own father.

She only wanted him to admit a little responsibility, then she would leave him alone.

But Harry didn't see it like this. All he saw was an attack and he sought to defend himself in the best way he knew, the way he always had.

"I'll tell you a story," he said and they should have seen that slight lack in confidence, the nervous flick of his eyes around the table as he tested their reaction to the idea.

Barbara and Ken had never heard one of Harry's stories before and they were, each in their own way, astonished by it, not so much by the content of the story, but rather the way it was approached, and they felt differently about him because of it, just as we feel differently about a man when we discover his secret passion is cabinet-making. There was, in Harry's stories, something of the skill of a cabinet-maker, the craftsman more than the artist. They were not usually stories at all, but incidents to which he applied himself with such dedication that, finally, the thing was like a folly or a carefully carpentered house for pigeons, a rotunda, a series of small pavillions with elegant roofs and perfect dovetail joinery.

There was something that happened to him when he told a story, a certain way he leaned back in his chair, folding his hands in his lap, half closing his eyes. If there had been anyone alive who had known Vance Joy they could not help but be amazed at the likeness, particularly certain American pronunciations and the slow, confident drawl which had a soothing, almost hypnotic effect on the listeners.

The words of the story could be of no use to anyone else. The words by themselves, were useless. The words were an instrument only he could play and they became, in the hands of others, dull and lifeless, like picked flowers or bright stones removed from underwater.

As usual the story was about and by Vance Joy. It came from the time of Vance's childhood and consisted merely of a journey undertaken by a small boy (Vance) with an old man (his grandfather) from the deep valley where they lived to the plateau country above them. It was called "Journey to the Sunshine" and it ended with the old man and the boy arriving to see the sun set and the boy misunderstanding the nature of the world outside the valley, for he had never seen a sunset before.

Yet when it was finished the room was quiet. The candles spluttered a little on the table and you could almost hear Ken nodding his head. Honey Barbara squeezed his hand so hard she might have broken it, to let him know, silently, that she had misjudged his power to throw off devils, and asking him to forgive her for her blindness. Harry, held by the soporific power of his father's story, had become quiet and gentle.

But Lucy would not let him go so easily. She had waited out the story, just in case. She thought, perhaps, it might have had a moral, or a meaning that related to Joel. But it was just another story, and he was using it to grease away from her.

"You misuse it," she said.

"What?"

"Your story. You use it to get away from having responsibility."

"It *is* about responsibility," Harry lied. "It is about love and care, and the father puts his hand around the boy's shoulder." But he could not look his daughter in the eye.

Lucy was a little drunk. She didn't know if what he said was true or not. He had thrown sand in her eyes. She had not meant to attack, but to clarify, to remove all doubt, but that all went with the wind and she attacked from another angle.

"But listen," she said, and heard meanness in her voice, "we never touched each other as a family. Aren't you being a hypocrite, telling a story like that?"

No one had ever talked about Harry's stories like that She was shocked with what she'd done.

"Go easy . . ." Ken said.

"We never did," she insisted. "Not like you hug Honey Barbara now. You never sat around hugging Bettina like that, or us."

Harry held out his long arm across the table, offering his embrace.

"No," she said.

He looked stung.

"Go easy . . ." Ken said.

"No." She did not recognize herself. "It's too late for that . . ."

"What's this got to do with Joel?" David said, and Harry held out his arms towards him.

"You come to me," David said. "I'm not going to you."

"You can kiss me, Harry," Ken said. He meant to make light of it, but the effect was not well calculated.

Harry stood slowly. He was hurt but not angry. It was their nature to all hurt each other. He bid them all, individually, good night, except Honey Barbara who he kissed silently and tenderly and without ostentation.

When he had gone they were ashamed of themselves, all except Honey Barbara who was furious.

"Why did you do that to him?"

"Well, he gets up himself," Lucy said sadly. "But you're right. I shouldn't have."

As became the pattern, they had another bottle of wine then, and even Honey Barbara had one more glass of Fleurie.

It was an old planter's house, designed to cool off quickly in the evening. To this end it was built on high stilts so that air circulated beneath the floor and the walls were only clad on one side, the inside, so that the uprights and cross-bracings became a decorative element in the exterior walls. As a direct result of this construction sound travelled easily from one part of the house to the other and those visitors who had been coy about the movements of their bowels had often left Palm Avenue severely constipated.

Yet, although everyone had gone to bed when Joel and Bettina arrived home, no one in the upstairs bedroom heard them, unless perhaps it was David Joy who had not yet slid into his labyrinthian dreams of Eldorado.

"Listen," Joel said smiling, "listen."

"You block your dirty ears," she said, but the creakings of the house were honeyed and erotic. "Come to the kitchen."

There was a murmuring, a slow sensuous stirring as if the house itself still contained, in its dry grey timbers, the sap of sexual pleasure, and it twisted, stretching against its nails, and through the huan pine ceiling came the moan of her daughter, soft as wool.

She put the kettle on and did not feel discontented. She read the note from Lucy asking her to wake them up if need be, but there was no need, and Lucy was certainly not asleep. It had been a long hard night in the casualty ward and sometimes a little frightening when the police were mentioned, but in the end Joel was bandaged, the police were not called, the knife was returned and now when Joel put his hand out on the table she covered it with hers. She had made so many decisions, hard steel decisions all locked together with little belts, cross-braced, double-checked. The easiest decision was not to fuck Joel any more because, although she loved him, it was she who was stronger. Weak men did not excite her. She had always known that.

"I am crazy in love, mooshey-mooshey."

Bettina smiled and patted his hand.

Honey Barbara had never felt her body so exactly. It felt oiled, every part of it taken to pieces and put back together again by a master watchmaker. Perhaps it was also partly the feeling of being in the heart of enemy territory, two good beings pitted against the dangerous and seductive forces of evil, or perhaps sympathetic paranoia can act as an aphrodisiac, perhaps it was this that made them move together so perfectly. They were in a cone of darkness in the centre of the world, and Harry was past questioning the nipping tortures of Hell, although had he been granted his secret prayer to be saved from them he would have been very bored indeed.

They did not hear Lucy's murmurs or Ken's moans, although they must have felt them, like you hear the sea at night or as you hear a river when you sleep beside it and, all night, water runs beside your dreams. They must have felt the current of pleasure pick them up and sweep them gently away from the bank and into the centre of the stream where the water is deep and fast and you can drown easily without caring and all that pours into your unresisting lungs is the sensuous liquid dark.

Honey Barbara had never been hypnotized, of course, but she had never had an orgasm either and tonight, for a reason she never understood, would be the first. Possibly it was a technical matter, relating to the gentle skill with which Harry had worked his tongue but in all likelihood it was not, and it seems much more likely that it was related to the whole erotic sway of the house which set up harmonic waves of pleasure and, the waves not quite co-inciding, produced beats, which are heard like droning. But whatever reason on that night, in that black room, she called out loud like a nightbird in the darkness, two loud musical cries and gave herself to herself, and herself to Harry Joy, and all her resistance to Palm Avenue seemed far away and she lay there afterwards, warm and wet, caught in its glistening web while Lucy's last cry fell through the house like an echo of her own. She drifted, mumbling, into sleep and began to dream of Bog Onion Road.

But when Joel shrieked, she sat upright. She was out of bed and running before Harry could stop her. She ran to the top of the stairs with visions of that pearl-handled knife, blood, mutilation, those waxy eyes, that soporific smile, the madness of his obsession.

Lucy and Ken met her on the stairs, and all of them rushed forwards, holding sheets and towels in front of them and behind them. And Harry followed, holding Honey Barbara's embroidered white silk dressing gown around himself.

God knows what they expected.

It certainly wasn't this: Joel flat on the kitchen floor, his pants around his ankles, surgical dressing around his chest, and Bettina on top of him, taking her last pleasure stroke while the kettle on the stove screamed with delight.

The winters at that latitude were like European summer. It was in winter that there was plenty: avocados, custard apples, new oranges and lemons, and even papaya, though these last would be pale yellow and sometimes a little sour in the winter, depending on where they stood and how they were fertilized. The vegetable gardens were also full of food: cauliflowers, cabbages, potatoes, peas, beans, spinach, tiny tomatoes, lettuces, artichokes. Winter was an easy time, Honey Barbara thought. The honey would have been spun, and the jars stacked and distributed. In the winter you could spare honey for your tea and you could spoon it onto your bread. The hard time was later, in the wet, and food would be scarce then and it would be pumpkins and cucumbers, papaya, watermelon, marrow, zucchini, wet squashy things which were fine for a while, but depressing later.

The first thing Honey Barbara did at Palm Avenue was begin the vegetable garden. While Ken and Lucy worked on the Cadillac on the front, she took to the back lawn with a spade and turned it into something useful. She added blood and bone by the bagful and started a compost heap. She ordered spoilt hay and mulched with it. She bought seedlings from Garry at the Zen Inn and soon had a garden going. Not everybody admired it.

She cleaned the house, helped with that Cadillac, wrote letters home and cooked the dinner and participated in those terrible nights around the table. To her shame she developed a taste for expensive wine and four weeks after her arrival could be found nosing a claret with some knowledge, not to say style, and holding the glass up to the light to judge the colour, in spite of which early elegance she still found herself becoming as loud and argumentative as the others.

So Honey Barbara was sucked into the madness which took place around the dining room table at Palm Avenue. The conversations often sounded more like the last moments of a wool auction with everyone screaming out their bids for salvation, attention, laughter or forgiveness, and if it was late, which it usually was, Bettina would be found sitting up on the mattress on the floor which she now shared with Joel, either asking them to shut-up or to pay attention, demanding Joel's presence or his absence, or simply screaming good-natured abuse at her daughter.

They always meant to move Bettina's bed (it hadn't been Joel's bed since she moved in). They discussed it. They argued about it. Plans would be made for the morning when it was to be shifted to the landing upstairs. A caravan was to be rented, a new wing built, a storey added, a cellar dug, a hotel room leased. But in the morning it always seemed more important to move the empty bottles and so the mattress remained on the floor and suffered spilt wine and cigarette ash and the irritations of its inhabitants.

Honey Barbara's marvellous eyes were becoming dulled and she found ways to avoid her gaze in the mirror. She made excuses for herself, the most practical one was that Harry was giving her money to send home. What alarmed her silent Victorian heart was that she was starting to enjoy the life. She was enjoying shouting and arguing which would have been considered boorish at home. She used salt in her cooking to make them happy. She complained triumphantly about her hangovers.

"At least they're alive," she told herself. At least they were not sitting back zonked out on dope asking each other questions about their gardens. She wrote long letters home giving detailed instructions for the care of the bees and demanding to know who was looking after them and requesting a personal account from those concerned. The letters weren't answered.

"I don't believe all this rubbish about cancer." Bettina jabbed the table with her little finger. "But I am prepared to discuss it. I am terrified of it but I will talk about it."

"You just *get* it," Lucy said, "don't worry. You either do or you don't."

"You don't just *get* it," Honey Barbara said.

"It's lies," Bettina said.

"You said 'discush'," Joel told her. "You're prepared to discush it."

"My mother", Lucy said, "has swallowed the whole thing. She believes the whole American myth. She believes General Motors are nice people. She thinks Nixon was unlucky. She thinks I.T.T. wouldn't lie. She believes in what she does." And she gave Bettina a hug and a kiss. "She is the real article. She is not a cynical manipulator."

"Get off," Bettina said, but just the same she was pleased.

"How you live", Lucy said to Honey Barbara, "might be fun."

"You don't know how I live," said Honey Barbara.

"No one knows," Harry said proudly.

"We know," Ken said.

"We guess," Lucy said. "We guess how you live."

"Lived."

"And will live again. But it is no better than this is. This society is fucked. You'll go down with it too. You won't escape."

"No!" Bettina stood up. She looked as if she wanted to propose a toast. Her chair fell backwards with a crash. "You're all so negative."

"I agree with you," said Honey Barbara, rising and clinking her glass against Bettina's.

Thus alliances were made and, in a similar fashion, broken.

Lucy and Bettina agreed that Honey Barbara was full of shit about food. Lucy and Honey Barbara agreed that everyone would get cancer. Honey Barbara and Bettina then agreed they wouldn't, but as Honey Barbara explained she only meant it for people who were careful with their food and where they lived, whereas Bettina was convinced that the whole cancer theory was a Communist conspiracy.

Joel always agreed with Bettina and when he spoke they all had to be quiet out of respect for Bettina. He was very boring but it was not permitted to shout him down. Bettina, watching him talk, smiled proudly and Harry, normally tolerant to a fault, allowed his moustache to reveal the sarcastic cast of his mouth.

Ken stood up and began to declaim Cavafy's poem. "Waiting for the Barbarians". His voice was as rasping as his teeth were jagged and he recited from memory as if his finger was dragging along printed lines, but there was a force in his rusty voice and David, for one, was impressed to hear things he did not understand.

"What are we waiting for all crowded in the forum?" Ken declaimed, struggling to his feet and glaring around the table. He held a finger high.

"The Barbarians are to arrive today," he answered.

"Within the Senate House why is there such inaction?
The Senators make no laws, what are they sitting there for?
Because the Barbarians arrive today.
What laws now should the Senate be making?
When the Barbarians come, they'll make the laws."

Bettina began to smell petrol in the second verse. She did not realize what it was and she was only aware of being depressed.

She listened glumly and when Ken finished she said: "No one talked like this before. All this gloom-doom business. It's since you came," she told Honey Barbara, "you encourage all this."

"It's not her," Lucy said, "it's Harry. He used to be see-no-evil, hear-no-evil, speak-no-evil."

But Harry did not speak. He sat, as he always did, and listened. He was a sponge in their midst.

"He used to stop us saying bad things," David said. "I think he was right."

"I can smell petrol," Bettina said.

"I washed," Lucy said.

"I washed too," Ken said.

It was the smell of her childhood, the fumes drifting up from the forecourt and in her open window. It was the smell of her father when she embraced him and, she swore, you could still smell the petrol coming from his coffin when he was lowered into his grave.

A dirty rag was found out on the verandah, and the subject of petrol was avoided by David who, eager to contribute something, told the table the entire plot of a spy thriller he had seen at the drive-in the night before.

So the matter of petrol, the Cadillac, Lucy's refusal to work, her wasted education, were saved for another night when it would take a predictable form, something like this:

"You are going backwards," Bettina would tell Lucy. "That's why we gave you an education, Lucy." She looked disapprovingly at Ken. "So you would not get involved with stinking petrol."

"You never told me," Lucy grinned.

"Please get a job," Bettina said.

"I don't want to be a boss."

"Be a worker."

"I don't want to be a slave."

And Lucy could paint a very convincing picture of the cruelties and iniquities of Hell. Harry listened to her describe the economic system, the blindness of profit seekers and so on.

"You are spoilt children."

"We are waiting for the Barbarians."

"You should learn how to feed yourself and protect yourself," Honey Barbara said sternly.

"No one will survive," Ken said, filling Harry's glass with Cabernet Sauvignon.

"I will survive," said Honey Barbara. "And Harry will survive. The rest of you are fucked."

But in the morning her eyes in the mirror were small and grey, and there were black marks like tiny freckles around her eyes: blood vessels she had burst vomiting.

As the weeks went on, the structural flaws in their relationship became apparent to Honey Barbara. It was, she thought, like being in a hut with a leaking rusty roof: you keep living in it, you try to ignore it, you mark the leaking parts with chalk and promise yourself you'll make temporary repairs with bituminous paint; but then, when it's dry, you forget about it. In the wet you live amongst plinking buckets but never enough of them, and you kick them over anyway, and everything becomes damp, and mould and mildew grow everywhere, even in your bed, until, in the end, it all becomes too much and you find your ladder and, just as the sunlight strikes the roof and the steam starts rising from it, you rip the fucker to pieces and the rusty iron disintegrates as easily as a dead leaf in your hand. Underneath it you find fat cockroaches, wooden battens white with rot, leaves, mulch, decay, mice, a tree snake with a yellow belly and some peculiar ice blue fungi growing from the rotten wood: a whole eco-system built on lethargy and failure.

In short, she knew she should have left him but she couldn't. She was doing what she had done years before with Albert (Peugot Albert, American Albert), finding herself in the middle of a situation she disapproved of, living with a man who was fucked, but who she stayed with anyway, like some novice board rider who tried to stay with a bad wave to its painful end.

She sought refuge in the garden and in the bedroom where she painted the frames of the windows three different colours: blue, red, purple. (Bettina sucked in her breath but said nothing.) She began a mural above the bed but didn't finish it. It showed a part of a small hut with blue, red and purple window frames, and an old Peugot, rust brown, which she intended to cover with creeper and long grass. On the verandah outside the red window she installed a hammock and sometimes, when Harry was more drunk or aggressive than usual, she would sleep out there. She had five yards of muslin for a mosquito net: she wrapped them around the hammock and lay there until the morning when he would come with red-eyed remorse and entice her back to bed and they would make peace and fuck until their eyes were wide and their mouths full of pillow.

With Bettina and Joel, Harry had formed a gang. Nightly they reported successes. They walked in the door clinking bottles and shouting. They had won this Account or that Account. They had sold a campaign. She could not be happy for them, although she had tried.

There was no joy in their triumphs, only anger, revenge, nose-thumbing, name-calling, and although Bettina provided the emotional tone, Harry followed it willingly and even lent to this unpleasant cocktail a dominant flavour of fear. She saw him encouraging these negative things in himself, as if by letting them expand and take over he would be better assured of success.

It was Honey Barbara who had instructed him in the usefulness of money, but now, a month later, when she questioned its value as a measure of worth, she was irritated to see what his moustache did not quite hide — his you're-only-saying-that-because-you-haven't-got-any smile.

She tried to make the bedroom a peaceful place. She made cushions and bought candles and tried to forget it was Harry's money. She lit incense and put wind chimes out on the verandah where she did her Tai Chi exercises every morning and night.

But still they argued. It seemed there was nothing that could be done to prevent the discord. No meditation, exercise, massage, or even prayer. Nastiness would creep in between them and push them apart. He defended fear and anger as necessary emotions and mocked her when she said there must be another way.

"How?"

"With love."

He laughed.

"It doesn't work like that." He lay against the pillows with a glass of wine in one hand and a bottle in the other. He was not the same person she had met in the Hilton. "You've got to be angry," he said. "It gives you strength. You commit yourself to win. Because if you don't get them, they get you. See?" He jabbed his finger. "You understand?"

"Christ," she said despairingly, "you know it's shit."

"Of course I know it's shit."

She compressed her lips.

"Don't you look so superior," he said.

She didn't answer.

"You drink my wine. You drive the Jag."

"I'd rather not."

He put his wine glass and bottle down and leaned towards her in such a way that she thought he was going to kiss her and her lips were already moving towards his when she felt the wine glass wrenched from her hand. He threw it out the window and she heard it shatter.

She was too tired to be angry. She hugged herself and felt cold.

He leaned back on the pillow. "If you don't want it, don't drink it."

After a moment or two he said: "Do you know how much you cost me?"

"A lot of money."

"You cost me a fucking fortune," he said, "so don't say you don't love me."

She wasn't even astonished. "You're getting poisoned with this shit you're doing Harry. You can't fuck around with it. You're catching it. You're becoming one of them."

She went and sat beside him. He stroked her hair sadly.

"It's what I've got to do," he said.

A silence.

"Come home with me," she said.

He stopped stroking her hair. More silence.

"It's safe there," she said softly. "We'll be fine." She touched the lambswool shoulder with the ends of her fingers.

"It doesn't sound safe to me."

Another silence (because he had never said this before and he was becoming angry and she felt betrayed).

"It is very beautiful," she said gently. "There is no shit at all."

"But not safe."

How could he sound triumphant?

"Yes, safe."

"But you're the one who's been to jail. I haven't been to jail. I haven't spent half my life worried about the police. They don't come here harassing us. My kids didn't grow up setting their alarm clocks for four in the morning."

"Maybe they should learn."

And it was, of course, with retorts like this, that she allowed herself to be drawn into it. He had become like a racehorse, or a dog bred for fighting.

"You are making this into Hell," she said. "You've decided that's what it is and that's what you're making it."

He shook his head and looked at the black night window. He would not discuss Hell with her.

"Whose Hell are you in?" she would say, trying to play his game. "Someone must be running it."

But that sort of talk only made things worse.

"You tell me," he'd say nastily.

"I don't know."

"How interesting."

And so on.

But just as there are dry days when even the rustiest roof can't leak, there were times when life felt very pleasant. There were miles of wide beaches both north and south of the town and at weekends they could surf and swim naked and let the sea tumble their bodies and rattle out their devils and deliver them on a blanket of white froth to the yellow sand. They lit huge fires on the empty beach and lay there at night watching the stars.

But it was, as she told him one Sunday night, only 2/7 of a life. The other 5/7 were devoted to fear and anger.

Once she had been silly and young, and she had seen Albert on the flooded creek with his Peugot and not known about hotels and restaurants and the city life. It was long ago. Even the creek was different then and everyone was naive enough to uncritically welcome its raging strength in the monsoon and it meant nothing to them but life. But two seasons later a twenty-two-month-old girl had been swept away and drowned just near that spot and the creek always sounded different after that and no one could cross the ford without thinking of that little girl and how, that cold July morning, they had waded the creek in the high dangerous water hoping they would not find her body and that, glancing into the undergrowth beside the creek, they would glimpse her making her way back home.

But they did find her and two weeks later Albert's Peugot was at the bottom of a gully and Honey Barbara was on her first aeroplane, high on cocaine, wearing high-heeled shoes. She didn't know what she was doing, or where she was going, but now, with another ten years gone, she had no such excuse.

Then what kept her at Palm Avenue? She confessed one morning, to the bathroom mirror: "Orgasms," she told her grinning face, "and flushing toilets."

David Joy was lying in bed in his room. He heard her laughter through the wall.

Bettina was burning brightly. She was consuming herself. She lost half a stone and had to buy new clothes. She could not sleep. She woke at 4 a.m. considering options, redoing ads, mentally rewriting letters to Americans about her future. Her mind was attuned to problems and she could not stand to see them unsolved, even for a moment, so that when the wine was opened in a restaurant she could not wait for the waiter to begin filling glasses, she pointed: there This too was her responsibility, this problem of the bottle of wine and empty glass with the glaringly simple solution.

She wasn't even aware that she did it, so she would certainly never have guessed that she was known to the wine-waiters of one restaurant as "The Glass-pointer" and Harry as "Mr Glass Glass-pointer".

And if she had known? "Well," she would have said, "I only do it to save time."

Perhaps one of the secrets of Bettina's success was that she applied herself as earnestly to trivial details as she did to big ideas. It was seven o'clock in the morning and Honey Barbara was sitting on the grassed edge of the vegetable garden with a glass of demineralized water. "Do you want to hear what happened last night?"

It was now near the end of Honey Barbara's third month in Palm Avenue (her deadline, and still she stayed!) and the dining room table had all but been abandoned as Harry and Bettina became (for business reasons, so they said) involved in the social life of the town. Bettina had produced a much-admired advertising campaign for the State Gallery (Art Schmart, she said, it's mouldy junk) and as a result of this Harry (Harry!) had been nominated and then elected as a trustee. In less than six months they had moved up that impossible last rung of the ladder and entered the very inner circle of society.

"Formal. No lovers." Bettina would announce when the invitations came. She would grin, and the lovers, laughing, did not always successfully hide their resentment.

"What happened? Nothing happened. The arseholes! Jesus, I'll be pleased to be out of this town. They all think it's Harry who does the ads. They automatically assume it's him. Oh, what a clever husband you have," she whined in imitation. "What a brilliant man. And what do *you* do, Mrs Joy?"

Then would come the latest bulletin in the campaign to get to New York. A letter from the famous Ed McCabe complimenting her on her work (she'd brought it to his notice, of course). A telegram from Mary Wells. She kept up a fast, furious correspondence with anyone who would answer her and her letters were tough, funny, and skilfully self-promoting. She wrote press releases for the New York trade press. She adopted Americanisms in her speech, remembering to say "Garage" instead of "Car Park", and "out back" instead of "out the back".

As she reminded Honey Barbara on this crisp, sunny morning: "This is only a stopping place for me. Another six months and I'm taking my samples and half the profits and setting up in New York.

"But let me warn you, he is starting to like it." He, in this case, was Harry. Joel was not liking it. Joel was waiting to go to New York. "They all think he's an intellectual. The less he says the more brilliant they think he is. That's always been Harry's goddamned talent. When you talk to him he looks at you as if you're saying the most interesting and original things he's ever heard in his life. No wonder everyone likes him. No wonder we all think he's intelligent."

"He is intelligent," Honey Barbara said sharply.

"Yes," Bettina said quickly. "He is, but you know what I mean. He's in his element. It's true. You should spray those cabbages They're getting eaten alive. I'll get someone to pick up a good spray for you."

"Bettina . . ."

"I know, I know, but what's the point of growing them if you let something else eat them?"

"There's plenty left for us."

"Mmmm," Bettina said, thoughtfully. She stared at the cabbages. "I've got to go," she said.

She tip-toed off across the lawn so as not to dig her heels into the grass. She found Harry shaving.

"You remember", she said, leaning in the doorway, "how Monsanto said they'd talk to us if we could think of a new product they liked."

"Mmm."

"I've got it."

"What?"

"Organic Poison."

*

He left Honey Barbara on her metal chair with her glass of water, sitting perched in the backyard like a muddy flamingo. She was like an exotic flower picked by a thoughtless child. He thought of bedraggled polar bears pacing their concrete-floored cages, their lukewarm water dotted with the soggy wrappers of confectionery.

Even the cabbages would not grow properly. They were poor and dwarfed, struggling to survive in the heavy clay soil. The compost heap, her pledge of hope for the future, had begun to smell. Rats came at night to raid it and possums gorged themselves as if it were a colossal pudding.

Harry sat back in the passenger seat of the Jaguar and felt depressed. Bettina, her seat pushed forward, hunched over the wheel and drove with damp-handed bravado, abusing the innocent through the safety of shut windows. The air conditioner made hardly a sound. It was seventy degrees Fahrenheit.

"Look at the mutants!"

They had stopped at traffic lights. Pedestrians streamed around the car, their faces marked by dull punishments. Harry was surprised at the intensity of her hatred for these Captives.

"Ugly," she chanted. "Ugly, ugly, ugly."

Bettina was not particularly beautiful. He mentally placed her in the midst of the crowd. He stole a drab overcoat from one woman, a string bag from another, and then, having dressed her with these secretly, let her walk in front of the Jaguar.

"It'll be the same in New York," he said. "Ordinary people in the street."

"Rubbish. They're so damned dull."

"What will happen", he asked, "if you can't get into America?"

"Cretin," she shouted, swerving in front of a truck and applying her horn as two men with a ladder jumped out of the way. "I'll get into America, don't worry."

"But if you can't."

"I will."

"What if something goes wrong?"

"Do you want something to go wrong?"

He didn't answer immediately. He was the Managing Director of a business whose growth and success was now based solely on Bettina.

"Come with me," she said.

He looked up, biting his lip. "Where?"

"New York." She gave those two words all their due. There was not a fleck of dust on them.

The bitten lip could not help but form a smile, and she could almost see the pictures in his mind, those idealized towers of glass, Vance Joy's magic, but also more recent dreams, as elegantly tooled as "The Talk of the Town" in the *New Yorker*.

"No," he said, and shifted his body a little so he could look out his side window.

"You can't even hammer a nail in straight."

"So?"

"You'll hate living in the bush."

"The hut is built."

"You won't go," she said swinging on to the freeway. "You're a city boy. You like soft things."

Like an expert jeweller she tapped the flaw, the long thin fault that ran through his character: he loved comfort, soft things, silk, velvet, words you could also use about wine.

"No," he said again. "I can't."

He was not prepared for what would happen when Bettina finally went. He chose to believe she would not go.

"I think we'll get a brand from British Tobacco," he said to change the subject. "Adrian says it'll be a two million dollar launch."

"I'll be gone by then. Come on, Harry, come to New York. We'll bring everyone with us."

He winced, thinking of his poor bedraggled Honey Barbara in New York.

"We can't walk out on the business, just when we've built it up."

"Sure we can."

"Our names will stink."

"Who cares. We won't be back."

"They'll hate us," Harry said.

"I hate *them*," she said simply.

The town had never taken Bettina seriously, which she felt might have been justifiable in the past, but not now. They gave her no credit. They treated her like a fool and sometimes at night she invented extravagant ways to punish them. She did not ask much from them, only credit for what she had done. But to the town she was no one: Mrs Harry Joy.

"Look at the fucking mutants."

They had come off the freeway and were waiting at the lights.

Harry huddled into his seat. He liked the smell of leather. He felt protected in this large rich car. He did not want blistering heat, mud, leeches and hard work. He could not hammer a nail straight, it was true. When Honey Barbara told him stories about Bog Onion Road she did not mean to terrify him, but how could snakes and police and bushfires and a hanging man ever be attractive to him? He pushed the Cancer Map away into the darkness and sought his safety here, under the protection of Those in Charge. They liked him, or, if not liked, at least valued him. He was in favour, in fashion, and his days were dedicated to staying there, his nights to dreaming about a fall. They patted him on the back and asked him to stay for drinks. They made assumptions about his beliefs which were incorrect. He smiled and nodded and pretended he didn't know what it was like to be inside a police station or walk the corridors of Mrs Dalton's Free Enterprise Hospital and see the trolleys carrying captives to their therapy. He looked them in the eye and they found him both courageous and intelligent. He loathed them.

He was a prisoner with special privileges making his captors tea, coffee, folding their socks, telling them funny stories for their amusement, ironing their sheets, warming their beds as they saw fit.

His soul stank of Californian Poppy hair oil: a weasling cunning little thing.

Honey Barbara and Ken and Lucy had taught him a lot about the structure of Hell. When he listened to the trustees of the State Gallery with their silky talcumed talk he could see exactly where they stood in the scheme of things. It was they who trafficked in poisons, controlled the distribution of safety, the purity of water and air, or, more probably, the lack of it. Not for them the nipping little tortures one Captive might inflict on another. It was their privilege to inflict many special diseases and even death, to withhold treatment from the sick, to beat the brave, and torture the poor.

The very smoothness of their skin frightened him, the perfection of their fingernails, the sharp white lines along which they parted their perfectly cut hair.

When he sat across the desk from the local Managing Director of Helena Rubenstein he could easily imagine that this smiling cultured man ("You've never read Conrad? We must remedy that."), that this urbane man could very easily torture him, not mentally, but physically, in an ordinary pale blue room on a sunny afternoon while the rest of the world went about its business. He saw fissures in their smooth exteriors and glimpsed the rage reserved for those who disobeyed.

"New York," Bettina said, "Imagine."

He did not imagine New York. He imagined Honey Barbara. Holding her, he was destroying her. All the things he loved about her were slowly fading: her strength, her confidence, her belief in herself, her food, her body, her mind. They made fun of her beliefs and called them mumbo-jumbo. They doubted the power of an OM. Her calloused feet had grown white and soft and where they once had been hard and strong they had now become big and ugly, city feet with flaking skin.

Bettina screeched the Jaguar down into the basement car park, skidded across an oil slick, and arrived in her spot. "What about it?" she said.

"Maybe," Harry said thus removing the subject from his mind.

"Maybe Baby," Bettina sang, and then stopped when she realized where Buddy Holly's words were leading her.

Honey Barbara drank Scotch with Joel. She didn't like the taste of Scotch; she mixed it with dry ginger.

While Bettina was away Joel became an expert on everything. He lay on his mattress eating Ken and Lucy's dinner and told her the best way to grow vegetables. He polished his glasses, rubbed his belly, wiped his ketchuped mouth with a napkin while she sat at the table and made patterns with the spilled dry ginger. She listed, for her own amusement, the things that Joel claimed to have done. He had edited a newspaper in Texas, run a trucking company and later a bus service, managed a rock-'n'-roll band, owned a travel agency, worked for McCann Erickson in Los Angeles and Caracas, imported brass goods from Pakistan, been a disc jockey, written a radio play which was performed by Orson Welles and spent five years at Day, Kerlewis & Joy. Although he was only twenty-six, Honey Barbara was prepared to believe him, but when he started to tell her how to grow cabbages she knew he was a fraud.

She yawned. He didn't notice.

The television was playing and he managed to look at this while he talked, occasionally pausing mid-sentence to let some hack comedian deliver a punch line and to join in the canned laughter. Harry and Bettina were hours away from rescuing her, and Ken and Lucy were out compiling their "Directory of Positive Things about

The End of the World". She wished they would come home. She would rather argue with them.

The only things that kept her alive were the things she hated most: argument, discord, acrimony, noise. She was disgusted with herself. She was disgusted to sit here and listen to this batteryfed man patronize her.

She was drunk when she stood up and that disgusted her too.

"Goodnight, Joel."

"Kiss," he demanded offering his lips like rose petals to be admired. Kissing was the social custom. When the others were out Joel would normally include a little fondling on his own account.

"Not tonight," she said.

She stumbled going out the door and he called out something which might not have been intended spitefully.

It was a house where she had learned to restrain noises signifying pain or pleasure. You choked them back, held them tight in your throat, buried them under blankets or drowned them in noisy water. But tonight the timbers of the house were saturated with the ultrasonic hiss of television and the canned laughter would drown her sobs as well as any pillow. She lay on the bed and cried. There was no pleasure or release in it, only self-hatred and the feeling that you might die from lack of air.

She had felt lonely before, and unwanted before, and even un-loved, but she had never felt unnecessary. She was a decoration on a poisonous cake. She was like the great bloated whale of a Cadillac that sat on the front lawn and consumed energy and enthusiasm and interest, all for no useful purpose. It was refitted with pleated silk door trim while its body rusted.

She felt his hand and pulled away.

"No, Joel, go away."

But it was David, his dark eyes full of sympathy, who sat gingerly on the edge of his father's bed.

"Here." It was a handkerchief.

David had changed his mind about Honey Barbara the night she told the story about the amphetamines.

"This is a story", she began, "about a million dollars' worth of amphetamines." She told the story, as seemed the custom, in the first person. Even Harry did this and it was sometimes confusing because he said "I" when the "I" in the story was Vance Joy and once even it was Vance Joy's father, but it was always "I" in Bogotá and New York.

The story was not hers at all; it belonged to her friend Annette Brownlee, or Annette Horses as she was more commonly known, who had once been involved, so she claimed, with this hoard of amphetamines which lay buried still in a city in Europe. Honey Barbara, always cautious about such matters, had changed Europe into South America, and it was just this change of geography which had so enraptured David Joy, who knew by heart the old city of Quito, and when she described the little plastic bags of white powder and the damp underground passages, he went very pale and his eyes contracted as if he had heard someone recite his dreams.

Days later Honey Barbara knew that something had happened, but she never ever guessed that it was Annette Horses' old story about the amphetamines which had caused it. After all, it was only one of the stories in the great repertoire of drug-paranoia stories, which were all a little too real to have any romantic interest for her.

Annette Horses, and therefore Honey Barbara, always ended the story with the claim that she was the only person in the world (only person in the world not in jail) who knew where these drugs were. Yet it was not avarice that made David change his mind about her — he had lived in Palm Avenue long enough to know that a good story always had a little extra romance than real life. ("Every good story should always have at least one tower in it," Vance Joy had said and, typically, having made the rule to suit a story about a tower, abandoned it in the desert, a puzzling shard that was polished and cared for by his descendants.)

So slowly that it was not at first remarked on, David Joy became polite to Honey Barbara and, once polite, helpful. He helped her to wash dishes and even, on one occasion, weed the vegetable garden, although he loathed the dry too-smooth feeling that settled on his dirty hands and he retired as soon as was politely possible to wash them and rub them with Bettina's Oil of Ulay. He did not go for walks with her like Harry did, or brush (suggestively) past her like Joel did, and he was certainly far too inhibited to ask for Kissing Rights. But he did, in his strange tight whisky voice, talk to Honey Barbara here and there and, at certain quiet times when the others were busy, make some confessions of his plans, his ideas about South America.

She had not discouraged his dreams. Better, she thought, that he got out of that job and actually did something.

He showed her selected sections of his dreams and she saw something black and glistening like oil, but not without beauty. While Joel looked at television she and David sometimes looked at the atlas together and she felt pleased that he liked her, for he had seemed so cramped, so tense, so unnatural that she thought about him in the way she thought about Bonsai trees which she always ached to liberate: to gently break their pots, unbind their roots, to take them back into the bush and let them grow. Her pride was that she was good with living things and she liked to see David Joy smile and she was proud to see him become calmer and more confident. At least, she thought, she could do something good at Palm Avenue, and tonight just when everything was so bleak he came and gave her a beautiful handkerchief made from yellow silk.

She lay on her stomach and he touched the muscles around her neck. "Knotted," he said softly.

He began to massage them and she was surprised, first that he touched her at all, and second that he massaged her well.

"I did what you said," he said. "I went to the workshop at the Zen Inn."

She felt his fingers breaking up the knots and smiled. She had taught him things he had begun by ridiculing, and she smiled that he had done these things in his secret way, and imagined how they would have handled him in the workshop, seeing him there in his shiny black shoes and expensive grey cardigan.

In her most paranoid moment she would never have imagined that David Joy had mentally rehearsed this moment for the last month, had nightly run over it in his mind, had taken the massage course for this, and only this, reason and moment. He had watched her with a cunning, a furtiveness that, to him, in no way contradicted the feelings of his heart. He had observed her slow collapse and had managed to at once welcome it and disapprove of Harry for causing it.

"I'll have to sit up here. O.K."

"O.K."

He massaged her back, working her spine through her singlet and she was the one who took it off. He went quickly to his room for oil. He massaged beautifully, with great sensitivity, and understood the importance of an uninterrupted stroke as he drew all the tension from her shoulders out through her fingertips.

When he turned her over, her eyes were shut and he gasped, privately behind his frozen face, to see the beauty of her breasts.

"Take your baggies off."

"I haven't got any other pants on."

"It's O.K."

She must have suspected that it might not be O.K., that he might have changed a little, but he had not changed that much, and he was still the same dark-eyed, furtive, inhibited boy who had begun by despising her and wanting her removed; but she was a sucker for massage and he had learnt his lessons well. He did her legs and then her arms and her neck and her stomach, and her breasts and she did not even know by then it was not O.K., but when he worked the fleshy mound of his palms between the petal lips of her vulva her wetness smeared his hand and gave the lie to it.

He had so many dreams, so many fantasies, revenges, loves, schemes, hopes, impossible Eldorados that when he felt this perfumed smear he was awash with emotions and his limbs felt so weak that he fell over trying to remove his clothes.

His body was surprisingly hard but also lithe like a snake in its sinuous movements and she took him into her with a sound which could have been heard as either a whimper or a sigh.

Through all the lovemaking her eyes were shut, and whatever she saw or thought she kept secret from herself. She felt him quiver and come before she was ready, but he did not stop thrusting and it was then she looked up into the eyes and saw specks of brown, almost gold, gleaming like cats' eyes in sunlight. He asked so desperately for her pleasure that she acted it for him and she dug her hands hard into his back and gave him, in a place that would not show, a bite that would glow sullenly for weeks.

Then she saw — just as, in a milling crowd, one might see a flash of a knife moving from pocket to pocket, just a glimpse the small glint as it catches the sun — the look in his eyes. It was triumph, a cold hard thing, like a spring on the lid of a box. She understood in an instant, that she was a dream he had caught in a net.

Damn you and your dreams. She carefully wiped his penis with the yellow handkerchief then placed the damp silk between her legs lest the marks of her infidelity show on the eiderdown.

She had come to this, this seedy betrayal, and she knew it was time to leave these people who had such trunk-loads of dreams, ideas and ambitions but never anything in the present, only what would happen one day, and it was time to get away from it and face whatever might be waiting for her at home and hope that it might be as it had been: better and deeper pleasures with smaller, more ordinary things, pleasures so everyday that these people would never see anything in them but tiredness, repetition, discomfort, and no originality at all.

The light in the room had always been bad, a sad little twenty-five-watt globe which produced an unrelieved cast of middle grey, from which nothing stood out except the tip of a yellow handkerchief which would, in a happier moment, have looked like the fallen petal of a jonquil between her legs.

It had stopped raining but, at three in the afternoon on that day in the unimagined future, a low mist still hung around the sides of the mountains and when David Joy descended from his truck he was careful not to muddy his suit. He lit a long thin cigar, and, when he put his matches back in his pocket, left his hand there with them.

The truck was just beyond the bridge where tourists took photographs and where truck drivers went to defecate. They had been stopped by the army on the Armenia side of the bridge and his passenger, the modest, infuriating man with the broad-shouldered shrug and the dark shadow on his face, had been shot dead as he ran towards the shelter of the round tanks, which turned out (Fabricá de Sulfato Amontaco) to be a fertilizer factory.

The local newspaper came out to take photographs of the man where he lay with his face in a puddle. The Major was too proud to indulge in any of this tomfoolery and when he spoke to the reporter he adopted a haughty air. His name was Major Miguel Fernandez. He was thirty-three years old. He had olive skin, a small mouth with unusually well-defined bow-shaped lips and hooded, soulful eyes. He walked with a slump of the shoulders, not a defeated slump, but the disguise of an athletic man who wishes, for some reason, to disclaim any special prowess. His love was not the army. His love was the literature of England.

"Now," he said, "perhaps we might go and drink coffee. Then we can discuss this."

Together they dodged the puddles.

It was a modern café built by its German owner to take money from the truck drivers and the bus passengers and in this he had been quite successful. He was a thin dried-out walnut of a man, who sat, in his white apron, on a special perch he had built for himself and his cash register. Here he spiked the bills, gave change, and surveyed the white and gold speckled floor, the neon lights (three different colours), the jet black laminex tables, the pinball machines and, through a system of mirrors, could check on anyone who might be considering leaving without paying.

But when David Joy and the Major entered his establishment he descended from his pulpit and, with a rare smile, escorted them personally to a booth at the window.

Miguel Fernandez sat where he could watch his men unload the truck. He was beguiled by what he saw as David Joy's Englishness. He liked the cool way he had climbed from his truck and lit his cigar, not exactly like David Niven, but like somebody, somebody English. He asked him questions about his place of birth, date of arrival in Colombia, papers and so on, but he managed to do it as one man of culture addressing another, and so supplied details of his own education and family history. But when he saw one of his men hold up machine guns from a crate, his stomach tightened, because there were simple orders to be carried out in circumstances such as these (officially a state of emergency) and he no longer had the appetite for them. In a year he would be out of the army. He would open a bookshop near the university at Medelin and sell Stevenson in translation but also in English.

"Mr Joy, what were you carrying in your truck?"

"Motor-cycle parts."

"If I told you they were guns, not motor-cycle parts?"

David Joy sipped his coffee. "I took the job," he said, "like any other. I can't spend my time opening crates."

Miguel Fernandez nodded in encouragement. "And he gave you money. You gave him a receipt perhaps."

"No, he gave me no money."

"It could be most important to you, Mr Joy, that he gave you money."

David Joy was not unaware of the respect being accorded him. He drew it into himself. He felt slow and lazy and he answered after a yawn. "He was to give me the money later," he smiled. "When the parts were delivered." He felt no fear, none at all. His head was perfectly clear, perhaps exaggeratedly clear, as if he was under the influence of a mild hallucinogen.

"But he had money." Miguel Fernandez had small pink-nailed hands which he had the habit of playing with, bringing the finger-tips together, then twisting them on an imaginary axis and so on. It would have been a more acceptable habit, David Joy thought, in someone with longer fingers.

"I trusted him," David said, edging out further on some imaginary tightrope.

"No," the Major said sadly, "you did not trust him. You do not drive for ten hours for a poor man who says he will pay you later."

David signalled the waiter for more coffee. The movement of his hand conveyed perfect authority.

"If you a businessman, you take money. You are a contractor. Perhaps the receipt has slipped your mind. Perhaps he paid you and you kept the receipt in your book."

"No," David Joy smiled. (This is not ordinary. I am not ordinary.) "I have no receipt."

"But you are not a Communist."

"Do I look like a Communist?" Now, in captivity, he felt freer than he had ever felt.

"Then in God's name write a receipt, Mr Joy."

"I cannot write a receipt because the man gave me no money."

"Then you are a Communist."

"You know I am not a Communist. The man asked me to carry goods for him."

"You are a very stupid man. Stay here."

David Joy was left alone at the table where he took pleasure in observing himself.

Major Fernandez was talking to Bogotá on the telephone. The line was bad. He pleaded for David Joy's life while David Joy sat by the window smoking a long thin cigar and drinking black coffee. Children came and stood in the doorway. He smiled at them and they hid. It was like a dream and it was, in some way, perfect. It was not the disgrace with the two knife-wielding spivs who had sent him scurrying back to the safety of his waiter's uniform. Everything he did was elegant, and proud. His movements were, just so. He lit another cigar with a flourish.

When the Major returned, David Joy observed the exotic nature of his uniform, the romantic quality of his face, his refined movements, the crumpled packet of cigarettes he placed on the table. It was like a film. It was as if he had never been in Colombia and had been dumped, just now, into this seat.

"You are trying to make me kill you," the Major said. "It would be simpler for you to just jump off the bridge."

David bowed his head and smiled. He appreciated the style of the

Major's comment. He offered him a cigar and was pleasantly surprised when he accepted it.

"You have my word I am not a Communist."

The Major looked at him with renewed hope. "You did not know about the guns?"

For a moment David allowed himself to despise the man's pleading eyes.

"I guessed," he said, "yes."

"I am not going to shoot you," Major Fernandez told him, "no matter how much you desire me to." And the rules of the game were thus, finally, stated.

Night came and they were still there. The soldiers crowded into the café and sat at the tables drinking coffee and playing cards. The German looked unhappy but did not complain. It appeared however that none of this was bad for business at all. Quite the opposite. Locals came to see the man in the white suit and they, of course, bought coffee and one or two purchased cigarettes. When the Major talked to Bogotá (who would pay?) the café went quiet as they listened to him plead for the life of the man in the white suit. The foreigner, the Major said, was not a Communist. He was a madman. He should be deported, perhaps, or locked up in an asylum, but not shot.

David Joy bought wine for the soldiers. The soldiers passed the bottles to the people from the town. David bought more wine. The German did not smile but his pen was kept busy and occasionally, behind the shelter of a ledger, he took out a small electronic calculator and fiddled with it before returning it to its place.

Major Fernandez was trying to communicate the essential quality of David Joy to the blockheads in Bogotá but he was only making a fool of himself doing it. He had family in the military. He irritated valuable contacts throughout the night trying to save David Joy, who played cards with the soldiers, danced (once, but to much applause) with a girl from the town, and answered questions which were translated back and forth by a throaty-voiced fifteen-year-old boy.

"Aren't you afraid?" they asked him.

"I was born in a lightning storm," he said.

A woman gave him a shawl to sit on in case the café chairs should soil his suit. He accepted it graciously, as his due. In return he told them stories which were translated a sentence at a time.

At about three o'clock in the morning Miguel Fernandez joined the table, a glass of wine in his hand, his uniform unbuttoned.

"David," he said, "you will only have to say where you were taking the guns." He was smiling, "That is all."

Some of the townspeople had gone home. But the fifteen-year-old boy was still awake to translate this for the audience. They waited. They looked at David Joy, their laughter ready, like pigeons, to fly around the room.

"No," David Joy said.

"*Non,*" the fifteen-year-old translated needlessly.

They did not know that he could not have provided the information anyway. But even if he had known it is doubtful if he would have weakened. He could not soil the perfection of this, this pure white perfect thing. The only perfect thing.

It is likely that the audience would have stayed to the bitter end, trooped out into the cold dawn and gone down under the bridge where the execution was to be carried out. But the Major cleared them out in a fury, screaming abuse at them.

"Carrion," he told them, "vermin. Go before it is too late."

So when the time came there was only the German to join the procession and he locked the café before following the party down the muddy embankment. It occurred to him, watching the Major and the man in the white suit, that it was the Major who looked as if he would be shot and the other who would do the shooting.

It was cold. David's balls retracted into his stomach and he knew his scrotum was a tough tight little purse. He wanted a piss. Would he piss himself after he died, as he died? He shivered. He stopped and turned his back to piss. The party halted. The men watched him. His penis had shrivelled in the cold. He turned his back because he did not want them to doubt his manhood. He watched the steam rise as his warm urine hit the ground. He felt like he had as a child on Sunday nights watching the highway full of cars returning home after a weekend.

He was not frightened at all. There had been no fear since the episode started. It had all been so easy. If he had known it would be this easy he would not have worried about it.

He was more distressed when, going down the embankment, he slipped and muddied the back of his suit.

"Fuck," he said.

But when he saw Miguel Fernandez's sick melancholy face it relieved him even of that pain.

"Cheer up," he told him, and felt again some of the bravado he had felt in the warm of the café with the soldiers gathered around him and the jukebox playing and that girl he had danced with, he had missed her name. "Cheer up, Miguel. You can have a big breakfast."

"You're a fool," the Major said bitterly.

"Possibly."

"It is unnecessary. Please, David . . ."

For a moment he hesitated. For an instant panic fluttered its wings in his ears.

"No," he said, "it is necessary."

And he went to stand against the embankment with his hands behind his back. He stood before the unhappy soldiers like a man posing for the photographer in the square of a tourist town. The mud was not visible to the camera.

"Come on," he said, "hurry up."

Miguel Fernandez did not wish to look at the body, but it was expected. As he walked towards the crumpled thing that had been a man he was not ready for the look of ugly surprise he would see on the dead man's face, nor did he know that one night nearly twenty years later, his son's wife would tell him the story of The Man with the White Suit. It was not quite the real story; it had become mixed with other stories David Joy had told that night.

The story of the man with the white suit ends formally, always the same, with the sun coming out as he falls, and they say *Pero era sólo una mariposa* (but it was only a butterfly) *que se volaba* (flying away).

The wrapper of a sweet confection delivered fifty-five years through time. But not even Miguel Fernandez knew that.

Harry Joy found Honey Barbara in the morning, one hundred miles up Highway One, and had he been two minutes earlier or ten minutes later, he would probably never have found her at all.

He brought the Jaguar to a stop in front of her and watched her run towards the car. At the passenger door, she recognized him.

"I'm not coming back," she said.

"I know."

"I'm going home."

"I'll take you."

She opened the door and looked at him, hesitating with her bundle resting on the seat.

"It's four hundred miles."

"That's O.K."

236

"Not all the way." She threw her bundle into the back seat and closed the door.

It was a difficult journey for both of them but at least they both knew there was nothing to say.

"I don't like you soft," she said once, touching the cuff of his sleeve.

He didn't understand and smiled painfully.

"I like you hard. Not all this silk." She clenched her fist and smiled.

"What are you saying?"

"We had nice times, Harry."

"Yes."

"We had some nice fucks."

"Yes."

They drove through Sunday traffic past giant fibreglass pineapples and bananas surrounded by buses and people with secret pimples on their arses.

"Can I come and see you here?"

"They'd think you were a spy."

"Who are they?"

"Realists," she said and sunk into her seat and watched the wipers slurp at the rain on the window.

It was five o'clock and getting dark when she made him stop at the turn off to Paddy Melon Road just on the curve of the bitumen where Paddy Melon Road goes downhill through the casurinas, a collection of puddles in a hard ribbon of mustard clay.

It had stopped raining for the moment but there were heavy inky blue clouds behind Mount Warning.

"It'll rain," he said.

"I don't mind the rain," she said. "They'll be waiting for it now. We have droughts in winter."

"Will you write to me?"

She bit her lip and they kissed uncomfortably, their bodies spanning the bucket seats and instruments of the Jaguar.

She took the bundle and closed the door without looking at him, and he stayed in the car with the engine running and watched her walk down the gravel road. He noticed that she flinched from time to time when a sharp rock bit into her soft bare feet.

It was noon on a Friday and the city was crowded. People stopped to look at Bettina, and it was not because of her cleverly cut black dress or the silk scarf with the signature of the famous designer she wrapped around her black bag, nor was it because of the strut, the prance (almost) of her plump legs, but the sheer quality of anger she contained. Her cheeks had flattened, almost hollowed, as they did when she was very drunk or very angry, and she was not drunk.

She bumped into people and did not look around.

She stopped at a traffic light and a whiskery old woman winked at her.

"Cheer-up, dearie."

"Mutant!" she said. Her dress was by Cardin, her shoes by Gucci.

She had so much anger she did not know what to do with it, no, not anger – rage. They had made a fool (what a fool, what an idiot) of Bettina Joy.

She walked into the corner pub opposite the railway station. It was the public bar. They made way for her and served her immediately. She ordered a double Scotch, drank it in a gulp, ordered another one and drank that.

Fifty-six men watched her in silence.

"That's it, girly."

Bettina curled her whole face into such a display of ugly contempt that the whole bar erupted into laughter. She threw money on the bar and left.

Until today life had been nearly perfect. In the three months since Honey Barbara had gone Harry had settled into work, they had all settled into work. Now there was no real reason to come home early, or even come home at all. They had heated soup in an electric jug, drank a little (but not a lot) white wine. They made toast. Whoever had the time would make the toast, it didn't matter. They changed the name to Joy, Joy & Davis, and that's what they were: a team. There was such a sense of excitement, of comradeship, and it was nothing (it was everything!) to work till three in the morning, or even, as they'd done on the second Mobil presentation, till dawn. They typed their own reports and bound them. There was nothing they couldn't do: she was good with ads, Harry was good with strategies, and Joel had revealed, finally, that he had a better eye for detail than either of them. Joel wrote the conference reports. He dotted i's and crossed t's with an enthusiasm that sometimes drove her crazy.

Just two weeks ago they had opened a letter and found they had sixteen entries accepted in the New York One Show. Copywriter: Bettina Joy, Art Director: Bettina Joy, etc.

Their profit projection for the calendar year was three hundred thousand dollars.

The New York trade press printed one of Bettina's press releases.

And then, this morning, in that grey dull little room with the wrought-iron balcony, that stale imitation of Paris with its waiting room stinking of meths, she had sat with no more trepidation than at the dentist's while he clipped the x-ray on to the screen and read a report.

"Mrs Joy," he said, "have you ever been exposed to petrol over a . . ."

"Tell me," she said.

He was tall and handsome and had a slightly roguish eye. She liked him even if she hated his business.

"This is something," he stopped and looked again. "This is something we normally only find in people who are exposed to petrol fumes over a very long period. Mechanics, service station attendants . . ." he faded away, smiling apologetically at such comparisons.

"Tell me."

"We'll get another opinion," he said, "of course."

"It's something nasty."

"Have you been exposed to petrol a lot?" He managed a smile. "Hardly." Then, avoiding her eye for a second, using the time to look down at her card: "It's a malignancy, I'm afraid. A rather nasty one."

"Yes." She could be very normal. She would be. In all the times she had imagined this scene she had gone to pieces. "Yes, it's alright. I think I knew." This was not true. SHE HADN'T KNOWN. SHE HADN'T EVEN GUESSED.

She had to find out the truth.

"It is a particular malignancy normally caused by petrol."

"Petrol causes cancer?"

He clicked his tongue sadly and pulled his lips back sideways against his teeth. "The benzine in petrol, to be precise."

"You'd think they'd tell people," she said wryly. She was proud of herself. She had style. They told her she had cancer and she was being sardonic. But he still hadn't told her.

"How long have I got?" she said the clichéd words. She said it to have it unsaid. He was going to say, oh, it's not *lethal*. That was the plan.

She tricked him only too well.

"Oh," he said, "you could have a *year*."

And only when the sentence was finished did he realize what a terrible mistake he had made, for he saw her face collapse and twist; defeat and rage battled with each other for control of her features, but both lost to the sheer force of her will.

"I need more than a year," she said.

"Mrs Joy ..."

"You're ridiculous!" she said. "I need three years to make it in New York. I can't do it in a year."

He folded his hands and when they rubbed across each other they sounded dry and papery.

"Why don't they tell people?" she said.

"I'm sorry ...?" He fiddled in his drawer where he had a 10-ml ampule of Valium.

"Petrol causes cancer. They were right."

He was ashamed of himself. He had bungled it. "Who was right, Mrs Joy?"

"The silly hippy was right. She said petrol causes cancer ..."

"There are many carcinogens in common use."

"Saccharin? PVC? ..."

"Yes," he said surprised.

"Well why don't they tell us."

He filled the hypodermic. "I'm going to give you a shot of this."

"What is it?" and her eyes were momentarily bright with hope.

"Valium," he said, his eyes downcast.

"Forget it," she said.

"It'll make you feel better."

"Nothing can make you feel better," she said, "when you have been made a fool of."

Her whole life had been built on bullshit.

Later, Harry was to think that if she had had more time to think it over she would not have done what she did, if Lucy had been home, if Honey Barbara had still been there, if Joel had not been driving out to Krappe and if he had not been lunching with Adrian Clunes.

He was wrong. Her actions were carefully thought out.

He remembered coming back from lunch and staring with disbelief at the torn-up Mobil story boards outside her door.

"What happened?" he asked Joel, who was sitting at his desk.

"Changed her mind."

"Good," he remembered saying. Bettina's best work always

happened like that, rejecting a good campaign and then doing a brilliant one. "Good."

That night they had all meant to go to the Krappe sales convention for "Sweet-tooth" but Bettina begged off because her ads were not finished. She put a note in Harry's diary saying the time for the Mobil presentation had been put forward till eleven, and that she would meet him downstairs in the coffee shop at 10.45.

When Harry came home she was asleep. When Bettina got up Harry was asleep.

She must have gone straight to the office.

As the tea lady remembered it, the whole thing had been very light-hearted. Everyone in the boardroom had been very relaxed and it seemed as if they were looking foward to the meeting. She heard Mrs Joy apologize for her husband's absence and Mr Jones, the Marketing Director, had suggested that they postpone the meeting but Mrs Joy had said: "No, no need. You're stuck with me."

They had laughed.

Mrs Joy had asked for a strong black coffee and when it was pointed out to her that all the coffee was one strength she asked for two cups. She had looked very smart, in a white linen suit with a large white hat. She did not normally wear hats, the tea lady thought, but it was very attractive, and the Chairman had commented on it. Bettina had coloured a little, pleased with the compliment.

They were short one cup, because Mrs Joy had had two, and the tea lady had returned to the meeting temporarily with a cup for Mr Bernstein just as Bettina was unpacking a large cardboard box. On the table she placed three large bottles of petrol.

Mr Cleveland said something about getting close to the product.

It seems unlikely that Bettina ever found time to present her campaign. Perhaps her natural impatience got the better of her. But one can imagine her standing at the head of the table and the men leaning back and smiling, enjoying the little theatre that comes from a good presentation.

"This," she might have said, "is petrol."

A joke, the sheer obviousness of it.

And if the wicks were not already in the bottles she might well have enjoyed the suspense as she put them in. She must have kept their interest — no one left the room just yet.

Did she say anything at all about her cancer?

If so, one imagines she would have had to do it quickly, as a curse almost, and there would have been no time for questions.

Miss Dobson, whose desk is outside the boardroom, beside the Managing Director's office, thought she heard Mrs Joy shout the word "Mucus" and then there was that terrible explosion, followed by two more in sharp succession and all at once the overhead sprinklers poured down, drenching the eighth floor and Mr Cleveland ran out of the boardroom and collapsed screaming in front of her. She had not recognized him. He rolled into the curtains and set them on fire.

Only one advertisement survived that inferno (certainly no people did) and beneath its bubbled cell overlay one could read the headline, set in Goudy caps and lower case: "Petrol killed me", it said and it is an interesting reflection on the art of advertising that it was four hours before anyone bothered to read the body copy and learned that the death in the headline was a death by cancer.

So when the police interrogated Harry for the first time, on the shocked grey ghastly day in that dull little office in the Mobil Research Department, there was only one motive he could think of.

"They must have rejected her ads," he said.

The faces at Palm Avenue had a grey waxy look. They were numbed and did not question the search but admired, in a vague distracted way, the style in which the police seemed not so much to search as to caress pieces of clothing, stroke objects, and when they slid their big blunt hands behind couches there was a deftness, almost a tenderness, that contradicted their gruff masculine manner. They stood on chairs and peered at the dead insects inside light shades; they worked their way along bookshelves and removed books with a gentleness that could be taken for respect.

There were only two of them, Macdonald and Herpes – whose red inflamed face suggested some connection with his unfortunate name – and although they were both titled Detective, it was Macdonald who appeared to be in charge. They were both big men but broad rather than tall, a physical type that is sometimes compared, often with admiration, to a brick lavatory. They wore shorts and long white socks. They carried clipboards.

It was Herpes who ushered everyone into the kitchen and

Macdonald who began to interview them, one at a time, in the dining room. There was little conversation in the kitchen and what there was centred on such problems as whether a person wanted coffee or tea and such prosaic details as names and dates and places of birth. To all this, they submitted meekly.

The more serious work took place next door and from time to time the smooth murmuring in the dining room would be broken by the lump of a sob as someone collided with some painful flotsam of memory.

It was the thirteenth of September, that time of the year when one night can be hot and steamy and the next bitterly cold, as if there were forces still arguing for a continuation of winter and others for the beginning of summer and summer would win one night, and winter the next.

The forces of winter were in control on the night after Bettina's death.

Breath hung in the air in the kitchen as they sat around the table like effigies of themselves with only their suspended breath to suggest that they were flesh and blood.

They were not yet told how or why Bettina had died. The police had only just read Bettina's body copy, and deliberately said nothing of her cancer. The questioning, they said, was routine.

The following interview with Joel was not atypical, although it could hardly be judged to be routine. Imagine then, the policeman sitting at the head of the dining-room table (how far away those lunatic nights seemed now), a radiator at his feet and some thirty books, mostly paperbacks, stacked neatly on the table. The titles of these books might suggest a house with a far more serious political bent than it had. Kropotkin's revolutionary pamphlets, Ernest Mandel on Trotsky, an Everyman edition of *Das Kapital* in two volumes, *Social Banditry*, and so on. These books were Lucy's, but the book that interested Macdonald most of all was *The Politics of Cancer* by Samuel S. Epstein, which Honey Barbara had bought and abandoned after its fifth depressing page.

"Do you have any particular theory about the cause of cancer?"

"No, not really."

"Do you think cancer is political?"

"I don't know."

"Is it someone's *fault*?"

"I suppose so."

"What do you mean exactly?"

"Well I've heard people say it's caused by chemicals, but I don't ..."

'Which people were these?"

"There was a woman, I don't know her real name, called Honey Barbara."

"Were there many meetings where this was discussed?"

"No, not meetings. Everybody just got drunk."

"Have you ever seen this book before?"

"No."

"But that is where you sleep, on that mattress?"

"That's right. I told you already."

"This book was under that mattress."

"Many people used the bed, all the time."

"Many people? You said you slept only with Mrs Joy!"

"Many people, during the day, to sit on, like a chair."

"And although you've slept on top of this book, you've never seen it?"

"No."

"How thick would you say it was?"

"Two inches."

"You slept on top of a two-inch-thick book and never felt it?"

"No."

"Do you think people who cause cancer should be killed?"

"I've never thought about it. Is that what Bettina did?"

"How tall are you?"

"Why do you want to know?"

"How tall are you?"

"Five foot six and a half."

And so on.

They saved Harry till last. He entered the room with every intention of co-operating, of being perfectly polite. In return he hoped to have some clarification of his wife's death. There was a feeling of shame in the kitchen. As if they had all done something wrong and would, in due course, be punished.

But Macdonald was soon asking him about Honey Barbara.

"I don't know."

"They said she was your girlfriend."

"No."

Macdonald looked at him and sucked his teeth. He had a big face with small ears like delicate handles on an ugly hand-made pot.

"Look here, fellow ..." he began.

He went no further. Harry had heard that tone before. It was the sound of a policeman who thinks he can get away with murder and he was not going to have it.

"Do you know who I am?" Harry said, pushing his face close to Macdonald's. "Do you know who my friends are? Do you realize," he stood up and it would have been ridiculous for Macdonald to stand up too so that Harry remained towering over him, "that the Chairman of Mobil was a close friend of mine. Not only my wife . . ." he hesitated, "is dead, but also my colleagues. Now if you wish to harass me, to cause me and my family trouble tonight I will be on the telephone and I shall have your arse kicked so hard you'll spit your teeth out."

Macdonald hesitated.

It is a measure of Harry's confidence in his safe position in Hell that his slow anger at the behaviour of the police, his grief, his irritation that Macdonald had commandeered the dining room rather than the kitchen, that no one was going to light the fire if he didn't, came forth in such a controlled silk-gowned display of rage.

Macdonald, having seen the house to be expensive but not of the first rank, was as surprised — more surprised — than the people in the kitchen who stirred expectantly and waited.

When Macdonald gave in it was not because Harry's face was red and his eyes yellow, nor that he was a widower, possibly an innocent one, nor was it the quality of his hand-stitched suit, whose expensive subtleties were lost on Macdonald, but that Harry said "*shall*" have your arse kicked so hard you'll spit your teeth out.

There was something in this combination of correctness and violence which he instinctively reacted to, and he decided to give him, at least for the moment, the benefit of the doubt.

"We have an unpleasant job to do," he said stiffly, lining up some pieces of paper on his clipboard, "and we try to do it as pleasantly as possible. I understand that you're upset."

Harry nodded and stepped back to allow the man to stand.

On this sort of night (wind rattling the tall windows in the dining room, the big fig scratching itself against the western wall) they would have eaten pea soup from big white bowls, baked vegetables and Honey Barbara's apple pie. They would have opened a magnum of Raussan Segla. Bettina would have sat in her wing-back chair, her face tired, a glass in her hand, while Joel nestled at her feet and gently rubbed her generous calves. And everyone would have been momentarily caught in a honeyed silence accompanied only by the oboe of the wind, the brush of the fig and the low percussive thump of the door.

Ah, Honey Barbara would have thought, all those dreams! And seen behind all those flame-flickered eyes the shimmering shapes of decadent utopias.

But tonight the room was dark and the street light threw down a blue sheen, like a spilled light globe trapped beneath the wax of the polished floor, and there was a deadness in their eyes that even the lights, once turned on, did nothing to change.

Only Joel burned bright and it occurred to no one that the energy he brought to lighting the fire and preparing the meal which no one had the stomach to eat (bacon, eggs, pancakes, maple syrup) was not fuelled by inexhaustible supplies of life but was more like that expended by blow-flies caught against the glass.

They admired his optimism and were irritated by it at the same time. They wanted a warm place to weep freely without shame but he placed sensible, practical things in their laps.

Yet nothing could prevent the mental image they all secretly carried: blackened, bubbling, Bettina's unseen corpse, this turd floating insistently before them, showing itself, unfolding, parading even before their open eyes.

Among the practical things they discussed, huddled around the fire on blankets and mattresses, was the need to remain silent about Honey Barbara. It was Harry's suggestion and they all supported it, except Joel who could not see that it was so important.

"I told them already," Joel said, "but they weren't interested."

"They were interested," Harry said, "they asked me. If they ask you again say you made a mistake."

"Why?"

"Because," Harry hissed, "she's poor. That's how it works, isn't it. We're rich, they leave us alone. We've bought our safety."

"You were fantastic," Lucy said, "you were wonderful."

"But we haven't done anything wrong," David said.

"Don't matter," Ken said. "I was busted once by the cops for dope and it couldn't have been my stash because it was in the teapot, a great big lump of hash, and they were drinking tea out of it. The stuff they busted me for, they planted on me, but I couldn't say that in court. Harry's right. They bust poor people."

"But we haven't done anything," Joel said.

"They don't need a reason," Harry said.

"Because Bettina has killed a lot of rich people," Ken said. "And rich people don't like to see other rich people get killed. It makes them go crazy."

They shared out tranquillizers solemnly and drank them with cognac to make them work better and then they built up the fire and bedded down beside it, without even discussing why they might do such an unusual thing. They huddled together on an odd assortment of mattresses, lumpy shapes under blue blankets and pale eiderdowns, like travellers in a waiting room in a foreign country.

Only Joel stayed awake, feeding the fire. At one o'clock Harry heard him cooking potato chips in the kitchen.

The noise was insistent and irritating, a continual bump, bump, bump. It was Lucy who wrapped a blanket around herself and went down the wet steps on that grey overcast morning.

The noise came from underneath the verandah and was caused, she later discovered, by Ken's electric drill which was hanging from its cord and being blown against one of the house's high wooden stumps: bump, bump, bump.

It was not the drill she saw, however, it was Joel, who had used its strong black cord to hang himself. His shining shoes were just an inch from the ground and the smell, the horrible stench of his shit, made it perfectly clear that, this time at least, he was not playing a joke.

There was no sympathy from the police. They put everyone back in the kitchen and started all over again, but this time there was a pale excitement in their faces and when Harry saw the thin impatient set of Macdonald's lips he knew that there was no safety for him in Hell. He was *persona non grata* with Those in Charge.

They yarded them like cattle, dragging them out for questioning one at a time, sometimes just for one question, for ten seconds, then back into the yard.

"In here." Lucy was called into the dining room where Harry stood.

"Say that in front of her," Macdonald said to Harry.

"I've never seen that map before," Harry said.

"O.K., take her back."

It was unnerving. Like standing in front of one of those machines that throw tennis balls.

"How tall are you?"

"Five foot eleven."

"When did you first meet Joel?"

No one was nice any more. Herpes did not show the photo of his holiday house. Macdonald told no jokes. Other policemen with beards and long hair began a search of the house which was neither stylish nor gentle. In the garage outside they used a rattling power tool to dismantle the Jaguar.

"You fink Joel was in on it, don't you?" Ken asked Herpes.

Herpes pointed a thick finger and narrowed his red-lidded eyes. Ken was quiet.

The police found passports, air tickets to New York, a cancer map. They did not doubt that Joel was in on it.

When everyone had been interrogated once, Macdonald came and leant against the doorway in the kitchen.

"This family", he said, "has been harbouring at least two terrorists, possibly more. I have had the unpleasant duty to spend most of last night in those homes where fathers and husbands have been murdered by two people from this house. So today," he bit the inside of his cheek and looked thoughtfully at Harry, "we won't be having any shouting or threats. At least," he smiled, "not from you." It was a pleasant smile, and more frightening because of it.

Finally, after one more round of interrogation, the police departed, leaving behind them a book-strewn house with a dismantled Jaguar still in the garage, its body panels stacked on the lawn.

"She had cancer," Harry said slowly, "She damn-well had cancer."

No one was listening to him. They had other things on their minds. They turned up the radio to protect themselves from bugs. They turned on taps and whispered conversations. They still wore big pullovers and thick socks although the afternoon had become suddenly hot. They prickled under wool.

Ken and Lucy were arguing with David. Ken was pushing a dirty finger at David's cashmere chest. David was looking frightened but he stood his ground.

"She had cancer," Harry said. "From this house, living with us."

David had stolen an air ticket from under Macdonald's nose, sliding it off the table while he looked the policeman in the eye. Ken was backing him against the refrigerator.

"It's my ticket," David was saying.

"I don't want your ticket, sonny," Ken said.

"You can't have it."

Ken closed his eyes in pain. He went to the kitchen table and sat down.

"The middle class are fucking disgusting."

"You can't stop me," David said, but he didn't move from where he had been pushed. "I was the one who hid his passport. If I want to go, I go."

"And leave us in the shit," Lucy said. "Typical."

"What shit? We haven't done anything."

"She had cancer," Harry said, but no one was interested. The radio played the traffic reports. The bridges were blocked. David and Lucy forgot about the suspected bugs and started shouting at each other. Ken sat with his head in his hands at the kitchen table.

Harry could feel the cancer in the air. It had been here all the time. It was impregnated in the walls, like spores, like a mould, invisible but always there in what they breathed, what they ate. He could feel the cells in his own body rising, multiplying, marshalling against him, to make him beg for mercy, for death, for release, slowly, agonizingly over an eternity of pain that they would call, euphemistically, A Long Illness.

What was about to begin was possibly the lowest, most shameful period of his life, five hours of panic in which he would abandon Ken and Lucy to the Special Branch and fight his son for money.

But his behaviour was not so different, in fact much milder, than the panic that was to run through the Western world (and parts of the industrialized East) ten years later when the cancer epidemic really arrived, and then it came at a time of deep recession, material shortages, unemployment and threatening nuclear war, and it proved the last straw for the West which had, until then, still managed to tie its broken pieces together with cotton threads of material optimism which served instead of the older social fabric of religion and established custom. Then the angry cancer victims could no longer be contained by devices as simple as Alice Dalton's Ward L, and took to the streets in what began as demonstrations and ended in half-organized bands, looting for heroin first, and then everything else, and Bettina's act in the Mobil office was no more than a brief eddy before the whirlwind of their rage.

So as you watch Harry Joy running around his own house in panic you have the comfort of knowing he is something less than freakish. His cancer map has come to life like some deadly pin-ball machine finally (the penny dropped) activated. His skin prickles.

249

His stomach hurts and he notices a strange coldness at the place where he imagines (incorrectly) his liver is.

And there he is, looting, going through his son's (nice boy, going to be a doctor) drawers looking for money, and yes, actually wrestling with the boy as they fight for a bundle of notes which fall from the desk top and float across the room. They scramble to pick them up. He catches his son's foot and sits on his chest, and from this position negotiates a puffing red-faced deal.

"Half. 50–50. O.K.?"

"O.K."

But once released the scramble is on again, and there must be another fight, and the son must be subdued again, and this time with a backhanded blow which will partly deafen him and cause him great pain on the aeroplane he will shortly board.

"You won't need it," Harry grunted, scrambling across the carpet. "I need it. I'm leaving."

"I'm leaving too."

"Where going?"

"New York."

They fought over a photograph of Bettina, and David won the bigger piece. Harry went to his room and packed a bag, cramming in silk shirts as if they were currency. He arrived downstairs just behind his partly deaf son. David had his suitcase with him.

"You think you're a real smart dude," Ken said to David, "but those coppers aren't dumb. They'll know you knocked off that ticket."

"Right under their nose," David said, but he stayed near the doorway, sitting on his case.

Harry sat at the table and let Ken pour him tea.

"You're a fool," Lucy told her brother.

He spat at her. "You're not so smart," he said, "limpet."

"Why don't you all shut up," Ken said quietly. He rolled a cigarette and looked at it closely while he did it. "Our only answer is just to be calm and stick together. We haven't done anything wrong. These coppers aren't like the drug squad – they're not all bent. They just think we're terrorists and they'll find out we're not. If you geezers run away we'll all be stuffed. They'll beat the shitter out of us and they'll catch you lot. It won't matter what you say, if they think you've done something they'll frame you."

"I know where to go," Harry said.

"Where?"

"The country."

"With darling Honey Barbara," Lucy said. "Honey Barbara thinks you're full of shit, Harry. They'd probably burn you as a witch."

But it was obvious then that no amount of reason or logic would stop either of them and David walked away without any farewell and Harry stayed. He stayed through a silent meal of sardines on toast. He stayed through the television until after it finished. He stayed sitting in the living room when Lucy and Ken went to bed.

They lay in bed and listened for noises. Nothing moved in the house.

"He's going to go," Ken said. "He won't be there in the morning."

At two o'clock they woke to a familiar noise.

"The Cadillac."

"Fuck him. Let him take it."

They lay and listened to him go backwards and forwards across the lawn as he manoeuvred the car out on to the drive.

"The creep," Lucy said as the Good Bloke drove away from Palm Avenue for the last time.

The Pan Am Jumbo took off, on schedule, at 8 p.m., into the waiting thunderstorm. Lightning filled the sky beside David's seat. Below him, in breaks in the clouds, he caught a glimpse of the yellow spiderweb of lighted streets which had, at last, released him.

He stood before the lightning and faced the monsters of the night.

Part Six
Blue Bread and Sapphires

Daze walked along the ridge looking for the blood wood. It was a hot November morning and the Razorback had a slight blue haze around it and the wind from the sea made the gums throw their khaki-silver umbrellas to and fro. He had slept in. Soon it would be too hot for this sort of work. He hefted the sledgehammer on to his shoulder and shook the small bag of wedges he held in the other. Only two wedges. People were careless with wedges. He could remember when there had been five of them, perfectly graduated from small to large. It had been a lot easier splitting fence posts then, but with only two wedges it became more difficult, particularly with blood wood which often had an almost corkscrew grain. It was harder with two wedges, but two wedges were still enough. Wedges were amazing things. He stopped on the trail to think about wedges.

He was over forty but his body was hard and stringy and the brown legs beneath his tattered shorts were a young man's legs. He had a pointed chin which hid beneath a sparse, slightly fuzzy beard, and a sharp inquisitive nose either side of which were small humorous eyes. He was stoned and kept forgetting why he had come.

The blood wood.

And he had been thinking about the wedge, the small wedge, and how amazing it was that the smallest wedge could finally split that old grey blood wood open to show its red secret heart. He did not think anything very profound, but he enjoyed his thoughts and he discovered and rediscovered things for himself all day in this manner. If he had had company he would have talked about the wedges, punctuating his meditations with "Mmms" and "Ahs" and his companion would be sometimes amused, sometimes bored, sometimes even enlightened by these meditations. Possibly (almost certainly) they would have explored the possibility of making new wedges and gone through the various methods by which this might be done, starting with smelting the iron, or even earlier, prospecting, perhaps on that rusty outcrop the Krishnas had on their land, and then the methods by which negotiations would have to begin with the Krishnas, perhaps sending Paul Bees or Honey Barbara first because they were permitted to place their hives in the Krishnas' ironbark forest in return, of course, for a percentage of the honey.

He nearly walked past the blood wood. It was just below the ridge, its dead grey trunk cut in ten places to show the hard red wood with the big empty pipe running up its centre.

"Mmm." He took the mandarin from his pocket and peeled it. He admired the fine spray it released as he pulled back the peel. One day they would have a goat fence right across the bottom of the property, up here over the ridge, and almost down to the rain forest at the bottom. There was no money this year because their crop had been ripped off, but it didn't cost anything to cut the wood and split it into posts. Later they would get the wire and strain the fence, but in the meantime there was plenty of work to do. He was still thinking about the Krishnas. They were not the most friendly people in the world but somebody over there understood something about growing corn. Their corn was huge and sweet and yellow, as succulent as yellow peas joined together on a cob.

That's interesting, he thought — they have yellow robes. Yellow corn. He tried to think of other yellow things the Krishnas had. Yellow truck, he remembered, and yellow pawpaws, but their pawpaws were not so good.

As he began to split the first length of blood wood he was still naming yellow things to himself, testing the magical power of the Krishnas when it came to yellow. He tried to remember the significance of yellow in Colour Therapy but couldn't remember. He would talk to Crystal about it.

When he was working, he worked hard, hoisting the sledgehammer and using its own weight to let it drop hard. Splitting posts was more a stop-start type of thing, and not as satisfying as using a scythe which is more rhythmic, and even sharpening a scythe is a pleasure, getting the edge at once sharp but also, just slightly, jagged, so that when the grass is cut it is not so much like a razor slice but a fine rip and the grass falls softly sideways, flop.

As he worked, his mind wandered from one thing to the next like a rivulet finding its way downhill. He had to kill three billies tonight. He never got used to that, never got used to death no matter what he pretended to Heather. They swapped the goat meat for meat other people had killed. He could not kill a Billy without thinking about his second son, even now, and it was ten years since that had happened. (His tiny hands.) They buried him down in the valley and they sent out Health Inspectors who dug him up again. Now they knew not to register births. They registered nothing. There were eighty-nine children here and no one else in the world knew about them. Two had been buried. If they'd been registered they wouldn't even have been able to do that. The bastards took your own dead from you and made you put them in their holes.

Shit!

Both wedges were jammed in the wood. He should have taken the tomahawk to use as a third wedge. He had been too cocky. He turned around looking for a piece of rock or a piece of wood he could use instead.

He wandered down the hill a little and it was then he saw, lying across a prostrate acacia, a creamy silk shirt.

This is dangerous, he thought.

He stood and looked at it, not touching it. Then he squatted down and looked around for a while, making small sudden movements with his head. He took his worn cotton shirt off then, and lifted the silk shirt from its prickly resting place.

He slipped it on. Hasn't been worn, he thought, finding the neck button done up when he already had it over his head. Could be dangerous. He brought his hands round and undid the offending button.

A perfect fit.

He stayed squatting. There was someone around dropping silk shirts. The police did not carry silk shirts. The Health Department did not carry silk shirts.

He rested on his knees. A little honey-eater came and hung off the acacia. He did up the cuff buttons on the shirt. Perfect. He stood up, slowly screwing up his face, waiting for something to happen to him.

When nothing happened he remembered the wedge and started looking for a piece of rock. He did not wish to be accused of being irresponsible again. Many people thought he was irresponsible. They had long memories. They did not give him enough credit for his fence.

Further along he found a pair of light creamy trousers.

He took off his shorts.

"Excuse me," he said to no one.

The trousers were too long and a little too big around the waist. He rolled up the cuffs.

These are good quality trousers, he thought. He undid them a little so that he could look at the brand name. He did not know brand names anyway, but he looked. There was none. Of course, he thought, these are tailor-made trousers. What sort of person would discard them? This could be heavy. They would have another meeting down at the Hall and accuse him of being irresponsible. He would deny being stoned. He would talk about the fence but they would not listen to him. Maybe it was some heavy-type criminal come to spy out the dope crop.

"Mooo," he heard.

The man was almost beside him, a man with a huge moustache clutching a broken suitcase to his chest. He was lying next to a fallen log and his face was bruised and his tongue was swollen in his mouth. His clothes were ripped. He had one shoe. He had a tick feeding on his face, just beside his right eye. The tick had been there for some time. It was fat and bloated with blood.

Daze hopped sideways like a magpie and looked at him.

"Unny," the man moaned, but his good eye was on the silk shirt. "Unny."

"Money?" Daze suggested, thinking that the man, in spite of his condition, was trying to sell him the silk shirt.

"Unny."

"I was just trying it on."

"Huh," the man said with enormous effort. "Huh-unny."

"You want to buy Honey?"

Neither Paul Bees nor his daughter sold honey here. Only narcs and estate agents came here trying to buy honey. Paul Bees and Honey Barbara travelled around with their bees and their van, taking the bees to the coastal ti-tree in the summer, the ironbark and stringybark in the winter, letting them feed on groundsel during the autumn. They sold their honey in the markets, visited other communities. Paul had become, because he had travelled for a long time, because they knew him, because he was needed by everyone, like an ambassador, a diplomat who was accepted everywhere not only by the Buddhists at Chen Rhezic, the Horse people at Lower Arm, but also by the Krishnas and the Ananda Marga who guarded their places, as they now did at Bog Onion Road, with a barred gate and, sometimes, a lookout. Paul's descendants would be a travelling family and before too long they would reveal themselves as not only bee-keepers but magicians, musicians, story-tellers, news gatherers and peace-makers, never quite belonging to any one place and treated with both respect and reserve in the places they came to.

"Unny Ba-ba."

"Honey Barbara?"

"Unny Barba." But the baleful eye did not leave the silk shirt and, looking down, Daze saw he had left two dirty thumb prints underneath the collar.

"Ah," he said, "Honey Barbara. You're a friend of Honey Barbara's."

He did not have a high opinion of friends of Honey Barbara's. He had not forgiven her for Albert, her most famous friend and even though they had got many useful parts from his crashed Peugot he had also brought the police and the newspapers to Bog Onion Road.

"I'll just take this tick out for you," he said, "and then I'll try and carry you down as far as Clive's."

It took him a while to pack, fitting the sledgehammer and wedges into the broken case, but in the end, after a few false starts, he managed to, carrying both the man and the suitcase, and they made their way back down the ridge with rests every two hundred yards or so.

It was cooler in the brick house, and the dirt floor they lay him on felt softer than anywhere he had lain for days. They put him on his back and he could see, through his good eye, that the naked man named Clive was too big for his silk shirts. He was barrel-chested and hipless, broader rather than taller. He pulled the shirt on, but his arms filled the sleeves.

"This is a little boy's shirt," he said. "It is just a little boy's shirt." The shirt hung open across his furry chest, hanging like a curtain beside his uncircumcised penis, which looked like a decoration for the window ledge.

Daze was sitting out of Harry's vision. He still wore the shirt and trousers.

Clive was trying to look at the back of the shirt with a round shaving mirror. "Do you think Heather would split this down the back for me," he said, "and put a patch down the back, and widen the arms?"

"You better ask *him* first."

"He's a spy," Clive said. "Anyway, we gave him water. We saved his life."

"He's a friend of Honey Barbara's."

"Honey Barbara's got too many friends. Do you think Heather would do that for me? I'll swap her two hours' work."

"You already owe her a day's work," Daze said tentatively.

Harry saw Clive lift his head and jut his jaw and let his gapped rabbity teeth show for a moment. "I pay my debts," he said.

"I'm going to get Honey Barbara."

Harry saw that Daze, when he crossed his field of vision, had taken off the tailored trousers. He was wearing the silk shirt hanging over the shorts. "I'll just wear this", he said to Harry, "until I come back. O.K.?"

"Take him with you."

"I'm not walking down the hill with him. I'll get Honey Barbara and come back."

Harry's mind was wandering. His throat was parched. He could hardly breathe. Sometimes he felt he had to make himself breathe or his body would forget to do it for him.

Some time later Clive's face, very big, loomed in front of his.

"If you turn out to be a spy," Clive said, "I'll hang you up by your left foot on that beam over there."

Harry could see the beams above his head. They were huge tree trunks.

"And I'll get my brush hook and I'll run a little line down your lovely soft tummy and then I'll open you up and wind your guts out on to a jam jar."

He smiled at Harry. He pushed his gap-toothed smile very close. He had a square head with a short, bristly hair cut.

"I bet you don't even know what a brush hook is," he said.

He held up a long-handled tool with a curved blade on the end.

"This is a brush hook," he said, and then he sat down on the floor and began to sharpen it with a file. While he did this, he talked.

"All sorts of vermin come looking out here," he said. "You understand? You know what a vermin is. A vermin is a rat, or a louse, or anything that carries diseases with it. All sorts of vermin, yes," he nodded his head, "that's right."

Harry could hear the file on the brush-hook blade. His head ached. He wanted to vomit.

"I'll use a file on this first and then when I've got it really sharp I'll get a stone, yes, and make it..."

Harry was frightened that if he vomited he'd choke.

"You ask anyone", Clive said, "about my brush hook."

Harry passed out. When he woke he could hear cooking. He could smell fat frying. The minute his eyes opened Clive was talking again. "You people think you can just come here. You see that concrete tank. You can't see that concrete tank because you're too weak, but if you could see it you'd know what work is. You look at those beams, mate. That's work. You look at that stone. You know how long it takes to lay that stone, to carry it? and all you buggers sitting in the city, sitting on your arses laughing, and when you finally realise what's happening you come running along to mummy. Mummy, mummy," Clive called, piling potato chips on to his plate and sitting on a cushion near Harry's head.

"No use you eating," he said. "You'd only chuck it up."

"You see those bolts there. No, there. You can see them, near the window." It hurt Harry to even move his eye, but he did not want to upset Clive. He looked at the bolts. He didn't know where he was. He knew it couldn't be Bog Onion Road.

"That's right. See, you can do it if you try. Well that's a machine-gun mounting. That's *right*," he laughed with his mouth full. "That's right, a *machine* gun. Yes. And if any of your vermin friends come running up the hill, I'll be here, mate. And when I run out of bullets I've got a lovely brush hook. I can take off into the bush and I won't die. You'll die. I won't. You can't even pull your own ticks out."

"Won't be long now," Clive said, "Any day now, next year, the year after, they'll come running up here, but you can't drive in your little motor car, can you?"

"I've got a dam down there", he said, "with five million gallons of unpolluted water. Perfect water. I've got fish in it, big fat bass. I won't starve. You'd sit down there and starve because you wouldn't know how to catch them."

Clive ate his last potato chip with regret and relish.

"You want some water? Don't fucking glutton it. Just a little bit." He snatched the water back. "That's enough."

"Years ago," he said, sitting down on the cushion again and

cutting up a large pawpaw, "when I was on the dole, there was a bloke just like you who used to interrogate me."

"'Mr Boswell', he'd say, 'we can't have this. You've been on our files for five years without a job.'"

Clive jabbed the knife at Harry's nose.

"'Well you tell me,' I'd say, 'What have you done to get *me* a job? How much do they pay?' I'd say. 'It's your *job*,' I'd say, 'to get me a job and you are incompetent.'

"'What do you do out there all day, Mr Boswell?'

"'Well', I'd say, 'I haven't got a car and I'm just trying to feed myself, but since you people have been harassing me I've been trying to teach myself to read so I can get a job.'

"'Very good', he'd say, 'very good, Mr Boswell.'

"'But', I'd say, 'I only had a Bible and a friend came over and told me how it ended, in the Apocalypse, and when I heard that, I couldn't see the point.'

"I said that", he told Harry, "because I thought he was a fucking Christian."

"'What have you done?' they'd say.

"'What have you offered me?' I'd say.

"They couldn't handle me, mate. I was on the dole longer than anyone in this district until they kicked us all off. I built this place on the dole.

"I don't need anything. You need everything. I don't smoke. I don't drink. I don't take drugs. I don't eat meat. I have fruit and vegetables. You look at that pawpaw. That pawpaw is fucking nectar. Look at this pumpkin. That's food, mate. Yes," he said, "that's right."

He buried his face in a quarter of pawpaw and didn't emerge until he had only thick skin left in his hand.

"Your shirts won't fit a man," he said, "but we'll take them anyway, for our trouble, for saving your life, and when Honey Barbara's daddy goes around with his honey he'll sell them and we'll have some pretty little Krishnas sneaking into town in your lovely suit, looking so straight everyone will think they're narcs like you."

It was the worst possible introduction to Bog Onion Road, but Harry Joy did not know that. All he knew was that he was going to be sick. He managed to turn his head sideways before he threw up water and bile.

Later he was being carried down a steep track in near darkness.

He was on some kind of stretcher. His head was jolted with every step. When they put him down there were sharp rocks digging into his back. He was delirious. He could smell damp, rotting, a smell of berries like sweat, eucalypt, a richer, muskier smell like death itself.

Above him there were giant trees crowding over the narrow track, their upper branches crossing the sky like clenched fingers joined in prayer.

Paul Bees had wanted Harry Joy. Now he could sit in the corner of his hut with his back against the wall and watch him like a treasure, a puzzle, a book, a number of books, expensive books with leather covers and gold embossing, containing information he had never thought to enquire about, as arcane as the social organization of armadillos and the crystalline structure of aluminium.

It is the nature, he thought, of bee-keepers that they will end up hopelessly addicted to stories, gossip, odd bits of information; a thirst that the local markets can never properly satisfy so that, after all these years, he was working over old diggings, being made jubilant by some pitiful spot of colour panned from the worked-over clay, the mullock heaps made by local life.

They had not been able to lift Harry up on to the sleeping platform, and Honey Barbara had been too angry to really try. She did not appreciate this visit from her friend, and it was true, her father reflected, that it did not help her reputation, but, as usual, they would forgive her, even if they would not forget. She had only stayed long enough to make a bed for him on the floor and to bend over his swollen face in the candlelight and look at it for a long quiet moment.

"You wouldn't believe his life," she said with both disapproval and awe, and that was as much as Paul managed to gather about his daughter's relationship with the stranger.

It was a small hut, one of the smallest in the community, and he had built it for himself in the rain forest, because he had always wished to live in rain forest, and also (the admission was painful to him) because Crystal at forty-eight still had the disturbing and hurtful habit of adopting new lovers and he thought he would be better away from her for a while. He retreated into the rain forest and built this small hut with a sleeping platform at one end, below which was a small book-enclosed alcove which opened on to a tiny verandah. It was here that he placed Harry

Joy, and here that he sat, a scrawny little man with a large black beard who gave the contradictory impression of great frailty (and be called Little Paul) but also not inconsiderable strength so that people felt compelled to remark on it admiringly with such expressions as "he's a strong little bugger."

They admired, respected, and pitied Paul Bees, holed up in his rain forest while Crystal lived in the old house up on the hill, bathed in bright sunlight, conducting a peculiar affair with a woodcutter from the Ananda Marga who had been seen, at night, slipping through the moonlit bush with his axe still in his hand.

On the other side of this little alcove, now illuminated with a soft yellow kerosene light, was a wood stove, a sink, and some cupboards. You could admire the way he had whittled cedar to make the handle for a drawer and the patient search he must have conducted to find the quandong branch which now made the curved banister of the stair to the sleeping platform.

The stove was alight and the kettle hissed gently. He rose and walked softly on his surprisingly large (huge toes) feet to the sink where he took a pair of scissors and began cutting lemon grass into three-inch lengths. When he had done this he stuffed them into a large brown teapot and poured boiling water over them. He carried the teapot, two cups, and a jar of stringybark honey, into the alcove where Harry Joy watched him from one good eye, the other being reduced to a mongoloid slit by a swelling, the legacy of the bloated tick.

"Bulk tea," he announced.

"Thank you." The gratitude in the man's voice was almost embarrassing. He had stopped him making speeches but he could not stop this excess of appreciation.

Harry had heard the things that Paul Bees had said in his defence. They had drifted to him through the ether of his delirium. It had not been a formal meeting at the Hall, no night procession of lanterns and blanket-bundled children, but an impromptu deputation as the story of the hunted terrorist came into Bog Onion Road by radio, spread through the valley and up the ridge. No one had criticized directly, not at first. That was not the way things were done. They talked, instead, about American Albert, and in doing so, of course, criticized Honey Barbara for threatening their safety by bringing criminals into their midst.

Garry had already found the Cadillac on Paddy Melon Road and he and Margot had gone to jump-start it and hide it in the bush for the night. It was not, they reflected, even a useful make for spare parts and they talked about the Peugot Albert had rolled into the valley off the hairpin bend.

Crystal said that the pattern of two new cars, two criminals, was not just a coincidence and must have wider meaning and it was Honey Barbara, who had endured all the comments in a hot prickling silence, who spoke up and said that this was bullshit because the Cadillac was not new and that she hadn't brought American Albert into the valley, that he had come here by himself, and he had been welcomed by everyone and that her romance with him had been actively encouraged by certain people who were old enough, at the time, to know better, but may well have been too stoned to know what was happening in front of their noses. Further, she said, she had not invited this man with the silk shirts to Bog Onion Road, but had left him behind in the city because he was fucked.

But it was Paul who reminded them that it was Harry Joy's American Express cards which had provided them with some money after the dope crop was ripped off and it was Paul who offered to take responsibility for his welfare.

"They won't find him here," Paul said, and finally he was allowed to stay because the rain forest was reckoned a safe place, guarded on its edges by lantana under whose barbed and secret arches leaf-paved paths led to Paul's house, and even from the air, it was thought, the dark roof of the hut would be invisible. The visitor was forbidden to leave the rain forest.

As it turned out, the visitor would have to be, finally, ordered out of it. He would not wish to leave. He understood the protection of the rain forest only too well and when Paul began to go out on the van again and help Honey Barbara with the hives and the spinning, Harry was more than happy to be left behind. He would, in time, left to his own devices, have become some slinking little animal, a furtive wingless bird of a drab colour and monotonous cry, a noise, rustling in the lantana on the edge of the forest, a disturbance amongst the dead leaves.

He ventured out of the hut, cautiously at first, amidst this twilight forest with the air festooned with creeper like some deserted vegetable telephone exchange. Even the creek below the hut was full of arm-thick roots and creepers, lying in the water like tangled pipes. The ground was soft and leaf-covered, littered with moss-green stones and laced with fine vine trip-wires which were best proceeded through without haste. And into this dark spongy world came slices of sunlight as sharp and clear as the cries of whip-birds and caught such jewels as the multicoloured pitta bird turning over a leaf, Harry Joy wearing the white baggy clothes Paul had made for him, the splendid green cat bird high in a palm, the unlikely owner of such a forlorn cry.

And Paul Bees, a month from this night, would not understand why Harry (who would sweep the floor, dust the books, collect kindling, split wood, collect water from the creek, bake vegetables for dinner, have warm water for Paul's shower) could not be persuaded to go to the open paddock fifty yards from the edge of the rain forest to collect eggs or fetch wood or release a bleating goat from its tangled tether.

Once he had gone to the edge of the lantana, at the top of the rise above the spring and, seeing the wide grassed paddock and open sky, felt almost faint. He scurried backwards, dragging sharp lantana across his heedless skin. The beginning of real agoraphobia.

But all of this, on the second night, was yet to come. The fever was leaving him and he could, at last, eat without vomiting. He did not know what the rain forest even looked like. He did not know the feeling that would come to him from trees, the dizzy ecstasy, the swoon almost as he looked up at the green canopy above him and felt these allies keep him safe from harm.

Paul Bees put stringy bark honey in his cup and grinned at his guest. He saw the stories. He was the first one to even guess at them.

As usual, she drove with her head out the window, looking up. It was a bee-keeper's habit. It came from staring up at the blossoms, and accounted for the lash of creeper that had drawn blood across her face. The Commer van lumbered on to the switchback and she stopped for a moment to look across to the Boggy Plains where, amongst the swampy country of tiger snakes, the ti-trees would feed the bees for the winter, those paper-barked trees which once, as a child, had meant nothing more to her than a source of mysterious paper to write secret messages on while her father had placed the hives.

The road was half washed out and the wet season hadn't even started. Her eyes were continually drawn between the problems of the truck and the possibilities of some unseen blossom. The community did not truly appreciate the problems of bee-keepers, and while they were happy enough to let the bee-keepers do the trading when they went to market, to barter a little milk or eggs for honey or the mead Paul Bees made from the groundsel honey, and even, on occasion, to make generous speeches on the subject, it seemed to Honey Barbara that not enough practical sign of appreciation was made.

It was five o'clock but it was still hot. Her bare arms were covered with a fine talcum dust and her eyes were red and strained. The others would be down at the dam. She thought about the water and everyone lying around, feeling satisfied with their day's work while she walked this lumbering old van down the hill. It was the only petrol-driven vehicle that used the roads now (they had wrecked the Cadillac bringing it into the valley and it lay rusting amongst the Peugots) and no one seemed to think that even this one van was necessary. That the roads were guttered and ripped was somehow seen as a desirable thing, and they did not think about her problems in actually driving these forest roads, a maze of cut-backs, dead-ends and deliberately contrived false leads which were interrupted by fallen trees. The old forest roads were being planted out as part of the reafforestation.

And the reafforestation, which they were all so smug about, was dominated by Clive and Ian and what was planted was what they thought was good timber, particularly tallow woods and blood woods, hard timber, one-hundred-year trees. There were also a few flooded gums because they grew quickly and made good straight poles for building. But no one really appreciated the problems of honey and they could have, if they'd listened to her, have planned for both honey and timber, and then the replanting would have contained more brush box, stringybark, red flowering gum, and there were even a few places where a ti-tree forest could have grown but they had timber farmer's eyes about ti-tree and called it scrub.

"Honey Barbara wants us to plant scrub." She could not get people to support her, and in the places where ti-tree would have grown they planted flooded gum instead.

"If you want it," Clive said, "you should plant it." Which was all very well, but she was busy enough doing what she had to do, and there were people like Harry Joy (that's right!) whose only job in the world was to plant trees and for that they managed to get great kudos, for one simple job any idiot could do.

Harry Joy was somewhere below the switchback, down there, planting-out road, and she felt irritable in anticipation of seeing him. He had fooled them all. And even though they liked to joke about how he had to be physically removed from the rain forest and set to work, they liked the way he had gone about it once they gave him the trees and placed him on the road. Paul liked to tell the story about how dark came and no Harry was in sight, how he had waited, smoked a joint, waited some more, gone to sleep, and finally woken up at about eight, and when he had finally gotten it together to walk down the track he found Harry Joy still digging this vast hole for one tiny tree because Margot, when she left him, had said: "The bigger the hole, the faster it'll grow."

Paul took him back and bandaged his hands and it was another two weeks before he could work again.

He still dug big holes. That was admired. A person who dug big holes for a tree and did not take short cuts was much admired here. "It looks like he'll be a good worker," they said.

But she knew. She didn't say, but she knew. He was digging those holes big so that the trees would grow and cover him. He was digging with negative energy, because he was afraid of the sky and the sun and he was chicken shit. He thought he was in Hell, and that was why he was digging big holes. He was driven by fear and did not love trees except for the wrong selfish reasons.

"Your friend," they said when referring to Harry Joy.

"He's not my friend."

And while they learned to accept him they continued to distrust her, she thought, because she had brought him there. If not, how come no one had said anything to her about going down with the dope crop this year? She did not want to go; she would certainly have refused but there was no doubt in her mind that she should be asked, and her advice sought on the disposal of the crop and now, it seemed, Damian was to go (God help us, she thought) and no one actually told her this but she found out by things half said and others unsaid.

"He is not my friend," she said out loud, straddling a particularly deep wash-away with the Commer and praying she would not slip in. He was not her friend. She had no friend. And although she had felt contented with her celibacy before Harry arrived, other things had happened which now made her lonely.

She had enjoyed her visits to Paul. She hadn't gone often, maybe once a week, but they had talked long into the night and even when she was alone in her hut she knew it was something she could do if she wanted to, but now she would walk down the little ridge above the rain forest at night and hear their voices (The Old Codgers) coming up from the dark of the valley floor and the damp fecund odours of the rain forest no longer seemed welcome to her and she would not enter. She was hurt that Paul had ditched her so easily in favour of a stranger.

Crystal was worse. She had adopted her new lover's politics, religion and dietary habits with an enthusiasm which Honey Barbara found unprincipled. She saw her mother adopting the mental wardrobe of the Ananda Marga just as she had with everything from Sufi dancing to Buddhism and Pentecostal Christianity, pecking at any idea with coloured beads or tinsel paper.

"You have the spiritual life of a crow," she told her mother.

She had been bad-tempered with everyone. Crystal, even now, sat on the hillside waiting for her daughter's apology. It was not forthcoming. Everywhere she went she heard bits and pieces of Harry Joy and his stories and that only made it worse. He had been, in every way, inconsiderate, and it had not even occurred to him that he should come and apologize to her.

He was down there. She had seen him when she drove out and now she would see him again in two bends' time. He was digging fucking holes and when she came round the corner he would be standing there naked with his crowbar or his shovel, standing back from his giant hole, waiting for a compliment.

Oh, they just loved the way Harry Joy dug holes.

She felt herself becoming angrier and angrier as she crossed the Saddleback and then back up a creek bed for ten yards and then sharply down. It was all unnecessary, this ridiculous complicated entry into the property, but it amused Clive and the other paranoids. If the cops wanted anything important, they'd do a helicopter bust. They didn't need roads.

And there he was.

She slid the Commer to a halt even though it was a steep and stony hill. He was planting out the junction with old Billy Road, or that, at least, was what they had called it on the forestry maps. He had three planted.

"Tallow wood," she said, "typical."

"It's good timber," he said.

Who was he to be suddenly such an expert on the timber at Bog Onion Road? What did he know?

"It's hundred-year timber," he said.

Repeating what he had been told.

"You planted one over there," she said.

"Yes," he said, "to make a pair, one on either side of the road."

She turned off the engine. "Do you realize," she said, "that when these trees grow, in a hundred years, you won't be able to get a van this wide through or," she said, anticipating the words ready to emerge from his opening mouth, "or a horse and cart."

The big moustache had now been joined by a beard and his long lank hair had been cut brutally short. He had some funny looking bumps on the back of his head. His naked body had taken the light honey colour typical of people who live with the sun so much that they do not seek it for pleasure.

He looked at her and smiled. "Yes," he said, "s'pose I better shift it."

"Hear you're building a place."

"Yes."

"Good one."

"Yes, should be good."

"Bush poles?"

"Yeah, bush poles. I'm going to try shingles."

"Hard to cut," she said, squinting at him.

"Might try anyway."

"Yeah, you should try."

"We should have a talk sometime," he said. "You should come over."

She started the engine. "Yeah," she said vaguely.

"I miss you," he said. /

But she was already concentrating on the next section of road, trying to keep the speed down so she wouldn't crack the sump on the crossing at the bottom. She did not have time to think about her feelings, but the bees knew, as they always did, and droned unhappily around the entrance to their hives.

It is a measure of how well Harry had adapted to life at Bog Onion that the hut which was planned for the late spring did not finally get under way until after the wet. There was no desperate rush and the subject of the hut, its design, materials, siting and so on, became the medium through which he came to know his neighbours and make new friendships.

He had become used to waking early, but on the morning he was to drop the five tallow woods he had marked out for his house, he got up even earlier. There was something he wanted to do before

268

Daze and Clive arrived with the horse to snig the logs out of the forest. He did not make tea. He did not fill the bush shower on the verandah, or do anything to make a noise because the thing he wanted to do was something he felt shy about, a small thing perhaps, but more important than he would have cared to admit; he might so easily have been laughed at.

He slipped into his shorts and pulled a dirty singlet on. Then he took the dirty singlet off and rummaged in the canvas bag which contained his few things. He took out a clean white singlet and put it on.

The axe was already sharp. He had sharpened it last night while he and Paul had sat on the verandah. He had sharpened it slowly, enjoying the sound. You could shave your arm with that axe and Paul, having examined it, declared it too sharp. Harry was learning confidence in his own ways. He left it sharp.

He did not wear shoes. There were none to be had and his feet had made up for the lack and grown their own thick soles. It is not hard to see the changes six months of hard work, clean air and less food have made to the man. It is a pleasure to watch him as he descends the steps of the hut and walks into the rain forest, a svelte shadow amongst the tangled roots and creepers. He had never ceased to see where he lived and, having begun with the aesthetic of a whip bird to whom the rain forest is shelter and cannot be left except nervously, he had, as the months passed, developed a more relaxed view in which gratitude to the trees and people of Bog Onion was not his sole emotion but had become blended with wonder and made volatile with some lighter spirit.

He nodded briefly (no one was there to see him) to the monsteriosa. No one could tell him with any confidence whether the monsteriosa was a native of the rain forest or an interloper but he felt he understood the way it wrapped its roots around the white blotched trunk of a cedar. Each morning when he passed through the rain forest he nodded his head briefly and compressed his lips and sometimes you might hear a small tsk of appreciation, a sound as light as a twig dropping, signifying, perhaps, the surprise he felt in being there at all.

He walked up the steps formed by tree roots, stooped to walk through the lantana hedge and emerged at the big burnt logs (like half-spent conversations) where they sometimes sat at night when the rain forest became too oppressive. They had lit some big fires here and told some good stories, and around this fire he had found himself remembering things he had not even known he knew.

He tried to talk to Paul about the trees but in the end, he thought, he had become boring and he felt that Paul would rather hear about other things, some story of Vance's, the episode with Alice Dalton, what an expensive whore house was like, what Milanos looked like, what the menu said, how much a glass of French wine would have cost. (Alright, Paul said, a bottle then — how much is a bottle?)

Paul Bees, however, was not at all bored by trees. He did not doubt that trees had spirits, that there was a collective spirit of the forest, but he could talk about these things with anybody, and Harry Joy had much more astonishing things to tell, for instance: how a television commercial was made and how much it cost.

Harry did not talk about trees and the forest as much as he would have liked, but nothing could stop him thinking about them. He had done what Honey Barbara had once told him to (back in the days when she still spoke to him), which was to place his arms around a big tallow wood when the wind blows and feel its strength and put his face against its rough bark. He could not walk through the bush now without feeling beneath his feet the whole inter-linked network of roots, some thicker than his leg, some as fine as the hair on his arm, the great towers of trunks, the columns of the forest, the channels between the world of the roots and the canopy of the forest which was not only alive with blossoms and leaves but which — sometimes he could almost feel it — breathed continually, interchanging carbon dioxide for the oxygen he would breathe in. All of this was new to him. He would walk through the forest, not in a calm way, but in the slightly agitated manner of someone feeling too many things at once.

He had planted peas and watched them grow. Could this corny, ordinary human act really be so earth-shattering to a man, that at the age of forty he is reduced to open-mouthed amaze-ment by the sight of a pea he has planted uncurling through the soil?

Everybody has pointed this out to everybody else before. They have made films about it and called them "Miracle of life" and so on. He may even have seen them, but when Harry Joy squatted on his haunches and contemplated a pea growing it did not matter a damn to him (it did not even occur to him) that his experience was not new. He was not interested in newness. When he was by himself he could say and think what he wished, and he was by himself the greater amount of the day. He could touch the deep rough scaled bark of a blood wood like someone else might stroke a cat, speaking not to be literally understood.

"When you talk about trees," Paul Bees said, pouring water into the pot, "it sounds like you want a fuck."

Which, in a rough and ready bush-carpentered sort of way, described Harry Joy's tone rather well.

He chose a certain route up the ridge so that he skirted the edge of Paul's small banana plantation which was still too young to bear any fruit. Then into some scrubby untidy bush which gave way to more lantana scrub and it was here, below Crystal's house, amongst the rusting Peugots, that the Cadillac waited for him, like a great dull beast, a stinking stranded whale he could not forget no matter how much he might like to ignore this painful reminder of his disgraceful past.

He had a new happiness at Bog Onion Road but he also had a new burden: he had done bad things in Hell. The guilt he felt about his past was the worst of the pains he now carried, but not the only one, for he had, if not daily, at least weekly, the reminder of Honey Barbara's hostility towards him. The Cadillac also reminded him of that pain.

"You stole it, didn't you?" she said to him on the day he came to her door.

"Stole what?"

"That car. That American thing." She stood at the door naked but there was no invitation. Behind her he could see the shape of a body lying in her bed.

"Yes," he said.

"How could I ever trust you?" she said.

There were dry leaves around the ground below her step. He touched them with his toe — the dry leaves and hard woody cases that had once held blossom — and he turned away without looking up. He had gone back to his holes in the road even though it was a rest day.

He had gained his burdens so quickly that the load was sometimes almost too much and he could physically stagger beneath them as if someone had dumped a bag of fertilizer too heavily on to his back. He felt some guilt, some remorse, about almost everybody he had known in Palm Avenue and although his work with the trees had begun as Honey Barbara had correctly guessed as a fearful response to his new environment, it had slowly become different, and from his fear, through his fear, he had discovered love and with his love he was trying to make amends.

He skirted around Crystal's house (where, living alone, she was making plans for the return of Paul Bees) and entered the big bush beyond it. On the edge of this bush there was only a little scrub, some groundsel, odd straggling lantana (yellow-flowered here) and then a patch of bracken, and beyond that: tallow wood, blood wood, red stringybark, black-butt, and the forest floor luxuriant with great blackboys, their thick black trunks hidden by their shining tussock-like crowns. This hillside had been cleared some thirty or forty years before but there were still a few giants left behind, trees so noble, Harry imagined, that no man could bring himself to cut them down, great gnarled old creatures which could harbour possums in their scarred wounds, white ants, insects, grubs and fungi, and still have the strength to draw water and nutrients into their tough old roots, suck them right up the enormous height of their sapwood, hold their leaves out to the sunshine and exchange gases with the world.

There was no wind. It was a perfect day for dropping trees, but he was not ready to start. There was something to do before the others arrived. Something to be done without rush. He leant his axe against the trunk of a young stringybark and went around gathering rocks which poked out here and there from the ground-cover of deep dead leaves. They were not the sort of rocks he would have preferred. He had imagined (that long time ago) something grey with a touch of some sparkling mineral (mica? anthracite?) which would later catch the sun. These rocks which littered the hillside were soft and red and looked like broken house-bricks.

As he gathered the rocks the forest seemed to become very quiet. A solitary honey-eater set up a sharp chatter down in the gully below him as he carried the rocks to the first tree which would provide him with stumps for his hut. It was already scarred, a small mark made by his own axe. Its base was half hidden by a tangled pile of twigs and leaves. He began talking, but not before he had looked around.

"I'm sorry," he said, "we have to do this. I need a house to live in. That's why we put the mark on you yesterday."

His voice sounded very thin and insignificant in the forest. He was not unaware of how he might look to people but was more aware of how he stood in comparison to an eighty-foot-high tree. If he was shy, it was not because of people. He was shy in the presence of the tree. He did not use the full words.

"I'm putting these stones here", he said, "as a promise. I will plant another tree here tonight, another tallow wood. I will dig a hole here beside you and plant it where these rocks are."

Daze sat quietly on the edge of the circle made by the trees they planned to drop. He had come down to tell Harry that Clive would be late with the horse. He had heard Harry's voice come through the forest and he had stopped to listen. He was going to roll a joint, but he decided not to. As he listened to what Harry had to say he was very moved. This was no bullshit story. This man was saying something that he felt. It was not the silky voice that Harry Joy had used in his city life, but something at once coarser and softer.

When Harry had done the first tree Daze gathered rocks and came and stood behind him. He nodded his sharp, inquisitive face and offered Harry two rocks.

"Go on," he said.

Harry began to shake his head, stepping backwards, colouring.

"Go on," Daze said.

Harry nodded. This time he used the proper words, the formal words, as they are known. His face burned bright red, but his eyes were bright.

"You have grown large and powerful. I have to cut you. I know you have knowledge in you from what happens around you. I am sorry, but I need your strength and power. I will give you these stones, but I must cut you down. These stones and my thoughts will make sure another tree will take your place."

Thus, with their stones, they moved from tree to tree. A small wind came and stirred the upper branches. Clive arrived with the old Clydesdale. Paul Bees came rubbing sleep from his eyes and yawning. Margot arrived too, and then Honey Barbara who remained standing at a distance with her arms folded across her chest.

"Stand around the tree," Daze suggested.

They joined hands around the tree and Daze said some of the words with Harry.

When it was time to chop the first tree they were all very quiet and it seemed to Harry that when he began to chop, the wood, famous for its hardness, was soft and yielding. Huge chips flew through the bush. (Later, when the logs had been snigged down to the site, Harry barked the logs and the flesh of the wood was yellow and slippery like a skinned animal.)

When the first tree fell, Daze walked back to where Honey Barbara was standing.

"Well . . ." he said.

"Well what?" Honey Barbara said.

"That was really amazing."

"I came to work," Honey Barbara said, "not to get involved in this Hippy mumbo-jumbo."

And to show she meant business she took one end of the cross-cut saw that Margot had placed across the fallen tree. "Come on, Margot," she said, "or did you only come for the mumbo-jumbo too."

Honey Barbara worked hard all day. She did not talk to Harry once and every time he passed her, she looked the other way.

The man with the clenched whiskered face wore suit trousers and a suit jacket which could never, in even the most bizarre time, have been part of the same suit. Heavy work boots showed beneath the trousers and there was string where once there may have been proper black laces. Above the right-hand boot was a white sockless ankle that something, perhaps a bush rat, had gnawed at before passing on to something else. This man (Jerusalem John by name) was lying in the sunlight on Daze's open verandah. A cheap thriller was sticking out of his jacket pocket. A couple of flies had laid their eggs on his gnawed ankle and he was, of course, perfectly dead.

It was still early enough in the day for one half of the valley to be in sunlight and the other in shadow, but up here on the ridge there was no shortage of sunshine. The trees, incorrectly known as wattles, glistened and two big king parrots swung around the branches of the one that grew over Daze's forever unfinished house, noisily eating the blossoms and dropping the hard wood casings on to the tin roof.

Honey Barbara, sitting with the others beside the rusting metal pipe which Daze had converted into a fireplace and boiler, did not need to be told what those small pinging noises on the roof were and, in her mind's eyes, she could see the red and green birds clearly against the bright blue sky. It had not been a good year for honey. Perhaps she might get a bit of a flow out of these wattles.

Daze was there, of course, fussing about washing cups. Paul Bees squatted on his big heels with his back to the fire and Crystal had moved a small three-legged child's stool to be close to him. She wore a long crushed-velvet dress on to which she had fastidiously stitched tiny shells. She wore wooden beads around her neck (the remnants of Paul's failed abacus) and the crystals from which she took her name were arranged, just two of them, in her jet-black hair.

Clive was there wearing, as usual, nothing but his boots. Richard was there, and Dani. Assorted children were sent outside occasionally where they could be seen squatting around the dead man. No meeting had been called. The gathering was prompted by the mysterious workings of the bush telegraph.

"What does he know about trees anyway?" Honey Barbara said to Daze. "He doesn't know anything. You don't know him like I know him. He's only into saving his neck. He doesn't believe in anything."

Daze didn't say anything, which irritated her even more.

"He knows good stories," Paul Bees said, "that's the point."

"You call yourself an anarchist!" she said to her father. "You people will follow anyone. You're all so bored that when someone new comes along you practically rape them. So the man's got nice stories. They're not his stories anyway. They're his father's. He even stole his *stories*."

"I don't see that matters," Richard said.

"I think," Dani said, "that it's O.K., so long as he *wants* to tell a story."

Honey Barbara groaned quietly.

Clive was leaning against a bushpole with his arms folded above his furry bear's belly. "I don't see why we don't do what we did for little Billy."

"What was that?" Crystal asked.

"We dug a fucking big hole," Clive said, and it was difficult not to believe that he was relishing it. "We dug a fucking big hole and we buried the bugger."

"We dig a hole for a person the same way we dig a hole for a shit bucket," Paul said.

"Well, that's right, isn't it?" Clive said. "It's the same. All goes back into the soil. I don't want any of you lot doing OMs over me."

"I think we should do something better for Jerusalem John than we'd do for a bucket of shit," Paul insisted.

"He's dead, mate," Clive said. "It won't worry him one way or the other."

Jerusalem John was not really their responsibility at all. He had made it his business in life to be no one's responsibility. He was an old hermit, a loner, who lived at the bottom of the gully that ran between Bog Onion and the Ananda Marga. He shot wallabies and read thrillers and the only thing that flushed him out were bushfires where, suddenly, you would find him stumbling out of the smoke to stand beside you with his wet sack or his hoe. No one would have found him but Richard had heard his fox terrier howling.

"You should have left him in the hut," Clive said, "and we could have just burnt it all down. Nothing in the place worth saving. The tin's rotted."

"I think we should get Harry to tell a story."

"You people are full of shit," Honey Barbara said, standing up and rubbing her bee-keeper's biceps angrily. "You're going to let him get control of you. You elevate him into something he's not."

"We're not elevating him into anything. He knows stories. He knows stories for trees..."

"He doesn't know shit about trees," Honey Barbara said. "You ask him to tell you the difference between a red stringy and a yellow, get him to show you a narrow-leaved ironbark, get him to tell you how old the buds on any of them are. He doesn't know. He can't do it."

But she knew she had made too much noise, gone on too long, and the only effect her speech was having was to annoy everyone except Clive who looked like he agreed with her. She was being negative, uncool, ungenerous, and there was no doubt that she had made them decide to ask Harry Joy to tell the story for the burial of Jerusalem John.

The next five years should have been the richest and happiest period of Harry's life, not only in Hell, but in any life he could remember. He built his hut above the creek on high stumps of tallow wood. He learned how to use a saw and chisel, and hammer in a six-inch nail. He built a fireplace from rocks and suspended a wide verandah over the creek and inside this new house you could tell, the way his silk shirts had become cushions around the walls, that this dry-looking man still loved his comfort.

He had many friends. He was not only liked, he was also necessary. He could dig a decent-sized hole for a tree; he could tell a story for a funeral and a story for a birth. When they sat around the fire at night he could tell a long story just for fun, in the same way Richard might play his old accordion and Dani her Jew's harp. He never thought of what he did as original. It wasn't either. He told Vance's old stories, but told them better because he now understood them. He retold the stories of Bog Onion Road. And when he told stories about the trees and the spirits of the forest he was only dramatizing things that people already knew, shaping them just as you pick up rocks scattered on the ground to make a cairn. He was merely sewing together the bright patchworks of lives, legends, myths, beliefs, hearsay into a splendid cloak that gave a richer glow to all their lives. He knew when it was right to tell one story and not another. He knew how a story could give strength or hope. He knew stories, important stories, so sad he could hardly tell them for weeping.

And also he gave value to a story so that it was something of worth, as important, in its way, as a strong house or a good dam. He insisted that the story was not his, and not theirs either. You must give something, he told the children, a sapphire or blue bread made from cedar ash. And what began as a game ended as a ritual.

They were the refugees of a broken culture who had only the flotsam of belief and ceremony to cling to or, sometimes, the looted relics from other people's temples. Harry cut new wood grown on their soil and built something solid they all felt comfortable with. They were hungry for ceremony and story. There was no embarrassment in these new constructions.

He did not become a leader or a strange man with a long white robe, not a shaman, a magician or a priest. He was a bushman. He was a bushman in the way he stood with one leg out and the back of his wrist propped on his hip. He dug holes, used flooded gum trees to out-grow and conquer the groundsel weed; he won Clive's respect by the energy with which he helped at the mill, where they cut packing-case timber from blackbutt and sold it to pineapple farmers in the world outside.

Yet the more he gained pleasure from his relationship with the people of Bog Onion (and the more he came to appreciate that Hell was a place of the most subtle construction which, on balance, he preferred to his other life), the more Honey Barbara's coldness towards him ate at his heart.

It came to dominate both their lives like a yellow cloud of smog that lay across an otherwise unpolluted sky.

Perhaps if they had been left alone, if well-meaning people who loved them both had not continually tried to help them, had not carried their not-quite-accurate messages from Honey Barbara's hut in the morning sunlight to Harry's hut in the shaded east, perhaps if they had just left it alone it would have sorted itself out in its own good time. But it was like a mosquito bite which is scratched and then scratched again until some organism hidden in otherwise benevolent soil can enter the broken skin and turn that mild irritation into a raging tropical ulcer with an inch-wide pus-filled centre reaching down as far as the bone, and there is no natural way to heal it, and only a trip into town to the hospital with all the attendant antibiotics and expense will effect a cure.

She had begun by being irritated at his lack of consideration in arriving at Bog Onion without being asked, but his own guilty confessions to Paul Bees had naturally leaked out on to the gossip circuit and they had come to fuel her indignation. She painted a big sign on the Cadillac which read: STOLEN BY HARRY JOY FROM HIS "FRIENDS".

She did herself a disservice. For, as anybody could see, Harry Joy was pretty much like anybody else, having his fair share of stupidities and conceits but also some reserves of kindness and love. For the most part he talked about the same things anyone else did: the state of the vegetable garden, how well the hens were laying, whether there would be a good wet and, although Honey Barbara mightn't like it, he could now tell the state of development of a swamp mahogany bud, whether it was one or two or even three years from blossoming, and by a series of questions and cross-questions and simple observation he had learned as much about trees as anyone in Bog Onion.

It is also possible that the sore might have cured faster if Harry Joy had not continued to love Honey Barbara, but he did, and she knew he did because he kept telling people that he did. No matter what she said about him, no matter what gossip reached his ears (and she made sure that there was plenty to gossip about) he refused to speak badly of her. He spoke of her only with admiration and when she heard about it, it made her angry — it seemed a trick, to make people side with him against her. When Daze came to discuss "these negative feelings you keep projecting on to Harry" she told him to fuck off and get out.

Sometimes she found Harry standing quietly on the edge of the clearing where her hut stood, the same hut which was still portrayed on the wall of the bedroom in the deserted house at Palm Avenue.

She tried to ignore him. He would leave some infantile present: a pumpkin, a wallaby, a handful of ironbark blossom he may or may not have climbed a tall tree to pick.

"You make it worse," she told him once, and then regretted it because he drew strength and confidence from anything she said to him.

There was a story she had heard that he had killed Bettina. He made her nervous. He skulked around in the bush by her hut. She heard him thumping around out there. "A man who believes he is in Hell", she told Crystal, "is capable of anything." She went down to Jerusalem John's and took the lock from the door. She fitted it to her own door (the only lock in Bog Onion) and kept it snibbed at night.

It is curious, but hardly surprising, that Honey Barbara, who spent the greater part of her time outdoors, on the road, her head out the window looking for new blossoms, carrying hives with aching arms through the bush, never walked a hundred yards into the bush around her own house. Sometimes her bees ventured in there when the blood wood were on, but the blood wood were not on in April. The only thing on in April was the groundsel weed which produced an inferior grade of honey of use for nothing much but the rather medicinal mead that Paul made each year. But then, one April, the bees began returning heavy laden and the hives were filling; not a heavy flow, but it was good honey, not groundsel.

Investigating this discrepancy she walked through the bush behind her house and found it planted densely with silver-leaved ironbark which was now in blossom. But there was also yellow box, a famous honey tree, and bottle brush and ti-tree and, if she had cared to walk amongst the so-called timber trees in the bottom thirty acres she would have found amongst the tallow woods and blood woods, stands of young trees carefully planned to provide blossom all year round.

It did not happen as Harry Joy had often (so very often) imagined it. Because there is his beloved Honey Barbara, her two hands around an ironbark trying to uproot it, whilst all the time her bees (whom one might guess, fancifully, to be in some confusion about their mistress's behaviour) feasted on a nectar which was far too good to be wasted making Paul Bees drunk at night.

He was sitting out on his verandah catching the late sunshine when she came into his house. He knew who it was. He had been waiting for two weeks. There was no one in the world who walked like Honey Barbara and when she strode across the bare boards of the living room he imagined he could hear the talcum dust of Bog Onion Road on her beautiful feet and that the whole of his house vibrated subtly with the rhythm of her body. He did not dare stand up. He rubbed his palms together as farmers sometimes do when they have to shake hands with people they imagine to be somehow cleaner.

He was clean-shaven that year and his face showed all the lines of his forty-five years, many lines around the eyes, and around the corners of the mouth. His brown eyes looked up towards the doorway and he brushed nis bare chest on which the scar of his initiation still stood, a pink ridge across a honey-brown terrain.

She stood at the doorway. She wore an old pair of khaki shorts and a loose white shirt tied at the waist. Her hair was short, cut as gracelessly as his. She was five years older than when he had known her and the only marring of her beauty was the suggestion of a tightness in the corners of her pale lips and for this scar he recognized his own responsibility.

"I am not going to waste my whole life," she began and his heart sank so sickeningly he had a sensation not dissimilar to suddenly losing sight. "I am not going to waste my whole life hating you."

He stopped breathing, waiting.

She also began to brush. She brushed her knee. She smoothed her cheeks. She squatted on the floor by the door jamb.

"You are forty-five," she said. "I am thirty-two. We're getting too old for this nonsense."

She leaned forward and held out her hand and took his, loosening it, releasing his palm from the closed trap of his nails.

"If you ever steal my Cadillac," she smiled (her moist eyes searching his face for signs), "I'll cut your bloody balls off."

It was so quiet they could hear a pitta bird down in the rain forest, rustling its bright feathers through the rotting leaves.

And now there is not much more to say about these lives, not, at least in a book that will be sold mainly in cities and to strangers at that. There were days, nights, meals, storms, fires, trees, bees, many things that were tedious, repetitive, as expected as peas uncurling through red soil.

There were stories, of course, in the natural course of things, which came to be told more slowly, with greater humour and with a pride that could not be mistaken for arrogance. Harry often seemed as happy to talk about the clay he dug, or the trees he planted (and a man who makes a forest has reason to speak about it with a little pride). In short he began to talk like a farmer and became the sort of character who makes city people laugh, drawling slow directions, complaining about rain or the lack of it, believing improbable (unscientific) things that more advanced people have discarded a century before, suspicious of new chemicals and things in packets, gazing off into the distance before answering easy questions, discussing a piece of fencing as if it were important.

He lived through thirty more wet seasons, seven droughts and two cyclones which happened, coincidentally, to have the same names as his new children.

So now there are only two stories left to tell, or rather two halves of the one story, and then it will all be done.

On the day of Harry Joy's death he was seventy-five years and two days old. He looked fifty. His face was deeply lined, you could even say creased, and it had been likened, by his children, to an old handbag. He walked with a slight limp, the result of a fall he suffered fighting a fire below the ridge at Clive's place. It was as close to a perfect day as might be possible, a warm sunny day in late October with the yellow box in flower and the 'Yard' bees travelling out from their racks (necessary to protect them from cane toad) out through the canyons and canopies of Harry Joy's forest.

He had only come out to look at the blossom, nothing more, but he walked amongst the trees like a true gardener and even removed a piece of groundsel weed he judged had no right to be there. Down below in the valley he could hear Dani singing.

Nothing will happen in this story, nothing but death. It is as inconsequential as anything Vance told. Soon the branch of a tree will fall on him. A branch of a tree he has planted himself, one of his precious yellow boxes, a variety prized by bee-keepers but known to forest workers as widow-makers (widder-makers) because of their habit, on quiet, windless days like this one, of dropping heavy limbs.

Any moment this thirty-year-old tree is going to perform the treacherous act of falling on the man who planted it, while bees continue to gather their honey uninterrupted on the outer branches.

There — it is done.

There is nothing pretty in this last death, this split head, this broken life. There was nothing beautiful in the cracking cry of Honey Barbara as it later resounded around the valley, swept and swooped like a great panicked crow in a glass cage, like a jet-black dove wings, the flapping overhead of flying foxes in the night.

But now the last story, and the last story is our story, the story of the children of Harry Joy and Honey Barbara, and for this story, like all stories, you must give something, a sapphire, or blue bread made from cedar ash.

He was dead, the yellow box branch across his head and arm, bees still collecting from the scanty blossom. He felt perfectly calm, and as he rose higher he could see Daze bringing the Clydesdale down the valley to where his grown-up children were dropping logs. He could see trees, trees he could name, and touch. Their leaves stroked him like feathers, eucalypt graced him with mint, rose, honey, violet, musk, smells, came to him. He was in a place he had been in before. His nostrils were assailed with the smell of things growing and dying, a sweet fecund smell like the valleys of rain forests. He did not wish to return to his body and instead he spread himself thinner, and thinner, as thin as a gas, and when he had made himself thin enough he sighed, and the trees, those tough-barked giants exchanging one gas for another, pumping water, making food, were not too busy to take this sigh back in through their leaves (it took only an instant) and they made no great fuss, no echoing sigh, no whispering of branches, simply took the sigh into themselves so that, in time, it became part of their tough old heart wood and there are those in Bog Onion who insist you can see it there, on the thirty-fifth ring or thereabouts of the trees he planted: a fine blue line, they insist, that even a city person could see.

He was Harry Joy.

He talked to the lightning, the trees, the fire, gained authority over bees and blossoms, told stories, conducted ceremonies, was the lover of Honey Barbara, husband of Bettina, father of David and Lucy, and of us, the children of Honey Barbara and Harry Joy.

Peter Carey
Exotic Pleasures

'Peter Carey's Australia is a land of nightmares, not a good place for the faint-hearted to wander through after dark. However, devotees of the short story should take a few deep breaths and forge ahead. The stories in this collection are as brilliant as they are bizarre' SATURDAY REVIEW

'Not since Ian McEwan's *First Love, Last Rites* has a book of short stories made such an impact on me. If you never read another short story collection read this one' WOMAN'S JOURNAL

Ian McEwan
First Love, Last Rites

Under Ian McEwan's manipulations, depravity may take on the guise of innocence and butterflies can become sinister. With equal power, he can show a child's life become fouled by the macabre, or distil the awakening sensations of first love, tracing its ritual initiations and infusing them with a luxuriant sensual imagery.

'A brilliant performance, showing an originality astonishing for a writer still in his mid twenties' ANTHONY THWAITE, OBSERVER

In Between the Sheets

First Love, Last Rites, Ian McEwan's first volume of stories and winner of the 1976 Somerset Maugham Award, was rapturously received as the work of a brilliantly original new writer. Here now is his second collection, as dark, dangerous and funny as the first.

'The most exciting fiction writer in England under 30' PETER LEWIS, DAILY MAIL

'Exact, tender, funny, voluptuous, disturbing' THE TIMES

Ian McEwan
The Cement Garden

'In many ways a shocking book, morbid, full of repellant imagery – and irresistibly readable ... the effect achieved by McEwan's quiet, precise and sensuous touch is that of magic realism' NEW YORK REVIEW OF BOOKS

'A little masterpiece of appalling fascination' DAILY MAIL

'For a first novel, it is a darkly impressive piece of work ... a touch of real fictional genius' THE TIMES

'Just about perfect' SPECTATOR

Richard Thornley
Zig-Zag

Three stories by a strikingly talented new writer: 'Gastarbeiter', in which a hitchhiker on the *autobahn* finds himself at the wheel of a juggernaut for the first time; 'Jewels' – a French anarchist commune under threat by sudden, savage storms; 'Tourist Attraction', in which a Jourdanian tatty-goods salesman in Florence finds that marriage to an American tourist is not necessarily the best way to make it to LA.

'Resourceful, restrained, deceptively casual, the writing proclaims the arrival on the scene of a born storyteller' GUARDIAN

'Not only a remarkable talent for characterization, but also that apparently innate gift for selectivity which is the sign of the true novelist' DAILY TELEGRAPH

D. M. Thomas
The Flute-Player

The country might be Russia, the city Leningrad – the places where totalitarianism attempts to destroy art. This is the story of Elena, the flute-player, who keeps alive the persecuted creative spirit of a generation of artists. Around them the city is in chaos – imprisonment and death, with brief intervals of freedom. The one constant is Elena – sexual and emotional inspiration, at once Muse and whore.

Winner of the Gollancz/Picador/*Guardian* Fantasy Competition.

'A fluent and lyrical clarity' GUARDIAN

'The story of the survival of poetry itself' SPECTATOR

Robert Sabbag
Snowblind
a brief career in the cocaine trade

The true story of Zachary Swan, whose genius flowered and peaked in a few short, mad years in the early seventies. From Latin America he brought better living through chemistry to those in New York who could afford it, inventing dazzling deceptions to baffle border patrols, always one step ahead of the narcs, and discovering in the process a hip and dangerous world, evoked by Robert Sabbag with breathtaking power and style.

'Dry wit, poetry, rock-hard fact and relentless insight' ROLLING STONE

Italo Calvino
If on a Winter's Night a Traveller

A fiction about fictions, a novel about novels, a book about books. Its chief protagonists are its author and his reader. Its progress traces the reading of a novel and the consummation of a love affair. In its course a whole shelf of novels are begun and – for reasons at the time entirely reasonable – never finished. Its characters are the myriads of beings involved with the process of creation, construction and consumption of The Book.

'I can think of no finer writer to have beside me while Italy explodes, while Britain burns, while the world ends'
SALMAN RUSHDIE, LONDON REVIEW OF BOOKS

Samuel Beckett
Company

'Imagine yourself old and reviewing your life. You are at the mercy of your memory, which dins in your ear stories of those scenes that made your life what it was. And if in addition you perceive yourself remembering . . . then you have split yourself yet again: into the voice of memory, the unwilling rememberer, and the unhappy perceiver. Essentially this is what Beckett has done in *Company*' NEW YORK TIMES

'There is in it a vivacious sense of despair that tears at the nerve ends. But its real richness lies in its language. What a master Beckett is . . . the finest verbal artist of the twentieth century' PETER TINNISWOOD, THE TIMES

Henry Green
Loving, Living and Party Going

Three novels by the man hailed by W. H. Auden as 'the finest living novelist'. Long neglected, the three novels published here deal with life in an Irish country house during World War II – *Loving*; working-class factory life – *Living*; and the comedy of manners of life in a London railway station – *Party Going*.

'A spellbinder . . . a true artist' L. P. HARTLEY

Nothing, Doting and Blindness

The publication of *Loving, Living* and *Party Going* in one Picador volume in 1978 signalled the end of years of unaccountable neglect for this fine writer. Three further of his fine novels are published together.

Nothing – a brilliant comedy of manners about a well-to-do widower and his debutante daughter.

Doting – a satire on the perils of romantic involvement between youth and middle age.

Blindness – Green's first novel, telling of a clever artistic boy, blinded in a senseless accident, who turns to writing with powers heightened by his affliction.

'A rare, strange talent recovered for another generation of readers' GUARDIAN

Max Handley
Meanwhile

From the depths of the ocean emerges a naïve male upon the world from which his sex was banished centuries before . . .

MEANWHILE, Ana, Matriarch of the Earth and Queen of the Steriles, waits with her grim armies . . .

MEANWHILE, in the Candle Palace, The Others begin their Full Moon Debauch . . .

MEANWHILE, from the swamps and bone yards come the crawling creatures of the night . . .

MEANWHILE, high in the mountains, twelve amnesiac males, sterilized for sacrifice, shuffle through the snow, sweeping away their footprints behind them . . .

MEANWHILE, come the Ecological Madmen; and the Last Child of Woman Born utters a first mewling cry. But is it already too late?

Picador

History of Rock and Roll	ed. Jim Miller
Lectures on Literature	Vladimir Nabokov
The Best of Myles	Flann O' Brien
Autobiography	John Cowper Powys
Hadrian the Seventh	Fr. Rolfe (Baron Corvo)
On Broadway	Damon Runyon
Midnight's Children	Salman Rushdie
Snowblind	Robert Sabbag
Awakenings	Oliver Sacks
The Fate of the Earth	Jonathan Schell
Street of Crocodiles	Bruno Schultz
Poets in their Youth	Eileen Simpson
Miss Silver's Past	Josef Skvorecky
A Flag for Sunrise	Robert Stone
Visitants	Randolph Stow
Alice Fell	Emma Tennant
The Flute-Player	D. M. Thomas
The Great Shark Hunt	Hunter S. Thompson
The Longest War	Jacob Timerman
Aunt Julia and the Scriptwriter	Mario Vargas Llosa
Female Friends	Fay Weldon
No Particular Place To Go	Hugo Williams
The Outsider	Colin Wilson
Kandy-Kolored Tangerine-Flake Streamline Baby	Tom Wolfe
Mars	Fritz Zorn

All these books are available at your local bookshop or newsagent.